"You married one of the richest men in Wyoming. That Range Rover alone could set you up for a while."

"He left me with nothing," she explained. "Chance inherits the bulk of the estate when he's twenty-one. I have fourteen days to vacate my house, and anything that isn't clothing or personal jewelry stays. I don't even want to go back there, knowing now what that monster did." She squeezed her eyes shut. "My dad's gone—and I'm alone. Except for my children. *Children*," she repeated, her voice breaking. "Look at what I have now. *Both* babies. I just need some time and a way to get back on my own two feet."

The emotion that settled on his face looked a lot like relief. "Of course I'll hire you," he said. "Anything you need, Sara. Always."

That same relief now flooded her. Okay. She had a safe place to land right now with her infants. She had a job. She had everything that was familiar and comforting. She'd be okay. This *had* been a good idea.

"Thank you, Noah."

He nodded and looked out the window as if regrouping. "I won't lose Annabel," he whispered, and he glanced back at her so fast she realized he hadn't meant to say it aloud.

and one of the richest men

Suddenly a Father

MELISSA SENATE
&
LAURA MARIE ALTOM

Previously published as *For the Twins' Sake*
and *Temporary Dad*

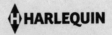 HARLEQUIN

ISBN-13: 978-1-335-61746-0

Suddenly a Father

Copyright © 2021 by Harlequin Books S.A.

For the Twins' Sake
First published in 2020. This edition published in 2021.
Copyright © 2020 by Melissa Senate

Temporary Dad
First published in 2005. This edition published in 2021.
Copyright © 2005 by Laura Marie Altom

Recycling programs
for this product may
not exist in your area.

This edition published by arrangement with Harlequin Books S.A.

For questions and comments about the quality of this book, please contact us at CustomerService@Harlequin.com.

Harlequin Enterprises ULC
22 Adelaide St. West, 40th Floor
Toronto, Ontario M5H 4E3, Canada
www.Harlequin.com

Printed in U.S.A.

CONTENTS

Melissa Senate has written many novels for Harlequin and other publishers, including her debut, *See Jane Date*, which was made into a TV movie. She also wrote seven books for Harlequin's Special Edition line under the pen name Meg Maxwell. Her novels have been published in over twenty-five countries. Melissa lives on the coast of Maine with her teenage son; their rescue shepherd mix, Flash; and a lap cat named Cleo. For more information, please visit her website, melissasenate.com.

Books by Melissa Senate

Harlequin Special Edition

The Wyoming Multiples

The Baby Switch!
Detective Barelli's Legendary Triplets
Wyoming Christmas Surprise
To Keep Her Baby
A Promise for the Twins

Furever Yours

A New Leash on Love

Hurley's Homestyle Kitchen (as Meg Maxwell)

A Cowboy in the Kitchen
The Detective's 8 lb, 10 oz Surprise
The Cowboy's Big Family Tree
The Cook's Secret Ingredient
Charm School for Cowboys
Santa's Seven-Day Baby Tutorial

Visit the Author Profile page at
Harlequin.com for more titles.

For the
Twins' Sake

MELISSA SENATE

For my wonderful aunt and uncle,
Rick and Arlene D'Alli, who came to visit me
way up in Maine just as I was finishing
writing this novel. XOXO

Prologue

Was that a baby crying?

Nah.

Noah Dawson turned over in bed and tried to go back to sleep, but he heard the sound again. A crying baby. Impossible on this isolated ranch in the Wyoming wilderness, but unmistakable. Yesterday, Noah had gone to Bear Ridge Groceries to stock up for the impending rainstorm that threatened flash flooding, and a woman in front of him on the long checkout line had had a baby in her shopping cart, wailing just like he was hearing now. A round of peekaboo had helped quiet the screecher. But, man, did he know a crying baby when he heard one.

Still, right now? He glanced at his phone on the bedside table—at 1:52 a.m.? He had to be hearing things. Dreaming. Imagining it.

"Waaaah!"

Noah sat up. The crying was getting louder—and coming through the window on the early April breeze.

Did he have a middle-of-the-night visitor and he'd missed the doorbell ringing or something? Did he even know anyone with a baby?

"Waaah-waaah!"

Noah bolted out of bed. That *was* a baby crying. And it was coming from just outside the window of his cabin, below which was the front porch. He grabbed his jeans from where he'd slung them over his desk chair, pulled them on and hurried downstairs.

The crying got louder. He pulled the front door open. Then he looked down—and gasped.

A baby—a girl, guessing from the pink blanket covering most of her in an infant car seat, a white cotton cap on her head—was crying up a storm. A small black tote bag was beside the carrier.

What the hell? Who would leave a baby here? He glanced around for a car, for someone, anyone, but all he saw were the distant evergreens in the moonlight. The ranch was silent otherwise.

"Hello?" he called out, looking in every direction. No one. "Hello?" he shouted.

No response. No person. Nothing but the breeze through the trees.

How long has she been out here? he wondered as he snatched up the carrier and bag and brought them inside, his heart starting to pound, his brain trying to make some sort of sense of this. A baby. Left on his porch at two in the morning.

He set the carrier on the big wood coffee table in the living room. He carefully moved aside the blanket.

Whoa. Noah didn't know much about babies, but this tiny creature had to be a newborn. He wouldn't be surprised if the baby had been born today. That's how small she was. Her pink footie pajamas were way too big for her little body.

Call the police. Call an ambulance. Call social services. So many thoughts ran through his head at once that he had to just stop, stand still and breathe.

He glanced out the window, the rain starting. Just drizzling now, but within ten to fifteen minutes the skies would open up. That was a problem. The ranch was forty minutes from town down some winding rural roads, and the storm was forecasted to quickly create flood conditions, which would come before anyone could safely reach the place. Doc Bakerton, who ran the clinic in Bear Ridge, had emergency hours, and his home was only a ten-minute drive from here. Noah could get the baby over to Bakerton's faster and safer than an ambulance or the sheriff could get here, and he knew these country roads and where the river would rise the worst. He could get back.

Decision made: he'd take her over to Doc Bakerton's place.

But right now, the baby was crying her head off. Should he comfort her for a few seconds? Noah had no idea what the hell to do. She let out another wail, and he shifted the blanket aside, not surprised she wasn't even buckled in.

Hand under the neck, he told himself, lifting her out as carefully as he could. He held her alongside his arm, bracketed by his chest, not sure he was doing this right.

He touched a finger to her little cheek. She wasn't cold or hot, and her color seemed okay.

A hot burst of anger swelled in his gut over whoever had left a newborn to the elements in the middle of the night. What if he hadn't heard her crying at all? What if she'd been out there all night? In the middle of the Wyoming wilderness, a rainstorm about to pour down. Granted, the large front porch of his foreman's cabin was covered on three sides as a point of refuge for future guests of the ranch to wait out any bad weather, but still.

He swayed his arms a bit, and the crying stopped. When the baby's strangely colored eyes—a grayish blueish—closed, his anger dissipated some. The little face looked content, relaxed, the tiny chest rising and falling, rising and falling, the impossibly tiny bow lips giving a quirk.

Whose are you? he wondered. Why would anyone leave you *here*? The Dawson Family Guest Ranch wasn't due to open for seven more weeks, on Memorial Day weekend, so the guest cabins were empty. And none of the small staff he'd hired lived on the property.

He glanced at the carrier and tote bag on the coffee table. Maybe there was a note. Or a birth certificate. Something.

He couldn't reach the bag easily without putting the baby down, and he thought he should hold her a bit— why, exactly, he wasn't entirely sure. To keep her warm? To comfort her? Make her feel connected to someone and something? His gaze caught on something small and white poking up from underneath the blanket in the car seat. He shoved the blanket aside.

So there was a note. Half a page. Scrawled, crudely, in black pen.

She's your baby, Noah Dawson. Your responsibility. You won't hear from me again.

Every cell in his body froze.

What?

My baby? he thought, the idea not penetrating.

Forget the police. Or social services. Until he could think, figure out who the mother was.

His baby? Seriously?

He grabbed the tote bag and rooted around inside it for a birth certificate or envelope or any kind of paperwork. Nothing but a baby bottle, a small container of formula and two tiny diapers.

The infant's eyes opened just then, then drooped, opened, drooped, then closed again. There *was* something familiar about the little face, something in the expression, the eyes, that he couldn't pin down. He *knew* that face. The baby's mother, a woman he probably was with one night... Or maybe the little girl looked a bit like him?

Just get her to the doc, he told himself. *Now.*

He very gently laid her back down in the carrier, one little fist moving, the lips quirking again. He buckled the five-point harness and settled the blanket around her.

From the looks of her, all scrawny and tiny, tinier than your average baby, he was pretty sure she couldn't be more than a few hours old. So her mother didn't want to keep her and dropped her off right after giving birth? That hardly made sense. Mothers who'd just delivered a baby didn't jump in cars and drop off their babies in the middle of the night. Unless they were desperate, maybe.

All he knew was that someone had left a baby on his

doorstep. No knock, no explanation. No concern for the infant's well-being.

No idea who that person could possibly be.

His baby? His brain wasn't fully firing right now from the shock, but as he lifted the carrier he managed to think back nine months. It was the second week of April now. Who had he been involved with last July?

There were a few possibilities. One of whom he'd seen in passing just last week as he'd parked in front of the coffee shop in town. She certainly hadn't been nine months pregnant.

Two or three others back then, one-night stands when his life had still been about drinking too much at bars and trying to forget his troubles with women whose last names he didn't know.

He wasn't proud of that time in his life.

He'd been a hot mess. Two years ago, the small ranch he'd managed to buy had gone under—like father, like son, he supposed. The woman he'd loved his entire life had told him she'd had enough and was moving on, unless he changed most things about himself. He hadn't known how, and she'd gotten tired of trying to help when all her advice fell on deaf ears. And so he'd driven her away and she'd married the biggest jerk he'd ever known. The downward spiral had continued.

And then five months ago he'd inherited the Dawson Family Guest Ranch with his five siblings, most of whom wanted nothing to do with the place. Suddenly, the man on the edge of the cliff had inched back to solid ground. Purpose. Determination. Heritage.

Before his father passed, before Noah had come back home to the formerly dilapidated guest ranch he'd grown up on, he'd had no idea heritage meant anything to him. But it clearly did. Because here he was. Not that he had anywhere else to go, but still. He wanted to be here.

And if this baby was his, she belonged here too. With him on the Dawson ranch. Until he figured out whose she was—aside from his—he'd keep his siblings out of it. Maybe he'd call his sister, Daisy, in Cheyenne. Maybe she'd come visit for a few days and help him out.

The tiny eyes opened, and her face scrunched.

"I'm taking you to the doc, little buddy."

It struck him that little girls probably weren't called "little buddy" the way boys were. He recalled how Sara—the one he'd driven away—hated that her father had called her princess. *I'm no princess*, she'd say. *Furthest thing from it.*

"You're no princess either," he told the infant. "You certainly did not get the royal treatment on your first day on earth."

Carrier in hand, he headed toward the door, setting it on the floor to put on his leather jacket. Then he picked her back up and headed out to the truck.

"I'm not gonna let anything happen to you," he said, latching the carrier rear-facing on the back seat, like the little diagram on the side of the carrier wisely showed. "You can count on that."

Chapter 1

Seven weeks later

"I, Willem Michael Perry, in sound mind and body, hereby leave my second-rate wife, Sara Mayhew Perry, absolutely nothing."

Sara sat in her late husband's attorney's office, not surprised by anything in the will. The insults. The disinheritance. She wanted to run out of here, put this— including her marriage to Willem—behind her, and go home with her seven-week-old son. If she even had a home anymore.

The lawyer, Holton Parrington, who'd grimaced through every word of the will as he'd read it aloud, put the document down on his desk and took off his glasses. "Sorry about all this, Sara," he said, shaking his head. "Willem wasn't exactly the nicest person, was he?"

Understatement of the year. Decade, maybe. But you make a deal with the devil... "No, he wasn't."

Her husband had died in a car accident five days ago. He hadn't been a good person, but Sara hadn't married him for his personality. She knew she wasn't perfect, but doing what needed to be done had always come naturally to her, and she'd hoped she could help Willem change, that she would rub off on him, that impending fatherhood would mean something to him, but he'd actually gotten meaner, more spiteful, more controlling.

She glanced at the stroller to her left; baby Chance slept peacefully. She kept her gaze on him for a moment longer; her son was all that truly mattered. Nothing else.

"Willem also left a letter to you and instructions that I read it aloud in the event of his death," Holton continued. "It's sealed, and I have no idea what's inside. Ready?"

Sara sighed inwardly. "For more bashing? No. But I guess this will be the end of it."

The lawyer nodded. He put his glasses back on, then slit open the envelope and pulled out one sheet of paper, written in Willem Perry's unmistakable, perfect handwriting.

"'Sara, if you're reading this, I'm dead,'" the lawyer read, pausing as if bracing himself. He cleared his throat and continued. "'I don't know what got me in the end, but I hope it was quick and painless and that I lived till at least ninety-three like my father.'"

Willem hadn't made it to his twenty-ninth birthday. He'd been reckless with the brand-new Porsche, a gift to himself for becoming a father, and had been going more than ninety around the rain-slick curve on the winding service road into town.

"'I debated about putting what I'm about to say on paper,'" the lawyer continued reading, "'but decided I couldn't—make that shouldn't—take it to the grave with me. Oh yes, I want you to know. You deserve to know. Brace yourself, darlin'.'"

She was already doing that. Who knew what Willem was capable of? She did, actually. She wished she'd known the extent of his cruelty before she'd agreed to marry him. She'd known he was a snob, but he'd been so kind to her before their wedding, and she'd had such faith she'd turn him around. Back then, she'd thought his worst trait was talking down to waitstaff in the nice restaurants he'd taken her to.

She'd never take anything at face value again. That was for damned sure.

She sucked in a deep breath. *Whatever it is, whatever his last laugh is, I can take it*, she told herself. *I'm stronger than I know. Just keep chanting that and maybe it'll be true.*

The attorney glanced at her, and she nodded.

"'Our son's twin sister didn't die during childbirth,'" the lawyer read on a gasp, his eyes widening.

Sara gasped too. *What?* They stared at each other, his face as pale as hers must be.

The lawyer sucked in a breath and continued reading. "'The female twin was frail, much smaller than the male. But very much alive. Thank God I'd insisted on a home birth with a midwife, or I'd never have been able to do what I did.'"

She grabbed the sides of the chair. Her mind went blank, the air whooshing out of her, blackness threatening. *What did you do, Willem? What the hell did you do?*

The lawyer leaned back, took off his glasses and scrubbed a hand over his face.

"Finish the letter," Sara said, hearing the panic rise in her voice.

What happened to my baby girl?

Holton nodded, his expression grim. "'I threatened the midwife and paid her off not to call for medical intervention and to back me up when I told you the female didn't survive the birth. Don't be too hard on the poor lady. She accepted the bribe for the same reason you married me. She desperately needed the money.'"

The lawyer glanced at her then, and Sara, feeling her face flame, lifted her chin.

"'I told you the baby died,'" the lawyer continued reading, "'then while you were sleeping, I drove it out to Noah Dawson's place—'"

Sara bolted up. "Noah? Noah has my daughter?"

Her head was spinning. Her daughter was alive? And with Noah Dawson?

"Let's finish the letter," Holton said. "There's only one paragraph left."

Sara nodded, tears brimming as she dropped back on the chair.

The attorney cleared his throat. "'With my male heir healthy, I had no need for a sickly-looking daughter. To be quite honest, I don't particularly *like* girls. They grow up to become conniving users, don't they? I drove the baby out to Dawson's cabin and left her on his porch with that starter kit the midwife had on hand and a note saying it was his baby and his responsibility. For all I know, the twins *are* his. Maybe you were cheating on me with him during our entire marriage. Since I don't know whether any of that is true, it means it could be.

Since it could also not be, I'll leave my son the bulk of my estate in trust for when he turns twenty-one. The rest will go to the development of a golf course named in my honor. You, as you already know, get nothing. Not a cent.'" The lawyer paused and put down the letter. "That's the extent of it. It's signed 'Willem Michael Perry.'"

My daughter didn't die. She's alive.

"For the past seven weeks, Noah Dawson has had my daughter?" she whispered, the blackness threatening again.

She tried to remember back to the moment when the midwife—a gentle woman in her early sixties who'd come highly recommended—placed Chance on her chest. Tears had been brimming in the woman's eyes over what Sara had assumed was the loss of the baby girl she'd helped deliver. Sara had felt so woozy, despite Willem's insistence she take no drugs. She must have fallen asleep hard after initially nursing Chance, because she'd woken up hours later, Willem letting her know Chance was sleeping like a champ in the nursery and that the midwife had gone home and that they'd taken care of the details for the loss of the twin.

She'd been so woozy still, her head feeling like it was stuffed with cotton, and she'd been so grateful that she hadn't lost both babies that she'd made her way to the nursery and held Chance against her. Her precious son had gotten her through the terrible truth that his sister hadn't survived. Over the next few days, Willem had resumed his usual twelve-hours-per-day work schedule, so she hadn't had to deal with him controlling her in person, though he'd left detailed emails about how to hold Chance, feed him, his nap schedule, and that no one was to visit until he'd had his shots.

Her baby girl was alive. And Sara wouldn't be the least bit surprised if Willem had slipped something into her water during labor, some kind of drug to keep her off balance and to make her sleep hard afterward.

Why would he take the baby to Noah, though? Willem had hated Noah Dawson.

"Sara, I'm afraid I have to prepare you for the possibility that the female twin didn't survive Willem's actions," the lawyer said, shaking her out of her question. "Left on a doorstep in the middle of the night? The second week of April, when it was still a bit chilly? Who knows when Mr. Dawson discovered the baby? If he was even home at the time? Didn't he very recently inherit the old Dawson guest ranch? I read that they're set for a grand opening this weekend, but I can't imagine how, given how run-down the place was."

She hadn't known Dawson's was reopening. She'd heard that Noah's widowed father had died and that he'd left the dilapidated ranch to his six children. She'd thought about going to the funeral but wasn't sure she'd be welcome. She'd been showing then and didn't want to make Noah uncomfortable, so she'd stayed home. She also would have had to get around Willem about where she was going, and she hadn't had the energy for that.

When she'd woken up about three hours after giving birth, the rain had been coming down hard. Willem had left their daughter on a ranch porch in the middle of the night during a rainstorm? The Dawson ranch in Bear Ridge was over an hour away from the Perry house in Wellington.

She swallowed back a wail building up deep inside

her. "I'm going to see Noah now. My daughter is alive. I feel it."

"I hope so, Sara," Holton said. "It seems clear that Willem expected this letter to be read decades from now. There are two bombshells, really. Your daughter. And the midwife's culpability. We can discuss options for how to proceed there."

She'd deal with that later. Right now, she only wanted to see her baby girl with her own eyes. Hold her. Get her *back*.

She reached for her long cardigan and put it on, then gripped the handle of Chance's stroller. He was fast asleep.

"Sara, again, I'm very sorry," Holton said. "I hate to bring this up right now, but I do need to tell you that you'll need to vacate the house within fourteen days. You may take your personal possessions, but everything else now belongs to the estate. If there's anything you'd like to take, do it before tomorrow, when the appraisals will begin."

She nodded again. She couldn't wait to leave that house. Where she'd move, she had no idea. But she did know where she was going now.

To see Noah Dawson. And get her baby girl.

"Should we give Bolt an apple slice?" Noah asked his baby daughter, snug in the carrier strapped to his chest.

He stood at Bolt's stall in front of the small barn beside his cabin, the mare nudging his arm for her apple. "We should? I agree." He pulled the baggie of apple slices from his pocket.

Annabel didn't respond, but according to the book

on your baby's first year, she wouldn't make sounds or coo for another couple of weeks.

He'd learned quite a bit about babies in the past seven weeks. He'd been right that Annabel had only been hours old when she'd been left on his porch. Doc Bakerton had been a grouch at being woken up at 2:20 in the morning—until he'd seen why Noah had come blazing over.

Because Bakerton was getting up there in years—nearing eighty—and had long been a rural doctor, he hadn't said anything about calling the sheriff or social services. Noah had showed him the note he'd found in the carrier, and that had been good enough. "The system doesn't need another abandoned baby when the perfectly good father is standing up," the doctor had said with a firm nod. Bakerton declared the infant healthy but small, recommended two possible pediatricians to follow up with and sent Noah on his way to beat the worst of the rain.

And so a little over twenty minutes after arriving, Noah had taken the baby home, shell-shocked but focused on the immediate here and now, not even tomorrow. The doc had given Noah some samples of formula and more diapers and wipes and had made a list of the basics Noah should buy in the morning.

Some of the shock had started to wear off while he'd been at Bakerton's, mostly because he'd realized he *could* simply leave the infant with the doctor, who'd call whoever needed to be called. The sheriff. Social services. And that would be that.

But what Bakerton had said kept echoing in his head as he'd watched him move that little stethoscope around the tiny back and chest...*when the perfectly good father is standing up.*

Noah Dawson, perfectly good father? He would have burst out laughing if the situation hadn't been so incredibly lacking in humor. Thing was, after all that he'd been through, all he'd lost, after the bad day he'd had with a sick calf, Noah had appreciated the extra show of faith in himself as a human being, and Bakerton had uttered the right words at exactly the right moment. The note said the baby was his. The perfectly good—or *able*, he figured Bakerton had meant—father was here with the infant, doing exactly what he should be doing. That was two for two on the faith scale.

He'd driven slow as his late grandmother's molasses back to the ranch in the pouring rain, and once inside he'd gone straight to his laptop, holding the tiny baby along his arm as he watched a YouTube video on how to mix formula, how to hold the bottle—how to hold a newborn, for that matter. Turns out he hadn't been doing that too wrong. He'd watched each video twice. By the time he'd closed his laptop, word had come that the river had flooded and two roads into town were impassable. He'd breathed a sigh of relief at the timing; the baby was safe and had been checked out, and Noah had what he'd needed to get through the night. The universe had been looking out for Noah lately.

They'd both survived that first night. While feeding the tiny infant, he'd realized he'd have to name her, and Annabel popped into his mind and that was that. He'd refused to let himself dwell on why.

Annabel Dawson. It wasn't official anywhere, not yet, but he'd have to deal with that too—getting Annabel a birth certificate while worrying that some bureaucrat would demand he hand his baby over.

His baby.

How Noah had gotten from where he'd been the night he'd found Annabel to *his baby* rolling off his tongue with ease was anyone's guess, but it had happened, and no one was more surprised than his sister. When the roosters had announced it was officially morning, he'd called his sister, Daisy, who lived out in Cheyenne, and boy, had she been in shock. She'd driven up by early evening and helped him so much—with Annabel and the ranch—the baby making her smile when he'd catch her looking so worried so often. Daisy had been close to five months pregnant then and wouldn't say a word about who the father was. She'd seemed relieved to have a reason to move somewhere, even to the family ranch, with its tangled roots and all.

Up until the moment he'd found Annabel, he'd spent the four months prior rebuilding the Dawson Family Guest Ranch. That had changed him, turned him around, made him a better person and had to have *something* to do with how immediately responsible he'd felt for the baby left on his porch—his baby. Add that to a tiny finger clutching his pinkie while feeding her. Being up all hours of the night checking on her—sometimes just to make sure she was still breathing. Googling "lullabies newborns like" and then playing them, and then singing them himself while sitting in the rocker he'd gotten from the town swap shop. Changing diapers. Playing peekaboo. Reading the pertinent pages of *Your Baby's First Year* and googling all the little things Annabel did that he wasn't sure was normal. Like burping so loud from that tiny body.

During the past seven weeks, he and Annabel had gotten even closer with all the walking around the vast property of the ranch, the baby against his chest in the Snugli and cozy footie pajamas. He'd told her all about the history of the ranch—how his grandparents had built it fifty-two years ago, how popular it had once been with tourists and locals coming to relax out in the country, to hike or ride on the vast trails in the woods and open grasslands, to learn to ride a horse, shear a sheep, spin fleece into yarn, milk cows and goats, and make butter and yogurt and his grandmother's award-winning ice cream, which she'd sold right in their own little shop in the main barn. Bess Dawson had always handed each of her grandchildren a little spoon and sample cup of her new flavors to make sure the ice cream passed the kid test, and every flavor always had. Noah could still taste his favorites: chocolate-chocolate chip, strawberry, Bear Ridge Mix—pistachio ice cream with peanuts. Noah had also told Annabel how his widowed father had destroyed it all within three years of inheriting the place, drinking and gambling away profits, savings, their legacy, his six kids eventually scattering across the West to get away from him.

Noah was the youngest and had been trapped there for a good bunch of those low years. Daisy, two years older, watched over him the best she could until she'd been driven away by their dad's self-destruction when she was eighteen. Noah had also left the moment he'd become a legal adult, all his pleading to his father to get his act together going in one ear...

Ten years later, the Dawson Family Guest Ranch had been a ghost ranch, rarely mentioned anymore except for someone in town to shake their head over its demise. But with the money Noah and his siblings had invested, he and a hardworking crew had gotten the place in shape—albeit on a smaller scale than the original—in just five months so they could open Memorial Day weekend. The day after tomorrow, Friday, was the grand reopening. His brothers hadn't responded to his invitation to stop by for the big day, and Noah wouldn't be surprised when none showed up.

"Let the place go," the Dawson siblings had all said to Noah one way or another at their father's funeral.

Except Noah hadn't been able to—and then his siblings had rallied around him, making a plan to invest in rebuilding because doing so meant something to him and would mean everything to their grandparents. Noah wouldn't ever let the ranch go. For many reasons. So many reasons he hadn't even told Annabel all of them yet. And he'd told her just about everything. His confidante was a seven-week-old, ten-pound, nine-ounce baby with chubby cheeks. There was a first for everything.

He heard a car coming up the drive and turned around. A silver Range Rover SUV was barreling up the dirt road toward the foreman's cabin. Did he know anyone who drove a Range Rover? The eldest Dawson sibling, Ford, maybe. But Ford had also said hell would freeze before he'd step foot on the ranch again.

Whoever it was sure was in a hell of a hurry to get to the cabin.

One hand protectively on the back of Annabel's head in the Snugli, he watched the SUV suddenly come to a dead stop halfway up the drive. The glare from the sun made it impossible to see who was behind the wheel. Why stop there?

The Range Rover suddenly started up again and inched forward, this time at two miles an hour.

When the SUV finally got within a few feet, he could see inside.

Holy hell.

Sara.

How long had it been? Almost two years. After she'd told him she was marrying Willem Perry—he could barely even think the name in his head without wanting to vomit or hit something—he'd then heard they'd moved out to Wellington, an affluent town an hour away. He hadn't seen or heard from her since. He'd been close with Sara's only living relative, her father, but Preston Mayhew had gotten very sick a few months before she'd married Willem. He'd also heard Sara had had her dad transferred from the county hospital to the state-of-the-art one in Wellington. Noah had once called about visiting hours and was told that all visitors had to be preapproved by Willem Perry. So much for that. It was better that there was no one to talk to him about Sara or what she was up to or how great her life was with that bastard Willem; Noah wouldn't have been able to bear it.

The car door opened and she stepped out, and his heart lurched. That wasn't a surprise. The sight of Sara Mayhew had always had that effect. Not just because she was so pretty with her silky light brown hair and round, pale brown eyes; his attraction to her had always been about who she was, not how good she looked. Though she did look good.

She must have heard about the Dawson Family Guest Ranch reopening this weekend and decided to check the place out for herself. After all, she'd grown up here too.

"I can't tell you how great it is to see you, Sara," he said, surprising even himself with his honesty. But it was bursting out of him. He'd missed her so much the past couple of years that he'd done regretful things to forget her, nothing working.

She shut her car door and walked toward him, her gaze on the Snugli, then moving up to his face. "You found that baby on your porch seven weeks ago? The early-morning hours of April 9?" Her voice sounded strange. Desperate and shaky.

He stared at her, his grip a bit tighter on the baby carrier. "How did you know that?"

"Because Willem—my late husband—is the one who put her there. She's mine, Noah. My daughter."

What? Noah took a step toward Sara, then a step back. "There was a note with her. It said she's mine."

Sara shook her head. "She's not yours. Willem told me she died during the home birth. But he just didn't want her because she was a girl and frail-looking when her healthy, robust twin brother—the male heir—had been born two minutes earlier."

No. That's insanity. On what planet does that sound believable? Even the worst of the worst like Willem Perry wouldn't do something like that. To his own flesh and blood? His newborn daughter?

She stepped forward, her gaze on the baby's head before looking up at him. "He left a letter for me via his lawyer detailing how he drove her here right before the rain started to come down in the middle of the night. I had no idea. I thought she didn't survive the birth." A sob escaped her, and she put her hand over her mouth.

Oh God. Unthinkable.

So unthinkable that it wasn't quite sinking in. All

he could do in the moment was look at Annabel, whom he'd taken care of for the past almost two months, whom he *loved*. She was his daughter. The note had said so. She was *his* child.

"That's my baby girl, Noah," she said, taking another step, then stopping. Maybe because of the expression on his face, which had to be something like horror.

For a second he could only stare at Sara, trying to process the craziness that had just come out of her mouth.

He thought about the first moments after bringing Annabel inside the night he'd found her. There had been something familiar about the little face, something in the expression, the eyes, that he couldn't pin down. He'd figured the baby's mother was a woman he'd been with for one night...

He and Sara had made love hundreds of times during their brief time as a couple, but the last time was right before she'd dumped him two years ago. He certainly wasn't the father of her daughter.

He glanced down at what he could see of Annabel's little profile, and yup, there it was, that slight something in the turndown of the eyes, the way the mouth curved upward. It was Sara's face. No wonder he'd felt so strangely connected to Annabel from the moment he'd brought her inside the cabin—before he'd even read the note falsely declaring the baby was his.

"I want to hold her so badly," Sara said. She reached out, and Noah felt the surrender everywhere in his body—the region of his heart most pointedly. This was Sara's baby. Not his.

Hell, he might break down crying. But he lifted Annabel out of the carrier. He handed her over with a stabbing awareness that this was it—it was over. His stint at fatherhood. He was proud of what he'd accomplished with the ranch, but he was proudest of what he'd accomplished with his daughter.

Not his daughter. He'd have to take that phrasing out of his vocabulary, out of his head. She wasn't his.

As Sara clutched the baby to her chest, tears streaming down her face, he closed his eyes, not surprised by the weight of sadness crushing his chest.

He loved Annabel. *That* was a surprise. But it was true.

"Is there somewhere I can go to spend time with her?" Sara asked, her gaze moving from the baby to Noah as she gently touched her wispy light brown curls, her cheek, her arm, her little fingers. "I just can't believe this is real."

Me either. He stared at his daughter—*her* daughter—and the jab in his chest intensified.

"You can take her into the cabin," he said. "She's eaten recently and been changed, so she's all set."

Now she stared at *him*, as if shocked he knew anything about Annabel's feeding and diaper-changing schedule.

"My son, her twin brother, is in the SUV," Sara said. "Could you take him out for me? I can't bear to let go of my daughter."

My daughter. My daughter. My daughter.

Noah's head was swimming, and his knees were wobbly. He nodded and lurched toward the Range Rover, mostly to have something to brace his fall if his legs did give out.

He pulled open the door, and there was Annabel's honest-to-goodness twin in green-and-white-striped pajamas. They looked so much alike—the wispy light brown curls. The slate-blue eyes. The nose. The expression. It was all Sara.

He took out the car seat and brought it around to where Sara stood. He lifted up the seat to Annabel's level. The baby that had been in his arms until five minutes ago. "Annabel, you're about to meet your twin brother."

Sara's mouth dropped open. "Annabel? That's what you named her?"

He nodded. It was Sara's middle name.

Tears filled her eyes, and she blinked hard.

"This is Chance," she said. "Chance, meet Noah Dawson. I've known him a long time."

A very long time. "Very nice to meet you, Chance." He gently touched a hand to the downy little head with its soft brown wisps.

"And Chance, this is Annabel, your twin sister," Sara added. "You're back together where you belong."

Oh hell. He was about to break down himself.

"I want to hear everything," she said, her pale brown eyes imploring. "From the moment you realized she was outside on your porch to the moment I drove up. I need to know about her life these past seven weeks. But first I just need some time alone with her. To let this sink in." She cuddled Annabel against her, her gaze going from her daughter to Noah and back again.

All these weeks that Annabel had been right here, with him, her mother had believed that her baby girl was dead. He had to stop thinking about himself and focus on that—what Sara had been through.

And how twin babies had almost been separated forever.

"I understand," he said, the sturdy weight of the car seat in his right hand making him both happy and miserable. "I'll help you inside with the twins, and you can have the place to yourself for however long you need. Text me when you're ready and I'll come fill you in."

She let out a breath. "Thank you, Noah. You can't imagine." She shook her head, her tear-streaked face his undoing as much as the situation.

He *couldn't* imagine.

They started walking to the cabin, which had once been her home when her father had been foreman. She stopped for a moment, staring up at the newly renovated two-story log house with the hunter green covered porch and flower boxes his sister had insisted on putting everywhere. Sara didn't say anything about the place, how it had changed, but she had much bigger things on her mind than the ranch.

He opened the door, then stepped aside so she could enter with Annabel. He followed her in, wanting to rip his daughter from her arms. He had to stop walking for a second; the pain in his chest was that severe, and dammit, he was worried he'd start bawling like a little kid any second.

He led her into the living room and set Chance's carrier on the floor beside the sofa. Sara dropped down on the sofa, crying, laughing, staring at the baby girl in her arms.

"Her baby bag is on the stroller by the door if you need anything," he managed to say. "Plus, there's a big basket of baby stuff on the side of the coffee table."

She couldn't take her eyes off Annabel. She nodded as if barely able to hear him.

"Take as long as you want," he said. "Text me when

you're ready for me to come back and we'll talk." He jotted his cell number down and left it on the coffee table.

She nodded, not taking her eyes off her daughter.

He wanted to grab Annabel away from her and run. Or just stay here, not letting the baby girl out of his sight.

Because no matter how many times he told himself she wasn't his daughter, he couldn't make himself believe it.

He forced himself out the door, his heart staying behind.

Chapter 2

Sara couldn't stop staring at the tiny baby nestled against her chest. Couldn't stop touching her, couldn't stop telling her she loved her, that she was so sorry she hadn't been there the past seven weeks, that nothing would ever come between them again.

On the drive over to the ranch from the lawyer's office, she'd kept thinking, *Please let my daughter be alive. Please let her be there. Please, please, please.* Her prayers answered, Sara's relief, her pure joy at being reunited with her baby girl, trounced her anger—murderous rage, really, at what had been done to the infant, done to Sara. *That monster took so much from us. He's not getting a second more of any piece of me. Not my thoughts or my emotions. Nothing. He's gone.*

"We have so much to catch up on," Sara whispered, in awe of everything about Annabel. Her ten fingers and toes. Her little nose and chin. The way her chest rose and fell in her sea-foam-green-and-white pajamas with little ducklings across the front. That she was really, truly *here*.

The baby's eyes were drooping, and Sara would be happy to sit here forever with Annabel napping in her arms. She glanced down at Chance, who was already asleep in his carrier. The siblings, twins, back together. She took in a deep, satisfying breath. Seven weeks felt like so much to miss out on, but she knew as time went on, she'd be grateful it had barely been two months.

She stood up, gently rocking Annabel, and walked over to the stone fireplace that dominated one wall of the living room, photos on the mantel. She'd lived in this house from the time she was born until she was sixteen, had sat on the sofa facing that fireplace night after night with her father after her mother passed away when she was nine. Talks, homework, reading, her dad's delicious sub sandwiches as they watched a series they could enjoy together. Her entire life was up in the air right now, but being here in this cabin made her feel safe.

"I grew up here," she whispered to Annabel. "Your grandma lived here. And your grandfather loved this cabin. He was the foreman here." Now Noah was.

She froze, biting her lip as Noah's words came back to her. *There was a note with her. It said she was mine.*

All this time, Noah had thought the baby was his. She glanced around the room, taking in the pale yellow playpen with its pastel mobile atop it by the bay window. The baby swing. The big basket of baby paraphernalia by the coffee table—she could see neatly folded burp cloths, a pack of diapers, a pink pacifier on a silver tray on the coffee table. An infant stroller was by the front door with a tote bag hanging from its handles.

Lots of photos on the mantel were of Annabel, a few of Noah holding her.

She gasped as it *really* sank in that Annabel had lived here these past seven weeks, that Noah had taken her in—as his daughter.

Was he relieved that the mother had come back to take her? Upset? Noah Dawson was the bachelor of bachelors. Clearly he'd gotten his act together to re-open the guest ranch, but perhaps his siblings were all involved in that. The Noah she'd known near the end of their relationship two years ago didn't wake until noon, despite having a ranch to run. Didn't take care of business. Didn't take care of their fledgling romance, the one she'd fought and kicked so hard for. Turned out Noah Dawson had been right about himself—that he'd only break her heart in more ways than one.

She always thought she knew better, didn't she.

Her future was in her arms. In the carrier beside the sofa. Her children. Hours ago she'd had only a son. Now she had twins.

Take the blessing and let that fill you, she ordered herself. Because letting herself get caught up in anger over the past—recent and not so recent—would only hold her back. She had a family to raise, money to earn, a life to start.

She took a deep breath and glanced at the other photos on the mantel, surprised to see one of her and Noah in their caps and gowns, their high school graduation. They'd both worked at the Circle D then, a prosperous ranch a half hour away. Sara had lived there as the foreman's daughter, and Noah was a hand. But a month later, when he turned eighteen, Noah had moved there too, so upset by the conversation he'd had with his dad a half hour earlier that he'd gone off alone. Sara still didn't know what had gone on during that discussion.

The other photos were of his siblings, the six of them together when Noah was sixteen. They'd still come home to celebrate his birthday, though they'd refused to have Christmas at the ranch with their dad and had flown Noah to one of their homes instead.

There was a photo of his mom, a pretty brunette with blue eyes who'd died when he was ten, something that had brought Sara and Noah even closer. They never had to talk about how awful it felt to miss your mother, to wish she were there. They just knew and could be together, quiet, skipping stones in the river, throwing bread to the ducks, climbing trees and sitting up there for hours.

She missed the Noah he'd been three-quarters of the time—even to the very end of their relationship two years ago. She missed that guy so, so much.

And she'd missed this cabin. She turned to look around. She had so many memories here, so much history. She knew every nook and cranny, which floorboards creaked on the stairs, how many steps it was down to the creek (182), how she'd sat on her bed in her room upstairs, writing *Sara Dawson* in hearts in her journal like the lovesick teenager she'd been.

"Where's my sweet baby girl?" a woman's voice called cheerily through the front screen door, followed by a set of knocks. "I need my Annabelly time."

Sara froze. Oh God. Who was this?

Noah's wife? Girlfriend?

"Noah? You here?" the feminine voice called.

Sara bit her lip. Should she go to the door? Pretend she wasn't here?

Curiosity got the better of her, since this woman might have helped Noah take care of Annabel the past seven weeks. Maybe, in fact, she'd done all the work. That was more likely.

She went to the door, and her heart soared. It was Daisy Dawson, Noah's only sister.

"Daisy!" Sara said, hearing her voice break and not caring. Her long honey-brown hair in a braid practically to her waist, a straw cowboy hat on her head, pretty, sweet Daisy had been a good friend from childhood until Willem had isolated Sara from everyone she used to care about. Daisy was also at least six months pregnant.

"Whoa—Sara?" Daisy asked with a shocked grin, pulling open the screen door and coming inside. She glanced at Annabel in Sara's arms. "This is a huge surprise. Did you come for Dawson's grand reopening?" Before Sara could even respond, Daisy added, "That rascal Noah—he didn't even tell me you two had gotten back in touch. God, Sara, it's so good to see you. You look amazing. So healthy and glowy. Is Noah here or did he have to step out to deal with something?" Daisy touched a finger to Annabel's cheek. "I'm so glad you got to meet my beautiful niece. Isn't she precious?"

My beautiful niece. Sara's knees buckled.

Sara tightened her arms around Annabel, more out of instinct than because she was worried she'd really drop to her knees.

Her every emotion must have been showing on her face, because Daisy tilted her head and looked at her. "Sara? You okay?"

"Not really," Sara said. "Not by a long shot. I'll be okay, though."

Daisy put a hand on Sara's arm, her warm blue eyes filled with concern. "How about we go talk in the kitchen? I know I could use a cup of decaf. I actually could use a big mug of real coffee. But I'm limiting myself to one cup a day, and I had that." She patted her belly.

Sara glanced at Daisy's left hand. No ring. She wondered what the story was there as she followed Daisy into the kitchen. Daisy always used to talk about wanting to be a mom one day, but she was insistent on picking the right guy so she'd never get divorced like her parents had, let alone thrice divorced like her dad. Sara had once pointed out that you could pick the right guy, as her own mother had, and leave him a brokenhearted widow at age thirty-six. You just never knew what life was going to throw at you.

As Daisy headed for the coffee maker, reaching for two mugs in the cabinet, Sara found her attention taken by the refrigerator door, all the things hung up with magnets. There was a checklist of baby-proofing essentials. A cutout newspaper ad for a local grandmother of five who did hand embroidery personalization on baby clothing and blankets and towels. The American Academy of Pediatrics' recommendations for feeding and napping schedules.

"Noah loves Annabel, doesn't he," Sara said, more a statement than a question, her voice sounding far away to her own ears as she stood in front of the fridge. "I can tell. I knew it as soon as I saw him with her in the Snugli."

Daisy tilted her head. "Of course. He loves that baby girl to pieces. Did you hear the crazy story? How someone left her on his porch right before that terrible rainstorm just about two months ago? There was a note that said the baby was his. He had no reason to doubt it. He even insists Annabel looks like him, but I don't see it. Don't tell him I said that!" She laughed and pressed a button on the coffee maker.

Sara almost smiled at the thought of Noah thinking Annabel looked like him. Once upon a time, when she'd still held out hope for marrying Noah Dawson and having a family with him, she'd always pictured little Noahs, two or three, with intense blue eyes and wavy dark hair, mischievous grins and big hearts.

"Daisy, I have a crazier story," Sara said. And told her everything. Not leaving a detail out.

Daisy was an expressive woman to start with, but the range of emotions that crossed her face was something. "Oh my God, Sara."

Sara nodded.

"Can I be really happy for you and really sad for my brother at the same time?" Daisy asked. "He must be out of his mind right now knowing you're going to take Annabel away."

Take Annabel away. Sara's stomach flipped over. She'd never really thought of coming to get her daughter as taking the baby away from someone. But now she kept seeing the look on Noah's face as he'd taken Annabel out of the carrier and handed her over.

It was anguish.

Oh, Noah, she thought. *This part of the story never would have occurred to me.*

This whole time, from the moment the lawyer had read Willem's awful letter, Sara had only focused on the fact that her daughter was alive, that Willem had taken her to Noah's cabin. She'd never stopped to think

about what had happened between then and now. Sara
had just wanted to find her child and reunite.

But Noah had taken her in, had been raising her as
his own, as he believed she was.

And that anguish on his face? Yes, he loved the baby.

Daisy poured two mugs of coffee and then opened
Noah's fridge. "Ooh, half a pecan pie. I think we're
gonna need a little of that too. Maybe a lot. Am I right?"

"Probably," Sara said. "I'm not sure if I can eat a bite
of anything, but since when don't I stress eat?"

Daisy nodded sagely and grabbed the pie and the
container of half-and-half, and Sara brought over the
mugs to the table. By the time Sara sat down and took
her third sip of the coffee and her second bite of pie, an
idea had started forming in her mind.

An either really good idea or a really bad one. She
truly wasn't sure.

Noah barely heard what his ranch hand was saying
about the hay bales, but the guy was smiling, so Noah
smiled back and nodded. Two days before the grand
opening was no time to have his mind elsewhere, but
every cell in Noah's body was focused on his cabin.
And what was going on in there.

He knew, actually. Sara was reuniting with the
daughter she'd never gotten to hold. Never gotten to
meet, let alone know.

And soon she'd text him that she was ready for him
to come back so they could talk, so he could fill her in
on the last seven weeks.

So he could say goodbye to the baby girl he'd taken
care of. His daughter who wasn't.

The pain gripped his chest again, and he sucked in a breath.

"You okay, boss?" Dylan asked, adjusting his cowboy hat as he peered at Noah. "You don't look so good."

"A-okay," Noah assured him. "So everything's in order in the main barn. What about the petting zoo?"

Dylan nodded, his mop of blond bangs shifting. "We're all set. I did inventory this morning. We won't need to place orders till Tuesday. Layla's feeding the farm animals now."

Noah nodded. "Thanks," he said. He'd hired several experienced hands for the land and animals and knew he could let go for a little while to deal with what was going on with Annabel.

He walked the quarter mile to his cabin and saddled up Bolt, riding her out to the gate a half mile down the gravel drive. He stopped and patted Bolt's flanks, staring at the hunter green metal that stretched across the road, Dawson Family Guest Ranch in gold letters, the silhouettes of a cowboy and a cowgirl on horses on either side. His grandparents had made belt buckles with the logo to sell in the gift shop, and one Christmas, he'd had six personalized with the grandkids' names. Noah still had his. In fact, he kept it on his desk, always had, and the past five months the buckle had served as a talisman, a lucky charm.

And for the past seven weeks, Annabel's presence had spurred him on to go even farther with making sure every detail of the ranch's reopening was perfect. This was going to be her future.

Now she wouldn't be part of it. She wouldn't be around at all.

His phone pinged with a text, and he reluctantly took

it from his pocket. The sooner Sara was ready for him
to return, the sooner she'd leave. With his baby.

But it was Daisy texting him.

U ok? Where R U? Heard whole story from S in the
cabin.

At the gate, he texted back. No, not OK.

She texted back, Be right there.

A few minutes later, Daisy rode up on her bike. She
jumped off, one hand on her belly, and threw her arms
around him.

"Sara's going to take her away," Noah said, letting his
sister comfort him for a second before pulling back. He
stared out at the woods beyond the road. "Just like that."

"I'm so sorry," Daisy said. "You know I love that
baby girl."

"At least Annabel will be with her mother. And Sara
will be with her daughter. I should focus on that. She
got her daughter back. It's a friggin' miracle."

Daisy nodded. "It is."

"And I guess Annabel as a Perry and not a Dawson
will have every creature comfort, certainly more than
I could ever provide." He knew the Dawson Family
Guest Ranch would do well; he was already booked
for the weekend and had bookings stretching all the
way to fall. Not every cabin was filled for every day,
but word of mouth would spread, and the ranch would
be a big success. He believed it. But he'd never be able
to give Annabel the life Sara could as richer-than-rich
Willem Perry's widow.

"You know what's crazy, Daize?" he said. "My

heart's been broken before, so I know what that feels like. This feels like that."

His sister put her hand on his arm. "Look, I don't know what happened between you and Sara two years ago. But maybe you can stay in touch, visit Annabel."

He could just see it now. "Uncle" Noah coming to visit every couple of months, bringing a stuffed animal. How could he become Uncle Noah when that baby had changed his entire life and world? She'd turned him into a father, something he wouldn't have seen coming in a million years. And dammit, he'd been good at it. Another shocker.

His phone pinged with a text, and his heart sank.

Come talk?—Sara

He stood there, his head hung, unable to move.

"I'm so sorry, Noah," his sister said again. "I know how much you love Annabel."

Even *he* hadn't known just how much he loved that ten-pound little human until this moment. More than he'd ever realized.

Chapter 3

Sara was sitting in the kitchen of the foreman's cabin, thinking, thinking, thinking, when the tap came on the front door.

"It's me," Noah called out.

How was it possible that his voice still had the power to send goose bumps up her arms, make her feel such anticipation? No matter what she'd been going through as a kid, as a teenager, the sound of Noah Dawson's voice…

"Come on in," she said, standing up, then sitting down. Why had she told him to come back so soon? Maybe she wasn't quite ready after all.

It felt funny inviting him into his own home, but what about any of this didn't feel surreal?

Like the fact that Sara had spent the last fifteen minutes—with Annabel napping in her carrier beside her brother—working over the idea in her head.

Good idea? Bad idea? Her only option?

Was she really hoping to count on Noah Dawson?

She was in dire straits. Nowhere to go, very little money suddenly, and two babies to care for.

And Noah had clearly changed these past two years. Reopening the Dawson Family Guest Ranch had always been his dream. He'd made it happen. And he'd taken very good care of Annabel the past seven weeks. According to Daisy, he'd done 90 percent of that on his own. Daisy had helped out, and a couple times he'd called their old sitter, Mrs. Pickles, whose real name no one could even remember at this point, when he'd had emergencies he had to deal with on the ranch. But for the most part, Daisy said that Noah Dawson had been a full-time, hands-on father, Annabel in that Snugli as he'd directed the crew, made his phone calls, sent his emails, dealt with the invoices.

She heard the screen door open. "In the kitchen," she called out.

And then there he was. For a moment, she couldn't take her eyes off him. Earlier, when she'd first arrived, she'd barely been able to think, let alone focus on the fact that she had been reunited with Noah Dawson after two years. Now, his presence in the cabin was almost overwhelming.

This was the man she'd loved her whole life. The tall, sexy cowboy she'd never stopped thinking about. The person who'd taken care of her daughter for the past seven weeks, despite being a single rancher reopening the family business and clearly having a lot on his plate.

Noah had believed the baby was his, and he'd stepped up. Of course, Sara would take Annabel to Chance's pediatrician and have her fully examined, but her daughter looked healthy and happy and alert. Noah had done a good job.

She could hardly believe it. Noah Dawson.

Annabel started fussing, her eyes opening and fighting to close. Her little face turned red and scrunched up a bit, and Sara's heart leaped as she stood to go pick her up.

"May I?" he asked, gesturing toward Annabel.

No. She's mine.

The instinct was so strong that Sara instantly felt guilty. "She's only napped for about thirty-five minutes."

Sara wanted to go to her baby girl. *She knows her mother now and wants her mama.*

That was what Sara wanted to believe, anyway.

Noah might feel very differently. Like that Annabel sensed her daddy was back and wanted to be held by him. Noah was the only father Annabel had ever known.

Oh God. She hadn't really thought about that until this moment.

Suddenly, her idea, either good or bad, seemed like the *only* idea, the best plan for right now.

"Sure," Sara said.

Noah smiled and knelt down in front of the carrier, unbuckling the harness and taking Annabel out. She watched the way he carefully cradled Annabel against him, gently rocking her, and she knew this was not the same man she'd left two years ago.

That Noah Dawson was in there, she was sure. But a new one had emerged. The one who was about to make her cry with how loving he was being to the baby girl, how tender, the care he was showing in how he held her, cooed to her, rocked her.

"Her eyes are shutting," Noah said. "There's a baby swing she loves in the living room. Can you go grab it for me?"

She popped up, relieved to have something to do, somewhere to go other than sitting right there and staring at Noah Dawson in wonder. She went into the living room and got the swing and carried it to the kitchen. She set it beside Chance's carrier; he was still sleeping.

Noah knelt down again and laid Annabel in the swing, her eyes slightly opening. He pressed Gentle Sway, and the swing began moving lightly, the softest of lullabies playing from the side speakers. The baby's eyes closed.

He touched a finger to her cheek, then looked at Chance for a moment, smiling so sweetly at her son that her eyes almost welled up. She was insanely hormonal. Willem had never looked at Chance that way, with that kind of tenderness, awe. Her late husband had only looked at his son as the trophy heir.

Yes, her idea was a good one. Not just for her and Noah. But for the twins' sake.

Noah stood up and walked over to the coffee maker. He switched out the decaf and brewed a cup. "Can I get you anything?"

"I had coffee with Daisy. I'm fine for now."

"She told me," he said. "We were talking by the gate until you texted."

There was so much to say, but she didn't want to say any of it. She just wanted to sit here and not talk.

"They're both asleep now," he said with a nod toward the twins.

She glanced at them, then back at him. "You really

seem to know what you're doing when it comes to babies. I'm very impressed, Noah."

She caught the way he glanced at her—the "when it comes to babies" hanging in the air as if he didn't know what he was doing in every other regard. Of course she didn't think that was true. Before Noah had started going a little too wild, heading down a road like his father had taken, he'd still been a good person, someone she could turn to. Steady. Trustworthy. Someone she could *always* count on. Until she gradually couldn't.

"I had to," he said. "I thought I was her father. Thank God for YouTube," he added.

She smiled. "I watched a few videos myself those first few days. Took me a while to get a good burp out of Chance. I'd been afraid to pat him too hard. Turns out I was way too gentle."

"Been there, learned that," he said with a nod, his gaze going to Chance. "Is Chance a family name?"

She shook her head. "It's a nickname I gave him the moment he was placed on my chest since I couldn't imagine calling him by his given name—Bancroft."

Noah rolled his eyes and she had to smile. "Willem's idea, I presume."

"His late mother's maiden name. I wanted to name him after my father, but he insisted that Preston wasn't stately enough." She shook her head. "If I could go back…"

"You had no choice but to marry Perry," he said. "Even I understand that. Barely, but I do. Your father was diagnosed with stage-two cancer when he had no health insurance. The bills took your savings, and then there was no way to pay for treatment when he needed to start radiation."

She felt tears well in her eyes. It meant so much that he *did* understand, that he didn't judge her. "I didn't realize how awful a person Willem was." She told him what was in the letter that Willem had written.

Noah's expression went from shock to horror to disgust. "Well, his sickening plan failed." He shook his head. "I'd like to scream every nasty thought I'm having about him from the rooftops, but I'll control myself because of these two," he added with a nod toward the twins. "I'd prefer never to hear his name again."

Exactly her thoughts since the lawyer's office. "Same here," she said.

She'd once really believed that Willem had loved her. He'd chased her all through high school, even though he was the town golden boy and she was the motherless daughter of a guest-ranch foreman who lived in the staff cabin she was in right now. Willem had truly seemed crazy about her—he listened when she spoke, told her interesting stories about his family, but she noticed the demeaning way he spoke to people, and she didn't like it. Besides, she'd *loved* Noah Dawson back then, and no one could ever compare.

Noah had been a wild child with a streak of good, and they'd been best friends since they were little. He'd always told her she was crazy for wanting him as a boyfriend and went for girls in his own circle instead, girls who skipped school and flashed boys in the hallway. Part of her always thought she'd dodged a bullet, but when they'd finally gotten together—for about six months—two years ago, when he had a small ranch of his own and was trying hard, she thought she'd help bring out the Noah Dawson who'd always been there. That was a mistake she'd made over and over, thinking people could change. They didn't, really. Maybe they could go a few degrees this way or that, but the core? That was settled. She understood that now.

So when Noah was sabotaging his fresh start on the ranch he'd wanted so bad, sabotaging their fledgling relationship, and then Willem Perry had started asking her out again, listening as she cried about Noah, about her sick father who would die without treatment, she'd let Willem take her away from her troubles. He'd promised her the moon, that he'd take care of her dad, and all he wanted in return was the woman of his dreams: her. She'd fallen for it all.

But what she'd really been was a notch. A conquest Willem had never been able to make until she'd been totally desperate. And the truth behind that made him resentful. And mean.

Just when things were so bad that she planned to leave her husband, determined to find a way to continue her dad's medical care, she found out she was pregnant—with twins. The news, for a while, turned things around; for a few weeks, Willem was kinder, until that changed too. He'd accused her of cheating with Noah, had gotten paranoid the twins weren't his. A prenatal DNA test confirmed they were Willem's, but his mind had gone twisted. He'd threatened her every time she told him she was leaving, and once, when she had left him, he sent a lawyer after her who scared the hell out of her that she'd lose custody of the babies entirely. She'd gone back home numb, not sure what she was going to do, how she'd get away from him and not lose her children. Then her father died, and she'd been too grief-stricken to even think about Willem.

All that was in the past, including her husband. The very recent past with lessons she'd not soon forget.

Noah came over to the table with a steaming mug of coffee. He sat down across from her, and again, she was overwhelmed by how close he was.

"Before I came here," she said, "I'd just heard from Willem's lawyer that you'd restored the guest ranch and are reopening this weekend. I immediately noticed the new signs on the road leading to the turn and the huge sign on the shiny gates. The landscaping, the foreman's cabin, the barn—you've done an amazing job. A lot of the place looks even better than when I lived here."

He smiled. "Thanks. Wait till you see the farmhouse, the cabins, barns, the pastures and the trails. We still have work to do, but the heavy lifting is done."

A wistfulness crept into her expression, her gaze moving around the kitchen. "It feels so good to be back here."

"That's how I felt when I first came home. My brothers, not so much. But I guess for some of us, roots have a grip, even when they're a tangled mess."

She nodded, her gaze shifting to the napping babies.

"I guess after we talk," he said, "you're getting back in that Range Rover and I'll never see any of you again."

There's your in, she thought. Good idea, bad idea, whichever—right now it was all she had. "Actually, quite the opposite, if you're open to my idea."

"What idea is that?" he asked, his eyes intense on her.

"I need a job and a place to stay," she said. "I'll work for you for room and board and a reasonable salary so I can get on my feet. There's a lot I can do on the ranch."

He looked at her like she'd grown an extra head.

"You married one of the richest men in Wyoming. Selling that Range Rover alone could set you up for a while."

"He left me with nothing," she explained. "Chance inherits the bulk of the estate when he's twenty-one. I have fourteen days to vacate my house, and anything that isn't clothing or personal jewelry stays. I don't even want to go back there, knowing now what that monster did." She squeezed her eyes shut. "My dad's gone—and I'm alone. Except for my children. *Children*," she repeated, her voice breaking. "Look at what I have now. *Both* babies. I just need some time and a way to get back on my own two feet."

The emotion that settled on his face looked a lot like relief. "Of course I'll hire you," he said. "Anything you need, Sara. Always."

That same relief now flooded her. Okay. She had a safe place to land with her infants. She had a job. She had everything that was familiar and comforting. She'd be okay. This *had* been a good idea.

"Thank you, Noah."

He nodded and looked out the window as if re-grouping. "I won't lose Annabel," he whispered, and he glanced back at her so fast she realized he hadn't meant to say it aloud. He picked up his mug and took a sip of his coffee. "I turned the spare room into her nursery," he quickly said, "so that's already all set up. You could take the guest room, and she and Chance can share the nursery. It's small, but hey, so are they."

"I'd prefer that to taking a room in the farmhouse. This cabin will always feel like home."

He glanced at her with such warmth in his eyes that she wanted to fling her arms around him and just hold him—for old times, for now. As a link to tomorrow and the next few weeks and months. But touching Noah Dawson had always gotten her in trouble in every way, and she had to rely on him enough right now—she wasn't going to mix up nostalgia, being grateful and need with anything else.

And anyway, she recalled that his grandparents had always kept two of the bedrooms of the main house available for emergencies regarding guests. Family members in arguments. Couples breaking up overnight. Plumbing issues. Right now, Daisy had a room and she'd need one for a nursery, so that left only two. It wouldn't be right to ask for one.

"I'm so used to Annabel being here," Noah said. "Honestly, I never thought she'd be going anywhere except when she graduated from high school."

She stared at him. "You really committed to being her father, huh."

He nodded. "I love that little girl. And I'll love her twin too. I want you all right here. Besides, the guest room is your old bedroom."

She did like the idea of staying in her old room. And she couldn't deny that Annabel looked happy and well cared for. *And* Noah had definitely turned the Dawson Family Guest Ranch around. But she didn't trust him—aside from knowing he'd never mean her harm. He'd taken her trust two years ago by sabotaging everything he held dear, including their relationship. Then her husband had obliterated what little faith she had left in people. She couldn't count on anyone but herself, and that was just the way it was. She'd do what she had to in order to fill a bank account with enough money to get back on her feet, then she'd figure out where she'd go from there. Maybe she'd leave Wyoming—not that could she could imagine it.

She'd go back to the house in Wellington tomorrow to collect her things, everything that was hers. Then she'd officially move to the ranch with the twins and start over. She could breathe here, make a plan here. Being a foreman's daughter meant she had ranch life in her blood and bones; she'd been assistant forewoman at the last ranch she'd worked at before she'd gotten married.

"Glad to have you at Dawson Family Guest Ranch, Sara," he said, extending his hand. "We can talk about what position you'd like once you're settled. I could use an experienced assistant, if you're interested. But there are a few open positions—from leading children's activities and workshops to being a cowgirl."

She nodded, so relieved at how this had all worked out. "I'm glad to be here."

He had no idea how glad she was. This had always been home. And now, for the time being anyway, it would be again. She'd get on her feet, figure things out and then off she'd go.

But Noah hadn't let go of her hand, and she wasn't pulling it away. Their history, their past, good and bad, lingered heavy in the air between them. There was *too* much to talk about, and right now, she just wanted to gaze at Annabel and get back the last seven weeks.

But then Annabel started fussing again, and Noah reached for her, then put up his hands and stepped back. "Old habits," he said. "I guess I don't have to jump anymore."

"It'll be an absolute treat to care for her," she said, holding the baby girl, who once again was struggling to keep her eyes open. "Something I'll never take for granted that I get to do after all."

He nodded and reached out a hand to hers, giving it a gentle squeeze. "Maybe we can put them both down in her crib, and then I can fill you in on the last seven weeks."

"Sounds good," she said, snuggling Annabel close, aware that Noah was watching her.

As he lifted Chance's carrier—the little guy was still fast asleep—she couldn't help but wonder what was going to happen, how this would all go. Could she and Noah share a cabin with all that had happened between them? Would the past flare up? Or would they both just ignore it?

She would definitely ignore it, she told herself. *No matter what he reminds you of or makes you think about, no matter how comforting it would be to be in his arms. Ignore it.*

This was her fresh start, her chance for a new life. Two precious little beings depended on her now, and she would *not* let them down.

"Oh, what a lovely room," Sara said, looking all around the nursery as they walked inside, each holding a carrier. She'd stopped in her tracks, her mouth slightly open as though she wasn't expecting this.

Noah realized that she'd probably been expecting the basics. Not a room fit for a...beloved baby daughter. "It helped that I couldn't sleep the past several weeks, between Annabel waking up every few hours and constantly worrying about something or other about the ranch or if I'd forgotten to take care of something. Made it easy to find the extra hours to turn this room into

something special for her. Now them," he added, nodding at Chance.

He watched as Sara spun slowly, taking in the furnishings. The white spindle crib with the pastel monkey
sheets. The stars and moon mobile that hung overhead
and played lullabies. The white floor lamp that he'd
stenciled matching stars and moons on. The big braided
rug in yellows and pinks and blues. The yellow glider
that he'd practically lived in the past seven weeks. The
white dresser topped with the changing pad and basket
of diapers and ointments. The bookcase he'd filled with
board books and baby books and lined with stuffed animals. And the window with the yellow velvet drapes,
tree branches and leaves and blue sky the view.

Every time Noah came in here, he felt so strongly
that this was all meant to be—that Annabel was meant
to be here. The first few days, his sister had asked if he
was worried about splitting his time between fatherhood and getting the final details taken care of for the
grand reopening, then less than two months away, and
for reasons he couldn't quite ever figure out, the answer
was more no than yes. Everything about Annabel in his
life had felt so right, his bond with her so immediate,
that he'd simply made it work. That was what you did.

He hadn't done it with Sara two years ago. Or with
the small ranch he'd tried to keep going. That was what
he'd thought about long and hard once he'd gotten his
act together five months ago and became the person
she'd wanted him to be then. Why had he let her go?
Why?

He didn't know. And he hated thinking about it.

"Thank you for taking such good care of her," Sara

whispered. "For giving her this beautiful home and nursery."

He managed a smile. He almost wished she'd stop reminding him that Annabel wasn't his. That was unfair; he knew it. But still.

This was going to be hard. However this new arrangement was going to go, what would happen. It would be hard. He had no doubt about it.

"How about if I put Chance down," she said, carefully taking her son from the carrier, "since I'm used to transferring him when he's asleep, and you put Annabel down?"

"Good idea," he said, reaching for Annabel and cuddling her close for a moment before dropping a kiss to her soft little head. *Love you, baby girl*, he said silently.

The moment she touched the soft sheets with the tiny pastel monkeys, she stopped fussing and her eyes closed.

He sighed inwardly with relief again. His baby girl wasn't leaving. He wasn't losing Annabel.

Thank you, universe.

"This is home for her," Sara whispered, her voice shaky. "Of course she likes her crib."

He eyed Sara, wishing he could take her in his arms and just hold her, comfort her. This had to be so damned hard for *her* on so many levels. "And luckily, Chance seems like a champion napper who can sleep anywhere," he said with a gentle smile.

She nodded, her face brightening a bit. "He's good that way." But her face fell a moment later. He knew her well enough to be able to tell she was suffering from regret-itis. Wishing things had been different, that she'd been with Annabel from the moment she'd been born.

"Hey. She's your daughter, Sara. And she'll be napping in your arms like she's been there from moment one in no time."

"How'd you know that was…" She trailed off and turned away.

"I've known you forever, Sara. Remember? Nothing escapes me about you."

She glanced at him, then gave a slow nod, and he wondered if he was getting too personal, if he should be more professional now, since they were going to work together. Heck, he was going to be her boss. "I guess we can leave them to nap and go talk," she said.

"I have a weird craving for a grilled cheese sandwich," he said. "Want one?"

"Actually, yes. An hour ago I couldn't imagine ever eating again. Now I'm starved."

Because your life is back on track, he thought. *You feel okay.* He hoped she did, anyway.

They headed down to the kitchen, and he told her to sit, that he had it. In minutes, she was sniffing the air appreciatively.

"Grilled cheese was always my comfort food," she said with a soft smile. "Whenever I was upset, if I couldn't sleep at midnight, my dad would make me a grilled cheese and I'd feel better. I think a lot had to do with him making it for me and sitting next to me at this very table while I took a few bites that made me feel so much better."

"Yup," he said. His closest-in-age brothers had been like that for him when there had been overlap with them staying on the ranch as he'd grown up. "And I'm not surprised Annabel conked out so easily. Meeting her mama was big stuff."

"It's only seven weeks, right?" she said, her voice shaky. "That's nothing."

She'd inadvertently thrown him a solid right hook in the stomach. Seven weeks had been more than enough for him to develop a serious bond with Annabel. Then again, he'd developed that bond within days. The weeks passing had just cemented it, his love for that baby growing every day. "A blip, Sara," he forced himself to say. "And you're together now. That's all that matters anymore."

"I'm glad she's staying here—for your sake too," she said.

"I'm not gonna lie. I'm very relieved. But I'm happiest for Annabel. I hope you know that. I love that baby. Truly love her, as if she were my own. I'd rather she had her mother and a twin brother and that she knew who she truly was than lived a lie with me for who knows how long."

And that was the truth, no matter how he felt about Annabel. If he loved that baby, he wanted what was best for her, not what was best for himself.

He thought about the letter Sara told him Willem had left for her. What if the rat bastard *hadn't* been reckless with that stupid Porsche? What if he *had* lived to ninety-three like his just-as-awful father had? Sara would never have known her daughter. He would never have known who'd left Annabel. All their stories would be very different.

"I believe that," she said. "You always had a big heart."

Again, so much of their past hung heavy in the air, regrets and good times. He'd let her down—hard.

Driven her right into Willem's arms. He'd never forgive himself for that.

"Why do you think he left her here?" he asked. "With a note saying she was mine?"

"Probably to create havoc for you, mess up your care-free bachelor's life, screw up your good thing with the reopening of the ranch, if he even knew about that. Was there press about the grand reopening? He must have read it."

Noah nodded. "The *Bear Ridge Daily* did a big story on it. So did the Converse County paper."

"I think he thought he was getting the last laugh," Sara said. "He knew how I felt about you and he couldn't stand it, even when I told him that was in the past. He never believed me. He resented you and prob-ably thought it was sweet justice that you'd think the baby he didn't want was yours."

He wondered how she felt about him now. Two years ago, after a drinking bender that had left Noah in no condition to drive her and her dad to his appointment at the county hospital since her car was in the shop, she'd screamed that she was done with him, then had sent him a text a few hours later: I'll never be done with you, Noah. Even if we never see or speak to each other again, I'll always wish you well in my heart. But goodbye.

Two weeks later, he'd heard she'd married the rat bastard.

He had a feeling he'd never be clear on why he'd screwed up with Sara once he'd finally allowed himself to be in a relationship with her. He'd had everything, and he'd let it all go. Sara. His starter ranch. He'd frittered away most of the savings account she wouldn't take from him on really dumb track bets. Then he had what he'd supposedly wanted, according to his sister, who'd eventually staged an intervention with his brothers: nothing.

"Well, I'm glad Willem chose me," he said. "Mine or not, it was an honor to take care of her the past seven weeks, Sara. Two years ago, I couldn't have done it. Two months ago, I did. I'm a different person now, if you haven't noticed."

"I noticed." She opened her mouth as if to say something else but apparently decided against it. He imagined she'd been about to say: *It's a start, anyway. Let's see where you are in six months. Or a year. Maybe you're one challenge away from messing it all up again.*

He could see in her face that she didn't trust him, and he didn't blame her. But things *were* different now—because he trusted *himself.* That was everything. He hadn't known anything about that two years ago or five years ago or ever. But when he'd taken on reopening the ranch, when his sister and brothers had told him he'd hit rock bottom and there was only one way to go from there, he'd grabbed control of his life with both hands. His siblings had believed in him when they'd had no reason to, when he himself had no reason to. By the time Annabel had been left on his porch, he truly was a changed man.

Sara leaned against the doorway frame, crossing her arms over her chest, her long brown ponytail falling against her neck. "What a mess this could have been had he left her with strangers. I could have had a custody fight on my hands for my own daughter."

"The universe was looking out for you all along," he said, lifting up an edge of the grilled cheese to see if it was golden brown. It was. He was surprised the conversation hadn't distracted him into burning down the entire kitchen.

"I think so." She nodded. "Wow, that looks good," she said, her gaze on the grilled cheese sandwiches.

"And here it comes, good old-fashioned comfort food," he said, putting the plates on the small round table by the window and grabbing two raspberry seltzers from the fridge.

"Thanks, Noah. I have a feeling I'll be saying that a lot."

"Sure beats the alternative," he said, then regretted it. She'd had some choice words for him back then. He didn't want to remind her of bad times. He wasn't that guy anymore.

But she gave him a smile and picked up half her sandwich. "I was wondering if I could borrow your pickup truck today. When the babies wake up, I can drive over to my house—my former house—and get Chance's things. Then I'll be done with that place."

He cracked open his seltzer. "I'll do you one better. I'll drive you and help you cart everything. And how about if we ask Daisy to watch the twins?"

Sara frowned. "I hate the thought of leaving Annabel for even a second when I just got her back."

"We could take the twins along if you prefer, but it would be a lot easier and faster to get the job done without having to worry about them or check on them."

She nodded. "You're right. And Daisy does seem to adore Annabel. Think she'd mind?"

"Mind? Annabel's her—" He clamped his mouth shut.

"Niece," she said solemnly. "Annabel sure had a lot of love here. I'm grateful. Your brothers too?"

He shook his head. "They know about her, but they all said they'd never step foot on the ranch again, that it was my thing and they were glad Daisy was here because it made them feel less guilty. I think a few of them were worried the baby news would trip me up about the ranch. I'm pretty sure they're all waiting to see how things shake down. No doubt Daisy fills them in."

She nodded. "Your sister can still be Aunt Daisy," she said, taking another bite of her sandwich. "He who won't be named and I were both only children. Annabel can use an aunt and four uncles."

He smiled. "And Daisy is six months pregnant and wants baby experience. She's loved her babysitting time with Annabel these past weeks. She's an old pro already. I'm sure she'd be happy to watch both."

"Okay, then. I'll take you up on the offer for help and your sister as babysitter."

He nodded and picked up his sandwich and took a bite. He'd eaten plenty of grilled cheeses here as a kid, just as Sara had had many meals in the main house. They'd been inseparable as children, the same age, when his five siblings had all been older and not so interested in the sprout tagging along. His eldest brother, Ford, was six years older, just a little more than a year separating all of them. They had three mothers among them. Daisy and Noah with the third wife. Axel, Rex and Zeke with the second, and Ford with the first Mrs. Dawson.

"Thank you again, Noah," Sara said, placing her hand on his. "For lunch. For the relief of a home and a job. For taking such good care of my daughter."

I'd do anything for you, he wanted to say, and it felt true, but when he'd needed to step up, he'd failed her. Gunk he didn't want to think about anymore but often kept him awake at night. For two years.

So he just nodded and squeezed her hand, then picked up his phone and called his sister.

A half hour later, Daisy was up in the nursery with the twins, happy to watch Annabel and Chance for however long they needed, and he and Sara were in his truck alone, heading down the drive until he realized they forgot about the Range Rover.

New plan. He'd follow her in the truck so she could return the fancy SUV to the house where it belonged, since the car, like everything else, was apparently in Perry's name.

Now he was behind her on the freeway, so aware of her in the silver SUV, never wanting to let her out of his sight again.

Chapter 4

Thanks to Noah's help, Sara got Chance's stuff and her clothing and toiletries and some personal items out of the Wellington house and into the pickup in under an hour—including the double infant stroller that Willem must have moved to a closet in the garage and then forgotten about. He'd gotten rid of the extras of everything they'd bought two of—a baby swing, a crib. The stroller was the only sign in the house that she'd been expecting twins.

Part of her wanted to leave it, but she'd picked out the stroller herself, knowing she'd be the one using it 99 percent of the time, drawn to the soft blue and white color. *It doesn't offend*, Willem had said when she'd shown him the online photo, so she'd ordered it. Ugh, that had been Willem's favorite description. *It offends*, he'd say about the most innocuous things.

She shivered as memory after memory hit her. *Just finish up and get out of here*, she told herself.

The shortest time possible spent in this house, the better. The three-story white Colonial with the black shutters and red door was classic and beautiful on the outside, and as cold and austere as a walk-in freezer on the inside. The walls were all the same cool gray, the furnishings white, black or cream. Willem had found color—and a whole host of other things—tacky. Since he'd passed away, out of Willem-ingrained habit she'd straightened the throw pillows if she'd sat on the sofa and shifted all the hand towels in the bathroom so they were perfectly aligned. More than once, Willem had called her upstairs as though something awful had happened and he'd point out that the shampoo and conditioner containers needed to face front, not one of them sideways or show evidence that they'd been squeezed with depressions in the center.

She'd lived like that for two years. And had lost her father anyway.

She'd tried, given it her all, done whatever it had taken to try to save her dad. Preston Mayhew had loved life and had been raring to go, to fight the traitorous cells with everything he had. She'd been given an extra year and a half with him. When he was first diagnosed, he'd told her he'd be fine with sticking around long enough to walk her down the aisle even with a cane, and the pure joy on his face when he'd done just that had let her know he'd go at peace, assured his only child would be okay without him in the world.

She had to get out of this house. "I think that's it," she said to Noah.

She'd sped through her bedroom, the room she'd

shared with Willem, where she'd given birth, where her husband had tried very hard to take something precious from her. She'd been unable to look at the bed or the pretty chair where the midwife had sat beside her for hours during labor, so encouraging, so kind. Granted, Sara hadn't gotten to know the midwife, Katherine, all that well, but she could only assume the woman was racked with guilt and unable to live with herself, no matter how much Willem had paid her off, no matter how desperate she'd been. What she'd done was reprehensible. Sara couldn't imagine any amount of money making what she'd done even a serious consideration. She'd have to deal with the midwife soon. Very soon. What if she was planning to assist with another birth? Sara would call the lawyer tomorrow and discuss it all.

Her stomach turning over, Sara pushed all that away, focusing on the man watching her right now. She let herself drink in the sight of him, so different from Willem. Noah was over six feet by a couple inches at least, lanky and muscular with warm, deep blue eyes and a mop of shaggy dark hair that curled by his nape. Movie-star hair straight from the shower or bed. He was incredibly sexy—objectively speaking. Women had always buzzed around Noah. Willem had been attractive but not sexy, tall and stocky with pin-straight light blond hair and ice-blue eyes that neither twin had inherited. They both had her coloring. Was it awful that she was grateful she didn't see him in them? Grateful as she was to have them.

She stopped in front of the fireplace mantel, chills running up her spine, and then walked past, leaving the framed photographs there.

Noah nodded at the mantel. "Not taking any?"

There weren't many, since Willem had also thought it was tacky to have personal photographs all over the place. She'd always loved the idea of stairway walls lined with family pictures, but the stairway wall was blank, a cold gray like the rest of the house.

"I really don't want them," she said.

He plucked their wedding photo off the mantel. "The twins might one day," he said gently. He looked at the framed photograph and shook his head. "Perry's expression says you're his trophy. Is that what it was like? He finally got the girl?"

"Yup. It was more about the conquest than anything. Then he resented me for it."

"I'm sorry you went through all that, Sara. All of it. I wish I could have helped with your dad."

"Well, you tried," she said.

When she'd told him how bleak the situation was, that the hospital couldn't continue with treatment because of the lack of insurance and lack of payment on the last bill, Noah had handed her a check that she knew was the contents of his bank accounts—business and personal. It meant he'd lose his small ranch that he'd wanted so badly, and the gesture touched and unsettled her. He'd give up his dream to help her, but the amount, generous as it was, would pay only the last bill and barely begin to cover the month ahead. He'd lose his ranch and she wouldn't be able to keep up with the payments anyway. It was lose-lose, and so she'd turned it down. That was the first night they'd made love, when they'd tried to be a couple, but it was all too much for him. The intimacy, she thought. Just too much. Within a few months he clearly couldn't handle it and so he began acting out in ways it took her a while to catch onto. By then it was too late for them. She'd ended their relationship after only six months together and started dating Willem, who'd actually seemed like a breath of fresh air.

Ha. Not that it was funny in the slightest.

Her phone pinged with a text. It was from Holton, Willem's attorney.

Hope I'm not overstepping but please advise re: the female twin.

She texted back, Alive and well. We'll all be okay.

Wonderful news, Sara. Also, I checked into the midwife's license. According to the Wyoming Board of Nursing, she allowed her license of thirty-seven years to expire just this month without renewing, and local hospitals and OBs that I checked with let me know she called them to say she had officially retired. At least she's out of business.

Sara shivered.

It was something, but not enough. She'd have to deal with the midwife at some point soon. But for right now, when she walked out the door of this house, she'd close this chapter of her life. She'd never want to hear the lawyer's name or her late husband's again. There was too much to process right now, too much to adjust to or she'd storm the midwife's home with the sheriff in tow. Or maybe just knock on the woman's door and find out what the hell Willem had threatened her with or what dire straits she'd been in to agree to such a heinous act. When the time felt right, she would do just that.

Forcing those thoughts away right now, Sara took the

photo out of Noah's hand and put it back on the mantel. "I plan to legally change Chance's name from Bancroft Perry to Chance Mayhew since I'll be taking back my maiden name."

"What do you think you'll rename Annabel?"

Sara held his gaze. "I can't tell you how touched I was when I found out you named her Annabel. *My* middle name. Unless that was a coincidence? You just happened to like the name?"

"Well, I do happen to, but it was no coincidence. You were always my best friend, Sara, no matter what. And I guess I wanted her to have a piece of the best woman I know. Who knew she had *all* of you?"

She smiled, the urge to hug him so strong. She forced herself to stay put. "I think Annabel is perfect for her. Annabel Mayhew, it is."

"I got a lot right with her. Don't know how, but I did. Gives me hope for the ranch."

"I believe in you, Noah. Always have."

"I know," he said, looking down, and she could tell a little of that old Noah was still there, the guy who couldn't handle too much emotional honesty without getting itchy or wanting to run.

She'd do him a solid and change the subject. "For the twins, for someday," she said, "I'll take one photo album that has an array of photos from when Willem and I first started dating to when we brought Chance home." She shivered. "But how will I explain why there are no photos of Annabel the day they were born?"

She burst into tears and covered her face with her hands, and Noah wrapped his arms around her. She'd been holding on, but it was the thing that whacked her legs out from under her. The idea of her children having questions she'd hate to answer.

"You have lots of time to figure out those details," he said, his arms tightening around her. "Right now, let's focus on what's necessary. Like getting the hell out of here."

He tightened his hold for just a second, and oh God, did that feel good. She let herself sag against him, needing this, his comfort, his strength, all their beautiful history like air right now.

But she couldn't need him this way. It was too, too much. She wiped at her eyes and pulled away, slightly embarrassed at falling apart, but then again, this was Noah Dawson, who'd seen her through just about all the rough times of her life.

And she couldn't lie to herself. Being in his arms again felt even better than she'd expected. Maybe because he had changed. Or maybe because she'd missed him so damned much. Either way, she had to be careful with how she responded to him. She had leaned on someone for the last time. Now, she'd only lean on herself.

"I almost forgot," Noah said as he drove down the freeway in his pickup, Sara's Range Rover left behind with her old life. "My dad left you something in his will."

Sara had had enough of wills and surprises. She couldn't even summon the polite words to feign interest so she just turned toward him.

"A garden plot behind the foreman's cabin," he said. "Apparently it was your mother's once?"

A spark of joy lit inside Sara, a warmth as memories rushed over her. Sara as a little girl kneeling in the grass in front of the wood-framed raised garden bed, her mother letting her drop in the seeds as she explained about vegetables you planted in the warmer weather, like tomatoes and green peppers.

"It was added to the letter he left me," Noah said. "'Tell Sara I bequeath her the garden plot behind the foreman's cabin. Her mother built it and grew all kinds of vegetables. Sara was a nice gal, so I wanted to leave her something.'"

"I can't tell you how moved I am," she said. "That is really kind, Noah."

He nodded. "My dad had his moments, didn't he? You should have seen the letter he wrote me. I cried for a minute straight. I seriously couldn't stop."

She looked at him. "Really? What did the letter say?"

"That he was sorry for ruining our family legacy and everything his parents had built and dreamed of. That he was sorry for letting us down. He said he owned the ranch outright, and the land, never sold any part of it, and he'd always paid his property taxes, even if he let the place fall apart."

Sara had been leveled by what his father had done to the place, how he'd slowly destroyed it. The final straw for her dad as foreman had been the afternoon that Noah's dad had drunkenly smashed his truck into the barn next to their cabin—though luckily her and her dad's horses were in the pasture and not injured. Bo Dawson had refused to pay for the repairs to the barn and left it as it was. Between not paying his bills, storm damage he wouldn't take care of, and time, the old word of mouth had spread, and guests stopped coming completely. Out of respect for Noah's late grandparents, her dad had stayed on for a few weeks more, trying to do what he could and reason with Noah's father, but the man was beyond hope, and they'd left. That was twelve years ago.

"He still cared about Dawson Family Guest Ranch," Sara said. "Even if he didn't show it or have the where-withal to do anything about it. The place itself meant something to him."

Noah nodded. "I used to think actions spoke louder than anything, and I've come to realize what people do masks all kinds of things they can't say or articulate."

She supposed that was true. Nothing was ever really black-and-white. She'd known that Noah had cared about her even when he was letting her down. People were complicated. Life was complicated. If anyone had told her five years ago that one day she'd be trapped in an emotionally abusive marriage, unsure how to get herself and Chance safely away, she never would have believed it. She would have smugly said she'd never *be* in such a marriage to begin with, let alone not be able to get out.

"My dad went on to say in the letter that he hoped I'd take charge of the place," Noah said, thankfully shaking her out of her thoughts. "That I'd reopen the Dawson Family Guest Ranch even on a small scale, that he felt awful he couldn't leave any money to make that happen. But that he knew I was the Dawson to do it. He said I had a streak of him running in my veins but more of my grandparents in me, and he was sure I'd reopen the place and have my grandparents smiling down at me and the ranch."

"Wow," she said, marveling at how people *could* surprise you. "To all of it."

He nodded. "He left us all letters. At the will reading after the funeral, I was the only one who shared my letter. My siblings wouldn't. Even Daisy, and she was never all that private, especially with me."

"What do you think he wrote in your siblings' letters?" she asked. "I mean, if he envisioned you reopening the ranch, what else was there?"

"Nothing as far as I know. He got so broke at the end that he even sold the chipped dishes and cheap silverware. I can't even imagine what he wrote in their letters. But whatever he did write had an impact, since they're all so tight-lipped about it."

"They invested in reopening the ranch," she added. "And they invested in you too. So he must have made some kind of amends."

He nodded. "They refuse to step foot on the property, though. Except Daisy. And only because she's pregnant and seems to be completely on her own."

"She's got you," Sara said. "And me."

He glanced at her. "I'm glad for that."

They were quiet for a few moments, the only sound the rush of the tires as they drove down the freeway.

"You know what's interesting?" she said. "That the last person you expected to change your life ended up doing just that. Your father."

He nodded. "I spent a lot of time thinking about exactly that as I was working on the ranch. My siblings and I had given up on him completely the last few years." He sucked in a breath. "I hate wishing I could go back. At the time, I felt justified in leaving him to his own destruction. We all did. He constantly told us to get lost and mind our own business, that it was his property and we were trespassing. So we stopped badgering him after a while. Once the drinking got really bad and he almost ran over Ford one morning, dead drunk at 10:00 a.m., we left him alone."

"I know all about wishing you could go back, Noah. I guess we just do the best we can at the time with what we know, what we believe is true and right."

He glanced at her and nodded. "I would have let you know about the garden plot, but I wasn't sure about getting in touch. I couldn't imagine you driving an hour a few times a week to tend to a twelve-foot-by-six-foot garden bed."

"To get away from Willem for a few hours?" she said. "I would have."

He reached for her hand and squeezed it. "Well, it's yours now. And time to plant."

"Being back at the ranch when it looks the way it does now, being with you, my old friend, it almost feels like the world's been righted for me."

He turned to look at her, and his expression was full of so many different emotions. He squeezed her hand and then returned his attention to the road, and she wondered if she'd said too much again, made too much of their reunion. To change the subject, she remarked on how beautiful the Wyoming wilderness was in late May when the leaves bloomed and wildflowers spread their gorgeous color across the brown and green landscape, the still-snowcapped mountain range in the far distance. He agreed, and then they were silent the rest of the way home.

As Noah drove through the gates of the Dawson Family Guest Ranch and up the dirt road past the foreman's cabin, Sara took in the manicured but rustic grounds, pastures and fields and wilderness in every direction. There were cute wooden signs posted with arrows, miles and timing to get to the main house, the foreman's cabin, the cafeteria, the lodge, Bear Ridge Creek, riding trails and the trail system in the woods that were part of the ranch. Wildflowers were everywhere, and there were hunter green wooden benches, picnic tables and wooden swings hanging from tree branches. The ranch looked so welcoming and inviting.

"Did you hire people to help besides you and Daisy?" she asked as they drove past a pretty, rectangular log cabin painted a rustic white with a sign reading Guest Cafeteria. Picnic tables were out front.

"I have a good staff. For one, my grandparents' old cook, Cowboy Joe, agreed to come back and take the job. No one makes better burgers or omelets or barbecue than him. He's nearing seventy, but I hired him two helpers. The caf will be open from seven to eight thirty, twelve to one thirty, and five to six thirty for dinner. Cowboy Joe will handle breakfast and lunch, and Daisy wanted to take the dinner shift. She's also the guest relations manager."

"Perfect," she said. "So you'll focus on the ranch and she'll focus on the guests."

"Yup. I have a great team assembled—maintenance, housekeeping, cowboys and cowgirls. It's a small staff, but we're starting small. We're having a final staff meeting before opening day on Thursday morning—you can come to that and we'll get your role squared away beforehand. Memorial Day weekend and through the rest of next week, all six cabins are booked with a retreat. Something about getting your groove back."

Sara smiled. "Really?"

He shrugged. "Some kind of female empowerment thing. It's led by a life coach. She's bringing her own protein shake mixes."

Sara laughed. "Sounds great. And are there bookings beyond opening weekend?"

"Not all the cabins all the weeks or weekends, but so far, so good."

"I'm really happy for you, Noah. Looks like the ranch will be a big success."

"I hope so. I know a lot can go wrong."

She glanced at him and saw for the first time the worry in his expression. Everything must be riding on the opening, she realized. His dreams and future. His siblings' investment. What he wanted to carry on for his grandparents—and now even for his father.

As the main house where Noah grew up came into view, Sara's jaw almost dropped. Once peeling with a rotting foundation, the white clapboard farmhouse looked pristine and gleaming as it stood in the sunshine, a white wood–fenced pasture beside it and several trails through the low and high grasslands leading into the woods about a hundred feet away. The guest cabins, which couldn't be viewed from the dirt road that ended at the house, were between the foreman's cabin and the creek, nestled privately in the woods. Given what the main house looked like, she knew the cabins had to be beautifully restored too.

"You've done wonders with the place," she said. "And it'll take off. I believe that."

"Here's hoping so," he said, parking along the side of the house.

They headed up the porch steps, and he pulled open

the screen door, Daisy coming over with Chance fast asleep in her arms.

"This guy got fussy a little while ago, so I walked around with him, rocking him a bit, and he fell back asleep. I couldn't bear to put him down. He's such a love bug." She breathed in the baby shampoo scent of him. "Ahhh. I know being a mom twenty-four-seven like I'll be in three months won't be all rockabye and baby shampoo goodness, but I don't care. I can't wait!"

Sara laughed. "Know what you're having?"

"I told the radiologist and my OB that I want to be surprised," she said. "Which was a surprise in itself, given that I've had enough of the unexpected lately for a lifetime."

Sara had a feeling Daisy was talking about the father of her baby, and she was so curious, but until her old friend wanted to tell, she wouldn't ask.

"Where's my baby girl—" Noah said and then froze and turned to Sara. "Sorry. I mean, where's Annabel?" He smiled but looked so uncomfortable that suddenly Sara felt equally uncomfortable. How hard this must be for him, to have to step back from Annabel, to accept that she wasn't his baby after all.

His phone rang, and he seemed relieved for the interruption. He read something on the little screen. "Oh man. I've actually got to run. Hermione—one of the alpine goats—escaped her corral, and Dylan, one of our cowboys, is having a hard time getting her back."

Daisy laughed. "That Hermione is a wily one."

"See you in a few," Noah said, looking at his sister and then Sara before sprinting out.

"Annabel's napping in the kitchen," Daisy said. "I

was just sitting at the table with the baby monitor on high volume making a list of all the things I'm going to need. Taking a peek inside the twins' baby bag helped me a lot. Taking care of two babies must feel like a huge change from just one."

"It is, but every time I look at Annabel, I almost can't believe she's real. That makes double the work a lot easier." She smiled. "And yup, sure is a lot of stuff," Sara said. "Of course for the past seven weeks, I didn't know I'd need two of everything after all."

Daisy shook her head. "I still can't process what happened. My ex—" She bit her lip. "He was this and that, but I don't think he'd ever do something like that. How *could* anyone?"

Sara felt her face fall. "It's the scariest thing, Daisy. That I didn't know what I was getting myself into. But it turns out I made a deal with the devil."

Daisy shook her head. "Don't do that to yourself. I remember you telling me how special Willem made you feel, how listened to, how important. Plus, he was instrumental in getting your dad the best care, Sara. He pulled the wool over your eyes with who he was, but he did help with your dad, so there's that. And there's also something else."

"The twins," Sara said, knowing what Daisy was doing. Letting her take herself off the hook. She put a hand on her friend's arm. "Thank you, Daisy."

Sara followed her friend into the kitchen, struck, as always, by how much she and her brother looked alike. Daisy had lighter hair—hers was a beautiful honey-brown—but they had the same blue eyes and gorgeous features. Though two years older, Daisy had always been warm and kind to Sara. When Sara had gotten her period for the first time, and her mother had been gone a year and half prior, it was Daisy she'd gone to, all nervous and worried and thrilled.

It was also Daisy she'd gone to about her first kiss and first crush, admitting it was on her brother Noah, which worried Daisy to no end, and under "no circumstances are you allowed to let him kiss you, let alone touch a piece of your clothing!" Sara had said she could only half promise, given that she was in love and only thirteen and driven by hormones and the brain of a teenager. She and Noah had been best friends, but he'd refused to date her, saying he didn't want to mess up the friendship, but she saw the girls he went for. C cups. High heels. Hips. She had none of those things. And then her father had told her they were moving when she was sixteen and that was that until Noah took a job as a cowboy on the new ranch her father managed and then moved there when he was eighteen. But he still wouldn't mess with their friendship.

That had gone on for years, and their romance had only lasted six months. No matter how helpful he was to her now, she'd never trust Noah Dawson with her heart again.

Sara saw Annabel's carrier on the floor by the window and rushed over, still amazed that she *did* have a daughter. The baby girl was sleeping and looked so peaceful. She'd made an appointment with a pediatrician in town for Annabel, but from what she could tell, the infant looked healthy.

"Coffee?" Daisy said, picking up the pot. "I was just about to pour myself a mug. It's decaf, though."

"I'd love some."

Daisy poured and brought two mugs to the table and sat down. "You should have seen Noah with Annabel the past seven weeks. I knew Noah was capable of surprising me, but he *shocked* me. When I called my brothers to tell them, they didn't believe it and thought I was exaggerating."

Sara added cream and sugar and took a sip. "Exaggerating what?"

"His devotion to that baby. The note said she was his, and that was all he needed to know. He loved Annabel from the minute he brought her inside, I think. You know how many times he watched a YouTube video about burping a newborn, how to position the bottle while feeding? Like twenty times. I went with him to the baby emporium in Prairie City, and he spent ten minutes picking out a wipes warmer." She chuckled. "Noah Dawson walking around the ranch holding a baby in pink footie pajamas, introducing her to all the new animals. One time she fell asleep, and he shushed the goats."

Again Sara wanted to smile and cry. "Our Noah Dawson. I wonder what happened to him."

"I think the ranch did, Sara. He was the one of us who loved this place. He was the baby of the six of us and the Dawson kid who lived here his whole life. Our half brothers were whisked away by divorce and only came to visit. I don't think it's in their blood the way it is in Noah's. And the letter our dad left him, wanting him to reopen the guest ranch? Something got fired up in him. Purpose. Legacy. A future."

Sara nodded. She understood all that. What she would never understand was why she hadn't been that for Noah when they'd been together. Maybe she was flattering herself or being whiny, but their friendship ran so deep and so long, and their attraction, which he'd denied both of them for years, had been crazy intense. But he'd let it all go.

Eh. Didn't matter anymore. She wasn't here to revisit their past or figure out the mind of Noah Dawson. She was here to get her life back, get back on her feet, be her own woman again. She'd save up and then she'd be on her way with her children, starting fresh.

"Did you and Noah figure out what your role will be on the ranch?" Daisy asked. "I'd love for you to help me out with the guests. Our first group is coming on Friday afternoon and staying the week. There are twelve of them sharing the six cabins. Each cabin can accommodate more people, but the group leader wanted each attendee to have a lot of space, mental and physical."

"Ooh, the female empowerment group. Noah mentioned them."

Daisy nodded. "The leader is a life coach. I might linger in the back of the room to eavesdrop on the sessions."

"Me too. Female empowerment is exactly what I need right now."

"Ditto," Daisy said. "Big fat ditto."

Sara took a sip of her coffee. "I just realized that Noah and I didn't talk about *any* of the details of my employment at the ranch. Childcare issues and all that. He did say we'd work out the logistics before the staff meeting on Thursday, when he'd introduce me to everyone."

"I'm sure he intends to be your childcare provider,"

Daisy said. "And Mrs. Pickles is available. And me too whenever I can. I really do need the experience."

"I feel really lucky," Sara said, taking a sip of her coffee. "You Dawsons were always wonderful to me."

"You're like family," Daisy said, touching Sara's hand.

"You're going to make me cry." She blinked back being such an emotional hormonal mess, but she was too touched and her eyes welled. "Did Noah tell you about your dad leaving me the garden plot my mom built behind the foreman's cabin?"

"Another thing my brothers and I couldn't believe," Daisy said. "The thoughtfulness involved in that. Just when you think someone doesn't care about a damned thing, including himself and his kids, he stuns us all with handwritten letters."

"You liked the letter he left you?" she dared probe.

Daisy seemed lost in thought for a moment. "It touched me. And I really fought it. But yeah, it touched me. I'm not really ready to talk about it, though."

Sara nodded. "Totally understand."

The screen door opened and there was Noah, and the sight of him almost had Sara blushing. He was just so intensely sexy. Without remotely trying. He had that tall, lanky, muscular physique, the low-slung dark jeans and dusty boots, the brown Stetson. And that face that she'd loved since she was so young, the star of her nightly dreams and fantasies.

The man who'd taken care of a baby girl left on his porch in the middle of the night. Who'd watched videos on burping and shushed noisy goats so she could nap while he walked her around the barn.

That old stirring ignited deep inside her, and she tried to toss some cold water on it from the bitter part of her heart, but then Noah came over and knelt down in front of the carriers, touching a finger to Annabel's cheek and then Chance's.

"How are these little rabble-rousers?" he asked, his expression so tender.

I. Cannot. Like. You. That. Way, she told herself. *Cannot.*

Heaven help her.

Chapter 5

"Wait," Sara said, putting her suitcases beside the bed in Noah's guest room, which would now be her bedroom. "This is your office."

"Not anymore." Noah took the big empty box in his hand and filled it with the contents of the desk by the window, then took the bulletin board off the wall and tucked it under his arm. The room had never felt like an office, and though he stored paperwork here, he didn't like to sit at the desk. He preferred the kitchen table with a view of the barn and Bolt's head poking out of her corral, which also afforded a view of the main drive up from the gates. He also liked to work in a corner of the living room with a view of the wilderness and a winding trail that led up to the main house. "Now it's your room."

"I don't want to displace you," she said. "We can move the bed into the nursery. The babies don't need their own room, really."

"Yes, they do. Because as you know, taking care of a baby is exhausting and you need *your* own space, a door to close."

She shot him an appreciative smile. "How'd you get anything done when it was just you and Annabel here?"

"I took her with me everywhere. In the ole Snugli. If I couldn't, Daisy or Mrs. Pickles would watch her for me. The crew I hired did the heavy lifting when it came to renovating. I directed."

She grinned. "I can just see you, telling the crew what to do with a pink-outfitted baby strapped on your chest."

"Hey, two of them were dads themselves. They high-fived me every day about it."

She bit her lip and turned away.

Uh-oh. What had he said? "Sara?"

She dropped down on the bed. "Just waiting for the other shoe to drop, maybe. This all seems too easy, Noah. Things falling into place for me—first with re-uniting with Annabel and having her safe and sound. Getting just the right job and place to live. You—my new boss, by the way—being this new person."

He got it. Her trust in everything had been shattered.

"You know what you need?" he asked.

She tilted her head. "What?"

"Some time to put your feet up and relax. Come down when you're hungry."

She raised an eyebrow, and he realized he was pushing it, being too much the host when she expected very little from him.

Which hurt, he also understood. He'd show her who he was.

Or not, actually. His entire focus could now be on

the ranch. For the past seven weeks, he'd had no idea how he was going to get everything done for opening weekend, the most important weekend of his life, with a baby in tow. But he had. Thanks to a solid team, thanks to Daisy, thanks to him caring about both the baby and the ranch more than he'd ever cared about anything.

Except Sara. And he couldn't let his residual feelings for her, which he'd been trying to tamp down since she'd stormed the drive in that Range Rover, get him distracted. The Dawson Family Guest Ranch wasn't just about him; his siblings had invested in the place. They'd entrusted him with their money and their faith, and he would not let them down. Or himself.

Just about two months ago, Annabel had been added to that list. But now he had to take her off—somehow. She wasn't his baby, and Sara wasn't going to stay here forever.

The real problem was that he couldn't imagine ever crossing Annabel off the list. Granted, it had been only hours since he learned the truth that he wasn't the baby's father. But inside, he was. And always would be.

A cry, slightly different than Chance's, came from the nursery across the hall of the foreman's cabin. Annabel. Sara's heart leaped, and she bolted out of bed with a glance at the clock—1:14 a.m.

Her first middle-of-the-night wake-up from the baby girl she thought she'd lost. She'd never been so happy to be pulled out of bed in her entire life.

I'm coming, sweetheart, she thought as she hurried across the hall into the nursery. *Your mommy's coming and will never let anything happen to you again. Ever.*

She stopped in her tracks in the doorway. A half-naked Noah sat in the glider by the window, Annabel nestled in his arms, the moonlight a soft glow around them. He was so focused on the story he was telling the baby that he didn't even seem to realize Sara was there.

"And then Hermione ran and ran and ran," Noah said, "and poor Dylan—he's one of our cowboys— tried every trick to get the black-and-white goat to come back. The *main* trick is to actually let the goat chase you. Yup, just start running in the direction you want Goaty to go and wham—back in her corral."

"Is that what happened?" Sara interrupted with a smile as she stepped into the room.

Noah looked up at her, his gaze lingering a beat longer than it normally might and she realized she was wearing her skimpy pajamas—a Wyoming Wildcats T-shirt and a pair of yoga pants with a heavenly stretchy waistline. No bra, and motherhood had done wonders with typically B-cup breasts.

He cleared his throat and smiled at her. "Hermione is especially strong-willed. She wanted the high grass on the far side of the field by the fence, so Dylan had to wait until she was ready to play chase." He frowned suddenly and carefully stood up, glancing down at Annabel, whose eyes were drooping. "I'm so used to rushing in at her every cry. I should have let you take care of it. Sorry."

"It's nice that two people care so much about her, Noah," she said, then instantly regretted those words. Did she want Noah to care about Annabel the way she did? Of course, she understood why he did right now, but once a little time passed and he got used to not being Annabel's parent, the bond would loosen, right? Seven weeks certainly wasn't a lifetime.

A blip, he'd called it. She realized now, based on how he was looking down at Annabel—like a loving, doting father, something her daughter had not experienced for even a second from her biological father—that Noah had been lying. Seven weeks weren't a blip to him. He'd said that for her sake—and Annabel's. Because he truly loved that little girl.

"Do you think Willem had a moment's pause?" she asked, unable to stop herself. "Did he reach into the car to get her carrier when he arrived at your cabin in the middle of the night, the rain probably having started, and look at her face and think, *this is my daughter, my baby girl, my son's twin sister.* Did he ever think that for one second?" A sob tore out of her throat, and tears threatened.

Bloody hormones.

She watched Noah gently lay Annabel in the crib beside her brother, then he walked over and pulled her into his arms and held tight. She let herself sag against him—again, his strength, the comfort he was offering everything she needed right now.

"I want to hope so, Sara. I think we should just leave it at that."

She nodded against his chest. His bare chest. Warm, hard muscle, soft skin.

Stop needing this so much, she told herself, unable to pull away. But in the difficult past weeks, the past few months, the past couple of years, allowing her husband to isolate her from friends to the point that she hadn't felt comfortable turning to anyone even after losing her baby daughter, she *did* need this embrace.

Noah didn't pull away either. "C'mere," he said, and led her by the hand out of the room and into her own.

He stopped in front of her bed and held up the pretty blue-and-white quilt, embroidered with little stars and crescent moons. Part of her frowned. The other part tingled. She could barely take her eyes off his chest, and when she did, his face was even better. The beautiful face she'd loved and dreamed about for so long, full of tenderness, his blue eyes blazing with what might even be desire.

But come on. "Um, I guess it's been the requisite six weeks doctors tell you to wait after childbirth, but it's only a week past." Why had she said that? It wasn't as if she'd let herself go there with Noah anyway.

He raised an eyebrow. "Sara. Get your mind out of the gutter," he said with a grin. "I'm putting you to bed—alone. Get your rest."

Oh. She felt her cheeks burning a little. *Embarrassing!* Maybe Noah wasn't attracted to her anymore anyway. *You are being jerked around by hormones*, she reminded herself. *Ignore yourself. Just go back to sleep like Noah suggested.*

She slid into bed, laying her head on the soft down pillow. He actually tucked her in and then leaned over and kissed her forehead. Oh God, now she might cry. Her dad used to do that. And she always felt so loved, so protected, so safe in the world.

"Sleep, Sara," he said, straightening. "If you hear a baby crying, just turn over. I've got it. I won't expect to see you until at least 9:30 a.m. That way we can talk over your role at the ranch before the ten o'clock staff meeting. It'll be a good time to introduce you to everyone."

She couldn't even speak. She was just too overwhelmed. By her thoughts, by him, by her life right now.

She nodded and then tried to find her voice. "Noah," she finally said as he neared the door.

He turned around.

"Thank you for everything."

"My pleasure," he said with such sincerity in his voice that her eyes did well up.

Danged hormones.

It *was* the hormones, right?

Brilliant sunshine streamed through the woven shades on the window, and Sara had no idea what time it was. Given how well rested she felt, how ready to bounce out of bed, it had to be past eight o'clock. When was the last time she'd slept in?

She grabbed her phone from the bedside table: 8:17 a.m. Heaven. She'd woken naturally, not from a crying baby or an alarm clock, though hers would have gone off at eight thirty.

The twins hadn't woken her because Noah had obviously taken care of the early-morning waking; she had no doubt they were either napping in the nursery or that he was downstairs with them right now, chatting away with them about ranch life or telling a story about the goats or sheep. Noah had gone from being someone she'd run away from to a man she trusted with the lives of her babies, including the baby girl she'd just been reunited with.

Still, part of her, a big part, felt uneasy about that. Putting her trust in anyone was a bad idea. Noah Dawson was going to be her boss. Their relationship was something different now. Another new normal she'd have to get used to.

After a quick shower, she dressed in white leggings and a floral tunic, which she hoped would be appropriate enough for the staff meeting, dried her hair and then headed into the nursery. The twins were asleep. Heart at ease and filled, she tiptoed out. If they were taking their morning naps, Noah had also gotten up with them at around five and fed them and changed them and taken care of them. He'd been up with them last night as she had, and he had to be exhausted right now. Today was likely to be a very busy day for him—tomorrow was the grand reopening of the Dawson Family Guest Ranch.

She headed downstairs, also appreciating the smell of coffee. Noah was sitting at the round table by the window, a clipboard with what appeared to be a checklist, various folders, his phone, a mug of coffee—and a baby monitor, of course, in front of him.

He was in jeans, a dark green Henley shirt and barefoot. Sexy feet.

"Sleep well?" he asked, taking a sip of his coffee. His gorgeous blue eyes were sparkling with energy. Or maybe just adrenaline. If the man was tired, he didn't show it. She realized he was on new-parent time—used to the crazy hours of caring for a newborn. His schedule and hers had been exact the past several weeks—an hour's distance from each other. There was no way he wasn't tired, but he made it work because he had to.

"I think I actually got almost seven hours, thanks to you. A new record."

"Good. You needed it. I can't even imagine what all that shock yesterday did to your system. You needed a solid night's sleep."

Huh. She hadn't even thought about that aspect. "I appreciate that."

He nodded. "So how about we talk about your job on the ranch, then we'll have the staff meeting, and then I can take you on a tour of the place, since it's changed from when we grew up here."

"Sounds good." She poured herself a mug of coffee, added cream and sugar, and sat down beside him.

"So, I figure you can either be the assistant foreman, as you were on the Circle D with your dad, or you can take on a specific position—I could use an education manager and workshops leader to run the information sessions and classes we'll offer about ranch life and the petting zoo. Or you can be a cowgirl and lead rides and teach the basics. Or a housekeeper, though Daisy already hired two. She also hired a receptionist who'll have the welcome-slash-check-in shed as her station by the gate, but we could use another. Cowboy Joe could always use another pair of hands in the kitchen. In terms of splitting the running of Dawson's, as I mentioned, I'm land and animals and maintenance and all that falls under that, and Daisy's guests, lodging, food and all that falls under that. As assistant foreman, you'd be both our right hands. It's a big job but one in your veins. And it pays well." He told her the salary, noting all employees would also receive holiday bonuses since the staff would have to work on most holidays, taking shifts so they could still spend time with family.

"Assistant fore*woman*, it is," she said, extending her hand.

She liked the idea of taking a job she knew and understood. She'd worked alongside her father for years as a teenager at Dawson's back in the day, and she'd been the assistant foreman—forewoman, in her mind—at the Circle D for years afterward, a position she'd loved. When her dad had gotten too sick to keep working, she'd switched to part-time to take care of him.

Willem had once told her that he liked that she smelled like goat when they were dating, because it made him feel like she wasn't a gold digger. Of course, she had married him for his money and he knew it; she'd never lie to herself that she'd loved him, though she had liked and appreciated him before she'd known who he truly was. It was how she'd not seen the real Willem back then that worried her. Maybe the truth was that she'd ignored what she'd needed to because what he'd promised had been more important than his snobbery and disdain of perfectly normal things.

Maybe she was doing something of that herself now. Ignoring her past with Noah because what she needed from him was more important right now. A job with room and board in a place that she loved, that felt comforting and familiar, where she felt on solid ground when she was anything but.

Just be smart, she reminded herself. *Build your trust in yourself and your judgment. You're in the right place for yourself and the twins for the right reasons.*

"Sara?"

She blinked and realized Noah was holding up his coffee mug in the air as if to clink in celebration over the job. She was glad to be pulled out of her thoughts. She held up her mug, and they gently clinked and took sips.

"Welcome back to the Dawson Family Guest Ranch," he said. "Assistant Forewoman."

His smile lit up his handsome face, and she was pulled back into seeing the old Noah—the one she'd been so in love with she could hardly look at him sometimes. How she'd loved that face, dreamed about it.

Noah was now her boss. Not the old love of her life. Not an ex. Her boss.

She'd keep her attention on that word, and she'd be okay. She now had a great job, was living in her old home, one where her father had never been sick or weak, one where her mother had still been alive for the first nine years of Sara's life. She had her mom's garden plot to revive. By summer's end, she might even have enough saved to start her new life, though now that she thought about it, she wouldn't have two built-in sitters-slash-bosses like Noah and Daisy. Things *were* going to be good here.

Maybe too good to leave, though. Which doubly meant she'd have to keep her distance from the way Noah made her feel. Safe. Everything felt so fragile, so tentative, so new, and there was no way she could count her chickens or think anything was squared away. Things could change in a heartbeat. People could turn. You just never knew.

Just earn your money, build your bank account and take care of your children, she reminded herself. That was her purpose. To be self-sufficient and never rely on anyone again.

"You remember Mrs. Pickles, right?" he asked her.

"Of course," she said, the image of a middle-aged woman with a long red braid and bright green wellies coming to mind. "The babysitter. Daisy mentioned she's helped out a few times." What she couldn't remember was Mrs. Pickles's real name; her surname had been long, so she'd told everyone to call her Mrs. Pickles, and it had stuck as she'd watched over Noah and Sara until Daisy was considered old enough to keep an eye on them and a couple of the ranch hands' kids too back when.

"She's been a godsend. I hope you don't mind that I called her and told her we could use her services for a few hours of wake time and a few of nap time for the twins going forward, and then I realized I had to tell her a bit of the story. She said she'd love to work for us. She has twin grandchildren herself, high schoolers now, so lots of experience."

"Perfect. I noticed their nap times seem in sync. Both were still sleeping when I checked on them a little while ago."

He nodded. "Annabel always woke from her morning nap around ten, so I'm thinking one of us can be home to do wake-up, feeding, a little playing, then hand over to Mrs. Pickles. She can watch them for three hours till the next nap, then stay for that three-hour stretch, so it gives us a good six-hour workday uninterrupted. Then, either one of us will be with them or we'll take them in the ole Snugli on the job when it's appropriate."

No wonder she trusted him with the twins. He was completely on top of everything—from ranch details to their schedules.

"They should sleep right through the staff meeting if Daisy and I keep it to no more than twenty minutes," he said. "It's really for everyone to meet one another. When the twins wake up, I figure we can put each in a Snugli and I'll give you the grand tour."

She liked that he wanted to take the twins with them, not just cast them off to a sitter the whole day. He truly wanted to be with the twins and to immerse them in the ranch life, because it was his life. *Their* life.

Once again she found herself overwhelmed at how thoughtful he was, how kind. She felt very lucky and wanted to wrap her arms around him in thanks.

She really had to force herself not to.

Chapter 6

"I'm real happy for you two," Cowboy Joe said after the staff meeting as everyone headed to their respective stations to make sure everything was in place for tomorrow. He stood in front of Noah and Sara, each with a baby strapped on their chest, outside the main house. "I remember you both running around the ranch as kids, getting into mischief. Now you're a family raising the next generation of Dawsons to carry on the legacy of this beautiful place."

Noah stared at the tall, skinny man—the ranch's cook—in the brown Stetson and shaggy gray beard, wondering what on earth he was talking about. Then he realized Cowboy Joe thought he and Sara were a couple—and the parents of the twins. Some of the staff had met Annabel when they'd come for interviews if he'd been unable to secure his sister or Mrs. Pickles, and of course he'd introduced her as his daughter. So when he'd introduced Sara as Annabel and Chance's mother, those who'd met Annabel naturally figured he was the dad and that there was a twin brother who they hadn't met before.

Hey, fine with him. He'd always feel like Annabel's dad, and he was glad to put Chance in the mix too. Plus, Cowboy Joe's presumption had not only given him a second shot with Sara, but a lifetime in the family sense. He liked that too. The *idea*, actually. Because romance was the furthest thing from his mind. Romance took over, kept you up nights, and he was already up nights—bleary-eyed but *clear*. He didn't need his brain and newfound structure and vision and purpose turned upside down over what his heart was doing. He'd never let himself mess things up with Sara again, anyway. Too much was at stake for that.

And he was flattering himself if he thought she'd ever give him a second shot.

"Come by the caf later to test out my new blueberry muffin recipe," Cowboy Joe said, giving each baby a gentle tap on the nose. "I'm planning on them for the welcome baskets Daisy asked me to make up for the group coming tomorrow," he added over his shoulder as he headed down the path.

"Will do," Noah called after him.

"So everyone thinks we're a couple and that you're the twins' father?" Sara asked.

"Probably."

She was quiet for a few seconds, staring off into the distance. "I guess the real story is a little too complicated."

"Way too complicated." He upped his chin toward the path. "C'mon. I'll show you the main barn."

As they walked in the brilliant late May sunshine, a perfect seventy-three degrees, which would hold steady for the entire week as some kind of cosmic gift, he pointed out the different kinds of trees and birds to Chance in the carrier on his chest.

"See that beautiful black-and-white quarter horse, Chance?" he asked, pointing straight ahead where Bea, one of the ranch's cowgirls, was grooming the horse in front of the big red barn. "His name is Batman. He's getting all spiffy for the big day tomorrow. One day, you'll ride him, Annabel beside you on Bolt."

Sara went quiet again. Until she said, "You should know… I'm not really sure what my future holds. I don't know how long we'll be here."

Sharp right hook to the kidney. "What?" he said, also feeling like a hay bale had just fallen on his head. "You just got here. I just hired you. You haven't even had your first day of work yet. Suddenly you're leaving?"

He looked at Annabel—well, the back of her, anyway—strapped in the carrier on Sara's chest. *That's my baby girl. She's not going anywhere. She belongs here.*

Dammit, dammit, dammit. He knew the truth of who Annabel's parents were. Why wasn't it helping?

"I didn't say that, Noah. I only said I didn't know how long we'd be here. By the time these two are old enough to get on a horse? I don't know."

He stared at her for a moment, not liking the direction this conversation had taken one bit. "Well, I don't know why we're even talking about that, then."

"I just want to be honest and open," she said, a hand

protectively on the side of the carrier. "I know you're attached to Annabel. So…"

Attached to Annabel. Attached? Was that all she thought it was?

"So I think we should continue with the tour," he said, a little grumblier than he probably should have.

"Fine," she said.

"Fine."

To have something to do, they both started walking over to where Bea stood with Batman.

"Hi," Bea said, putting down the grooming brush. "I finally get to meet this little charmer up close." She bent toward Chance in the carrier on Noah's chest. "Aren't you precious. Just like your twin sis. I'll name the outdoor petting zoo enclosure for you so you'll each have your own special honor."

"Special honor?" Noah repeated.

"Go see," Bea said, gesturing at the petting zoo a quarter mile up from the main barn. The gleaming yellow barn with its white trim had several enclosed pastures for the animals, the goats and sheep grazing. Their two alpacas were in their own large area, as were the six ponies. "I wanted it to be a surprise for opening day," she added with a big smile. "I checked in with Daisy a couple days ago—she said you'd love it."

Oh hell. A couple of days go, everything was very different than it was today. A couple of days ago, he was someone's father. Now he wasn't. "Well, thanks in advance," he said, knowing Bea's heart was in the right place. "That was sweet of you, whatever it is."

He glanced at Sara, who smiled at Bea, and then they headed up the path to the yellow barn. Inside, the top half doors open to bring in the light and fresh air, the floors freshly swept and the pens recently cleaned, his attention immediately fell on a large sign handwritten in colored chalk on the wall of the barn: the Annabel Dawson Petting Zoo Barn. The sign listed rules of the barn. Not to feed the animals inside the barn. Not to enter the corrals. To wash hands before leaving. That was listed three times to stress its importance.

He glanced at Sara. She was staring at the sign, her expression...tense.

Annabel Dawson.

"Bea didn't know," he said quickly. "Nor did Daisy a couple days ago when Bea checked in with her. It's just chalk. It's easy to erase Dawson and write in Mayhew. Or we can just erase the whole thing."

Since you won't be here long anyway.

She reached a hand to Annabel's head in the sea-foam-green cotton cap, her shoulders slumping. "I keep forgetting how hard this must be for you," she said, turning to face him. "She's been your daughter for almost two months. A Dawson like the sign says. Now here I come, erasing her last name on her specially named barn. Talking about leaving one day." She stared down at the ground.

Right? he wanted to say. Smugly. Honestly.

Ragingly.

Until he thought about what *she'd* been through the past two months.

His phone pinged with a text, and he was grateful for the interruption, because what the hell was there to say about all this? The truth was what it was, and Sara had been through hell. Potentially losing Annabel to her rightful parent—and distance—was nothing compared to what Sara had had to deal with, what she could have believed her whole life.

He pulled out his phone. The text was from Carly, the receptionist and gate greeter.

Four guys who look like you just drove up and are heading toward the welcome shed at the gate.

What? Four guys who looked like him sounded like his brothers, but there was no way they'd be at the gate.

Yup, I called it, Carly added. They said they're your brothers, here to see you.

Whoa.

He pocketed his phone in what felt like slow motion, his brain not quite catching up. "I can't believe I'm actually about to say this, but my brothers are here."

"Wow," Sara said, her expression brightening. "Didn't you say they all refused to step foot back here?"

He nodded. "Wonders never cease." That rolled off his tongue, but nothing was truer in his life right now than that old adage.

"You go meet them, Noah. I'll take myself on the tour. I know my way around, even if things have changed."

Things had changed, but not the basic paths, and Sara knew those walkways and trails, including the ones that led into the woods, with her eyes closed. Plus, he had no doubt she needed a little space right now. From him.

"I'll just need to get the double stroller from the cabin."

"No need to walk back there. See that shed?" he asked, pointing out the half door. "I keep a lot of different supplies in there, including for Annabel. There's an infant stroller. I can put Chance in and you can take him on the tour with Annabel in the Snugli."

"Is there anything you don't think of?" she remarked.

He glanced at her, catching the surprise in her eyes, her tone.

"Not anymore. It's my business to think of everything."

She half smiled and they headed over to the shed, where he took out the stroller, diaper bag attached.

"You really do have this parenthood thing down," she said, staring into the diaper bag. "Pacifier, wipes, a changing mat, diapers. A bottle, bottled water and a small container of formula."

"I worked at it." *Harder than I ever worked at anything, even rebuilding the ranch.*

She held his gaze for a moment, and he couldn't read her expression, so he took Chance out of the front pack and put him in the stroller, not a peep out of him. He unstrapped the Snugli and folded it in the stroller's basket.

"If you need me," he said, "just text or call, and I'll be wherever you are in a heartbeat."

She held his gaze again, and he still couldn't read her. She nodded. "Go see your brothers. We'll be fine."

As he watched her continue up the path toward the guest cabins and the creek beyond, he couldn't move. And suddenly it didn't just feel like Annabel was moving away from him with every step, but all three of them.

His phone pinged again—Carly at the welcome shed. They said they'd meet you at the farmhouse.

He turned and headed in the other direction, forcing himself not to turn around to watch Sara and the twins get farther away.

Focus on your brothers, he told himself. Hadn't Ford said hell would freeze over before he'd come back to the ranch? Hadn't Rex said he was done with the place to the point that it bugged him to think about Noah getting it back up and running?

They were here, and that was all that mattered.

Same with Sara and the twins.

As Ford—who as oldest still declared himself in charge of the grill—put the perfectly cooked steaks on a platter, Noah glanced around at his four brothers and sister sitting around the patio table in the backyard, unable to believe the Dawson guys were really here. They'd spent the first half hour making small talk and catching up a bit, then Ford had gotten busy cooking. Apparently, the siblings had planned the surprise visit to the ranch a week ago, so they'd shopped in town for a pre–opening night celebratory dinner involving New York strips, baked potatoes, asparagus and craft beer.

Surprise didn't begin to describe how Noah felt. Shock was more like it.

But here they all really were. Ford. Axel. Rex. Zeke. And Daisy, who he was used to seeing, of course, but he certainly didn't take her being here for granted. When he'd first arrived at the farmhouse and seen his five siblings in the yard, he'd gotten all emotional and had to take a moment. Now, they were yakking like they saw each other all the time; it was always like that when they finally did get together.

Despite having three mothers among them, the siblings looked a lot like. They had varying shades of brown hair, some very dark like Axel's and some almost blondish like Daisy's, and they all had their father's clear blue eyes. The six of them were tall, including his sister, who was five foot nine. Everyone always said it was lucky she got the tall gene too because standing up to five brothers, four of whom were older, was easier when she at least reached their chins.

Ford was from their dad's first marriage, which apparently had lasted two months before his mother found Bo Dawson cheating not once or even twice but three times and finally left, then discovered she was pregnant, dropping off little Ford every other weekend for years. Axel, Rex and Zeke were from the second marriage to one of the other women who'd left hard-living Bo for the reliable, friendly mail carrier, whom Bo had tried to beat up but had been too drunk and ended up punching himself out. Axel, Rex and Zeke had all been too young and small to carry him inside, so they covered him with a few sleeping bags and put a bag of frozen peas on his purple-and-black eye and let him sleep it off.

Noah and Daisy were from Bo's third attempt at marriage, which lasted until their mother died in a car accident when Noah was nine. *He's trouble, but he's my trouble*, their mom would say, thinking she had the smarts, sense, work ethic and financial savvy to manage both their lives and their children's, so she could be with the man she loved, despite his flaws. She'd been kind to the four older kids too when they'd come for their visitation. Daisy had once told Noah she thought their mom was romantic *and* half-crazy, that she'd never be so reckless with herself. Anyway, after their mother's death, Bo had gotten a vasectomy, and word among the women who hung out in the sticky-floored bars he liked to frequent was that he carried around a letter from his doctor confirming he'd had the procedure so that no one could pin a pregnancy on him. A good-looking man, tall and lanky with an easy smile and flirtatious manner, he still managed to bring home lots of women, who never stuck around long. The Dawson name still carried weight in those days.

"I thought you said something about hell freezing over," Noah said to Ford as they all got busy digging into the plates and bowls on the table, thanks to Ford, who'd nixed their offers of help with dinner. Ford had always been the Dawson who could do anything and everything—from cooking to wrangling troublemakers—he was a police officer out in Casper.

"Well, it kind of did," Ford said. "Daisy let us know that not only were all renovations on schedule and according to plan, but that the place looked even better than it did when Gram and Gramps ran it. And that you pulled it off with a baby strapped to your chest the past two months. Tipping my hat to you, Noah."

The praise felt good. "Well, a little determination and all your help, and the Dawson Family Guest Ranch is back."

"Our help?" Axel repeated, heaping butter on his baked potato. "What did we do, Noah? You did it on your own." A search and rescue worker, Axel had always had big expectations for the word *help*. He spent his days and nights rescuing the lost and injured from area mountains. His most recent mission—involving a toddler whom he'd eventually found and reunited with his mother—had almost done him in.

"Um, he had our *financial* help," Rex pointed out with a grin. What Rex did for a living to have helped so much in that department was anyone's guess. He clearly had money and liked nice things, so he did *something*, but he'd always been cagey about it. Noah and Daisy used to joke that he was a CIA agent. For all they knew, he could be.

"And Daisy was here," Noah added, twisting the cap off his beer. "I had her help too."

Daisy raised her sparkling water. "Sometimes I think about how if you hadn't found a baby on your porch, I might still be in Cheyenne."

"Speaking of daddies," Ford said, eyeing Daisy. "You ever going to tell us who the father is?"

She frowned just slightly, and Noah could see how conflicted she was about the guy. "The two of us are talking again. We weren't when I first found out I was pregnant. So let me see how things go, and then maybe I'll introduce him. Maybe I won't ever get the opportunity. We'll see."

"Sounds complicated," Rex said. "You need to sic your brothers on him, you say the word."

Daisy's eyed widened, then she grinned. "Why do you think he's still anonymous?"

There was some reminiscing about the times they did face down any guy who'd dared mess with their little sister. Even Noah, two years younger, but closer to Daisy than any of the Dawsons, had been protective of her.

"Well, speaking of *babies*," Zeke said, turning to Noah, "when do we get to meet our little niece? Who's watching her right now?" Zeke, second oldest, was the businessman of the bunch, a corporate cowboy who wore suits with boots and was never without a black Stetson; in fact, he wore one right now. Noah had been in touch with Zeke the most of all his siblings besides Daisy, since every month he sent Zeke his ranch ledgers, and every month Zeke sent back a satisfying: *I'm impressed. You know what you're doing on all levels, kid bro.*

Noah took a swig of his beer. "That's kind of complicated too."

"Which part?" Ford asked in his cop tone.

"After dinner, you'll hear the whole story," he said, glancing around at all of them. "And meet Annabel."

He was about to add *and her twin brother,* but that would pause forks and beer bottles and require immediate explanation. As he'd walked up to the house to meet his brothers just an hour and a half ago, he'd texted Sara to ask how she wanted to handle said explanation, and she said she'd like to come over for dessert, twins in tow, and tell the story on her own terms.

There were some raised eyebrows and shrugs and everyone resumed eating. Daisy sent him an encouraging nod. For the next fifteen minutes they talked about the guest ranch's bookings; Noah had a solid lineup of guests coming all summer and into fall, and Zeke said he had no doubt word of mouth would fill out the empty cabins along the way. All the brothers agreed the place looked great, that the more modern aesthetic—rustic-luxe spa meets dude ranch—would appeal to a wider range of people, and it had. Noah had stormed the offices of every small and big newspaper in the county— the daily and the free weeklies—with press releases Zeke had helped him write from afar and photos as soon as prime spots were camera ready, like the cabins. The Dawson Family Guest Ranch 2.0 had gotten solid press, and the phones started ringing with bookings. People remembered the place—many locals and those spread around the state had spent their family vacations at the ranch, so that had also worked in its favor.

"Well, let's eat up so we can meet Annabel and hear this complicated story," Ford said, eyeing Noah. Again, cop face. Nothing got by Ford Dawson. Noah knew his older brother had long felt responsible for his younger siblings, living with them only part-time growing up, and now at a distance of hours.

Luckily Noah had already finished his steak and a heap of the roasted asparagus in garlic butter, his favorite vegetable. Because his appetite was shot.

"Hey, is that Sara Mayhew?" Rex asked as he and Ford came out the sliding glass doors to the back patio with three kinds of pie for dessert.

Noah turned and shielded his eyes from the glare of the sun, just beginning to make its descent. Sara was coming up the path from the foreman's cabin, wheeling the double stroller. She wore a long black sundress and sandals, a straw hat on her head, her silky brown hair in a braid down one shoulder. She looked like a vision and he could barely take his eyes off her.

"Sara *Perry*, right?" Zeke corrected. "I occasionally saw photos of her and Willem Perry in the society pages of the *Converse County Gazette*. Once I ran into them at a fund-raiser and hugged Sara hello, and Willem practically grabbed her away from me. I'm surprised he didn't take a swing at me." He tilted his head. "I read he died in a car accident a couple months ago. Is Sara okay?"

Noah glanced around at the shocked expressions, barely hearing the murmurings of "how awful" and "he was so young" and "poor Sara." None of them knew Willem the way he and Sara did—Sara most of all, of course—because the three of them had been the same age, had come up in school together. "She'll *be* okay," Noah said, offering her a smile as she got closer.

As Sara arrived on the patio, the group got up to say hello and offer condolences. She handled that well with brief thank-yous and nods, accepted their hugs, and then conversation thankfully turned to oohs and ahhs about the babies.

And then, from Ford, his focus on the twins: "So who's who? I assume one is Noah's daughter and one is yours, Sara?"

"Actually, they're both mine," Sara said, adjusting the sun shade on the stroller so the Dawsons could get a better look. "Annabel and Chance are twins."

"Wait," Axel said. "Daisy told us Noah found Annabel abandoned on his porch in the middle of the night—right before a major rainstorm." As a search-and-rescue specialist, those details would be foremost in his mind. "Since I'd have a hard time believing *you* left your daughter like that, there has to be a story here."

Four sets of blue eyes turned to Sara, then Noah. Daisy already knew the details, of course, but even she was staring at Noah.

"There is," Noah says. "And it's ugly. I'll let Sara tell it," he said, sitting down. The brothers took his solemn cue and all sat back down at the table.

"Why do I think we're going to need whiskey for this?" Rex asked, leaning back and crossing his arms over his chest.

"It's as ugly as Noah says," Sara began and then launched into the story.

The expressions on his brothers' faces said it all.

"Wish I could arrest the bastard," Ford said, shaking his head. "I've seen a lot in my time on the force, but this?" Disgust was palpable on his face. "Have you spoken to police about the midwife's actions?"

"Not yet," Sara said. "Willem's lawyer did a little digging for me after we found out what Willem—and she—had done. She officially retired the next day."

"How are you planning on handling that?" Ford asked.

"I'd like to pay the midwife a visit," Sara said. "I know there's no excuse for what she did, given her job, her responsibility to her patient and the baby she was hired to help deliver. But I also know that Willem threatened her and that he had something on her. I'll plan on seeing her in the next couple weeks. I've just got a lot to focus on right now."

"If you need help or an escort for the visit, you let me know," Ford said.

"I will. And thank you."

"You know what I can't stop thinking about?" Daisy said. "How lucky it was that Noah actually heard Annabel's cries at two in the morning outside his window. He's always been a light sleeper. A herd of buffalo couldn't wake me up."

"Oh, trust me, one tiny peep out of your little one and you'll be bolting up," Sara assured her. "Mother radar is strong stuff."

Daisy smiled. "Glad to hear that." She took a sip of her seltzer. "You know, given what your late husband did, Sara, things sure worked out all right. Noah *did* wake up. He saw the note saying she was his and took immediate responsibility—he even had her checked out by Doc Bakerton at 2:30 a.m. And then just seven weeks later, the truth is revealed in that letter. Willem's whole terrible plan was interrupted within two months. Someone up there was sure looking out for you."

"I think about how it could have been decades," Sara said, shaking her head.

"Cosmic justice," Axel said. "Sorry if I'm speaking ill of the dead, but…"

No one disagreed. That the plan had been foiled so early because Willem had been killed in an accident and had left that "last laugh" letter for Sara did seem like cosmic justice.

Noah loved Annabel with everything in him, but now that he knew the truth of her parentage and her brief history, he wasn't Team Ignorance Is Bliss. It wasn't—and never was. Annabel deserved to know her mother; Sara deserved to be with her daughter. Things had worked out for the best for the two of them. Except when it came to what Noah would have to give up when Sara—as she put it—left one day.

"The twins are beautiful, Sara," Axel said, standing up and peering in the stroller.

"And look just like you," Ford noted.

"Didn't Noah say that Annabel looked just like him?" Rex asked with a grin. He peered closer at the baby girl. "Uh, maybe the coloring—hair and eyes. But that nose, that chin, the shape of the eyes, even her expression—all Sara."

Humph. Noah really had thought Annabel looked something like him; he had from the moment he'd brought her inside. Yeah, she'd looked more familiar than like him, but *still*.

"And both twins are safe and sound," Zeke added with a nod.

They all raised their bottles to that.

"Well, hell," Axel said. "I say they're our *honorary* niece and nephew."

As everyone clinked to that, Noah noted that Sara's smile was genuine.

So what did that make him? Honorary dad?

As the group crowded around the stroller to take closer looks and photos of their honorary niece and nephew, Ford held back.

"You okay?" his brother whispered.

"Somehow," Noah said. More glumly than he meant to.

"Probably because you care more about Sara than you do about yourself," Ford whispered back. "Always have, right?"

Noah sucked in a breath. He was always surprised at how well his siblings knew him when they didn't get together very often the past ten years. But suddenly he understood why Ford, who'd led the intervention in Noah getting his act together *and* rallying the siblings in support of Noah's determination to rebuild the Dawson Family Guest Ranch, believed in his youngest brother. Because Ford *did* know him. And that confidence in him meant the world to Noah.

Yes. He did care more about Sara than about himself. Always had, always would. Except for those months two years ago when he'd finally given in to his attraction to her, despite how bad he knew he was for her, when he'd been at rock bottom without realizing it, putting on a good show with the small ranch he'd bought until he couldn't hide who he was back then: his father's son.

As Ford joined the others in fussing over the twins, Noah couldn't take his eyes off Sara, who'd never looked more beautiful, Annabel in her arms.

Everything that meant anything to him was in this backyard, on this property right now, including the ranch itself. And the best way to take care of Sara and the twins was to make sure the ranch was a big success. Annabel and Chance would always have a home here, Noah's own grandparents' home for many years. There was family history here for them, and he wanted Dawson's to succeed for them.

He owed his siblings that too—for their investment in the ranch and in him. He couldn't fail, couldn't lose sight of the prize: steady bookings, good reviews, word of mouth. Nothing could get between him and making this ranch everything it needed to be for his family— and Sara's.

So keep your distance from her, no matter how attracted you are to her.

Not going to be easy, since they were not only sharing a cabin, but essentially a workplace. He was her boss, and he was going to have to keep things very professional between them.

And his thoughts were anything but professional as he took in how beautiful she was, how sexy, memories of their brief romance hitting him left and right.

If you care about her, you'll keep your hands and lips to yourself.

He made that silent vow, then headed over to where the group stood around Sara and the babies, his head clear, his heart guarded.

Chapter 7

After a brief tour of the guest ranch and more hat tipping to Noah at what he'd done with the place, the Dawson brothers—except for Ford—got back in their rented truck and headed off to the Airbnb they'd booked in town. There were free rooms in the main house and a bunch of comfortable couches in the lodge, but between being honest about the place still having too many bad memories attached *and* not wanting to distract from the big day tomorrow, Axel, Rex and Zeke opted to stay elsewhere. Sara had gotten the impression that Noah understood; he still seemed to be marveling over the fact that they'd come at all. Ford had been cryptic about why he wanted to stay at the house, and Noah hadn't pushed, but Sara sure was curious. Ford was the Dawson sibling who held the worst memories of the ranch.

Now, just after 9:30 p.m., she and Noah were in the nursery, putting the twins to sleep in their crib. She stood beside Noah as he told a story about Batman, an Appaloosa, escaping his stall and running all over the ranch in search of the perfect carrot. Noah's voice was so soothing, so beautifully familiar, that even Sara almost fell asleep, but the twins were out within two minutes.

"My work here is done," he said with a smile, but it quickly faded.

"Everything okay?" She knew he had a lot going on, a lot on his mind, but she had a feeling he was still thinking about their conversation in the barn earlier that day.

"Are you planning to leave?" he asked, finally turning his head to look at her. "If you are, I want to know. I need to prepare myself so I'm not blindsided by losing Annabel."

She liked how direct this new Noah was. But then again, this wasn't a conversation she could have now. How could she possibly answer him?

"I have no idea what I'm doing, Noah. Right now, I want to be here. I *need* to be here. That's all I know."

He crossed his arms over his chest. "So maybe you'll stay for a couple of months."

"I really don't know. I guess it depends on how things between us are. And right now, they're not good."

He stared at her. "In general or this minute?"

She felt herself relaxing. "This minute. And the minute earlier in the barn."

"I don't want to run you out of here," he said, taking her hand. "I want you to stay."

If she wasn't mistaken, he'd been about to add the word *forever* but then clamped his mouth shut.

So why did that make her feel so…prickly? Because

that *want* had nothing to do with her and everything to do with his love for the baby he'd thought was his daughter?

Maybe. That should make absolute sense to her. It wasn't as if she wanted Noah Dawson to be romantically interested in her. Did she?

Oh hell. She did a little. Because she was still reeling from all that had happened and needed a pair of strong, familiar arms? Or because her residual feelings for him would never, ever fade? Noah was her first love. Her only love. Yeah, she'd been married. She'd also had some short-term relationships over the years that hadn't gone anywhere—maybe because she'd never felt about anyone the way she'd felt about Noah. Despite how wild he'd been, how she hadn't been able to tame him. He'd done that reining in himself, now that she thought about it. Maybe that was why she was even remotely thinking about him *that* way.

When she was ready to find love again—though that felt very far off—she'd look for a man who'd be a great father to her twins. Like Noah.

She'd look for a man who was responsible and reliable in ways she could plainly see. Like Noah.

She'd look for a man who sent little chills of anticipation up her spine at the thought of kissing him, of being in bed with him. Like Noah.

Oh hell. She was sunk!

She wanted to flee the room *and* fling herself into his arms. That's how much she couldn't get a handle on herself.

She needed fresh air and more open space, somewhere his tall, muscular, sexy being couldn't dominate.

She gave his hand a squeeze. "Let's go enjoy the gorgeous night. We can sit outside and *not* talk."

He laughed. "Let's do that."

Downstairs, he grabbed a baby monitor from the hallway console table and they headed out to the front porch, so big and welcoming. His sister had told her she'd planted all the beautiful flower boxes that hung from the windows, and there were four white rocking chairs and a porch swing along the side porch where it wrapped around. They opted for the swing, Noah giving them a push with his foot.

She had the urge to wrap her arm around him, and whether she should or not, she was going to. Doing so earned her a smile and Noah scooting a bit closer. "How many nights did we sit here and look at the stars and not talk because there was too much to say and we both knew what the other thought anyway?"

"I feel like that's both the case and not, now, though," he said. "We do have a lot to talk about, but it's so complicated—and not—that there's really nothing to say at all." He shook his head. "Did any of that make sense? Was it actually English? Between you saying things like you're leaving and my brothers' surprise visit, I'm a little out of whack."

"What if I promise I'll stay the summer at the very least?" she said, turning to look at him.

He got up abruptly and walked to the porch railing, facing away from her, then turned around. "Great. So three more months of getting attached to Annabel and now her brother and then you'll leave? That's great, Sara."

"I thought we weren't going to talk because it's too complicated."

"I don't push things under the ole rug anymore," he said. "You talk or you fester and implode. I'd rather talk."

"I suggested the summer because you'll know we're staying put for at least that long."

"I *love* Annabel, Sara," he said, a fierce edge in his voice. "She's my daughter. There, I said it. She's my daughter," he shouted into the sky. "I know she's yours, but she's mine too."

Sara gasped. "I get it. I do."

"Marry me. Let's get married. That's the solution. Annabel stays forever. And not only that, but I get to be dad to her twin brother too. The twins grow up in the place where they have so much family history. Both Annabel and Chance will have a loving, devoted father. You'll have the security of the ranch that means home to you. And to sweeten that end of it, I'll split my share of the ranch with you fifty-fifty. You'll be an owner, with the same share as I have."

She gasped again. It was all too much to take in. The marriage proposal. The security. The ranch ownership. *The marriage proposal.*

All because he felt like Annabel's father in his heart, in his blood and veins and every cell in his body.

Security—for the twins and for herself when she was penniless with maybe $1,100 in jewelry to sell if she needed to.

Home—when the Dawson Family Guest Ranch was home and always had been.

And if the place went belly up, if Noah reverted to his old ways and ran the place into the ground?

He won't, a voice inside her knew full well. *He cares*

too much now. His family is involved. Annabel is involved. And now you and Chance are added to the mix.

And you believe in him.

"I need some time to think," she said, turning away.
It was all too much.

"Am I being selfish here, Sara?" he asked, stepping
closer. "I know what you went through with Willem.
Why you said yes. Am I asking the same thing of you?"
He took a step back, regret all over his face. "You know
what, forget I even brought up the word *marriage*. After
everything you've been through, it's not fair to you."

She studied him—hard—and his sincerity was clear.
His sincerity had never been the issue. "I don't think
you're being selfish. I understand where you're coming
from. You're making me an offer, Noah. What Willem
did, what I accepted, was very different. Or it *feels* different, anyway. But I do need time to think."

He nodded. "Take all the time you want. I'll go do
my rounds on the animals. Need anything before I go?"

A hug. A bear-hug.

She shook her head. "I'll just sit out here awhile and
then probably go up to bed."

He nodded. And then she watched as the man who'd
just proposed to her headed down the path toward the
red barn.

Marry Noah Dawson? Once, that had been her
dream. Now it might be her only option for security for
herself and the twins. But more, she understood Noah's
depth of love for the baby he'd rescued, had thought was
his, had raised, even if it was for barely two months.
How could she take Annabel from him when the baby
meant so much to him that he was willing to give up
his freedom for her?

Maybe that was what put a check mark in the no column. When she'd dreamed of marrying Noah Dawson, love was the biggest factor. Now, it wasn't even on their radar.

Noah moved sideways through the stables, giving each of the thirty-two horses a pat and a little pep talk for tomorrow. He was expecting twelve guests, which meant twelve horses would christen the new and improved Dawson Family Guest Ranch's trails and fields. And though Noah would do his best to match rider to horse based on the guest's level of experience or lack thereof, sometimes, they'd have to see how it went. Which meant having lots of solid, sweet, well-rested horses to choose from. "Based on the initial questionnaire the guests filled out," he said to horse twenty-seven, Blaze, "you'll definitely be paired with our most experienced rider. Do me proud tomorrow." He gave Blaze a pat.

He'd gotten up to horse number thirty, Sugar Cube, when he finally broke, when he couldn't pretend to have only the ranch at the forefront of his mind.

"I proposed, Sugar Cube," he said to the silvery-white quarter horse with the soulful brown eyes. "Proposed marriage. What if she says no? What if she says yes?"

Sugar Cube didn't respond, but she still got her pat. Noah moved to the next stall, Goldie, and told the gorgeous palomino with her gold-colored body and white mane that he had no idea what Sara's response was going to be. "Think she'll say yes? She might? Then we'll both have what we want and need. Right?"

He'd still considered Sara his best friend the past

two years when they hadn't spoken or laid eyes on each other, when they'd known nothing about each other's lives. That was how strong their connection was. To him, anyway. That seemed like a solid basis for marriage. Much more so than the hot and cold of fleeting love with all its passion and arguments. Best friendship: lasting. Real. He'd let passion intrude on that friendship two and a half years ago, and what happened? He'd run Sara off into the arms of a psycho.

He'd be able to raise Annabel and Chance. They'd be his children for real. And his precious Sara, whom he cared about to the moon and back, would be beside him, sharing his life, his world.

"It wasn't impulsive," he told Bluebell in the next stall, giving her a pat. "I mean, it was. I didn't think of it until that moment, but it's probably the smartest thing that's come out of my mouth ever." He reached the end of the stalls, patted King and felt the tension leave his shoulders.

As he was leaving the stables to head back toward the main barn, he noticed his brother Ford walking about a hundred feet ahead, just around the side of the pasture fence. Ford was staring at a piece of white paper, then looking down, then around. He had something in his other hand. Looked like a narrow pitchfork.

What the hell was he doing?

"Ford?" Noah called out.

His brother jerked his head up, clearly surprised. "Just looking around."

"Sure you are," Noah said, walking over to him. He glanced at the piece of paper in his hands, which looked like some kind of crudely drawn map. "What's that?"

Ford sighed. "My legacy from Dad."

"Ah." He suddenly realized why Ford "Hell Will Freeze Over Before I Step Foot on the Ranch" Dawson had decided to stay the night at the main house.

"A map of some kind?" Noah asked.

Ford nodded. "It was folded up in the letter he left me. The letter rambled on about how one night when he was drunk and angry at my mother over an argument, he put her diary, which he'd jammed open with a knife, in a metal box and buried it somewhere near the stables. Or he thought near the stables."

"Her diary?" Noah repeated. "You sure you want to find that?"

Ford sighed hard. "Apparently my mother had a secret. That Dad knew about. He wrote that my mother flew into a rage and tore up the property looking for the diary but never found it. Then I guess she gave up on it, figuring he was too much of a drunk to ever dig it up himself and use it against her, since he'd likely never find it."

"Any idea what the secret is?" Noah asked.

He shrugged. "Who the hell knows. I'm not sure I want to know. But Dad's letter said it's something I *should* know, that he's sorry he wasn't a better father to me or any of his kids. I figured while I was here tonight, I might as well try to find it, since Dad made a point of saying it was far off any of the trails or paths. I didn't want to do anything to mess up the grounds the night before opening day. I've just been poking into the dirt, hoping to hit on something hard."

"I'll help," Noah said.

For a minute there, Noah thought lone-ranger Ford was going to say, *nah, you've got a big day tomorrow, I've got this*, but Ford replied, "I'd appreciate that."

Noah jogged over to the stables and got a sharp-ended tool, then jogged back over to where Ford was poking the ground in circles. "Let me see the map."

Ford handed it to him. "This seems to be the area," Noah said, taking in where his dad had drawn the stables with a few horse heads poking out, the tree line, the five-hundred-plus-acre pasture. There was an X on a tree trunk—a tree that seemed to stand alone. And the only tree that stood alone was close to where Ford was poking with the pitchfork.

They poked and poked and poked, walking in circles and squares, but both came up empty.

"I had a feeling I wouldn't find it," Ford said. He shrugged. "Just thought I'd give it a try."

Noah glanced around at the grass. There was just too much land to cover. "I can keep looking when I get the chance. And you can always come back."

Ford ran a hand through his hair. "I might. We'll see. Sometimes it's better not to know." He shook his head. "I'm not sure I mean that. I don't know."

Noah got the sense his life wasn't the only complicated one.

"I'll be heading out first thing," Ford said. "Good luck tomorrow. I know this place will be a big success."

Noah extended his hand, and Ford glanced at it, then pulled his youngest sibling into an embrace.

"You did good, Noah," Ford said. "With the ranch, with Annabel. With whatever's going on with Sara and both twins, considering that they're all here."

Noah nodded, Ford's words of praise a boosting balm as he embraced his oldest brother. "I'm trying. Hard." *To the point that I* proposed.

Let her say yes when I get back to the cabin, he thought.

* * *

Sara sat in the kitchen, on her third cup of decaf, picking at the leftover peach pie that Daisy had packed up after dinner for Noah to take to the cabin. She heard the key in the lock, and her pulse leaped.

Yes, no, maybe so. She had no answer yet. Her answer was all of the above.

Noah came into the kitchen and gave her such a forced casual smile that she laughed. Sara could plainly see how tightly wound he was right now and how he was trying to fight it.

Because he'd proposed and wished he hadn't? Because he worried she'd say no?

She took a sip of her coffee. "I'll get right to the point. If we're going to put a marriage on the table, we'd better square away some important details."

She could see the relief in his eyes, the way his shoulders relaxed some.

He got himself a bottle of water, then sat down. "At least it's up for discussion."

She was about to blurt out, *Well, I did it once before with a monster, so why not with my one true love?*

Which just made her feel worse, more tied up in knots over the whole damned thing.

"Noah, marriage is supposed to be sacred. It's supposed to mean something more than a mutually beneficial partnership."

"That's what it is for everyone who gets married," he said. "A couple is madly in love. That's mutually beneficial, so they marry."

She raised an eyebrow. "You know what I mean."

"I do. And my point still stands. We've got a lot of water under the bridge, Sara. And we have some very good reasons to band together and do this. Unless you think your soul mate is out there, waiting for you to be ready. Do you?"

She stared into her coffee for a moment, his words jabbing her in her chest. "You obviously don't think either of ours is. Or you wouldn't be proposing what's basically an arranged marriage."

He took a swig of his water. "I guess different things are more important to me now. I figure to you too."

She stood up and walked to the window, looking out at the night, at the pasture, at the Wyoming wilderness beyond. "What the hell happened?" she asked.

She could see in the reflection from the window that he stood up.

"What do you mean?" he asked, concern deepening his voice.

She turned around. "This entire conversation. A marriage of convenience. How the hell did my life come to this?" She stalked over to the chair and sat down. "I'm just whining and feeling sorry for myself. I'm pissed, Noah."

He sat back down too. "You have every right to be angry. But that isn't my aim—to dredge up bad feelings. If that's what the proposal is doing to you, let's forget it. You stay here as long as you want. I just want you to be happy and feel safe."

She glanced at him, her eyes welling. *I just want you to be happy and feel safe.* A person who said that was a person who cared about her. And he was the only person saying anything like that. Her family was gone. Her friends scattered. She had no one left.

"I used to believe in soul mates," she said. *You, you*

big dope. You were my soul mate. "I don't believe in that stuff anymore, Noah."

He leaned forward. "Let's be each other's family, Sara. You, me and the twins. A family, right here where it all began for both of us in so many ways. And you'll have half my ownership of the ranch."

Could this work? If she didn't believe in love and romance anymore, if her first marriage had blown everything she'd once cared about to bits, then why not accept a partnership with Noah Dawson? They'd set terms. They'd treat each other respectfully. They'd get what they needed.

"I'd never take any part of your share of the ranch, Noah. But yes," she added, standing up again. "I will marry you."

Before Noah could stop himself, he got up and held out his arms, and Sara rushed into them. He could feel her holding herself a bit stiffly, which he completely understood. This hug was about gratitude on both sides, about the friendship that would never fade, no matter what. It was their handshake on an agreement.

"I was so afraid you'd say no, Sara." He found himself holding her an extra beat too long, inhaling the balsamy scent of her hair, remembering how good having her so close against him used to feel.

She stepped back and leaned against the counter. "We should discuss logistics, of course."

He nodded and sat back down.

She did too. "Let's just go to the town hall. There's no waiting period in Wyoming. We could be married in the morning."

"My head might explode," he said. "Getting married

right before the ranch reopens. How about we wait till the first group leaves? That'll give us time to decide if we're telling people about this or keeping it our secret. If we're wearing rings." He took a drink of his water.

"But there are some issues we can settle right now," she said, looking everywhere but at him.

"Like?" he asked.

"Separate bedrooms. No sex. No kissing, no touching, no hanky-panky of any kind, Noah Dawson. We're making a deal for those mutually beneficial reasons you listed. I don't want any confusion about what the marriage is."

He wasn't so sure they had to make any proclamations. Who knew how things would evolve?

Then again, sex had destroyed their relationship once and sent her away.

On one hand, he could see them returning from a long day, a problem with a guest, a sick calf, and having the urge to take her in his arms and kiss her, hold her, this beautiful woman he'd loved for so long and who'd share so much of his life going forward. He'd always been so physically drawn to Sara, including right now. How would he tamp down these feelings?

He'd just have to. Because on that other hand, the confusion she'd mentioned had the potential power to ruin their arrangement entirely and send her away again. He couldn't risk that.

He took in one last long drink of her luscious body, her pink lips, her brown eyes and long silky brown hair. He closed his eyes for a half second, vowing that when he opened them, he'd see her as discussed: off-limits.

"Agreed," he said. "We're friends. We won't let anything get in the way of that and what we're doing."

She gave him something of a smile that didn't last very long. "Good. Then we have a deal."

The problem was that the vow he'd just made to see her as off-limits wasn't working. She was still sexy as hell. But if there was one thing Noah Dawson had developed the past few months, it was self-control.

He'd do this because he *had* to.

Chapter 8

The next morning, at just after 11:00 a.m., Sara stood beside Noah and Daisy outside the Dawson Family Guest Ranch lodge as a silver van pulled up in the parking area. The first guests had arrived, and she could feel the Dawsons practically vibrating with excitement and nerves.

The weather couldn't have been better—blue skies, brilliant sunshine, low humidity and sweet breezes in midseventies temperatures. Sara smoothed her hunter green polo shirt with the ranch's logo on the pocket, Staff spelled out in caps on the back. Last night, Noah had knocked on her door and said he'd forgotten to give her an employee shirt; all staff would wear the green shirts and jeans during working hours.

When he'd held up the shirt in her doorway, she'd been so moved by it, by her memories, that she'd wanted to pull him into her bedroom and never let him go. She'd had a Dawson's staff T-shirt when she was a teenager. She still had it, though she was a size small back then and seven weeks after giving birth, Sara was a definite L for large. The old one was a burnt tan color, and she liked the forest green even better. The new shirt reminded her of all good things, of new beginnings. Before Noah had knocked on her door, she'd wondered how she'd sleep with questions of their pending marriage looming in her thoughts. But somehow the green shirt representing her employment, money coming in, *security*, had her falling asleep within a half hour.

The twins had woken her up twice, and a third time, very early this morning, she'd gone into the nursery to find Noah already taking care of business. He'd looked wide-awake and alert, excited about his first guests. Mrs. Pickles was with the twins now in the cabin, and Sara liked that she just might see the sitter wheeling them around the grounds in the stroller during the day.

A thirtysomething redhead stepped off the van, shook hands with Noah and Daisy, and then Noah introduced her to Sara as Connie Freedman, the life coach running the retreat.

As the retreat participants came off the van—eleven aside from the coach—Connie introduced everyone. But Sara was surprised—and thrilled—to already know one of the women, an old friend from high school named Tabitha Corey. Since the retreat was getting underway immediately, Sara would have to wait to catch up with Tabitha until this evening.

As guest relations manager, Daisy led the group to their cabins to settle in before the tour, opening session and meet and greet of the horses Noah had chosen for each participant. But Sara couldn't help but notice most of the guests looked kind of…glum.

"Is it my imagination, or do the guests not look very excited to be here?" Noah whispered.

"Oh wait," Sara said. "The retreat is called Get Your Groove Back."

"What does that mean—exactly?" he asked, tilting his head. "I thought it was about getting some R and R."

"Well, that too, but getting your groove back generally means you've lost that spark and you want to find it. A recharge kind of thing for the heart, mind and soul."

Noah raised an eyebrow. "I just ride Bolt when I need that."

She smiled. "That's why they're here. Nature helps. Horses help. Inspiring talks help. Like-minded people who won't make you feel like you're whining or just need to man up or chin up. Hopefully they'll look very different in a week."

He nodded. "I'm pretty sure I recognized one of the guests—and her name too. Tabitha Corey. We went to high school together, right?"

Sara nodded. Tabitha looked very in need of a recharge, even if she was in full Western regalia, the kind of outfit that said she'd gone all out on new riding gear and Stetsons and Western-style shirts when plain old jeans and T-shirts would do. Sara couldn't help but be curious about why Tabitha had signed on for the retreat. She had been a golden girl, the kind you couldn't hate because she was kind and friendly to everyone, even if she was a queen bee. She'd recently gotten engaged to a tall, good-looking endodontist Willem had played squash with, but they hadn't socialized as couples. Willem would insist on showing up for fund-raisers and important events, but then he'd want to leave after fifteen minutes, which had always been fine with Sara. She'd noticed the diamond ring on Tabitha's finger. Huge. And she looked like a million bucks, despite the lack of light in her eyes. Sara couldn't help but wonder why Tabitha was here.

As the afternoon went on, Sara helped both Daisy and Noah in various capacities, and she found herself loving the fast pace and constantly changing duties. This morning, before the guests had arrived, she'd double-checked the cabins with Daisy to make sure they were all ready with welcome baskets and fresh wildflowers and had all the necessary supplies. She'd helped Noah and Dylan in the main barn with lining up the saddles the guests would likely be using. Since the group would hit the cafeteria for lunch at twelve thirty, she'd stopped in a bit before to see if Cowboy Joe needed any help. He had everything under control with his small staff. Lunch was his specialty, chili and corn bread, and the entire caf smelled amazing.

At two, the life coach and retreat director, Connie, was giving a talk called "What Happened to My Groove, Anyway?" in the lodge. Sara had been assigned to work the concessions counter, offering coffee and tea and lemon-infused water and snacks, and she'd been riveted by Connie within a minute. The life coach was in her late thirties with pretty shoulder-length red hair and dark brown eyes, in a forest green pantsuit that managed to look woodsy and professional at the same time. Connie stood at a podium in front of the eleven seated participants, who all held little silver notebooks. Sara had never met a life coach before, but Connie's talent at public speaking and conveying her message was an immediate given.

"Feeling stuck," Connie was saying. "Knowing you're stuck and knowing there are probably steps you could take to get yourself unstuck but being too down in the dumps to do anything but mope on your sofa with a stack of tabloid magazines and the remote control and a family-size bag of sour cream and onion potato chips. And a two-liter bottle of soda. And a big bag of fun-size chocolates." She gazed at the group. "How many of you can relate?"

Sara's hand shot up in the air before she could stop herself. She pulled her hand down, but not before Connie sent her an encouraging smile. Twelve hands, including Connie's, were up. Sara wanted to stick hers back up too. Hell yeah, she could relate.

"But guess what?" Connie said. "All of you, every single one of you, has already started the process of getting yourselves unstuck, getting your groove back. Because you're here. You did something proactive. You got off the sofa, figuratively and literally." She smiled. "Round of applause, ladies." Connie clapped, and so did everyone else, including Sara, down low under the table.

Maybe she shouldn't be cheering herself on, though. She hadn't gotten herself off the sofa—figuratively speaking. She'd been propelled off it by Willem's death. She'd learned the truth about her daughter, sped over to the ranch and here she was. In a new life entirely.

But she had to wonder just how long she would have lived under Willem Perry's thumb. Being chastised for installing the toilet paper roll the "wrong" way. Night after night, unable to dislodge the lump in her chest, in her throat.

"We all have our breaking points," Connie continued. "You're all here because you're either close or you've reached it and you're ready to break out, break free, be who you actually are."

The part about the breaking point made Sara feel better; she'd reached it—she'd briefly left during her pregnancy and had been pulled back out of fear, but she would have figured out a way to leave again. She was sure of that. And anyway, going over this was pointless. She was in a new life—with her son and daughter. What mattered was what she did with her present and how she planned for her future—their future.

She frowned as she recalled how sure she'd felt earlier about accepting Noah's proposal. But had she been operating out of fear, out of feeling like she was stuck? She had a job, a place to live, a good roof over her babies' heads. She was earning her way here. Noah had offered her half his share of the ranch to sweeten the security deal, but she didn't want that from him. She'd never take that from him.

Suddenly she was only 50 percent on the idea of marrying.

There was a solid week between now and when they'd go to the town hall to legally become husband and wife. She'd see how things felt.

"Sometimes, the hardest part can be doing just that—getting up, asking for help, making a commitment to yourself," Connie went on. "And sometimes the hardest part might be yet to come—really examining what you want and how to achieve that. Sometimes we don't feel like we deserve what we want, let alone to actually get it. I'm here to tell you, we all do deserve it. So at this retreat, let's commit to giving ourselves a chance.

Baby steps, big steps, whatever you're ready for. We're all on our way!"

Yeah! Sara almost cheered as she straightened the bananas in the pretty blue bowl on the table.

Connie handed out schedules and outlined the rest of the day—next up was being matched with horses, so the group got up, a few stopping at the concession table for the lemon-infused water or a coffee or a piece of fruit. As the participants left the lodge, former golden girl Tabitha hung back, then came over to the table and made herself a cup of coffee. She looked amazing—gorgeous long blond hair, light makeup that looked completely natural, the fancy Western outfit and dark pink cowboy boots. But she sure didn't look happy. Newly engaged to a young Brad Pitt endodontist or not. And, of course, she was here at a retreat for getting her groove back. Sara would have never in a million years thought Tabitha Corey had ever or would ever *lose* her groove.

You never know what goes on in someone's private life, Sara thought as Tabitha stirred her coffee. *Appearances are deceiving. Yup, I know all about that.*

"So far, so good," Tabitha said, a hopeful light suddenly in her pretty hazel eyes. "Right?" But then the light disappeared and she seemed so conflicted. Something was definitely bothering her.

Sara reached out a hand and covered Tabitha's. "I'm not even a participant in the retreat and I feel empowered." She smiled.

Tabitha nodded and seemed about to say something, then she lifted up her coffee cup as if toasting in agreement and shuffled out, catching up with the rest of the group.

Sara wanted to run after her, give her a hug, tell her

she was here for her if Tabitha wanted to talk, but she could see Connie now standing next to Tabitha, chatting away as the group headed to the barn. She had a good feeling about Connie and what this week would give all these women. Maybe even Sara herself.

Her phone pinged with a text. Daisy.

Have fifteen minutes to help set up the meditation room in the lodge? Second floor event room.

Meditation? Sara thought. *I might lie down and stay there myself.*

Be right there, she texted back.

Between the retreat and her job, Sara just might get her own groove back. If she watched her step with Noah Dawson. And she would.

The barn hadn't collapsed. A horse with a guest on its back hadn't gone rogue, throwing her fifty feet in the air. No one had gotten food poisoning from Cowboy Joe's chili (not that they would). These and many more were the irrational fears that had kept Noah up at night when he should be getting any chance of sleep he could, particularly with two babies in the cabin. But opening day of the Dawson Family Guest Ranch had gone off without a hitch so far—knock on every piece of wood in the vicinity.

He stood at the small barn beside his cabin and gave Bolt, whom he'd just returned to his stall, a piece of carrot. Then he lifted his face to the gorgeous late-May sunshine and breathed in the warm, breezy, fresh air. Between the weather and the total lack of problems, he could almost relax, but he'd save that for the end of the week. He'd spent the past hour with the retreat guests in the barn and pasture, first making sure they were matched to the right horses for their level and comfort and then joining in on their first ride in the huge expanse of prairie to the right of the main barn. Satisfied that the group was comfortable and set for the time being, he'd left them in the horse leader's capable hands with Dylan and Bea, the ranch hands, who'd ride alongside the group as backup.

About to walk the paths to keep a general eye on things, Noah saw Mrs. Pickles come out of his cabin with the twins in their double stroller, using the ramp he'd built. That tiny burst of joy, still so unexpected, went kaboom in his chest at the sight of the babies.

"There are my sweet twins," Noah said, walking over with a smile. He leaned over and unbuckled Chance, carefully lifting him out of his infant seat.

He froze, just for a moment, sucking in a breath. *My twins?*

Reaching for Chance as easily as he would Annabel?

The little cowboy had worked his way into Noah's heart just as his sister had. And just as fast. He couldn't really even think of Annabel without thinking of Chance; they were a pair, a package, a set. Individuals, but he loved them with equal ferocity.

Oh God. He did love them. Both. Hard.

"I was hoping to run into you, Mrs. Pickles." Sara's voice came from down the path. There was tension in that voice, if he wasn't mistaken.

He turned around, Chance cradled against his chest. Sara was coming from the direction of the lodge. As it had earlier, the sight of her in her Dawson Family Guest Ranch staff shirt shot straight to his heart, and despite his vow to keep his mind off how attracted to her he was, every cell in his body went on red alert. "Same here. And I did."

She smiled sort of vaguely, her gaze on the baby in his arms. What? Why did she seem uneasy?

She leaned over the stroller and gave Annabel a kiss on the head, then got as close to Chance as she could while keeping her body as far away from Noah as possible, and deposited a kiss on her son's head.

Hmm. She was definitely bothered by something.

"These two are such good babies," Mrs. Pickles said, grinning at her charges. "I love watching them. And what a lovely day for a walk."

"Well," Noah said, putting Chance back and running a finger down Annabel's cheek. "I won't keep you." He turned to Sara. "I was about to take a walk of my own on a grounds check. Join me?"

"Sure," she said. She leaned over the stroller. "'Bye, sweets," she cooed to her twins. "See you later. I love you," she whispered.

Then they both watched as Mrs. Pickles wheeled the stroller toward the lodge.

"There goes my heart," Sara said, her expression wistful as she stared after the sitter and the stroller.

He stared after them too, then looked at Sara. "I know what you mean."

She frowned, took one last look at the retreating figure of Mrs. Pickles, then turned for the path toward the main barn.

So he was not mistaken that something was bugging her. And it was something *he* was doing.

"You seemed uneasy before, when you saw me holding Chance," he said, walking beside her.

She turned and looked at him. "I hate that you know me so well, Noah Dawson."

He grinned. "Actually, us knowing each other so well might make things easier. Because it makes us talk about even uncomfortable stuff."

"I also hate talking about uncomfortable stuff." She bit her lip. "I guess I'm just taking everything in, Noah. The idea of getting married. What that will mean going forward. About the twins too."

He stopped. "What do you mean?"

"You already feel like Annabel's father," she said. "You're going to feel like Chance's father too."

He was already beginning to.

She crossed her arms over her chest. "And I'll have to factor you in when I think about what's right for me and the twins. How did that happen? When did you become a vital part of my plans for my life?" She frowned and turned away.

"When—"

She whirled back around. "Rhetorical question. I know, I know. When you brought Annabel inside and took responsibility for her. When a note said she was yours."

Damned right. But he understood how strange that must be for her. And yeah, maybe even unsettling. He wasn't Annabel's father. He'd met Chance the day Sara arrived on the ranch. Noah shouldn't factor into Sara's decisions for herself.

But he also couldn't help how he felt or that circumstances had unfolded as they had. Her baby girl *had* been left on his porch. He *had* taken her in. He *had* claimed responsibility. And he *loved* Annabel. She'd always feel like his child. Chance now did too, because he was Annabel's brother, because they were living in his cabin, and the little guy had grabbed hold of his heart and wasn't letting go.

"Ah," she said with an exasperated tinge to her voice and throwing her hands up in the air. "I get your side. I get my side. But I need to get *my* groove back, Noah. Sounds cute and all on retreat flyers, but it's serious stuff and hard work, and I don't know that coming into my own means marrying you for security." She shook her head. "In fact, it doesn't."

Oh hell. He understood that too well. He'd had to fight his butt off to stand up again—and the only person he'd been fighting was himself. He'd found his way. He wasn't going to stand in Sara's while she worked out her past.

"If you're telling me you've changed your mind about getting married, I...understand," he said, holding her gaze for a moment, and then he had to look away and let the disappointment sock him in the gut. She'd leave. She'd leave and take the twins. Not immediately, not even in a few months, but a new year always meant something to Sara, stood for new beginnings and possibilities. She'd probably leave by then.

"That would kill you, wouldn't it?" she asked. "If I told you I changed my mind. I think that's what bothers me, Noah. That it would."

"Should I be honest? It would. And you know why."

"Yes, because of Annabel," she said.

"And Chance. They're a pair."

Tears welled in her eyes, and he took a mental step back. He was overwhelming her, and that wasn't fair. She knew he meant it—that he loved Chance too. And that was killing *her*.

He put his hands on her shoulders. "Look, Sara. I want to be very clear. I like the idea of getting married and what that means for me as the twins' acting father. If you change your mind, yes, it'll knock me to my knees, but I'm all about getting up again. That's who I am now."

She stared at him. Almost looking confused.

He removed his hands and stuffed them in his pockets. "But I'll tell you something else. Yes, I have my good reasons for wanting this marriage, wanting you to stay with me forever. There are reasons involved that have nothing to do with the twins."

She tilted her head. "Like what?"

"Like that you've been my best friend since I was a little kid. Separated for the last two years or not. You mean a lot to me."

She gave a slow nod. "Same," she whispered.

He let that sink in for a moment, and it gave him the courage to say what had been building inside him the past couple of days. "And because—" He shut up fast. He couldn't say *that*. He took off his Stetson and ran a hand through this hair, glad he hadn't blurted out the rest of that whopper.

"And because what?" she asked, staring at him.

He had no idea why he thought she'd let him off the hook.

Hell. Just be honest. Say what's on your mind. "And because maybe, somewhere in there, months, years from now, whatever feels right—if it does—" Man, he was rambling. "Maybe there's a possibility of a second chance."

There, he said it.

He caught the intake of breath, the shielded surprise in her eyes.

But should he have said it? If he meant it—and he did—then why not? Why not put his cards on the table, say what he meant and felt? Even if it did get him knocked to his knees. Ignorance was never bliss. Everyone knew that.

His phone buzzed with a text.

"You should take that," she said fast. "I'll go check the main barn." She walked away—even faster—before he could say anything else.

A conversation we'll finish later. Or not.

He grabbed his phone. Carly, the welcome manager.

There's a reporter here from the Converse County Gazette. He says he's interested in writing a story about the grand opening. Should I let him through?

Noah's stomach flipped. Then flopped. A reporter. Press for the ranch: good thing. Bad press: bad thing. What if the reporter didn't like the looks of the place? What if something went wrong just as the reporter happened to be there, taking pictures and notes? An accident on the trail. An unhappy guest complaining about the water pressure, which was actually just fine.

You put your heart and soul into the reopening, he reminded himself. *Hired a top-notch crew. Everything is set for today. Everything is going great. The article will be glowing.*

Maybe. Or maybe not.

Cripes.

Why the hell was everything in his life so up in the air?

By the main barn, he could just make out Sara giving a wave to Mrs. Pickles, who was over by the small

barn, pointing out the goats to the twins. *I have to believe in this place—for Sara, Annabel and Chance. If
I don't believe in what I've rebuilt here, no one will.*

Noah's Magic Eight Ball answer had to come from
himself: *It is decidedly so.*

Sure, send him up to the lodge, Noah texted back
to Carly.

This was make or break for the guest ranch. Just like
Sara marrying him was make or break for his heart.

Chapter 9

Avoiding Noah in a twelve-hundred-square-foot cabin wasn't easy. Once Sara was officially off-duty, she'd rushed back to the cabin to take over from Mrs. Pickles and was there when the twins woke up from their nap. Over the next few hours, she told them all about opening day, her surprise at finding herself wishing she could sit in on every retreat lecture, and the even bigger surprise of running into Tabitha Corey. And then she started talking about Noah, how he'd rebuilt the ranch, how proud she was of him and how she couldn't figure out what to do.

Should I marry him?

Make a pro and con list, she could hear her mother saying any time she couldn't decide what to do about something, when both sides of the issue had check marks. She'd have to make it a mental one since she certainly didn't want to accidentally leave a piece of paper around with all that info for Noah to come across.

She sat on the sofa, Annabel finishing her bottle, Chance half-asleep in the swing on the floor beside her. *Okay, here we go, guys,* she told the twins.

Pro: I've known him forever. He will always feel like family, no matter what. I don't want to trust him, but dammit, he's given me no reason not to this time around. His sincerity leaps off him. I know the twins are safe with him. I do like the idea of them having a father—a father who actually loves them and cares about them and wants what's best for them, not himself. The sight of Noah Dawson gives me goose bumps. Everywhere.

Was that also a con? It was, given that the marriage Noah had proposed was like a business arrangement of sorts. Well, as businesslike as it got when children were involved. Scratch that, there was nothing businesslike about sharing a home and raising children together. This would be very personal. And Noah had said he liked the idea of a second chance—down the road.

Perhaps another con. How could she keep her heart out of things in that case? When Noah did give her goose bumps?

Another pro: she adored his family. Daisy was right here. The ranch would be Sara's home on a permanent basis, and she did love this place. Everywhere she turned today, memories filled her. Her mother teaching her how to ride a two-wheeler. Her dad teaching her everything he knew about horses, his great love. Noah showing her a few secret trails he'd made that led to the river, where they'd fill backpacks with chips and the occasional stolen bottles of beer from both their houses, Sara hoping against hope he'd make his move, despite what he'd said. He never did. Not once. He'd written himself off as a jerk and told her she deserved the world. He'd seemed to believe that about himself to the point that it was automatic for him not to touch her.

She hated remembering that. And she'd hated remembering that he'd turned out to be right. Not about being a jerk; he wasn't. But about being wrong for her, unable to pull himself up and out of the hole he'd fallen into.

Pro: all these memories. Con: all these memories.

She sighed, cuddling Annabel against her and peeking over at Chance, who was just lying peacefully in the swing, gently swaying, fighting sleep as his little eyes drooped.

"Noah loves you both," she said to Annabel as she tilted up the bottle. "I really see that. If he acted like only you mattered, Annabelly, I could have reason to make some sort of fuss. But of course, he adores Chance too."

Every time she felt that frisson of fear about Noah getting too involved—as if there was anything more involved than the two of them marrying—she'd think about how he truly did seem to love both babies, and she'd feel that rush of gratitude that the twins were loved by someone else in this world. Someone pretty special, at that. She had no family, and Willem, an only child, had lost both his parents during the past five years. Noah really was the closest thing to family that she had.

Just when she thought she was acting out of devotion to the twins, making decisions for their sake, she'd feel that tap on her shoulder with the flip side, the other hand, the "yeah, but."

So am I marrying him or not? she silently asked both twins. *Am I committing to life with him as my best friend and my twins' acting father? Or am I committing to my-*

*self and finding my own way without needing security
from anyone else?*

She heard his key in the lock, and on cue, goose
bumps ran up her spine and along her arms and the
nape of her neck.

"How are the twins?" he asked as he came into the
living room.

She kissed Annabel's sweet-smelling head. "Fed,
burped and ready for their cribs."

"Would you like to do the honors or should I?" he
asked.

"It's kind of amazing that after hours and hours of
work and running around, you're up for putting them
to bed." *Because he's committed to them. Because he
loves them.* "How about we both do the honors?" she
said, getting up.

He smiled and took Chance out of his swing. The
little guy fell asleep in Noah's arms before they even
hit the stairs.

With both babies in their cribs, the lullaby player on
a low setting and the door ajar, they headed back downstairs to the living room. Because Noah was Noah and
would probably go into the kitchen to whip them up a
three-course meal when he had to be exhausted, she
beat him to it.

"I'm going to make us dinner," she said. "You sit
and put your feet up."

"Dying to," he said, dropping on the sofa and putting
his legs up on the coffee table beside the baby monitor.
"Ah, that does feel good."

"Pasta with prosciutto and peas in a creamy pink
sauce and garlic bread coming right up." She still had
cravings for rich comfort food and had been dreaming

of that very dish all day yesterday. A quick trip to the market last night, and she had the missing ingredients.

"Hurry," he said. "Now that you said it, I want it immediately. Five minutes ago."

She grinned and got to work in the kitchen, enjoying the domesticity.

Ah, another pro, she thought as she put the water on to boil and grabbed the prosciutto from the refrigerator and a cutting board from the cabinet. She liked cooking for herself and Noah because she liked Noah. Cooking for Willem had been a chore because he'd been so picky and finicky. Once, early on in their marriage, she'd grabbed his plate away when he'd complained how his steak looked before he'd even tried it and told him to make dinner himself, then stalked off. His passive-aggressive behavior that followed for days had ended up shaping more of her behavior and response to him than she'd realized. Willem had a been a gaslighter, making her feel crazy for complaining, and in her eyes, he controlled whether her father lived or died. So she'd kept the peace. And destroyed herself in the process.

Not exactly good companion thoughts for making a nice dinner. She poured herself a glass of lemonade and drank half, letting it refresh her, then set her thoughts on her twins and the hot guy on the sofa with his feet up.

Her head set back on straight, she sautéed the prosciutto and garlic, the delicious aroma taking over and making her stomach grumble.

"Can I help with anything?" Noah called from the living room.

Another for the pro column. "I've got it, but thanks," she called back.

How many times had she stood in this very spot at the

stove, beside her mother or her father, and shared cooking duties with them? Her dad's specialty was his favorite dish, chicken parmigiana with a side of very saucy spaghetti. Her mom loved making every kind of seafood and salads with vegetables from her little garden.

There were times, particularly lately, when she thought about her parents and felt so sad that she'd need to sit down and just cry. But right now, sweet memories were coming at her, making her smile. Her parents had loved each other so much.

Con: marrying a man who doesn't love you that way.

Addendum: she used to believe that Noah *did* love her that way, even when they were teenagers, and that he truly was protecting her from himself. She'd believed he loved her during their brief and disastrous relationship two years ago. It was now that she wasn't too sure about. Noah was such a different person these days, and sometimes she couldn't even read him when she'd been easily able to before. His focus was brand-new to her, and it wasn't on her or a good time or sex. He was all about the success of the ranch—and now the twins.

But with that little hint of possibility he hadn't meant to utter aloud, *Maybe a second chance for us...*

Marrying Noah Dawson would be a leap of faith. Plain and simple. Who knew what would happen?

Con: she didn't know what was going to happen.

She'd been the one to say their marriage would be strictly business—no hanky-panky, no confusion over what they were doing. So there would be no sex to muck anything up, making her feel closer to him—or farther away, depending. Her feelings for him would be based on how they operated together, how they got along, worked together, took care of the twins together.

"Smells amazing!" she heard Noah call from the living room.

She gave the sauce a stir, not even guilty that it was from a jar. Hey, infants and working and making dinner? Sauce from a jar.

Five minutes later, she had everything stirred in a big blue ceramic bowl and brought it to the table. There was no dining room in the cabin, but the kitchen was eat-in and big enough for a round table for six by the window.

"Come and get it," she called out.

He appeared in the kitchen doorway, looking at her like he intended to do just that. His blue eyes were intense on her. This wasn't about appreciation for cooking or anticipation of eating. This was desire—for the chef.

"Now that I put it out there," he said, "I can't stop thinking about it."

"About what?" she whispered, a plate of garlic bread in her hand.

"Second chances. Everything I am is about second chances right now. I screwed up things the worst with you, Sara. I'd give anything to make everything right."

She put down the garlic bread. And rushed into his arms and wrapped her legs around him like she was Rachel McAdams and he was Ryan Gosling in *The Notebook*.

Not bad for seven and a half weeks postpartum, she thought, their mouths meeting, their bodies pressed so tightly against each other that she truly felt like they were one. They kissed so fervently that her legs couldn't retain their hold and they slid down. He pressed her against the counter, kissing her harder, hotter, his hands roaming into her hair, down her back, up her back under the light cotton tank top she'd changed into.

Just go with it, she told herself. *Go with what you feel, what you want. That is how you get your groove back. Stop overthinking and just feel.*

"Uh-oh," he said, putting her hands on his shoulders, his forehead against hers. "You said this was a no-go if we get married."

"My way of taking some control of things," she said. "I don't know what I'm doing, Noah. I just know that I wanted to kiss you."

"Me too," he whispered.

"But, but, but, I don't want to get emotionally caught up in you. That's not good for me. That's what I need to avoid. And yes, sex will absolutely push me into that." She threw up her hands, then grabbed the plate of garlic bread to have something sturdy between them. "What am I doing?"

This was nuts. A minute ago, she was feeling and going with it. Now she was overthinking again and letting that do the controlling.

Why was this so damned hard?

Because she was scared, she suddenly realized. That was it. Scared of losing herself again. And getting hurt again.

"Let's eat, okay?" she said, pushing past him to the table.

"I'll try not to look at you like I want to devour you again," he said. "That wasn't a fair move."

For a woman who hasn't had sex since she conceived? So true. At least she was pretty sure that night was the last time. Willem had been obsessed with her menstrual cycle and planning, and once he'd hit on the right window, he'd ignored her.

Anyway. It had been a long time since anyone had

looked at her the way Noah had just then. Kissed her like that. Made her want so much more.

She sat down and heaped some pasta on her plate, then busied herself eating. The rich, creamy pink pasta and bacon and peas were every bit as delicious and comforting as she'd expected.

"Mmm, this is so good," he said, reminding her of sex again. She paused, her fork in midair, and watched him twirl a forkful into his gorgeous mouth. He took a drink of his bottled beer, then looked at her. "I'm going to take your lead from here on in. On whether we get married, whether we continue that kiss. No pressure from me, Sara."

"I appreciate that."

"Oh, and I should qualify that comment about the second chance. I mean just having you with me. My partner. My wife. Having you back." He glanced down, then cleared this throat. "But not in a romantic sense. Just like you said. We tried that, and we both know what happened. There's way too much at stake to mess anything up between us."

She stared at him. Was he backtracking or did he mean that? Was he truly worried that he'd drive her away again? She wasn't sure.

She cleared her throat and then just nodded.

Great, she thought, pushing her pasta around on her plate. She had no idea what she wanted, what she was doing. But what he'd said helped put things in a stalling pattern, which was exactly what she and they did need.

Feeling better, she took a bite of garlic bread. She really had to get herself assigned to another of the retreat seminars. Because she felt a part of her groove burning brightly back inside her—the red-blooded woman who'd thought that piece of her was gone.

Thanks to Noah just *looking* at her, she knew it wasn't.

After dinner, Sara had excused herself to her room and tried to read a book from the living room shelves on animal husbandry, but she couldn't concentrate. What she needed was a walk, some space from Noah where he wasn't upstairs or downstairs, so aware of his presence in the cabin, despite the closed door and a gleaming gold lock on it.

That kiss just loomed a little *too* large.

Wow.

Now she'd had a taste of what it was to be an actual sexual person again, and there was an incredibly sexy man in the vicinity who made her legs feel all rubbery.

She found Noah in the kitchen, drinking a cup of coffee and going through a stack of invoices, his laptop open in front of him.

"Can I help with anything?" she asked, standing in the doorway.

He looked up at her, and for a split second she saw so much in his eyes, in his expression, but then he flipped neutral. "Nope. Just reconciling some inventory."

"I thought I'd go for a walk," she said. "Get some air. You've got the twins?"

"Absolutely. Go ahead."

What a luxury. To be a single mother of infants and to be able to do anything on her own, let alone take a refreshing walk. That was thanks to Noah.

He glanced at his watch. "The retreat group's final lecture of the evening is scheduled to go on until nine thirty, so you might want to head away from the lodge if you're looking for time alone."

Hmm. It was 9:10 now. Maybe she would actually head straight for the lodge and make sure all was well, that the lodge fridge had enough bottled waters and that the fruit bowls weren't depleted. She could catch the last of Connie's talk from just outside the doorway.

She checked on the twins, then headed back to the kitchen. "The babies are fast asleep. Thanks for letting me get some air. I appreciate it."

"Anytime," he said. "I mean that."

He did. That wasn't in doubt.

As she turned to go, she could feel his eyes on her. The pull to turn back, to just walk up to him and hug him for so many different reasons, was almost too strong. She forced herself to the door.

The moment it closed behind her, she let out a breath. Up ahead on the path toward the lodge, she saw a slim figure with long wavy hair. A retreat participant? She couldn't tell in the dim lighting offered by the light posts that dotted the paths every now and then. But when the woman turned slightly toward the sound of an owl hooting in the distance, she could see a pregnant belly. That was definitely Daisy Dawson.

"Daisy!" she called out in as hushed a voice as she could muster.

Daisy turned around, and Sara could tell she was straining to see. "Sara?"

Sara jogged over. "Taking a walk, getting some air, a breather. Noah's watching the babies. Well, they're sleeping, but he put himself on twins duty."

Daisy grinned. "How'd he become father of the year?" she asked, then her eyes widened and she touched Sara's arm. "I'm sorry. I keep putting my foot in my mouth about that. I know he's not Annabel's dad. Or Chance's, of course. And clearly, you two have worked something out. But I need to stop thinking of my brother as Annabel's dad."

"He still thinks of himself that way. Of both babies. Talk about taking responsibility," she added with a chuckle, trying to make Daisy less uncomfortable.

"So…how does that work, exactly?" Daisy asked. "I mean, you're playing house, but you're not a couple and he's not their father."

She'd always admired Daisy's forthrightness. Her brother shared that with her. "Can I swear you to secrecy? I only want your discretion because I'm not sure I should be sharing your brother's private business, you know?"

"Promise," Daisy said, holding up two fingers.

"He proposed to me. A marriage-in-name-only kind of thing. He'd get to be the twins' father. I get the security of a home on the guest ranch I was raised on. He even offered me half his share of the place, Daisy. That's how serious he is."

Daisy stopped on the path, the moonlight filtering through the treetops and capturing her amazed expression. "Wow. I mean, I'm not surprised to hear any of it. But wow."

"Wow is right."

Daisy stared at her. "And *you* said, I ask nosily?"

"I said yes, then basically said I don't know. I *don't* know. For all the reasons you can imagine. You know my history with Noah. And after what I went through in my marriage, I want to stand on my own two feet. No one is dying. I'm not desperate. I'm not trying to save anyone's life. It'll be hard, but I can do this on my own.

I have this great job now. A place to live that makes me feel safe and comforted."

"I get it," Daisy said. "It's like you want to say yes for some reasons and no for other reasons, and no side is stronger than the other."

"Exactly. So what do I do?" Sara asked on another chuckle but immediately sobered.

"Sometimes my secret dream is that someone amazing will propose to me," Daisy said, a hand on her belly. She sighed and stared up toward the moon. "I was dating the father for three months. The condom broke, and then suddenly he was scarce. When I found out I was pregnant and told him, he said he was really sorry but he wasn't serious about me and he was only in Cheyenne temporarily, and then he just disappeared."

"Oh, Daisy, I'm so sorry."

"I don't know what's in my future. Well, except being a single mother."

"I'm here for you," Sara said. "Anything you need, I'm here."

Daisy pulled her into a hug. "Thank you. A lot." She stepped back, and they resumed walking. "Is it terrible that I'm finding reasons to listen in on Connie's talks? She's so good."

Sara smiled. "I know! I'm doing the same thing. In fact, that's why I'm headed toward the lodge. To check that the fridge is stocked with enough water bottles."

"Um, that was *my* plan," Daisy said with an evil grin. "There's only about fifteen minutes left, so I don't feel too guilty."

They linked arms and kept walking, the pretty white clapboard lodge with its steeply pitched roof and wraparound porch coming into view.

"Let's go check that water," Sara said.

"And the fruit bowls and granola bar bowl," Daisy added with a nod.

They headed inside and walked over to the kitchenette in the corner. A rectangular bar table separated the kitchen from the room, and they stepped behind it, both quietly "taking inventory." Sara made a note to add more apples to the bowl for the morning.

"So let's go over the most important step to getting your groove back," Connie was saying to the participants seated before her in a semicircle. "Figuring out what you *want*."

Sara glanced at Daisy, who was riveted by Connie. Daisy pulled a small notebook and pen from her back pocket and jotted something down. Sara could just make out that it said, *What do I want?*

"Maybe you want your husband to cook two nights a week," Connie went on. "Maybe you want a more satisfying job. Or a raise. One hour to yourself every night. Or your teenaged daughter to stop talking to you disrespectfully. Maybe you want more intimacy with your husband. Or a divorce. Or to stop arguing with your mother. Maybe you want a week's vacation at a beach. Or to see Italy. Maybe you want to read more. Become a mother. Or not. Maybe you want to learn to knit or take a German class or go skydiving. Whatever it is you want, identify it. If there's more than one immediate thing, write down the top three things you want, no matter how big or how small."

"Man, she's good," Daisy whispered, jotting down the assignment and then flipping her notebook closed and returning it to her pocket.

Sara nodded, her attention on Connie's words. *What is it that I want? Really want?*

I want to feel safe in the world.

The answer came faster than Sara thought. There it was, loud as it could be in every part of her. *Safety.*

"And the next step?" Connie went on. "Making a list of what steps you can take to get what you want. For example, let's say you want more intimacy with your husband, who watches the game, then a movie, and you've barely said two words since either of you got home. Maybe you suggest *going* to a movie, even if you have to see something you're not all that interested in. Maybe you suddenly give him a neck and shoulder massage. Maybe when you get out of the car in the Home Depot parking lot, you take his hand. You can start and see where it leads. Little things can lead to results."

Huh. *Steps to feeling safe in the world. What makes me feel safe? Feeling financially secure. Being able to take care of my children. So having a good job, which I now have. A nice home, which I now have, even if it's not the most traditional living situation.*

And somehow, out of nowhere, Noah Dawson makes me feel safe.

So, I'm doing exactly what I need to in order to get what I want.

"Tomorrow, we'll talk more about what to do when those steps don't feel feasible," Connie said. "But tonight, our homework is to think about what we want and if we feel comfortable, to start making those lists of steps we can take to achieve our goal or goals." She looked around at the participants with a warm smile. "It's been a great first day, full of wonderful new experiences. This time is your own. Perhaps for an evening walk or back to your cabins to rest up for tomorrow. The lodge's fridge is stocked with beverages and snacks that are free for the taking, so help yourselves."

"We're a bit low on fruit for the morning," Daisy said.

"I'll go pop by the kitchen and replenish, then I'll head home. I want to start my homework right away."

Sara grinned. "See you tomorrow, Daize."

She watched Daisy leave, feeling buoyed for both of them—and thinking she should pay Connie for eavesdropping so much on just the first day. She smiled as two women approached to grab bananas and noticed Tabitha Corey heading out of the lodge. Instead of turning right for the cabins, Tabitha went straight on the path that led to the creek.

Go talk to her. If she doesn't want company, her body language or expression will let you know and you'll give her space.

Sara grabbed two waters and two small bags of pretzels and followed her, hoping she wasn't overstepping.

She saw Tabitha sitting on one of the large rocks that faced the creek, her knees pulled up to her chest, her arms wrapped around her legs. Almost like a self-hug.

"Hi, Tabitha," Sara said gently so as not to startle her.

Tabitha turned around, eyes wide, but she seemed to relax when she saw it was Sara.

"Water and pretzels?" Sara offered, holding them out.

"Sure," Tabitha said. "I wanted to stop and take something to drink and nibble on, but I didn't want to get caught up in chatting with the group. I'm feeling pretty talked out, and I've barely said ten words all day."

"I know what you mean."

Tabitha tilted her head. "I'm sorry about your husband. I would have attended the funeral, but I didn't hear a thing about it."

Sara opened her water. "Willem was very clear about not wanting a funeral. He instructed his lawyer to spread his ashes in the Bear Ridge River at sunset."

Tabitha raised an eyebrow and looked a bit surprised.

"Our marriage was pretty awful," she admitted, and it felt good to say it aloud to someone besides Noah. The truth was the truth.

Tabitha gasped. "I thought you had this perfect life!"

"Oh, I'd say it was quite the opposite. I'm working on creating the right life for me and my twins, though."

Tabitha looked confused again, as if she'd probably thought Sara had only one child, a baby son. But Sara didn't want to get into the details.

"I've been eavesdropping on Connie's talks," Sara admitted, popping a pretzel into her mouth. "I find her so inspiring and helpful and comforting. I only caught the last five minutes, but luckily it was a wrap-up and I applied the question to my own life. What do I really want? I was surprised to have an immediate answer."

"Me too," Tabitha said. "I mean, I know what I want. How to achieve it, another story."

Sara was so curious. But she couldn't just ask Tabitha what she wanted. It was personal, and if her old friend wanted to share, that would be one thing.

"From the outside, I probably look pretty blessed," Tabitha said. "Well, if you don't look too closely at me lately." She flipped up a hank of her frizzy hair.

"You're clearly engaged," Sara prompted, gesturing at the at least two-carat diamond ring sparkling in the moonlight. She'd seen Tabitha with the endodontist with his movie star–like blond hair and easy laugh at a fund-raising barbecue once. They looked like the perfect couple. But who knew better than Sara at how deceiving appearances were?

Tabitha stared at her ring. "I opened up to my mother about how I'm not sure I even love Philip, that I'm not sure I can go through with the engagement. Want to know what she said to me this morning before I left for the retreat?" she asked, looking up at Sara. "She said, 'All this finding yourself nonsense will find you alone and miserable. Your father and I will be very disappointed if you ruin your opportunity for a good life.'"

"By marrying your fiancé?"

Tabitha nodded. "He's the son of close friends of my parents. I've known him a long time. He checks a lot of the boxes."

"Which ones?" Sara asked, hoping she wasn't going too far.

"Well, for one, my parents are often disappointed in me for this or that, and I had their absolute approval for, I think, the first time in dating Philip and 'getting yourself proposed to,' as my mother put it. She actually told me she was proud of me for accomplishing that." She shook her head and turned away.

"So you *don't* actually love him?"

"He's all right. He's a good person. He's a mansplainer and we don't agree politically, and there's not a lot of chemistry in bed, if you know what I mean." She sighed. "He has a lot of good qualities, though. And I'm twenty-nine and single, as my mom points out often. She always says, 'I don't know who you think is out there that would be better than Philip. No one you meet will be perfect. Especially a guy you fall madly in love with. He'll be the *worst*.'"

Sara thought back to the Noah Dawson of two years ago. Even overbearing mothers had a point sometimes.

"Over the years I did get my heart broken a couple times by guys I fell hard for," Tabitha added. "So I know what she means. But still. Am I really supposed to settle like this? Marry the guy who seems right but really isn't?" She burst into tears and covered her face with her hands, her ring glinting on her finger.

"I'm so glad you came here, Tabitha," Sara said. "At the very least, you have a week away from your parents and Philip to really think. And to apply Connie's questions."

"What if my mother is right? What if it's guy after guy, one who wants me, one I don't want, never two of us in love, and I end up alone? I want a husband. I want children." Her voice broke. "I met a guy in the coffee shop the other day. A cowboy. He said he was a bull rider, hoping to win big in the rodeo. The way he talked about the rodeo and his love for it, how his dad took him to rodeos every weekend as a kid, he just stole my heart. He wasn't even necessarily flirting with me. He was just talking, Sara. He probably has a serious girlfriend, because he left, no name, no number, no nothing. But he made me realize that guy *is* out there. A guy who could rivet me that way, you know?"

Sara nodded. "I know. I always felt that way about Noah Dawson. That no one would ever compare. He wasn't ready when we were actually a couple. But he's ready now."

But was Noah actually ready now? He'd told her he fully agreed their marriage should be strictly platonic. That meant he didn't really trust himself with her or with their relationship."

Still, they were working toward something. "If circumstances hadn't brought me back to him…"

Huh. She hadn't really thought of it like that until just now. Circumstances had brought her back. That was how life worked.

"So if you hadn't lost Willem," Tabitha said, "you'd

still be in your awful marriage when the man of your dreams was waiting here the whole time."

Sara gasped. That was exactly it. She nodded, vaguely, trying to take it in, digest it, process it. Things with Noah weren't going to be a fairy tale, but right now, Sara needed to think of the twins.

"That means the right guy for me might be out there too. I can settle and have my parents' approval. Or I can work toward finding the right man for me. Who knows, he might be in line in front of me in a coffee shop. Or leading the advanced riding lessons at the stables I love going to every chance I get."

Sara gave Tabitha's hand a squeeze. "Sounds like you're answering a lot of your questions."

Tabitha nodded. "I need to go do my homework. Write down what I want and how to achieve it. One of the problems has always been that I do want my parents' approval. I always have. If I give Philip back his ring, they'll be not only disappointed but furious. They won't understand."

"Well, maybe it'll help to write down the steps you could take to deal with that," Sara said. "If a harmonious relationship with your parents is very important to you, then write down some ways you could keep that while doing what *you* need to do to be happy. Your parents aren't living your life. *You* are."

"I keep telling myself that, hoping it'll sink in," she said. She stood up, and so did Sara. "I'm so glad you came to talk. This has been really helpful."

"For me too," she said.

They hugged and then headed back up the trail toward the lodge. Tabitha turned left for the cabins and Sara went right for the foreman's cabin.

Ping. A text. She took out her phone. It was from Noah. Even the connection by text gave her a line of goose bumps up the nape of her neck.

Just got a text from the Converse County Gazette. The review of the ranch is running tomorrow. I have a stomachache.

The review will be glowing, she texted back. The place is amazing and the guests love it. 5 stars.

He texted back a smiley emoji and a thumbs-up.

It struck her that you could only control so much. Noah had done the hard work and should be proud and pleased and expect that glowing review. But who knew if the reporter was a jerk or prickly or didn't like the color forest green or chili or the horse Noah had chosen for his mini trail ride.

All she knew was that she wanted to get back to the cabin—to be close to him. To think about what she'd said, what Tabitha had said. The man of her dreams waiting here for her this whole time… Maybe the timing was finally right, even if they were talking about a platonic marriage. And maybe she should grasp onto how she felt and not let go. Taking a leap of faith was hardly a way to feel safe in the world.

Except Noah *did* make her feel safe.

And the exact opposite.

Chapter 10

B-rrrrring! B-rrring!

Noah opened an eye, then aimed it toward his alarm clock—6:14 a.m. His alarm would go off at six thirty, but someone was pressing the doorbell to his cabin like it was on fire.

Ping! Ping-ping!

Now someone was texting him. He grabbed his phone. It was Daisy.

Oh my God, oh my God, oh my God, his sister texted. Open up! Hurry!

He pulled on jeans and rushed out of his bedroom, meeting Sara in her bathrobe on the stairs. "Something's wrong," he said, panic edging his voice. "The ranch or Daisy's baby?"

Sara's eyes widened. "Oh God." She practically flew down the stairs and unlocked the door.

Daisy came in, clutching her phone.

"Is the baby okay? Should I call nine-one-one?" Noah asked.

Daisy stared at him as though he had two heads. "The baby is fine! The review is up!"

Noah felt himself relax for exactly one second, then all his muscles bunched up again, and his stomach flip-flopped.

"Did you read it?" he asked. "Positive or negative?"

Daisy shook her head. "I haven't read it. I just saw the headline and hurried over."

"How's the headline?" Sara asked.

"Very neutral," Daisy said. "'Dawson Family Guest Ranch has grand reopening in Bear Ridge'"

Noah sucked in a breath. "Okay, read it."

Daisy nodded. "'The once famed and popular Dawson Family Guest Ranch, which reopened Friday after years closed, is an absolute delight.'" She jumped up and down as much as a six-months-pregnant woman could. "An absolute delight!" she repeated.

Noah's legs almost gave out in pure relief. He dropped down on the second step.

"'From the immaculate grounds to the family-friendly vibe,'" Daisy continued, "'the guest ranch is a paradise tucked away toward the woods in Bear Ridge and offers riding and lessons, retreat space, a full-service cafeteria, a lodge, a petting zoo, and bountiful, well-marked trails, including several that lead to the creek. Fishing gear is available for free rental. The cabins, like the entire ranch, manage to be rustic and modern at the same time and contain everything a guest might need. The horses are gentle, and even the sheep look happy to be living at the Dawson Family Guest Ranch.'" Daisy did a little dance, turning completely around. "Even the sheep look happy!" she repeated. "Could this be any better?"

"Congratulations, Noah," Sara said. She gave him a quick hug—too quick.

Then his sister did. "I say we celebrate with decaf and bagels and cream cheese. I have such a craving. Please tell me you have veggie cream cheese."

"I actually bought some the other night," Sara said with a grin. "Sesame bagels or plain or everything?"

"Everything, of course," Daisy said.

They headed into the kitchen, Daisy going for the coffee maker, Sara for the bagels and Noah for the fridge to get the cream cheese. When everything was ready, they all sat down and toasted with their coffee mugs.

"To the Dawson Family Guest Ranch," Sara said.

"Hear, hear," Noah added with a clink.

Noah's phone lit up. Every one of his brothers either called or texted, and Cowboy Joe texted, as did several of the staff.

I did this—and I can be the husband and father of your children that you want, he sent silently to Sara. He slugged down a gulp of coffee. Where the hell did that come from all of a sudden? Well, maybe not so all of a sudden, since he'd been lobbying for the position for days. But earning Sara's yes meant everything to him.

What are you thinking? he wanted to ask her as she sipped her coffee and read the review for herself on Daisy's phone.

A yes from Sara and his life would be complete.

A cry came from the nursery, and Sara headed upstairs. He wanted to go with her, to take care of the twins together, to be true partners. In the platonic sense of the word. At first he'd been hoping they could be more than platonic, but then he'd realized that was asking for trouble. He'd messed up terribly once with Sara and couldn't risk that again.

"Everything okay, brother dear?" Daisy asked, peering at him over the rim of her coffee mug. "You suddenly look like a guy who didn't just get a rave review from a major newspaper."

"I proposed to Sara," he whispered. "I don't think she's going to say yes."

"Well, I have one piece of advice for you," she whispered back. "And you can thank Connie Freedman and her talks for that. Find out what she wants—what she really wants—and see if that's something you can provide. Maybe she's unsure."

He stared at his sister. What Sara wanted? Didn't he know? "She wants security. After everything she's been through? The rug pulled out from under her? Lies and deceit? Being left penniless? She wants security. I can provide that on every level."

"Okay, she wants security. But I said what she *really* wants. You're going to have to dig deeper under the umbrella term, Noah."

"Umbrella term? *What?*"

"Security. What does that actually mean for Sara? To Sara? Is it about money? She has a good job. A comfortable home? She has that now. So what is it she *really* wants?"

Oh God. He was bad at this. "If you know, please tell me. Right this second."

"I don't know. But if you want to marry Sara, you need to find out. And make sure you can give it to her. Or there's no point."

What did Sara really want? Women were kind of

mysterious. Everyone knew that. Was this some deep, dark puzzle or something simple?

Sara came down the stairs, eyes shining with love for the baby in her arms—Chance. "Annabel's still asleep."

As his sister doted on Chance and Sara made a bottle for him, Noah stared at his bagel, wondering what Sara wanted and if he'd ever find out.

Over the weekend and the following days of the Get Your Groove Back retreat, Sara continued her—now sanctioned—eavesdropping on Connie's talks and did her homework. She'd let Connie know the second morning how inspiring she found the talks, and the life coach invited her to listen in on all the lectures. Daisy joined her often, writing in her notebook, and Sara thought her friend seemed more at peace about the idea of being a single mother. Sara had tried to engage Tabitha a few times, but her old friend had told her she just needed to do some deep soul searching and take long walks and rides and do her homework. On the final day of the retreat, Sara thought Tabitha looked as conflicted as she had the first day.

"I don't think my friend Tabitha got her groove back," Sara said as they straightened chairs in the lodge. "I wish I had all the answers."

"Me too. Because you could tell me if I should trust Jacob."

"Jacob?" Sara repeated.

"The dad," Daisy said, patting her belly. "He showed up on my doorstep last night and said he felt guilty about just running away. He isn't sure what he wants, though."

There was a lot of that going around.

"What did he say?" Sara asked.

"He just kept saying he felt guilty and a man shouldn't shirk his responsibilities and that maybe we could just take it day by day. What the hell is that? I'm six months pregnant. This isn't a dress rehearsal." She sighed. "Or maybe it is. Maybe we should get to know each other through this stage, knowing the baby is coming in three short months. Maybe we'll really see who we are." Daisy always looked so sure of herself, and right now, she seemed anything but. "What do you think, Sara?"

"Sounds to me like you want to try," Sara said.

"I have to, right? I feel like even though he disappointed me once, he is the baby's father, and he is asking for a chance. If I don't at least try, I might regret that."

"Do you still have feelings for him?" Sara asked.

Daisy nodded. "There's something there. I tamped all that down over the past months. I don't know if it's him or the fact that he is my baby's father and it's more that than anything. I just don't know, and I hate being so out of tune with myself."

"I know what you mean," Sara said, giving Daisy's hand a squeeze.

"Here's a photo of Jacob." Daisy held up her phone. "The face helps, and it shouldn't."

Sara stared at the picture of an extremely cute blond surfer cowboy–looking guy with twinkling green eyes and a wide smile.

"I feel like I was getting my groove back, and now here he comes, throwing everything up in the air again. I feel so off balance."

Sara nodded. "Factoring someone else in when you need to keep yourself steady isn't easy. I know that for sure. Want to know what else I know for sure?"

"What?" Daisy asked.

"Our kids are going to be besties raised together," she said.

Daisy brightened. "Instant BFFs."

Sara nodded. They both drank their waters and settled back.

"Does that mean you're going to marry Noah?" Daisy asked.

Huh. Maybe it did. "I decided that when I wake up tomorrow, the retreat over, I'll know. At least, I think I'll know."

Things between her and Noah had been a little odd the past several days. They'd kept to their routine with the twins, which worked really well, but she constantly had the feeling he was trying to figure something out about her. The way he'd listen—hard—when she spoke, narrowing his eyes as if working to figure out some hidden meaning.

"Don't keep me in suspense," Daisy said. "Promise."

She and Daisy had gotten so close. Sara didn't know what she'd do without her friendship. "Pinkie swear," she said, wrapping her little finger around Daisy's.

Daisy's phone pinged. She took it from her pocket and frowned. "Uh-oh. It's a text from Connie Freedman. Tabitha Corey seems to be missing. She didn't show up for a scheduled activity and she's not in her cabin. Connie said she did a brief search on horseback in all the usual places Tabitha seemed to like to go but couldn't find her. Connie's worried about her state of mind since she skipped the talk and dinner last night too."

Sara bolted up. "I'll let Noah know right away. You stay here so you can be a ground support for Connie and the other participants. We'll find her."

Daisy nodded but looked worried.

Sara rushed off toward the foreman's cabin, texting Noah along the way.

Sara walked the creek bank again, Noah about ten feet away doing a sweep of the area from the path through the woods. Dylan and Bea, two of the ranch hands, were also searching the grounds since they'd come to know the nooks and crannies so well. She and Noah had checked and rechecked all the usual places Tabitha might be. She hadn't left the property, per the cameras by the gates on the road leading out of the ranch. The horse she'd been assigned, Nutmeg, was in her stall in the barn. All the bikes were accounted for too. Tabitha had gone off on foot.

Where are you, Tabitha? she wondered, scouring in between trees and down the edging of the creek toward the water, praying she'd find her old friend sitting curled up. Noah had said they'd give it only another half hour, because it was possible Tabitha might be injured and unable to call for help, and he'd bring in the big guns—his brother Axel, the search-and-rescue expert, and his yellow lab, Dude, an expert tracker. They'd find Tabitha in no time.

But Sara was 99 percent sure that Tabitha was safe and just hiding herself away because it was the final day of the retreat and she wasn't ready to go home, hadn't figured out what to do about her problems.

She scoured the creek bank, straining to see in the sunny glare. Wait—was that movement? And a glint of something purple?

Sara slowly inched forward, craning her neck. Yes!

That was a hand. And a sparkly purple sneaker. Tabitha wore sparkly purple sneakers.

She took out her phone and texted Noah. I think I see her! Yes, it's her! Give me a little time. I'll text you if she's hurt and needs help. Otherwise I think we should just talk a bit.

Okay, he texted back. I'll let Daisy and Connie know she's been found.

Sara pocketed her phone, then softly called out, "Tabitha?"

Tabitha didn't turn around.

"Can I sit beside you?" Sara asked.

"'Kay," came a teary voice.

Oh God. What had happened?

Sara approached where Tabitha was wedged between two big rocks, which now explained how they'd missed her on the first sweep. There was brush cover on both sides of the area she was sitting. Sara sat a good foot away, facing the same direction as Tabitha so the woman wouldn't feel stared at or crowded or pressured.

"Why do I have the feeling you came to a decision someone didn't like?" Sara asked gently.

Tabitha's eyes were teary. She lifted her head and leaned it back against the rock. "I called Philip about an hour ago and told him I was very sorry but that I couldn't marry him. I was honest and told him I cared about him but felt pressured into the engagement by him and my parents but that it wasn't what I wanted."

"Oh wow. How'd he take it?"

"He was upset, but in the end he said he admired my courage and wished me well. And he hung up."

"So why are you so upset?" Sara asked. Then she

realized Tabitha must have called her parents next and told them her news.

"I called my mom afterward. It was so hard to make that call. But I explained that I didn't love Philip and I hated to disappoint her but I had to do what feels right to me."

"Good for you!" Sara said—despite knowing full well her mother must have come down hard on her.

"I thought so. I felt so proud that I was standing up for myself and my future. And I believed, really believed, that I'd come first with my mom, you know? That she'd care more about me and how I feel than about appearances. Well, she didn't." She dropped her head onto her arms and sobbed.

"Oh, Tabitha, I'm so sorry." Sara scooted over closer beside Tabitha and put her arm around the woman's shoulders.

Tabitha glanced up with a tear-streaked face. "My mom said marriage wasn't about dumb lust and why did I think there was a 50 percent divorce rate. She said it was about partnership and well-matched couples building a future together."

Sara swallowed. Her own marriage to Noah would be a lot like the one Mrs. Corey described.

"But how can I sacrifice my happiness like that?" Tabitha asked. "It doesn't make any sense. It's sick, is what it is. But now my parents probably won't talk to me again."

Would Sara be sacrificing her happiness if she married Noah in this platonic arrangement? She would be happy feeling settled and secure. She would be happy living on the ranch. She would be happy that her twins would have a father, someone who loved them from the get-go.

But she wouldn't have a real marriage, the one she'd always dreamed of, the one Tabitha deserved, the one everyone deserved. Marriage with someone you loved and wanted to grow old with. Not a marriage that was first and foremost a business arrangement. Noah had her feeling so unsure about what he really felt, what he really wanted.

"I love my parents," Tabitha said. "I've never been able to handle when they're upset with me. And now they probably will disown me."

No way. That was nuts. Because she didn't want to marry the guy they thought she should? Because ending the engagement would cause a potential rift with their friends? "Do you really think so? They'll cut you out of the family?"

Tabitha could barely nod.

"Well, hell, Tabitha. That's not about love either. That's about control, and it's not fair. People who love and care about you and truly want the best for you don't cut you out of their life for not marrying the guy they think is right for you." Man, she was spitting mad. Sara felt like kicking something and shot up and did kick a small rock across the ground.

Tabitha hugged her knees to her chest. "I guess I'm really on my own now. In one fell swoop, I lost my fiancé and my parents of my own free will."

"The fiancé, yes. Your parents, no. I think you should write your mother an email, Sara. Right now. Speak directly and honestly to her, tell her exactly how you feel and why and how brokenhearted you are. You started on this path of honesty and being true to yourself. Continue on it. Your mother just might come around. And one parent is all you need to push the other."

Tabitha gave the smallest of shrugs. But Sara could see a glimmer of hope in her expression. "You think that might help?"

"I do."

Tabitha stood up, as well. "I'll go write it now." She glanced around at the woods. "I know I got a bunch of texts that I ignored—a few were my parents yelling at me, so I shut off my phone. I'm sure you guys and Connie were worried about where I was. I'm sorry."

"All that matters is that you're okay," Sara said.

Tabitha leaned over and hugged her. "Can we keep in touch after I leave tomorrow morning?"

"Of course!" Sara said. "And any time you need to get away or a place to go, you come straight to the ranch."

Tabitha gave a shaky smile. "Thanks. I just might."

They headed up the path to the lodge. Connie and Noah were waiting out front, and Connie came over.

"I'd love to talk a little if you're not too tired or done for the day," Tabitha said.

Connie squeezed Tabitha's hand. "How about over iced tea and really good cookies that I saved from dessert tonight?"

Tabitha smiled, then turned to Sara. "Thank you again. For everything. I'll see you in the morning to say goodbye?"

"Definitely."

She watched as Tabitha and Connie headed toward Connie's cabin, aware that Noah was walking over to where she stood by the directional sign.

"She okay?" he asked.

"She will be. She's on her way."

"Good," he said. "Ready to go home?"

Home. God, yes. How she loved the sound of that word and that it applied to here. The ranch. Dawson's. And the foreman's cabin.

She *was* home. But would she ever be truly settled?

It was pitch-dark when shrill cries woke Sara up. She glanced at her alarm—2:57 a.m. She couldn't tell which baby it was, but someone was making a racket— and these were higher-pitched cries than normal. Something was wrong.

Sara bolted out of bed and ran into the nursery to find Noah already there, lifting Chance out of his crib.

"He's really hot," Noah said, concern in his eyes. He laid a finger to the baby's forehead. "Very, very hot."

Sara put her own finger to Chance's forehead and gasped. She ran for the thermometer in the bureau as Noah laid Chance down on the changing pad. Chance's temperature read 103.2. "That's way too high. I'm calling the pediatrician." She rushed into her room to get her phone, grateful she had the doctor in her contacts. The service answered right away, despite the fact that it was almost three in the morning. She explained about Chance's high fever and raspy breathing, and the service said the doctor on call would return her call as soon as possible. It took just a few minutes.

She flew back into the nursery, where Noah was pacing, gently bouncing Chance in his arms, which didn't affect the crying. And it usually did. "The doctor said the temperature was high enough that we should bring Chance to the ER since the fever is combined with fast breathing." Sara's eyes welled. She stood there, taking deep breaths, barely able to think.

"I've got Chance," Noah said. "Call Daisy and ask her to hurry over for emergency babysitting. It's 3:00 a.m., but that's what sisters are for."

Sara's body unlocked; a mission she understood. She called Daisy, who assured her she'd be right over. A few minutes later, Daisy had arrived in her pajamas and flip-flops.

Sara and Noah rushed out with Chance in his carrier. For the twenty minutes it took to get to the clinic, Chance was shrieking, his face ruddy and sweaty. A half hour after that, he'd been diagnosed with a common respiratory virus that had flared out of control. He'd be absolutely fine.

Sara wasn't, though. This was the first time one of the babies had gotten very sick. The panic she'd felt had taken over, and she'd appreciated the calm, cool and collected voice of Noah, giving instructions, knowing, somehow, what to do.

Feeling safe in this world meant a lot of different things. Having her person, someone she could always lean on, count on, trust, was paramount to her, more so than she'd ever realized.

That person was Noah.

She needed to be practical, not hold out for something she'd stopped believing in.

The answer to what she really wanted was summed up in how they'd operated tonight. They had been true partners.

"I've been doing a lot of thinking this week," she told him when they shut the door behind Daisy, who'd gone back to the main house. Chance was upstairs in his crib, sleeping comfortably now that he'd had medication to bring his fever down. Annabel would be staying in the bassinet in the living room for a couple days until Chance was more on the mend. "About what I really want. And what I want is for us to get married in the partnership you proposed."

That he liked what she said was evident in his expression. "We were a pretty good team tonight," he said, shutting off the hall lights and heading for the stairs.

She walked up beside him. "Exactly. We were. I panicked and you were calm, cool and collected. I needed help, and you were there. Daisy was there. I like having support. It's vital."

"It is. And you can always count on me. Always."

"I believe that. Let's go to the town hall once Chance is well enough. Probably even tomorrow."

At the landing, he took both her hands. "This is going to be the start of something great for both of us. Try to get some sleep."

"You too," she said, walking across the hall to her room. "Good night."

He held her gaze. "Good night."

Back in bed, she pulled the quilt to her chin. In just a couple days, she'd be married. Noah Dawson would be her husband. Her life would be completely different than it had been a week ago.

She was where she should be, making plans that would benefit everyone—her, Noah and the twins. Plus, Daisy would truly get to be Aunt Daisy instead of just an honorary aunt.

She smiled and closed her eyes, but sleep eluded her. Nerves about marrying a man she had so much history with?

So many what-ifs ran through her mind. She turned over and pulled the pillow over her head.

She was marrying Noah Dawson. For her sake. For his sake. For the twins' sake.

She was marrying Noah Dawson because she *loved* him. She flipped off the quilt and got out of bed. Before she could stop herself, she walked out of her room and down the hall, and knocked on his door.

"Come on in," he said.

Please mean that. In every sense.

She opened the door and closed it behind her, which made Noah sit up in bed and stare at her.

She walked over to the bed and sat beside him. Then kissed him. Then again. And again.

Don't stop this, she sent to him telepathically. *Because if I'm marrying you, I'm marrying you right. With everything I feel.*

"You're sure about this?" he asked, his blue eyes glinting with desire.

"Very," she said and kissed him again.

"And it's safe?" he asked. "Timewise?"

"It's safe," she assured him.

He peeled off her tank top, his hands all over her breasts. She watched him take in every inch of her bare torso and could feel him hardening underneath her. She took off his T-shirt and tossed it aside, and then he flipped her over and removed her yoga pants, leaving on her none-too-sexy pink-and-green granny panties with the little bow.

"I think those are incredibly hot," he whispered, hooking a finger at the waistband.

She swallowed, her insides feeling like liquid heat. "I think you're incredibly hot."

In moments, his sweats joined her pants on the floor. He lifted up over her, bracing himself on his elbows, staring down at her, kissing her, his hands in her hair, on her breasts, her shoulders, moving down her stomach…

She writhed underneath him, needing him so badly she couldn't take it. His kisses trailed up her neck, then his mouth caught hers so passionately she heard herself moan. She was kissing his collarbone and chest as he reached into the bedside table and pulled out a condom, making quick work of putting it on.

The moment he was inside her, all thought left her head and she only *felt*. *I love you, I love you, I love you* echoing in her head.

She hadn't forgotten how amazing Noah Dawson was in bed. He easily brought her to climax and then went wild to the point she was surprised the bed didn't collapse. The Wild West every night? That was more than all right with her.

And suddenly he was lying on top of her, kissing her neck, her cheek, breathing hard. "Oh, Sara. That was something."

"Yes, it was," she said. "And I guess this means our arrangement will now need some modifying."

She felt him freeze. *Crud.*

He turned onto his side. "What do you mean?"

"Well, we just had sex, Noah. And we're getting married tomorrow or the next day."

"I thought—" He clamped his lips together.

Oh hell. "You thought *what*?"

"I thought this was about tonight," he said hesitantly. "About the culmination of a rough night. Our marriage is supposed to be—" Again the lips clamped down.

"A platonic partnership," she finished for him, the ice in her voice surprising even her.

And clearly it surprised him, because his gaze swung

to hers. "Sara, being platonic was your idea and a good one. A necessary one for me to make sure the marriage is a success. We need to be on the best path forward."

The best path forward? Good God. What self-help podcasts had he been listening to? Could he really want a platonic relationship at this point? Did he really not love her enough to make it work in all regards this time around?

Maybe he didn't.

"I think I hear Annabel," she said, grabbing her top and yoga pants and quickly putting them on. She darted out of the room and into the living room, where Annabel was sleeping in her bassinet for the time being.

She dropped down on the sofa beside the bassinet and looked out at the glow of moonlight amid the darkness. Noah had never veered on what he wanted; she had to remember that. He hadn't played games. He hadn't made sexual innuendos. He'd been crystal clear. Yeah, he'd brought up a second chance but then explained what he'd meant. A second chance to do things right by her. Not *with* her. He wasn't a man in love.

He wanted the twins and his former best friend to share his life on the ranch that he'd rebuilt.

She took a deep, steadying breath, feeling much calmer.

Well, at least she'd gotten great sex before entering into a sexless marriage. Tonight had been so damned good it would hold her for quite a while.

Or make her wish they could be together every night.

Partnership, partnership, partnership, she told herself. *Feeling safe in the world. Having someone you count on without all the craziness of lust and passion getting in the mix.*

A future to count on.

She heard footsteps coming down the stairs. "Sara? Can we talk?"

She stood, trying not to notice how incredibly sexy he looked. Trying to remember every moment of the past half hour. "I'm all right," she said. "Annabel's fine." She smiled and gestured to the bassinet. "Okay, that was an excuse to run away from you. But I'm fine."

"So...we're okay?" he asked. "*You're* okay?"

"I am," she assured him.

But she wasn't all that sure.

Chapter 11

The next morning, there was the expected awkward sidestepping as Sara and Noah ran into each other in the cabin a couple of times. Sara always had the mornings with the twins before Mrs. Pickles came so she could go to work, and Noah did his rounds on the ranch, but they'd been in the same place at the same time twice, both not quite looking at the other.

Last night, he'd accepted her "okay" and had followed her lead when she'd gone back to her room. The moment she'd heard his bedroom door close, she'd let out a huge sigh and then stared out the window at the night for what felt like hours. One moment—a half hour—they'd been so close, as close as two people could physically get. The next, separate bedrooms.

She'd felt really alone last night, but so aware of him down the hall, as always, and the dichotomy of

that made her nuts. She had no idea how she'd managed to fall asleep, between thinking about their night
together and what would happen in the morning: a trip
to the town hall.

Now, they stood in front of the lodge at seven fifteen, preparing to say goodbye to their first guests.
She forced her thoughts away from Noah as each of the
participants shook their hands and let them know how
much they'd enjoyed the ranch and what their favorite
aspects had been. One guest, Zoe, admitted she'd cried
saying goodbye to her horse, Lolly, with whom she'd
felt a special bond, and she was already planning a future stay. Sara couldn't help but notice that Tabitha was
looking particularly happy—and her engagement ring
was no longer on her finger.

Her old friend pulled her aside for a hug. "So I did
email my mom," Tabitha said. "I was very honest and
emotional and put it all out there. That I couldn't marry
a man I didn't love and didn't want to grow old with,
but that I also couldn't bear to lose her and Dad's love
over it, and if they were ready to disown me for disap-
pointing them, I'd rethink the marriage."

Sara was surprised at that last part.

"I was bluffing," Tabitha admitted. "And seriously
praying I knew my mom as well as I thought I did. I
know my parents love me and I just had this feeling
that if I really explained how I felt, my mother would
come through."

"And she did?" Sara asked. From Tabitha's happy
expression, that much was obvious.

Tabitha nodded. "With several hours to digest the
news, my mother softened and said she realized what
she was doing to me—the exact thing her own mother

would have done to her. She said she was horrified when she realized that. She had a long talk with my dad, and they called me this morning and said I came first, it was my life, and they wanted me to be happy."

Sara was so relieved for Tabitha that she pulled her into another hug. "I'm so glad, Tabitha. Now you can go out there and find your true happiness."

"Exactly. Thank you for helping me see that and for giving me good advice. I'll never forget that."

"Aw, that's what friends are for. We'll keep in touch?"

Tabitha nodded, and they exchanged cell numbers, and then it was time for the group to board the van.

"What was that all about?" Noah asked as they waved at the van pulling away.

"Tabitha Corey got her groove back," Sara said. *By standing up for herself. By knowing what she truly wanted beyond the obvious and finding a way to make it happen. She broke her engagement and kept her parents in her life.* Sara was very impressed.

Noah grinned. "Good. The six new groups coming today aren't part of any retreats. We have two sets of couples, a few families, and friends looking for some nature time."

"They're all set to arrive at one o'clock?" she asked.

"Yup. We'll have a group orientation. After this, the orientations won't be in big groups—it just worked out that way since they were all arriving around the same time on the same day. Some of the guests will be staying a couple days, some four, some a week. Things are going to get a lot busier around here now that we'll have constantly arriving and departing guests. It's all thanks to the great review in the *Gazette*. We're booked, every cabin, every day, throughout midfall. I even have some bookings through winter at this point."

"That's great!" she said, wishing she could hug him. But she stayed put. "And Chance's temperature has been normal for over twelve hours, so I'm confident he's on the mend. We have a few solid hours to go get ourselves married before we'll need to be back and focus on the ranch."

Thank heavens for Daisy; she'd gone to the foreman's cabin about a half hour ago to babysit while Sara and Noah said goodbye to the guests, and she'd watch the twins until they returned from the town hall.

With gold rings on.

Noah was staring at her, clearly looking for hesitation, for upset, for a change of heart, but she had her neutrally pleasant face on. She wanted to do this. "Well, the staff knows what they need to do to get ready for the coming guests, so we can go anytime."

"I'd like to change, of course," she said. "I mean, I know it's not a big-deal wedding, but I don't want to get married in an employee shirt and denim shorts."

"Me either," he said with a nod.

They walked back to the cabin, both briefly chatted with Daisy, who was with the twins in the living room, and they went upstairs, disappearing into their separate rooms. They'd agreed to meet downstairs at eight.

It was just past seven thirty. A half hour to decide what to wear to marry Noah Dawson. She went for a pale yellow sundress that skimmed her body but was forgiving with its drape, and her bronze sandals. She left her hair loose, dusted on a little makeup, put a small dab of perfume behind her ears and that was it. Ready to get married.

A knock at the door made her jump. Didn't Noah know he shouldn't see the bride-to-be before the ceremony? She rolled her eyes at herself. As if it was that kind of wedding.

But it wasn't Noah at the door, it was Daisy.

"Just checking if you need any help getting ready," Daisy said, sitting down on the edge of Sara's bed. "From the looks of you, you *are* ready. You look so pretty, Sara."

"Thank you for saying that, but it's not like it matters. *Pretty* and *romantic* aren't key words for these coming nuptials."

Daisy bit her lip and twisted her long hair up and let it drop over one shoulder. "Kind of reminds me of my own love life. Or lack thereof. Every time Jacob uses the phrase I *want to try, I* want to scream," she said. "I almost feel like the two of us are only getting back together for the sake of the baby. Not because there's anything between us anymore. But maybe that should be all that matters. The baby."

"I guess people end up together for lots of different reasons," Sara said. "What really matters is what *you* want, Daisy. What's right for you. I do believe that marrying Noah is right for *me*. Yeah—for the twins too, but for *me*. For a lot of reasons."

Daisy nodded thoughtfully. "And like I said, I'm just glad we finally get to be sisters." She stood up, a hand on her belly. "You've always felt like family, and now you will be. And I get to be Aunt Daisy for real."

Sara grinned and hugged her sister-in-law-to-be. "I don't know what I'd do without you."

Daisy grinned and glanced at her watch. "You'd better get downstairs, or you'll be late for your own wedding."

The town hall opened at eight thirty. Noah wanted to be among the first so they wouldn't have to wait around. She wasn't sure she would survive that.

Downstairs, she found Noah in a suit and his black Stetson. She hadn't expected him to dress up.

"You look very handsome," she said. She could barely take her eyes off him. Memories of last night hit her, and she forced the images of a completely *undressed* Noah Dawson out of her head. There would be no more of *that* in their lives.

"And you look absolutely beautiful," he said, the reverence in his voice catching her off guard. She could feel him staring at her, taking her in, liking what he saw.

But you prefer a lifetime of platonic partnership, she wanted to scream. *Safety over—*

Huh. She'd been so focused on how *she* needed to feel safe and secure that she hadn't really focused on why he was so dead set on a passionless marriage.

She knew that he needed the safety too. It wasn't just about keeping Annabel and Chance in his life. It was about *her*. The thought hit Sara uneasily in the stomach, and she wasn't sure why. It wasn't as though she didn't know he was *avoiding* how he really felt or what was between them by insisting on a platonic marriage.

"Ready?" he asked.

Was she?

She found herself nodding, and they headed out, the brilliant sunshine and low seventies temperatures wasted on a quickie town hall ceremony that would last all of ten minutes. No reception. No wedding night.

Just…security. And maybe a couple of photos to

commemorate the day. Taken by strangers, employees of the town hall who'd serve as witnesses.

She sighed as she got into his truck. She'd had the real wedding, complete with a princess ball gown, only white flowers—per Willem's decree—a jazz quartet and exceptional catering. Willem had hired a high-priced wedding planner and had apparently directed the woman not to let Sara make any changes to anything he'd already decided. Sara hadn't really cared. Back then, she was all about her father trying to fight prostate cancer, and that she'd danced with him at her wedding meant the world to her. The look on her father's face as he'd stood up with all the strength he could muster for that dance had been priceless.

Life was about choices, and Sara had made hers for reasons she would always stand by. She would do the same about today's wedding.

Fifteen minutes later, they arrived at the brick building in the center of Bear Ridge. Sara saw a few people she knew out and about, folks heading into the coffee shop, the diner, and waiting for the post office to open. Just people going about their lives while she was about to undertake something so big, so important. She was getting married and barely getting married at the same time.

Upstairs, they found the Weddings Performed Here sign on the second door on the right. Inside the large waiting area with benches and chairs and a lot of mirrors on the walls, another couple was already there, also clearly wanting to beat any possible rush at eight thirty on a random weekday. Sara imagined the couple was in a similar boat to her and Noah. An arrangement-type marriage. Needing to get it done before work. Even if the bride was in a strapless, above-the-knee white ball gown and white cowboy boots, and the groom was in a tux with a neon purple tie and black cowboy boots. Even if the bride held a beautiful bouquet of pink and red roses. Sara did not have a bouquet. Still, she liked to imagine the couple was getting married out of necessity instead of deep, abiding love. *Petty and small, Sara Mayhew*, she silently yelled at herself. *Don't wish a lack of love on anyone!*

She need not have worried. She watched the groom take the bride's face in his hands, staring deeply into her eyes, and say, "I'm the luckiest person on earth. To get to spend my life with you. I still can't believe it."

The bride leaned up on her toes to kiss her tall groom, wrapping her arms around his neck. "No, I'm the luckiest. I can't wait to become your wife."

Sara's shoulders slumped as pure envy socked her in the heart. She caught Noah eyeing the couple before turning away from them and fidgeting, pulling at his blue tie.

A door opened, and a middle-aged woman dressed in a powder blue suit with matching heels called the Hartley-Monkowski party. The couple made squealing sounds and hurried through the doorway after the woman, who closed it behind her.

"Guess we're next," Noah said, taking in a breath.

She nodded, biting the inside of her lower lip. A sheen of sweat broke out on the nape of her neck, despite the air-conditioning. Her sundress felt itchy. Her sandals suddenly felt too small. Her throat was dry and scratchy.

And standing next to her, looking like he might either faint or jump out the second-story window, was *her* groom-to-be. He seemed preoccupied, wasn't looking at her and did not remotely seem ready to do this.

To get married.

"Are you all right?" she asked him. *Please say no. Because this isn't feeling right.*

Why had it last night but not now?

"Just hitting me that we're actually getting married," he said. "Legally. Husband and wife. I'm about to become a married man." His expression was half wonder, half something else. Like fear.

"Strictly platonic partnership," she reminded him, peering at him closely.

"Platonic," he repeated. "But still it's legal. Official. We'll be married, and we'll both know it."

"Meaning?" she asked, staring at him. Where was he going with this?

"Meaning vows are serious stuff, Sara. We're about to vow to love, honor and cherish each other till death do us part."

And we're not going to mean it the way the first couple will, she thought. Sadly.

A small sob built deep in her throat. *Just remember why you're both here and doing this. Remember how you felt last night. Remember how scared and panicked you were. How grateful that you had Noah to count on. Partnership is a good thing. Not getting emotion and sex involved means things stay on an even keel. Always.*

In other words, settling for certainty. Not that that word could ever be applied to anything in life. She thought about Tabitha, coming into her own, not settling for a life she didn't want. Sara might want the life Noah had offered—the husband, the family, the father for her kids, the ranch, the partnership, the team...but not the platonic part. How was she supposed to live as husband and wife with the man she loved—as essentially his *roommate*?

"Mayhew-Dawson party, we're ready for you," called a voice.

Sara glanced to the left; the woman in the powder blue suit stood in the doorway of the room where the ceremonies were performed. Beyond her, Sara could see the justice of the peace at the front of the room, standing in front of the windows.

She swallowed. Partnership. Safety in the world. Noah Dawson, her friend. The man she'd always loved.

And did love.

Oh God, she realized as she slowly turned toward the smiling woman in blue. She loved Noah too much for this.

Noah stood in front of the justice of the peace, a man he'd never met, let alone seen before, Sara beside him, looking like she might throw up. Her complexion was kind of pasty and green at the same time. Her expression at the trying-to-keep-it-together stage.

This was not how this was supposed to go. Butterflies were one thing. Nausea quite another.

He wanted this marriage. But not at the expense of Sara's happiness.

"Sara, if your heart isn't in this," he whispered, "let's just go home."

She frowned. Actually, she looked pissed as hell. "Just one moment," she said to the justice of the peace, then took Noah by the hand and led him toward the back of the room.

"My *heart* isn't supposed to be in this. It's not supposed to count at all, remember?" she muttered. She shook her head. "Tabitha almost married a man she didn't love to make her parents happy. Your sister is trying to figure out how she feels about her baby's father after he disappeared on her the past six months. I'm not sure doing the right thing should be this damned hard. And I'm not sure this is the right thing anymore. Do you want to know why, Noah? The beating-heart reason why?"

He had a feeling he was finally about to learn what it was that Sara really wanted.

"Yes," he said.

"Because I love you. Not like a friend. Not like a partner I happen to be close to. I love you with everything I am, every part of me."

He sucked in a breath and stared at her. Of all the things she might have said, he hadn't been expecting *that*.

"I had to settle once before," she added. "And I paid dearly. I won't settle again. So unless you're in love with me too, I'd like to return to the ranch and spend my morning with my twins."

Something shuttered inside him—what thing exactly, he didn't know. A wall went up or a gate came crashing down.

He didn't want to talk about love. Or think about it. That wasn't what this marriage was supposed to be about. Teamwork and partnership and knowing where they stood and what they wanted from life and the future. A solid family.

"Sara, I—" He stopped talking, unsure what he wanted to say, what he felt.

"You know what, Noah? I don't think I'm flattering myself by saying that I think you do love me. And I mean love me in *all* the ways, every way, with every part of *you*. I think you always have, since we were teenagers. But you were scared then, and you're scared now."

He didn't like being told how he felt. At all. "Regardless," he said, that wall or gate making his voice sound so...cold. "We tried having a real relationship. Remember what happened? I drove you away."

"You're not that guy anymore. Everyone knows that. Especially me. And *you* know that."

Did he? He'd stepped up, yes. He'd changed his life. But wasn't he the same Noah Dawson he always was? Wasn't that guy who'd lost everything still inside him? Of course he was. Able to take over at any time.

"Then I guess we're going home," he said. "Wedding's off," he called to the justice of the peace and walked back through the door, two more couples in the waiting area now staring at them. Both women were looking at Sara as though she'd been cruelly left at the altar.

"She changed her mind," he snapped. "Not me." Oh God, now he was acting like a seven-year-old.

He glanced at Sara, whose cheeks were red. Oh hell. He'd screwed this up.

But he'd proposed something specific. She'd agreed. Then said no. Then said maybe. Then said yes. Then said no a few minutes ago.

Love, the kind she was talking about, the kind she wanted, was not supposed to be part of the arrangement.

And now you're going to drive her away again, he chastised himself as she stalked out the door and down the steps. She barged through the door into the parking lot. He wasn't even sure he'd find her waiting by his truck when he trailed after her.

He hurried downstairs and out the door. She was there, arms crossed over her chest, steam practically coming out of her ears.

"Sorry," he said. "Just got caught by surprise and let it get the better of me."

All that anger that had been on her face, in her body language? It turned to sadness. Defeat. "Same here, Noah. Same here."

What the hell was he going to do?

The new guests required all his attention, and he barely got to speak to Sara all afternoon. A few times they'd worked together, leading trail rides, supervising the petting zoo and going over the rules with the three sets of kids of varying ages, and pairing horses and riders. But they hadn't been in a position to talk. He'd have to wait until tonight.

And say what?

He was walking the path back toward the main barn when he saw his sister up toward the farmhouse with Jacob, her boyfriend, if he could be called that. The father of her baby. Noah had only met him a couple times, but something about the guy irked him. Jacob was polite, seemed okay enough, but there was just something that Noah couldn't put his finger on. And Daisy didn't look happy when he saw them together. He got the feeling his sister was forcing something she didn't feel.

Relationships didn't seem easy for *anyone*.

A few minutes later, he saw the boyfriend driving down the gravel road toward the gates. Daisy was heading toward him. She looked upset.

"Everything okay?" he asked her.

"You know it's not. This morning I expected to have a sister-in-law. Now I don't."

He almost smiled. "I know you love Sara, Daize. And I tried. But she wants more than I can give."

She stared at him. "You're lucky I'm not holding something. Because I'd bop you over the head with it. She wants more than you can give? Are you serious?"

He turned away, hardly interested in talking about this with his sister. "I've got a lot going on. At first, I just wanted to protect my interest in Annabel. Then her twin brother got ahold of me, and I started feeling like a father to them both. So I came up with an idea that would keep me and Sara in one place, give us both what we need."

"A roommate?" Sara asked, scrunching up her face.

"A *partner*," he corrected. "Without all the nonsense."

She snorted. "The nonsense of love? That nonsense?"

"How's Jacob?" he asked. Then regretted it. His sister was just calling him on what seemed ridiculous, and he could see how it might look that way to someone who wasn't him or Sara. They'd been through the wringer in different ways, and their needs were different. Daisy was six months pregnant and trying to make it work with her baby's father. He got that too. "Sorry," he said. "Been a long day. It's going to be a long night."

"Jacob is fine, by the way," she said. "We're trying. I don't know if it's working, but we're trying. The more time I spend with him, the less close I feel to him. How is that possible?"

"You probably just have no chemistry or much in common. Except for the baby," he added, eyeing her stomach. "I think it's great that you're both trying to make it work. But don't force something that isn't there."

"You are," Daisy said.

He stared at her, narrowing his eyes. "*I* am? How?"

"Trying to marry a woman you don't love," Daisy said. "So I'm not sure you should be giving advice on this subject."

"Who says I don't love Sara?" he asked, then froze. Of course he loved her. He knew that. But until he said the words out loud, he hadn't admitted it to himself. Or anyone else.

"Aha!" Daisy said, pointing at his chest. "I knew it. You are in love with Sara."

He scowled at her. "Doesn't matter. I'm not looking for romance. I just want a partnership marriage with certain parameters so nothing gets messed up. There's too much at stake."

"Mom once told me that no matter how bad things seemed at home between her and Dad, that marriage was a beautiful thing and I should know that I'd find my Mr. Right when I was ready and that marriage could be wonderful. I always felt bad because she didn't seem to really believe that—she just wanted to put it in my head, make up for what we were growing up with, seeing every day."

Their father had cheated on their mother a bunch of times. He and Daisy had both heard the arguments, the tears, the *I'm sorry, I'll never do it again*. Until the next time. And then his mother died, and his father was never quite the same. He still ran after women, but the loss had changed his father.

"I didn't need Mom and Dad's example to tell me

relationships don't last. None of mine ever have. Including with Sara."

"You sabotaged that on purpose. Only you know why, Noah."

He rolled his eyes.

"Don't roll your eyes at me, Noah Dean Dawson. You weren't ready then in any way, shape or form. You *got* ready and you changed your life. To the point that I came back when I swore I'd never live here again. You showed me what you can do, who you are, and I came home to be part of this. And because I was scared myself and needed a place to go where I could relax, where there was someone I could count on. You."

Oh hell. Now she was getting him all mushy. "Of course you can count on me, Daisy. I'd never let you down."

"I know you won't. And don't let *yourself* down. That's what you'll be doing if you let fear hold you back. You've got to be in it to get anything in this world. You know that."

"I'm doing that with the ranch. There's no way I'd blow the investment you all made in me. I've got enough riding on this place. I can't take more risks, Daisy. Not when it comes to Sara and the twins. I lose them, that's it."

"Well, Sara wants something very different, so you're going to lose her anyway. Kind of dopey of you not to *try.*"

His phone pinged with a text. *Saved*, he thought. He pulled out the cell. His cowboy, Dylan. "Dylan needs me in the petting zoo. Runaway sheep."

"This conversation isn't over," Daisy said. "You and Sara both deserve better."

"Gotta run," he said and headed in the opposite direction.

Sisters, he thought. Good thing he had only one. His brothers liked to challenge him, but they didn't stand around talking about relationships the way Daisy did.

He headed over to the pasture beside the main barn, and between him and Dylan they got the runaway sheep back in his pen. He passed the petting zoo, stopping to watch his youngest guests, five-year-old Liam and his twin sister, Lyra, offer the little goats some pellets.

That'll be Annabel and Chance in just a few years, he thought, his heart close to bursting. He could just see them running around the ranch, playing with the farm animals, learning ranching by living here.

And because of you, they might not *be running around the ranch at all. In fact, they might be running around some other guy's ranch, someone else their father.*

If he couldn't give Sara what she wanted, she wasn't going to stay.

He couldn't live with that either.

Chapter 12

Sara wasn't sure why, but she couldn't stop thinking about Katherine Palmer. The midwife. She'd pushed the woman out of her head since the day after the bombshell in the lawyer's office, when Holton had assured her the midwife had retired, per calls he'd made to area hospitals and clinics and local OB practices she could be affiliated with and the Wyoming State Board of Nursing. Palmer's license had expired last month and she hadn't renewed it for the first time in thirty-seven years.

Holton had wanted to file a claim against Katherine Palmer, but until Sara had spoken to the woman herself, she didn't want him to do that. She knew what Willem had been capable of and could only guess what he'd threatened the midwife with. Once Sara had been assured the woman was retired and could never do anything remotely like what she'd done to Sara and Annabel again, she'd relaxed some and put Katherine Palmer out of her head until she was ready to confront her.

For some reason she couldn't put her finger on, the midwife had entered Sara's mind on the drive home from the town hall, along with the few lines Willem had written about her in his letter. She suddenly wanted to talk to Katherine, to understand why she'd done something so heinous. *How* she could have done it. No matter what Willem had threatened her with. A person who'd devoted her career to bringing new life into the world for almost forty years?

Sara sat on the couch in the foreman's cabin, the twins in their swings, staring at the sparkly mobiles hanging high above them, trying to figure out why it suddenly felt like time to pay the woman a visit. Maybe Sara was simply in fight mode. Maybe what had happened at the town hall, coming so close to marrying under terms she couldn't live by, had her ready to deal with everything that wasn't right.

She wasn't sure what talking to the woman would accomplish, but it had been hanging over her head since she'd learned the news back in the lawyer's office, and it felt like time to entirely put her past to rest.

When she heard Noah's key in the lock, she took a deep breath, preparing herself for anything. For him to say, *Actually, I don't love you, sorry.* Or, *Actually, I do, you're right, but sorry, I can't.* Either way, she lost. She'd confront the midwife, get that off her to-do list and figure out what she was going to do next. This new Sara Mayhew didn't leave things hanging. She might not exactly have her groove back, but she felt as if she was on her way.

"Crazy day," Noah said, coming into the living room.

"Start, middle, finish and every moment in between. I wished I could have had just ten minutes to see you, talk to you."

"About what?" she asked. None too nicely.

"Just to check in, I guess."

"Thought so." Again, none too nicely. "I've made a decision," she said.

He paled, and she was struck by two things. One: that she knew him well enough to know he thought she was talking about leaving. And two: that it would truly tear him apart if she did leave.

But not enough to blast through the wall he'd erected where she was concerned. So that they could have a real relationship. Start a real future together.

He stood beside the coffee table, waiting. Looking... nervous.

"I'm going to see the midwife," she said. She expected him to relax since she wasn't talking about leaving at all, but he seemed more anxious, actually.

"Really? Why all of a sudden? Not that I don't think you should talk to her—I do. But just curious about why right now."

"Taking care of business," she said. "I need to close that chapter. And I need to hear why she did what she did. I need closure."

"I'm not sure she's the closure you're really after," he said.

She scowled. "Meaning? That I'm deflecting being upset about you? Yes, I'm upset about you. And us. But I'm done running away and seeking safety, Noah. Life is about risk. Being a parent is about risk. Love is about risk. I've avoided dealing with the midwife. But I'm going to face her."

He grimaced. "I'm coming with you whether you want me to or not."

"Good, because I do want you to," she said.

His entire body relaxed, and he sat down beside her, running a finger down each baby's cheek in their swings before turning his attention back to her. "And after you speak to her? Then what?"

"Then I move on mentally and emotionally from what Willem attempted to do. I have my children—both of them. I close that part of my life so that I can start a new one. One in which I'm not scared or looking for anyone to take care of me."

"Sara, I—"

She was done with *Sara, I...* followed by either silence or Noah trying to explain himself. Unless he could say the words she needed to hear to marry him, any discussion of marriage was over.

"You know what?" she said, her eyes widening as something occurred to her. "I thought that feeling safe in the world was what I wanted and that I needed to give up other important values to have it for myself and the twins. But what I really want is to feel safe in the world at *my* own hands, Noah. Stand on my own two feet. I will never make another deal about my security, because I can support my children myself. It might not be easy, and as a single parent, my paycheck isn't going to stretch so far, but I've done the math, and I'll be fine if I'm careful. And I have been."

He stared at her, hard, and she knew his mind was churning, but she had no idea what he was thinking.

"You've always impressed the hell out of me," he said. "I understand. And I admire you."

That was all well and good. And if she were honest

with herself, she'd admit he'd touched her deeply with that. But what she wanted, really wanted, was his *love*.

According to an online search, Katherine Palmer lived at 132-B Harris Road in Wellington, the town Sara had moved to when she'd accepted Willem's proposal. A quick map check showed Harris Road was near the center of town.

She decided to just show up, not call. If the woman wasn't home, Sara would simply wait until she turned up. It was kind of nutty, but the entire situation was insane, so there was no right way to go about it. Noah was unsettled about the whole thing but agreed that alerting Katherine that she wanted to talk to her might make the woman flee, and Sara would never get answers.

Because Wellington was an hour way, they'd decided to leave at eight this morning so they could be back by ten thirty or eleven at the latest, figuring they'd spend an hour or so with Katherine. Mrs. Pickles would babysit since Daisy needed to be on the job.

She was quiet on the way there, and she was grateful that Noah didn't try to fill the silence with conversation. He seemed to know she needed to just sit with her thoughts. She couldn't begin to explain how she felt at the moment anyway.

When Noah pulled up in front of an apartment complex, Sara could see 132 was the middle of three identical rows of garden apartments in a U shape around a green. In the driveway for apartment B, there was a small dumpster and a pod truck—as if someone was moving out.

"Maybe we got here just in time," Sara said. "Maybe she's moving." She sucked in a breath. "Let's knock."

They got out of his truck and headed to the front door. A small silver car was parked in front of the dumpster, so it looked like someone was home. Sara found herself unable to lift her arm to ring the bell. Her stomach churned, and she closed her eyes for a second. She squeezed Noah's hand, and he squeezed it back with an encouraging look at her. She was so damned grateful he was here, that he'd insisted on coming, because she wasn't sure if she would have asked him to otherwise, despite wanting him with her. Some things she could do alone. Some things she didn't want to. *This* was a didn't want to.

"Okay," she said under her breath and rang the bell.

She could hear footsteps. Sara's heart sped up. Katherine Palmer was about to open the door.

But the woman who appeared in the doorway was in her early thirties at most. The midwife was sixty-five years old. "Can I help you?" she asked.

Was this Katherine's daughter? she wondered. There was a definite resemblance. Similar auburn hair and hazel eyes, a similar fine-boned face.

"I'm looking for Katherine Palmer," Sara said. "My name is Sara. I was a patient of hers. Her last patient, actually."

"Oh," the woman said softly. "I'm sorry to tell you, but my mother passed away three days ago."

Sara turned to Noah, her throat closing up, her legs feeling like rubber. Of all the scenarios that had gone through her head the past several hours, this wasn't one of them.

"I'm sorry for your loss," Sara managed to say.

The woman gave a closemouthed smile of sorts. "You said your name is Sara. Sara *Perry*?"

Sara stared at her. "Why do you ask?" What did Palmer's daughter know? *Did* she know?

"My mom left a letter addressed to a Sara Perry," the woman explained. "I haven't had a chance to mail it or even drop it off. Between crying and trying to get the house sorted before the bank takes it…" She waved her hand by her face and then shook her head, her eyes welling. "Ignore me. Things are a mess."

She glanced at Noah. That the midwife had had financial problems wasn't a surprise. Willem had bribed her. She'd known that from the start.

"I am Sara Perry," she said. "And I am truly sorry for your loss. I lost my parents, and I know how painful it is."

The woman offered a small smile. "I'll just go get the letter. It's on her bedside table. I think she wrote it the night before she passed. I was here the week prior, knowing how sick she was, and it wasn't there earlier."

"Was it cancer?" Sara asked.

The woman nodded. "The diagnosis came too late to do anything about it. I'll just go get the letter."

Katherine's daughter left the door ajar and walked up the stairs. Sara turned to Noah, unable to form words. He squeezed her hand.

"Another letter from beyond the grave," she finally said, shaking her head. "I don't know if I can bear it."

"Sounds like it might be a deathbed confession," he whispered.

She gnawed her lower lip. The woman returned, holding a letter, and she handed it to Sara.

"Thank you," Sara said. "And again, my condolences."

She nodded and closed the door.

Sara and Noah headed to his truck. She was done here, at least. She had a letter, which might explain things.

They got into Noah's pickup. "How about I drive a bit away from here, so you can read it in privacy. Without being right here, I mean."

"Actually, let's get out of this town entirely. Wellington is doubly ruined for me forever. Let's go back to Bear Ridge. You can park in town near the coffee shop—I'm going to need a boost of caffeine."

He nodded and started the truck, and once again she was so aware that he was right here when she needed someone who could see her through whatever the hell was in the letter. Explanation? Apology?

She held the letter in her hand as Noah drove the hour back to Bear Ridge. Finally, he parked near the coffee shop on Main Street.

"Ready?" he asked, gesturing at the letter.

"No. I wasn't ready for Willem's letter either. I almost wanted to flee the office before the lawyer could read it to me. Good thing I stayed."

Noah nodded. "I'll be right here. You can read it aloud or to yourself. Whichever you want."

"I'd rather read it aloud. So you hear what I hear." She cleared her throat and slit open the envelope. Inside were two pages, typed on white paper. It was signed with her full name—Katherine Marie Palmer—in black ink. She glanced at Noah, needing a gulp of him before she dived in. "Okay. Here goes."

Dear Sara,
Two weeks ago I was diagnosed with ovarian cancer, stage three. My doctors tell me it's inopera-

ble. I did something terrible that I need to rectify. I can't fix it, but I can tell you the truth. It's only two months later, and though that must feel like a long time to you, I feel better knowing it's not.

Your baby daughter didn't die at birth. Your husband, Willem Perry, told me he'd make up a devastating lie about my daughter and ruin her life if I didn't comply. He also bribed me by paying off tens of thousands of dollars of debt, which my late husband accumulated through gambling. Anyway, it's true that your daughter was born frail, but she was alive. He told me to back him up that she died during the birth. I was horrified but said I would for the reasons I stated. Then he muttered something about "Dawson." I don't know what that refers to, and as I left your home that evening, hoping to make it home before the big thunderstorm, he left too—with the baby in a car seat. I don't know where he took the newborn. But she was alive when she was born. Maybe the word Dawson will mean something to you? A start for finding your daughter?

This letter will be a shock. I don't know why your husband didn't want the girl. I only know that I can't go without making this as right as I can. By telling you the truth. May God forgive me. I won't ask your forgiveness, because I don't deserve it. And I've taken enough from you. I'm deeply ashamed. I don't know what your husband would have done to my daughter had I refused, and because your daughter did look so frail and small compared to her brother, I rationalized that she would probably not make it. That was not

my decision to make. I hope I was wrong. I hope
you find your daughter healthy and get her back.
Sincerely,
Katherine Marie Palmer

Sara just stared at the words on the pages, unable to speak.

Noah took the letter and put it back in the envelope, then shoved it in his glove compartment. He leaned over and took her in his arms, and she let him, wrapping her own arms around him tightly as she cried.

He didn't say a word; he just held her, which was exactly what she needed.

Fifteen minutes later, she wiped under her eyes. "I'm ready to go home," she said. "I have my closure. And I never, ever want to think about her or Willem or what they did or why again."

"Want to get some coffee first?" he asked, pointing at the coffee shop two stores down.

"And a Boston cream doughnut," she said. "Maybe two."

He smiled and squeezed her hand. "Coming right up. Want to wait here or come in with me?"

"I'll wait here."

She watched him head in, her head clearing already. By the time he came out with a white bag and two coffees in a tray, she was ready to put her past behind her.

She had no idea what the present would hold, though. Or where she and her twins would be in the near future.

Noah told Sara to take the day off. He'd matched her with a horse when she'd first agreed to take the assistant forewoman's job, and he was glad when she agreed that taking Bluebell for a ride in the acres of open pasture would be therapeutic after the heavy morning. The moment she'd ridden off, though, he missed her and wished he were beside her on Bolt. He didn't want her to be alone, even though he knew it was probably best for her right now.

He checked in with his staff, glad to hear everything was running smoothly. He was going to lead a trail ride for parents and kids who were new to horses, Dylan as his backup. As he met the group of six in the barn, three parents and three kids, he couldn't help but notice how the moms and dads doted on their children, listening to them, assuring them, being excited about the horses along with them. This was what he wanted for himself with Annabel and Chance, and because there was something fundamentally wrong with him deep inside, where he couldn't commit to Sara the way she needed, he was going to lose the twins.

With the kids on the gentlest of ponies and the adults on sweet quarter horses, they entered the small pasture and did a slow trot around the perimeter. There was hooting and laughing and big smiles from the entire group, and Noah gave easy instructions as he rode alongside the middle of the pack, Dylan at the rear.

And then out of nowhere, somehow, a little girl fell off her pony. Lyra Barnett, five years old.

Her face crumpled in tears under her helmet, and she just lay on the grass, not moving. Her father, a very fit man in his early forties named Mike Barnett, was beside her on the ground in a heartbeat, as were Noah and Dylan.

"I'll text our on-call doctor," Noah said, pulling out his phone.

The man held up a hand. "Hang on a second." He turned his attention to his daughter. "Where does it hurt?"

The girl just cried.

"Daddy, is Lyra okay?" her twin brother asked, still on his pony.

Her father touched her leg, slowly inching his hands around both feet and the entirety of her legs. The girl didn't wince.

"I'm a doctor," Mike explained. "Nothing feels broken."

Noah's heart was beating like a hundred wild horses galloping. She was okay. Thank God.

Lyra cried harder, then wiped at her eyes. "I stink at riding horses."

"You were doing good until you fell off," her brother put in.

"I really was, right, Daddy?" Lyra asked, wiping under her eyes.

Her father smiled at her. "You sure were. Accidents happen, right?"

"Right," her brother said.

Lyra scowled at him. "Right," she said louder.

Mike Barnett smiled, and Noah had to also.

"Dylan, why don't you take the group into the next pasture," Noah said. "I'll have Sara join you." He quickly texted her.

Dylan nodded and helped Lyra's brother off his pony so he could sit beside his family, and then he instructed the group to dismount, helping each kid off, and they all led the ponies and horses into the next pasture. He could see Sara already coming up the path in the golf cart, her expression grim.

"I'll run her over to the clinic in town," Mike said. "We're locals, so we're familiar with the place." He turned to his son. "I'll call Mommy and she'll take you to the creek to see if there are beavers and badgers and porcupines hanging around."

"The porcupines are my favorite," the little boy said.

Sara rushed over, concern in her eyes. Noah explained the situation, and she texted Daisy to pick up Mrs. Barnett from the lodge, where she was taking some R&R with a book and Cowboy Joe's lemonade and peach cobbler.

"Your wife will be here in two minutes," Sara assured him. She turned to the little girl. "Hi, Lyra. I'm Sara. Was this your first time on a pony?"

The girl shook her head. "My third time. I rode a pony at our birthday party."

Sara smiled. "I've been riding horses a long time. I fell off one time. I was thinking about something, and plop, right off on the ground. Luckily I wasn't hurt."

"I don't feel hurt anywhere," Lyra said. "I'm upset that I'm not on Cupcake anymore." She looked at the sweet brown-and-white pony.

Her dad grinned and patted Lyra's back. "Well, let's have you checked out as a just-in-case, and if nothing is broken or sprained, we'll get you right back on Cupcake, okay?"

"'Kay, Daddy," she said.

Her mom arrived, and Daisy drove off in the golf cart with the family—father and daughter to their car by the gate, and then mother and son to the creek. Noah dropped back down to the ground, leaning his head against a fence post. "That was lucky. And close. If she'd gotten hurt…"

"Little kids get hurt. It's what happens. I like her dad's point of getting right back on the pony. That's the lesson, Noah."

"I don't need a lecture right now," he said, squinting up at her in the bright sunshine. "I feel bad enough as it is."

"I understand that," she said. "But you absolutely do need a lecture," she added, pushing her straw cowboy hat farther on her head and taking off down the path.

Every minute he pushed her farther and farther away, when all he wanted was to have her beside him.

Chapter 13

As Noah finished his chores and rounds and got a welcome text from Mike Barnett that Lyra was absolutely fine, no broken bones or sprains or torn anything, he let out one hell of a breath. He knew that little kids got hurt. Of course he knew that. He'd broken at least five bones over his childhood from being too rough with himself and from incidents he had no control over, like tripping over a hole in the ground that his father hadn't taken care of. Kids got hurt. And yes, the important thing was to teach them to dust themselves off, if possible, and get back up.

He wasn't afraid of Annabel and Chance falling off ponies; of course they would. Of course they'd have illnesses and mishaps. That was life.

So why the hell could he commit so fervently to them and not to Sara? Granted, he wasn't afraid of her getting hurt. He was paralyzed at the notion of giving in to the full range of his feelings for her. Once he did, he wouldn't be in control. That he understood, because he'd thought of little else the past two days. He had to remain in control of himself or he'd drive her off, one way or another. He couldn't ruin what they had—he wouldn't. And keeping things as professional as possible between them, as friendship based as possible, was the answer.

As he closed the main barn door, he saw Daisy coming toward him, on foot this time.

"So I have news," she said, stretching out her hand.

There was a ring on her finger. A small round diamond in a silver band.

"You're engaged?" he asked, his mouth dropping open.

"Jacob proposed this morning. He said he felt ready to ask me last night, but didn't have a ring, so went off to the jewelry shop to buy one." She looked at her hand.

"You don't look particularly happy," he said, then regretted it. This wasn't his business. Or maybe it was. Of course it was. He was her brother.

"I feel good about it," she said, her eyes still on the ring.

"You feel good about it?" he repeated.

"Noah. I'm almost seven months pregnant. My baby's father proposed. We're going to make this work so that we can be a family. It's the right thing to do."

"Except you don't love Jacob. Does he love you?"

"He cares about me. He's committed to our family and our future, and he thinks we'll get there as time goes on and we share a life with our child."

He stared at her. "Get *where*? To love?"

"Yes, to love. We'll be raising a child together. Our

goal will be the same. We'll be parents, committed to our baby. That alone will help us grow as a couple."

"God, Daisy. Is that how it's supposed to be?"

Now she stared at him. "Um, hello, pot talking trash about the kettle."

He scowled at her. "My situation is different. I'm protecting my stake in those twins. In not destroying my relationship with Sara."

"*Riiight*, little brother. With the woman you're madly in love with."

He froze, realizing how true that statement was. He was deeply in love with Sara.

"How can I not try?" Daisy asked, tears welling in her eyes. "Things might work out great with Jacob. He's my baby's father." She stared at him—hard. "I personally don't know how you *cannot* try, Noah."

With that, she walked off, leaving him so unsettled he had to sit back down against the barn.

Had a hay bale fallen on his head? That was how he felt. Absolutely gobsmacked.

And not sure where the hell to go from here.

To make this as easy on the two of them as possible, Sara was packed before she told Noah that she planned to move into the main house. She'd been thinking about doing just that ever since she'd left the town hall without a wedding ring on her finger. There'd been a lot going on and she'd pushed moving out of her head, but there was no way she could continue living in the cabin with Noah. Yes, he'd lose home access to the twins, but the way she saw it, that was his own damned fault.

Stubborn gets what stubborn deserves, she thought, instantly feeling bad for him. She didn't know exactly what it was going to take to get through to him, to blast through the concrete he'd built around his heart. She just knew she had to protect herself.

She had spoken to Daisy, swearing her to secrecy until she could talk to Noah about her decision, and Daisy had offered her a bedroom in the farmhouse across from the nursery, which the twins would have. The downside was that the living arrangement was temporary. Daisy was newly engaged to her boyfriend, Jacob—boy, had Sara been surprised to hear the news—and Jacob would move in after the wedding. He was a businessman, something to do with imports and exports. She understood why Daisy wanted to marry him, despite, despite, despite.

Daisy and Jacob had talked about a July wedding, a couple weeks before her due date so that Daisy could have the wedding she wanted—a church ceremony and a big reception at the ranch with family and friends. If they were going to do this, she wanted to really do it.

Sara understood that more than anyone. And, at least it gave her a solid month in the farmhouse with her good friend until Daisy married and her husband moved in and Sara would move out, finding a place she could afford in town.

Now, Sara stood in the kitchen of the foreman's cabin, making a pot of coffee, knowing that Noah would be home in about ten minutes.

She was on her second cup of the bracing brew when she heard his key in the lock.

Her suitcases were beside the table. She'd thought about collecting the twins' baby stuff and putting it all near the door so that they could get into his truck quickly, but she knew what the sight of the swings and stroller and mats would do to him.

Her stomach churned. She hated hurting him. But he'd left her no choice but to do exactly what she was doing. She couldn't live this way with him, this quarter of a life.

"I smell coffee," he said with a smile as he appeared in the kitchen doorway. Then his gaze moved to the suitcases, and the smile disappeared. "You're leaving?"

"Moving up to the farmhouse. The twins will take the nursery that Daisy has already begun creating. The three of us will leave right before her wedding, when Jacob will move in."

He sighed and crossed his arms over his chest, quiet for a moment as he seemed to take in what she'd said. "I don't think she should be marrying him so fast. I get that they want to get married before the baby comes, but why not see how things go before committing like that?"

"Because they're committing," Sara pointed out.

He shrugged. "I guess they are." He stared at her suitcases. "I don't want you to go."

"Feel free to stop me, Noah." She tried a smile, but tears welled and she shoved her half-drunk coffee mug away.

"Sara, I…"

Oh God, not that.

Maybe the real problem with Noah Dawson was that he didn't love her. Maybe that was what he—and she—couldn't face.

But she'd bet everything she had that he *did* love her—very much. She knew it, she felt it, she believed. But until he could admit it to himself and open up the gates inside him, they were stuck.

"Will you help me load up the twins' stuff?" she asked. "I know it'll be hard for you, but I can't do it alone."

He grimaced. "Of course." He poured himself a cup

of coffee, added cream and sugar, and took a couple long sips, then put the cup in the sink. "For what it's worth, I am sorry, Sara."

Tears stung her eyes. "Well, it's not worth all that much to me. I don't want you to be sorry. I want you to love me. I want us to raise Annabel and Chance together, be a family. I want us both to be happy. And if you really think you can be happy by shutting off half of yourself..."

He couldn't. But she was done talking, done arguing, done trying to convince him. It was time to go.

The expression on his face as he picked up one of the baby swings almost broke another piece of her heart.

But they silently loaded the pickup. Once back in the cabin, all that was left were the babies themselves in their carriers. She picked up one, then the other. Heavy, but she had this.

He stared at her, and then reached forward to take both carriers himself, but she walked out the door toward the truck before he could.

She could feel him just standing there and had no doubt his own heart was breaking. But by his own hand.

Noah had done double rounds on the ranch and finally made himself go home. Then he tried to stick to his bedroom, where he wouldn't be overly reminded of Sara or the twins. But he'd made love to Sara in this room. And every time he closed his eyes, he'd see them in bed. He'd never been so aware of how much he felt for her as he had that other night, when he'd stopped thinking so much and just let himself *feel*.

That he loved her like crazy wasn't in doubt.

He thought he heard a cry and bolted up and into the nursery, but the cribs, which were still there, were empty. Daisy had enough of a setup in the nursery she'd started making for her own child that they didn't need to move the cribs and dresser and glider right away.

He stood in the room, his gaze on the letters spelling out Annabel's and Chance's names on the cribs. He'd painted their names himself. He dropped down in the glider, where he'd sat so many nights, a baby in his arms, telling a story or just marveling at the precious infant he held. He thought about hearing Annabel's cries the night he'd found her. The note saying she was his.

The terror that had gripped him.

He'd been so damned scared of screwing up, but he hadn't. Hadn't screwed up at all in the seven weeks he'd taken care of Annabel.

And now he'd lost not only her but Chance, as well.

Instead of focusing on that, he kept going back to the previous thought. That he *hadn't* screwed up. Huh. Why the hell was he so focused on destroying his relationship with Sara when there was nothing to indicate he would—well, other than a history of doing just that? He had a history of failure, but he'd given himself an A-plus when it came to rebuilding the ranch and an A-plus in raising Annabel those first seven weeks.

He could handle a newborn baby as a bachelor rebuilding his family's legacy, but he couldn't handle his own feelings for the woman he loved with every fiber of his being?

He shot off the chair. Wanting to go get her. Get his woman. His life, his future, his everything. His Sara.

He sat back down. Once he'd allowed himself to really go there, there was no turning back. He'd be cracked wide-open. And his least favorite word in the English language: *vulnerable*.

He thought about the most vulnerable he'd ever felt. The day he'd read the letter his father had left him in his will. The whoppers in there. About how his dad believed he was the one to restore the Dawson Family Guest Ranch, that Bo Dawson hoped he would. *I believe in you,* his father had written. *I'm sorry I was such a failure. I know you can make things right, Noah. I know it. And knowing it gives me peace at going.*

Noah felt his eyes well. He took out the letter and read it for the fifth time, then put it back in the envelope and under his socks in the top drawer of his dresser. Even his father had owned up to his failures and looked to fresh starts—for Noah, at least, if not himself.

And Noah was going to sit in this empty, silent cabin when the woman he loved was a quarter mile up the road with the family he'd already made his own?

No, he wasn't. He opened his dresser drawer again, reaching under the socks until he felt a small velvet box that had been there for two years now.

Sara sat outside on the porch of the farmhouse where she'd spent so much of her childhood, running between this house and the cabin. She loved this house as much as she did the foreman's cabin, and she was grateful to have a room here. She might not have what she really wanted in a getting-her-groove-back way, but at least she wasn't settling for what she didn't want. That was a no-go.

She and Daisy had had a long talk when she'd arrived with her stuff, after a grim-faced Noah had brought everything in, making a thousand trips up and down the stairs. Then he was gone, and she'd let herself burst into tears, Daisy comforting her. They'd talked for the past two hours, Daisy assuring her she was doing the right thing, Sara assuring Daisy she was too. Trying was paramount. Now Daisy was in her bedroom, working on her wedding plans for July. She'd asked Sara to be her maid of honor, and Sara had joyfully accepted. According to Daisy, they were still honorary aunts to each other's children, even if they weren't going to be sisters-in-law.

Daisy heard a truck coming up the road, then saw the headlights. Was that Noah?

She stood up as he parked. It *was* Noah.

If he was here to try to convince her to come back, he was wasting his breath. But damn, it was good to see him, and they'd only been apart for two hours.

He came around the side of the truck and walked up the porch steps. "I've been doing a lot of thinking."

Don't get your hopes up, she told herself. *He's going to suggest some kind of compromise.*

"You're absolutely right," he said, his blue eyes intense on her. "I'm letting fear control me. It's what did my father in, I understand that now. He failed, and then instead of picking himself up, he fell deeper into the hole."

She stared at him, her heart surging. Maybe she *could* hope a tiny bit.

"I've loved you so much for so long that you're a part of everything I am," he said. "I'm you and you're me and we're separate but the same. There's no me without you, Sara."

Tears welled in her eyes. She'd let herself hope a second ago, but he was taking her to the moon and the stars.

"I love you, Sara Mayhew. I'm in love with you. I want to spend my life with you and the twins. I want to be your husband in every sense of the word. I want to be Annabel and Chance's father. I love you. Even more than you could possibly want."

She grinned. "Is that possible?"

"Anything is possible now," he said, the moonlight shining down on him as he got on one knee, opening a little black velvet box. "Do me the honor of becoming my wife. Will you marry me?"

Sara gasped and barely managed to whisper, "Yes," before jumping into his arms and wrapping her arms around him. "I love you too."

He kissed her and she kissed him back, then he looked at her, and she could see the change in his eyes, in his expression. He slid the beautiful ring on her finger, then kissed her again. So passionately her legs buckled.

"Get a room!" called a voice from an upstairs window. "At the cabin so you don't wake the twins. I've got them till the morning. Go, lovebirds," Daisy added with a grin.

Noah laughed. "Thanks, Daisy. I owe you."

"Yeah, you do," his sister called back with a smile before poking her head back in.

"Let's go get that room," he said, taking Sara's hand.

And then they got in the truck and headed home, where they both belonged.

* * * * *

Laura Marie Altom is a bestselling and award-winning author who has penned nearly fifty books. After college—go, Hogs!—Laura Marie did a brief stint as an interior designer before becoming a stay-at-home mom to boy-girl twins and a bonus son. Always an avid romance reader, she knew it was time to try her hand at writing when she found herself replotting the afternoon soaps. When not immersed in her next story, Laura plays video games, tackles Mount Laundry and, of course, reads romance!

Laura loves hearing from readers either at PO Box 2074, Tulsa, OK 74101, or by email, balipalm@aol.com.

Love winning fun stuff? Check out lauramariealtom.com.

Books by Laura Marie Altom

Harlequin Western Romance

Cowboy SEALs

The SEAL's Miracle Baby
The Baby and the Cowboy SEAL
The SEAL's Second Chance Baby
The Cowboy SEAL's Jingle Bell Baby
The Cowboy SEAL's Christmas Baby
Cowboy SEAL Daddy

Visit the Author Profile page at Harlequin.com for more titles.

Temporary
Dad

LAURA MARIE ALTOM

This book is dedicated to the wonderful game of Scrabble, and to all the lovely folks with whom I've had the privilege to play.

John Chew, webmaster extraordinaire for the National Scrabble Association—thanks so much for your generosity in sharing the particulars of the National Scrabble Championship. Any errors in official protocol are mine.

Chapter 1

Waaaaaaaaaaaaa! Waa huh waaaaaaaaahh!

Sitting in a cozy rattan chair on the patio of her new condo, Annie Harnesberry looked up from the August issue of *Budget Decorating* and frowned.

Waaaaaaaa!

Granted, she wasn't a mother herself, but she'd been a preschool teacher for the past seven years, so that did lend her a certain credibility where children were concerned. Not to mention the fact that she'd spent the past two years falling for Conner and his five cuties. Considering how badly he'd hurt her, the man must have a PhD in breaking hearts.

Baby Sarah had only been nine months old when Conner brought his second-youngest, three-year-old Clara, to the school where Annie used to teach.

Their initial attraction had been undeniable—Annie's affinity for Clara and Baby Sarah, that is.

The two blue-eyed blondes were heart-stealers.

Kind of like their father, who'd gradually made Annie believe he'd loved *her* and not her knack for taking care of his children.

The man had emotionally devastated her when, instead of offering her a ring on Valentine's Day, he'd offered her a position as his live-in nanny—right before showing off the diamond solitaire he was giving the next female on his night's agenda.

Jade.

His future bride.

Trouble was, Jade didn't much care for the patter of little feet—hence Conner's sudden need for a nanny. But beyond that, he explained that the exotic brunette was one hot ticket. *Us all living together'll be like a big, happy family, don'tcha think?*

Waaaaa ha waaaah!

Annie sighed.

Whoever was in charge of that poor, pitiful wailer in the condo across the breezeway from hers ought to do *something* to calm the infant. Never had she heard so much commotion. Was the poor thing sick?

She plucked a dead leaf from the pot of red impatiens gracing the center of her patio table, then returned to her article on glazing. She'd love to try this new technique in the guest bath that was tucked under the stairs.

Maybe in burgundy?

Or gold?

Something rich and decadent—like the decorating equivalent of a spoonful of hot fudge.

The house she'd grown up in had been painted top to bottom, inside and out, in vibrant jewel tones. She'd lived with her grandparents, since her mom and dad were engineers who traveled abroad so often that once she'd become school-age, it had been impractical for her to go with them. Her second place of residence—never could she call it a *home*—had been painted mashed-potato beige. This was the house she'd shared with her ex-husband, Troy, a man so abusive he made Conner look like a saint. Lodging number three, the apartment she'd run to after leaving her ex, had been a step up from mashed potatoes, seeing how it'd been painted creamed-corn yellow.

This condo was her fourth abode, and this time, she was determined to get not only the décor right, but her life. As much as she loved spending five days a week around primary colors and Sesame Street wallpaper, in her free time, she craved more grown-up surroundings.

Waaaaa waaaa waaaaa!

Waa huh waaaa!

Waaaaaaaaaa!

Annie slapped the magazine back onto her knees.

Something about the sound of that baby's crying wasn't right.

Was there more than one?

Definitely two.

Maybe even three.

But she'd moved in a couple of weeks earlier and hadn't heard a peep or seen signs of any infant in the complex—let alone three. That was partially why she'd chosen this unit over the one beside the river, which had much better views of the town of Pecan, Oklahoma's renowned pecan groves.

The problem with the other place, the one with the view, was that it catered to families, and after saying tearful goodbyes to Baby Sarah and Clara and their two older brothers and sister, not to mention their father, the last thing Annie wanted in a new home was children.

Conner had packed up his kids, along with his gorgeous new wife and Scandinavian nanny, moving them all to Atlanta. The children were just as confused by the sudden appearance of Jade in their father's life as Annie had been. She sent them birthday cards and letters, but it wasn't the same. She missed them. Which was why she'd left her hometown of Bartlesville for Pecan. Because she'd resigned herself to mothering only the kids at work.

Conner was her second rotten experience with a man. And with trying to be part of a big, boisterous family. She sure didn't want any daily reminders of her latest relationship disaster.

No more haunting memories of running errands with the kids at Wal-Mart or QuikTrip or the grocery store. No more lurching heart every time she saw a car that reminded her of Conner's silver Beemer on Bartlesville's main drag.

She needed a fresh start in the kind of charming small town that Conner wouldn't lower himself to step foot in.

Annie looked at her magazine.

Glazing.

All she needed to feel better about her whole situation was time and a can or two of paint.

Waa huh waaaaaaa!

Annie frowned again.

No good parent would just leave an infant crying like this. What was going on? Could the baby's mom or dad be hurt?

Wrinkling her nose, nibbling the tip of her pinkie

finger, Annie put her magazine on the table and peered over the wrought-iron rail encircling her patio.

A cool breeze ruffled her short, blond curls, carrying with it the homey scent of fresh bread baking at the town's largest factory, a mile or so away. She had yet to taste Finnegan's Pecan Wheatberry bread, but it was supposedly to die for.

Normally at this time of year in Oklahoma, she'd be inside cozied up to a blasting central AC vent. Due to last night's rain, the day wasn't typical August fare, but tinged with an enticing fall preview.

Waaaaaaaa!

Annie popped the latch on her patio gate, creeping across grass not quite green or brown, but a weary shade somewhere in between.

The birdbath left behind by the condo's last owner had gone dry. She'd have to remember to fill it the next time she dowsed her impatiens and marigolds.

Waaaaaa!

She crept farther across the shared lawn, stepping onto the weathered brick breezeway she shared with the as-yet-unseen owner of the unit across from hers.

The condo complex's clubhouse manager—Veronica, a bubbly redhead with a penchant for eighties rock and yogurt—said a bachelor fireman lived there.

Judging by the dead azalea bushes on either side of his front door, Annie hoped the guy was better at watering burning buildings than poor, thirsty plants.

Waaa huhhh waaa!

She took another nibble on her pinkie.

Looked at the fireman's door, then her own.

Whatever was going on in there probably wasn't any of her business.

Her friends said she spent too much time worrying about other folks' problems and not enough on her own. But really, besides her broken heart, what problems did she have?

Okay, sure, she got lonely now that she lived an hour south of her grandmother. And her parents' current gig in a remote province of China meant she rarely got to talk to them. But other than that, she had it pretty good, and—

Waaaaaaa!

Call her a busybody, but enough was enough.

She couldn't bear standing around listening to a helpless baby cry—maybe even more than one helpless baby.

Her first knock on the bachelor fireman's door was gentle. Ladylike. That of a concerned neighbor.

When it didn't work, she gave the door a few hard thuds.

She was just about to investigate the patio when the door flew open. "Patti? Where the—oh. Sorry. Thought you were my sister."

Annie gaped.

What else could she do faced with the handsomest man she'd ever seen—hugging not one baby, not two babies, but three? Each red faced and screaming. Triplets?

On teacher autopilot, she reached for the most miserable-looking one, automatically cradling the poor, trembling thing against her left shoulder.

"Hi," she said, lightly jiggling the baby while at the same time smoothing her fingers down the back of her head—her judging by the pink terry-cloth pjs. "I'm your new neighbor, Annie Harnesberry. I don't mean to be nosy, but it sounded like you might need help."

The guy sort-of laughed, showing lots of white teeth. "Yeah. My, um, little sis left me with these guys over twenty-six hours ago. She was supposed to be back at two yesterday afternoon, but—"

Annie's triplet had calmed, so she brushed past her neighbor to place the child gingerly in a pink bunny-covered car seat. Then she took another of his screaming babies for herself.

"Don't mean to be pushy," she said, "and please, go on with your story about your sister, but occupational hazard—I just can't stand hearing a child cry."

"Me, too," he said, wincing when the baby he held launched a whole new set of screams. "I'm a fireman. Jed Hale. What do you do?" He awkwardly held out his hand for her to shake.

"I'm a preschool teacher now, but used to work with infants in a day care. I ran a pretty tight nursery." She winked. "No crying allowed on my watch."

"Admirable." He grinned, and his boyish-yet-all-man charm warmed Annie to her toes.

She soon calmed the second baby, then put him—judging by his blue terry-cloth pjs—alongside his sister in a blue giraffe-upholstered carrier.

She took the remaining infant in her arms, and, like magic, after a few jiggles he fell into a deep sleep.

"Wow," the boy's uncle said with a look of awe. "How'd you do that?"

Annie shrugged, easing the last snoozing triplet into his seat. "Practice. My major was premed with a minor in child development. Seems like I spent half my college career in the campus nursery studying infants. They're fascinating."

He leaned against the open door. "Sounds pretty

bookish for a preschool teacher. I didn't even know you had to go to college for that—I mean, not that you *shouldn't* have to, but—"

"I know what you mean. I always wanted to be a child psychiatrist. Not sure why. Just one of those things." She didn't have a clue why she was standing here in this stranger's home, spilling her guts about stuff she hadn't thought of in years. Reddening, she said, "Sorry. Didn't mean to ramble—or barge in. Now that you've got everything under control, I'll just mosey off to my magazine." She backed out of his condo and hooked her thumb toward her patio. Whew.

The man's eyes were gorgeous. Brown shot with the same flecks of gold she'd like on her bathroom walls. Opulent and rich and definitely all grown-up. As yummy as that spoonful of hot fudge swirled with caramel! The decorating version of course...

Although she wasn't in the market for a man herself, should she try fixing him up with one of the other teachers at her school?

"Don't leave," Jed said, hating the needy whine in his tone. He'd always prided himself on never needing anyone, but this woman he didn't just *need,* he had to have. He had no idea what magic she'd used to zonk out his niece and nephews. However, if his sister didn't arrive to claim her offspring in the next thirty seconds, it'd be a pretty safe bet he'd need Annie's special brand of baby tranquilizer all over again. "Really, stay," he said, urging her inside. "I've been meaning to bring over a frozen pizza or something. You know, do the whole Welcome Wagon neighbor thing. But we've had some guys out sick and on vacation, so I've been pulling double shifts." He glanced at his watch. "In fact,

I'm due back in a few hours, but my sis should be here way before then."

Now who was the one rambling?

Jed could've kicked himself for going on and on. Not only did he have a desperate need for this woman, but now that he'd been standing next to her for a good fifteen minutes, he was starting to admire more than her babysitting skills.

She was cute.

Hot in a G-rated sort of way.

Loopy blond curls kissed her shoulders and neck. A curve-hugging white T-shirt gave tantalizing peeks at cleavage and a great, all-over tan. And seeing how she was now up to a PG-13, how about those great legs in the jean shorts?

Damn.

Not too long, not too short. Just right for—

Waaaaaaaaa!

Triple damn.

He sure loved Patti's little critters, but they were in serious need of a few lessons on how *not* to screw up Uncle Jed's chances with his hot new neighbor.

"He's probably hungry," she said, marching over to the carrier and picking up his squalling nephew. "Got any bottles?"

Her lips. Man. When she talked they did this funny little curvy thing at the corners. Made him want to hear her talk about something other than babies. Where she'd moved from and where she one day wanted to go. Why she'd wanted to be a child psychiatrist but ended up teaching preschool.

"Jed?" Annie grinned. "You okay? If you'd just point

the way to the bottles, I'll go ahead and feed this guy while you take a breather."

"I'm good," he said with a shake of his head. "The bottles are in here."

He led her to the kitchen. A tight, beige-walled cell of a room he usually avoided by eating at the station or feasting on takeout in front of the TV.

He took a bottle from the fridge, then turned to the woman behind him. "Want me to nuke it?"

She grimaced, kissing his nephew on top of his head. "It's probably best to put the bottle in a bowl of hot water, otherwise it gets too hot."

"Oh."

She headed toward the sink.

Speaking of hot...

Nudging on the faucet, she asked, "Got any big bowls?"

Jed retrieved the only bowl he owned—a promotional Budweiser Super Bowl VIII popcorn dish he'd won playing sports trivia down at his friend's bar. "This work?"

She eyed it for a second, then said, "Um, sure."

Over an hour later, Annie had fed and diapered the infant trio. Jed had confirmed her earlier assumption of their being triplets. The five-month-old girl was named Pia, and the boys, Richard and Ronnie. Jed explained earlier that morning, he'd lost the ribbon bracelets his sister kept on the boys to help tell them apart, so now he wasn't sure who was who.

"Man," he said, arching back his head with a yawn. "I don't know how I'll ever repay you. When Patti finally shows up, she's going to catch heat the likes of which she hasn't felt since I caught her smoking in church."

"Bit of a wild child, was she?" Annie asked, as she fastened the last snap on Pia's pink jammies. She found a tiny pink Velcro bow stuck to the terry cloth, pulled it off, and attached it to the baby girl's thin tufts of hair.

He laughed. "That's an understatement. The happiest day of my life was when she said her *I Dos* to Howie. Finally, I thought, she's someone else's responsibility."

"You been looking after her for a while?"

"Yeah. Our folks died my freshman year of college. Patti was okay as a kid, but once she hit her teens, she was nothing but trouble. She started pulling all this rebellion crap. Smoking. Drinking. Exclusively dating guys whose gene pools were only half-full. Most times, I knew she must have still been upset about Mom and Dad. But then there were other times I swear she did every bit of it just to piss me—" He winced. "Sorry."

"That's okay," Annie said, hugging the sleeping beauty to her chest.

"So lately," he said, "she's been kind of depressed. Howie—her husband, my savior—got laid off from his job here in Pecan, so he took a new one that has him traveling out east a lot. The company won't pay for the whole family to relocate, so until he can find something closer to home, this is what he's doing to pay the bills. Patti hasn't handled it all that well. Before this happened with Howie, she'd been a bit shaky on the whole motherhood thing—not that she hasn't done a great job. It's just that she gets pretty frazzled."

"Who wouldn't?" Annie said, starting to share Jed's concern for his sister, this precious infant's mother. She stroked Pia's downy-soft hair and breathed in her innocence and lotion.

"Anyway, that's why I offered to watch these guys for her. I figured she could use a little break, but her being gone overnight…" He shook his head. "I never agreed to that. I've checked her house, called her neighbors and friends. Mrs. Clancy on the end of her block saw her tear out of her driveway yesterday about twelve-thirty in my truck. Since I can only fit one baby seat in my truck, she probably thought it best to leave me with the Baby Mobile. No one's seen her since." He raked his fingers through his hair.

The muted sound of a running vacuum came from next door.

"When she was younger," he said, "she ran away a few times. I'm scared she's choosing that way out again. But it could be something else. Something bad…"

The vacuum went off.

Annie leaned forward, her stomach queasy. "Have you called the police or tried getting in touch with Howie?"

He shrugged, then pushed himself up from the sofa and began to pace. "I've got a couple friends down at the police station, so I've been calling them like every hour. They've entered my plates and Patti's vitals into the national missing persons base. Anyway, the cavalry's been called, but they keep telling me the same thing. Wait. She'll come home. There's been no sign of trouble. Odds are, with Patti's history of running, the stress of the babies probably got to be too much for her and she just took off."

"And her husband? Did you ever get hold of him?"

"Nope. His cell keeps forwarding to voice messaging—same as his office phone. Apparently, not a single real live person answers the phone at that high-tech fortress where he works. I'd go to see him, but he's out in Virginia somewhere."

"Sorry," Annie said. "Wish there was something I could do."

"You've already helped," he said. He shot a glance at his nephews. "Sometimes when these guys—and girl—start on a crying jag, I get panicky. Maybe my sister felt the same and split."

Annie's eyes widened. "She just left her babies?"

"I don't want to think that of her, but what other explanation is there? I mean, if there was an emergency or something, wouldn't she have called?"

"I'd think so, but what if she can't?"

"Oh, come on." He stopped pacing and thumped the heel of his hand against a pasta-colored wall. A snow-capped mountain landscape rattled in its chrome frame. "In this day and age, I'll bet you can't give me one good reason why a person *couldn't* call."

Annie wanted to blurt dozens of comforting reasons, but how could she when Jed was right?

Chapter 2

Patricia Hale-Norwood glared at the ICU nurse manning the desk phone. "*Please.* I'll call collect. I just need to let my brother know where I am. I left in a hurry, and he'd taken my triplets to the Tulsa Zoo, and so I couldn't—"

"I'm sorry," said the steely-eyed, middle-aged dragon disguised as a nurse. "Hospital policy. This phone is for emergency use only."

"This *is* an emergency." Heart pounding at double the rate of the beeping monitor in Room 110, Patricia clenched her fists. From the call that'd interrupted her bubble bath telling her Howie had been in an accident and was barely alive, to the hasty trek down the front porch stairs that had badly sprained her right ankle, then the endless flight and rental car drive that led her to this North Carolina hospital where her husband now drifted in and out of consciousness, this whole trip had been a horror show that just kept getting worse.

The nurse sighed. "I'm sorry, but unless you're in need of a blood transfusion or have an organ you'd like to donate, I can't let you use this phone. There are pay phones and courtesy phones located throughout the hospital for your convenience."

"Look." Patricia slapped her palms on the counter. "I don't know if you're aware of this or not, but over in that fancy new wing y'all are building, some yo-yo sliced the phone cables with a backhoe. So now there isn't a single phone on this whole freakin' square mile that works—except for yours—which, I've heard through the hospital grapevine, has its own separate emergency line."

"*Please,* Mrs. Norwood, lower your voice. We have critically ill patients here."

"You're damned right!" Patricia said shrilly. "My husband happens to be one of them. He's hanging on by a thread, and you're acting like he's here for a bikini wax. Now, we've been through this already. My cell batteries are dead. My charger is back home two thousand miles away. My ankle's swollen to the size of a football, making it kind of excruciating for me to get around. *Please* let me use this phone."

The nurse cast Patricia a sticky-sweet smile. "Perhaps a family member of one of our other patients has a cell they'd allow you to use in the special cellular phone area on the sixth floor?"

Jed slammed his cordless phone on the kitchen counter.

What was the matter with those guys down at the police station? They were supposed to be his friends.

Hell, Jed had been the one who'd thrown Ferris his police academy graduation party. And now the guy was claiming there wasn't a thing more he could do to find Patti?

He glanced at his niece and nephews, thankfully all still sleeping.

What would he have done without the help of his new neighbor? What was he going to do when all three babies woke at the same time, demanding bottles and burping and diaper changing?

Jed had earned many medals for bravery as a fireman. Yet those snoozing pink and blue bundles made him feel like a coward.

The phone rang and he lunged for it before the next ring. "Patti?"

"She's still not back?" said Craig, one of his firehouse buddies.

"Nope."

"What're you gonna do? We need you down here, man. There's a brushfire on a field by the country club, and we just got back from a house-fire call over on Hinton."

"Anyone hurt?"

"Nah, but their kitchen's toast."

"Bummer." Jed had been on hundreds of scenes like this. Witnessed lots of *why me's* and crying. Crying. Occupational hazard.

Annie said the same about her job. How she hated hearing babies cry. Jed hated hearing *anyone* cry. It was great that he saved lives, but the emotional toll taken by fires was every bit as horrible as the physical destruction.

Fire didn't just ruin lives and houses, it also stole memories.

Snapshots of Florida vacations.

Golf and baseball trophies.

Those goofy little clay ashtrays kids make in kindergarten.

Little brothers.

He sighed into the phone.

"Jed, the chief's real sorry about your sister, but we need you down here. Want me to call Marcie and ask her to watch the triplets for you?"

Marcie was Craig's wife.

And yeah, she could come sit with the babies, but that would be about the extent of it. Those two didn't even own a dog or a guppy. What did she know about taking care of three newborns?

But Annie...

She'd know what to do.

The way she'd calmed his niece and nephews earlier that day—it'd been a bonafied miracle.

"Jed? Want me to tell Chief when you'll be in?"

"I'll be there as soon as I can."

"Will do," Craig said. "Catch you later."

Jed pressed the phone's off button.

He hated asking for help.

After his parents had died, he'd looked after not only himself but his sister, who'd been ten. He was nineteen then, and he'd done a good job. Their folks' life insurance hadn't lasted long, and when it'd run dry, he'd finished college at the University of Tulsa, taking night classes. Worked his tail off during the day making sure Patti had everything a kid could want.

The bank took the house they'd lived in with their

parents since after the fire, but he'd found them an apartment over the old town theater. The whole building had long since been condemned, but back then, they'd played dollar movies there on Thursday, Friday and Saturday nights.

When Patti was still a sweet kid, he'd taken her to most of the shows. No R-rated ones, though—his mom wouldn't have approved.

He'd come close a few times to having to sell the cabin in Colorado that'd been in their family for generations. Money had been crazy tight, but somehow, he'd made things work. That cabin was the only tangible reminder of their parents. A part of Jed felt that he owed it not just to Patti, but to his own future children to keep it in the family. No matter what the personal cost.

He'd single-handedly raised his sister. He'd gone over her homework, helped her study for tests. Gone looking for her when he suspected she was hanging with the wrong crowd. Grounded her when, sure enough, he'd caught her guzzling beer down by the river.

He'd even been there to rub her back when she'd thrown up those beers a few hours later in the apartment's rust-stained toilet.

He'd covered college applications and tuition. Book and dorm costs.

Through all of that, he'd never asked for any help himself.

Never wanted it.

But now...

Somehow this was different.

Helping Patti study for a test? That he could do. Dragging her home from a party? Paying her student loans? He could do that, too. But figure out how to care for three babies while launching a full-fledged investigation into Patti's whereabouts?

He groaned.

If this afternoon was any indication of the fun still ahead, his sister's latest stunt just might do him in.

Jed sighed, resting his elbows on the kitchen counter. "Patti, where are you?"

Ten minutes later, propping his front door open with a bag of rock salt he'd found in the coat closet, Jed did the unthinkable—knocked on Annie Harnesberry's door to ask for help.

"Jed. Hi." Annie ran her fingers through the mess on her head. Ever since leaving her neighbor's, she'd been hard at work on her guest bath, scraping the shoddily applied popcorn ceiling, making way for something grander. A nice, restful Scrabble game would've been more fun, but difficult with only one player. Hmm... Someday she'd have to see if her new neighbor liked to play.

"Looks like you've been busy." He brushed a large chunk of ceiling from her hair.

Not sure whether to feel flustered or flattered by his unexpected touch, Annie fidgeted with the brass doorknob. "One of the reasons I chose this condo was its great bone structure. Redecorating is a hobby of mine."

"Great. Maybe you could tackle my place when you're finished. We could talk tile over pizza."

"Maybe." Though his tone had been teasing, something about the warmth in Jed's eyes led Annie to wonder if he might be at least a little serious about wanting to see her again. Was that why he was there?

To ask her out?

Wow. She'd just made this big move designed to steer her clear of all men, yet here she was, faced with another one. Even worse, the old optimist in her, the one who so badly wanted to find that elusive pot of gold at the end of the dating rainbow, had almost said yes. After all, the guy *was* movie-star gorgeous.

Not that appearance mattered in the scheme of things. Look what had happened during her first go-around with a good-looking guy. Her ex-husband, Troy, had been gorgeous. He'd also turned out to be her worst nightmare.

"Do you like Scrabble?" she blurted, not sure why. Both Troy and Conner had hated the game that was her family's passion.

"Love it," Jed said. "Sometime, when my life calms down, we'll have to play. I warn you, though, I'm pretty good." He winked.

Her stomach fell three stories.

No. No matter how handsome her new neighbor happened to be, she wasn't—*couldn't be*—interested. Yes, she'd date again because she couldn't bear the thought of ending up alone. But not yet. Her head and heart just weren't ready.

"Well—" He shuffled his feet.

From across the breezeway, Annie noticed his propped-open front door, and beyond that, the corner of a blue bassinet. "Your sister's still not back?"

"No. I'm really starting to freak out."

"I don't blame you," she said, squelching the urge to comfort him with a hug. At work, she hugged parents and students and co-workers, but in this situation, a hug might imply a certain affection she shouldn't want to share.

"The reason I'm here," he said, shooting her a beautiful smile that did the funniest things to her breathing, "is that all hell's breaking loose down at the station and they need me ASAP. So, anyway, I was wondering if you could hang out at my place for the next twenty-four hours? That's the length of my shift—but I'm sure Patti'll be back way before then."

"You mean you want me to babysit?" Handsome Jed Hale wasn't here to ask her on a date but to care for his sister's triplets.

She should've been relieved, so why did Annie's heart sink? Why didn't men see her for *her,* but only for her knack with kids?

Worse yet, why did she care?

Hadn't she just established the fact that she had no current interest in any man?

"Yeah. Babysit. Oh—and of course I'll pay. What's the going rate?"

Bam. Annie's ego took another nosedive.

Now the guy was even bringing money into it?

Why couldn't he just offer to take her out for a nice *friendly* steak dinner once his sister finally showed up?

"Annie? What do you say? Can you help me out?"

Noooo, she wanted to scream.

Hanging out with kids was her day job.

At night, she did grown-up things like scraping ceilings and glazing walls and sipping wine and playing Scrabble.

And if she was honest…

Dreaming of what her life might've been like had she met a guy who didn't hit or take advantage of her ability to move an infant from screaming to sleeping in twenty seconds.

What were the odds of a woman being so cursed in love?

"I know it's short notice and stuff," he said, those intriguing brown-gold eyes of his eloquently pleading his case. "But I really could use your help."

"Okay," Annie finally said, hating herself for being so easily drawn in by Jed's puppy-dog sadness. She had to remind herself she wasn't doing this for him, but for the babies.

If she'd learned anything during her years with Conner, it was that guys with ready-made families were only after one thing. And it had way more to do with heating up formula than anything that went on in the bedroom. "What time do you want me over?"

He winced. "Would now be too soon?"

Annie looked up from her seat at the end of Jed's black leather sofa and came uncomfortably close to keeling over in an old-fashioned swoon.

Wow.

He stood at the base of the stairs, dressed in plain uniform navy cotton pants and a bicep-hugging navy T-shirt with a yellow Pecan Fire Department logo on the chest pocket. His choppy, short dark hair was damp from the shower.

He'd shaved, and the scent of his citrus aftershave drifted the short distance to where she sat. The mere sight of him, let alone his smell, implied clean, simple, soul-deep goodness. He was a fireman, charged with keeping helpless grandmas and grandpas and babies and kittens safe from smoke and flames.

It probably would've sounded crazy had she tried to explain her sudden reaction to the man. But in that moment, she knew he would never hurt her—at least not physically, the way Troy had.

"I can't tell you how much I appreciate you doing this for me," he said.

"Sure. It's no big deal."

"Yes, it is." He walked the rest of the way down the stairs. "You hardly know me, yet you're giving up your time to help me out. In my book, that makes you good people."

His words returned the warm tingle to her belly. She stood, not sure what to do with her flighty hands or dry mouth. "I already told you," she said. "It's no biggie."

He looked at her for a long moment, then peered down at his black uniform shoes. "To me, it's a very big deal. Don't discount the value of what you do."

The urge to hug him came back. In those opulent eyes of his she'd caught a glimpse of sadness. Fear for his sister? Or something more?

Before she had time to ponder the question, *he* was hugging *her,* wrapping her in his all-masculine scent and strength.

And his touch wasn't awkward or inappropriate, but comforting and warm. And then, just as unexpectedly as the sensations had come, they were gone, and Jed was waving and walking out the door. Thanking her again. Smiling again. Alerting Annie to the undeniable fact that she was very much in trouble with a man and his adorable children—all over again.

Hours later, Annie woke to a ringing phone.

It took a few minutes of fumbling in the dark to realize she'd fallen asleep on Jed's sofa instead of her own. Another few minutes to actually find the phone—or not.

Somewhere, an answering machine clicked on.

Hey—congratulations! You've reached Jed. Leave a message and I'll call you back.

Annie grinned.

During the time they'd spent together, Jed hadn't shown any signs of having a sense of humor. The notion that he did made him that much more appealing.

"Jed," a woman's voice said. *"Good grief, it's after midnight out there. Where are you? Are my babies okay?"*

Patti.

Hoping she'd find a phone attached to the machine recording the woman's voice, Annie hustled up the stairs.

"You wouldn't believe the trouble I've had finding a phone. Anyway, I'm all right, but—"

By the time Annie got to the top of the stairs, dashed across the short hall and into a master bedroom that was the mirror image of hers, it sounded as if the woman had been cut off.

Annie found the phone on a nightstand beside a badly rumpled king-size bed.

She answered but was too late. The dial tone buzzed in her ear.

She turned on a lamp and checked the phone for caller ID, but the cordless model didn't have an ID window. She tried *69, but got an error message.

Great.

If the woman on the phone had been Patti, it seemed that she either didn't want to be found or was having technical difficulties.

Annie sat on the edge of the bed.

From talking to Jed, she got the impression that he

thought his sister had suffered some kind of emotional breakdown, then taken off on a joyride. But the woman on the phone sounded weary—not at all like she was off having fun. Her voice was full of concern—quite the opposite of a woman who'd abandoned three newborns with her bachelor brother. A brother who obviously didn't know the first thing about caring for infants.

Waaaaaaa huh waaaaaaa!

Maybe it was time to quit playing detective and start playing temporary mom.

She smoothed the down-filled pillow on the bed and breathed in the room's heady male scent.

Oh, boy.

Annie had the feeling she'd entered a definite danger zone.

Bedrooms were highly personal places.

They told a lot about people.

But since she was wasn't interested in dating just yet, Annie didn't want to know how sumptuous Jed's navy-blue sheets felt against her skin. Or how they smelled of fabric softener and just a touch of his aftershave that had already made her heart race.

She especially didn't want to see the really great framed print over his bed. Gauguin's *And the Gold of Their Bodies*.

She'd always loved that painting.

Interesting that Jed did, too.

The full-figured island women evoked paradise and pleasure.

Waaa huh!

On her way out of the room, Annie trailed her fingertips along the cool, dust-free surface of an ornate antique dresser.

She loved antiques.

The stories behind them.

Where had this piece come from? Was it a family heirloom? Or something Jed picked up at auction? Did he like auctions? Annie did. Maybe they could go together some time? Share a Frito-Lay chili pie during—

Waaaaaaaaahh!

Casting one last curious look around the room, Annie hustled downstairs.

She'd scooped Pia out of her carrier and was feeling her diaper for thickness when the phone rang.

If it was Patti, she wasn't missing her.

Running up the steps, Annie cursed herself for not bringing the cordless phone downstairs.

"Hello?" she said, out of breath. By the glow of the lamp she'd forgotten to turn off, she stared into the blue eyes of a grinning, wide-awake baby.

"Hey, Annie. Good—you found the phone." There went that curious flip-flopping in her stomach. Could it be because Jed sounded as hot over the phone as he did in person? No. And to prove it, she changed her focus to plucking Pia's pink Velcro bow off her pajama sleeve where it was once again stuck to return it to her hair.

"Were you hiding it?" she asked.

"What?"

"The phone."

"Nah, I keep forgetting to move it. Lightning fried the one downstairs."

"Did you serve it with ketchup or tartar sauce?"

He groaned. "That stank."

"Sorry. Couldn't resist."

"You're forgiven. So? Everything going okay?"

"Sure. Pia's up, but the boys are still sleeping. Oh—
and your sister called."

"You didn't get to talk to her?"

"It took me forever to find the phone, and by the time
I did, she'd been cut off."

A long sigh came over the line.

Annie asked, "Want me to play the message for
you?"

"Sure."

She pressed the red button beside a blinking light,
then held the phone to the speaker. When the woman's
voice abruptly ended, she said, "Well? That tell you
anything?"

"Yep. Tells me to call off the cops and move on to
Plan B."

"What's that?"

"Going to get her."

"But you don't know where she is."

"Oh, yes, I do."

Annie shifted the cooing baby to her other arm.
"Care to let me in on the secret?"

Chapter 3

In the specially designated cell phone waiting area, Patti held an ancient-model cell phone over her head, waving it back and forth in the hope of finding a signal. The man she'd borrowed it from, Clive Bentwiggins of Omaha, was visiting his mother. Clive was at least ninety-eight and on oxygen. The hissing from his portable tank sounded like wind shushing through the Grand Canyon.

"Get one yet?" Clive asked, cradling a cup of black coffee.

Edging toward the Coke machine, holding up her phone arm, Patricia shook her head. "I had one over by that fake ficus, but I—oh, here. Right here." *Yes.* Between the Coke machine and a corral of IV poles, the light indicating a signal glowed an intense green.

"Dial fast," Clive said. "Don't want you getting cut off again."

She cast her phone benefactor a smile and dialed Jed's number. It rang three times before the answering machine picked up. After the beep, she said, "Jed? Jed, honey, are you there? Jed!" She heard static on the line. *Crap.* She inched closer to the IV poles, but the green light disappeared.

Wheeling his hissing tank behind him, Clive walked toward her. "Losing it again?"

Patti nodded, tears welling in her eyes.

Where could they be?

Something had to be wrong. It was too late for Jed not to answer his phone.

He didn't have a woman over, did he?

She should've known better than to leave her babies with him.

The green light came back on, but all she could hear was the hissing from Clive's tank.

Covering the phone's mouthpiece, she said, "Would you mind scooting your tank just a little bit that way? I'm having a hard time—" Too late. The signal was gone.

Patricia sighed.

Clive patted her back. "I raised six kids and twenty-three grandbabies. Trust me, your flock is fine. It's that busted-up husband of yours you need to worry about."

"Hello?" Annie said, hands on her hips. "Care to finally let me in on your big secret?"

Jed had been home from his twenty-four-hour shift for five minutes. In those five minutes, he'd replayed Patti's latest message ten times. Now he *definitely* knew where his sister had gone.

He shot into action, barreling into the kitchen. He'd

take everything Patti left with him. There were only a few cans of formula and three or four diapers, but that should at least get him over the Colorado state line. In Denver, he'd grab whatever else he needed.

"Jed?" Annie's sweet voice jolted him from his to-do list.

Arms laden with his few requisite supplies, Jed looked up on his way back to the living room. "Yeah?"

"What are you doing?"

"Packing."

Annie's eyes narrowed as she kissed the top of Pia's head. "Please tell me you're not planning to load up these sweet, sleepy babies and trek them wherever you think your sister may be."

"Hey," he said from the living room, dumping the baby grub into the diaper bag, "I can see why you might think I'm crazy to go traipsing blindly across the country. But for your information, I happen to know exactly where Patti is."

"Oh, you do?" She followed him into the living room and gently set Pia on a fuzzy pink blanket on the floor. "Mind telling me how you worked it out, Sherlock?"

"Love to, Watson." He grinned. "You like those old movies, too?"

Frowning, she said, "I prefer the books."

"La-di-da."

She stuck out her tongue. "Just get to the part where you unravel the mystery."

"Simple deduction." He snatched the diaper wipes from the coffee table. "Remember all that hissing and shushing on the answering machine message?"

"Yeah…" she said, arms crossed, eyebrows raised. "Can't wait to hear where this leads."

"She's at our family cabin just outside Fairplay, Colorado."

"You've got to be kidding. Patti hardly said two words on that message, and from that you've deduced she's holed up in some cabin?"

Snatching a few teething toys—plastic key rings and a clear plastic thingamajig with fish floating around inside—Jed said, "You know babies, right? Well, I know my sister. Ever since having the triplets, she's had a rough time of it."

"Duh."

He shot his smart-mouthed neighbor a look.

She shot him one back.

Try as he might to stay on topic, Jed couldn't help thinking that he liked this feisty side of her. As soon as he got things settled, he just might tackle a whole new case—figuring out how to take Annie's PG-13 rating to a wicked-fun R!

He shook his head to clear it of the sweet sin threatening to muck up the next task on his road-trip agenda.

"Well?" she asked. "You're zero-and-one. Gonna go for zero-and-two?"

Jed glanced up as he stuffed a blue blanket into his now-bulging duffel bag. "Anyone ever tell you that for having such a fine package, you sure have a sassy mouth?"

Annie's face reddened and she looked away.

Hmm… Apparently he'd just pulled off his first TKO. "For your information, Little Miss Sassy Pants, all that hissing on the answering machine wasn't *hissing,* but wind. Wind whistling through the pines and firs outside our family cabin to be specific. Cell-phone service is touchy up there, which explains why she constantly gets cut off."

As much as Annie hated to admit it, Jed's warped logic made perfect sense.

"Patti loves the place. When our folks were alive, we spent every summer up there for as long as I can remember. After they died, Patti and I went there as often as we could. Here in town, she was all about keeping up appearances. I guess she felt she had to put on this cool act. But up at the cabin, she was herself. A sweet kid who allowed herself to have fun."

"But Jed—" Annie crossed the small space cluttered with stuffed animals to touch his arm "—she's not a kid anymore. She's a grown woman with a family of her own. If your assumptions are true—that she ran off to figure out her life—maybe what she *doesn't* need is her big brother charging in for a needless rescue. Maybe she needs time to get her head on straight. I mean, that's essentially why I moved here. I miss my grandmother something fierce, but it was time for me to grow up. To face a few issues on my own. I'm betting Patti feels the same."

Annie looked down to see that she was still touching him, and she marveled not only at his physical strength—tightly corded and radiating heat beneath her fingers—but at his sheer mental will.

"Look," he said, "I realize that I probably seem a little psycho right about now."

"A little," Annie said with a smile.

He didn't return her smile.

Instead, he dropped the baby bag and sat hard on the bottom step. He cupped his forehead. "There are some things about me. My past. Patti's. There's no time to rehash it all now. You just need to know that I have to get up there. See for myself that she's all right."

"Okay." Her tone softer, Annie nudged him aside to sit next to him.

Big mistake.

The entire right half of her body hummed. All the way from her shoulder to her thigh to her bare ankle that almost touched Jed's bare calf. The ankle felt a twitchy, electrical buzz of attraction that she—and her ankle— had never come close to feeling before.

This was wrong.

Here she was, trying to comfort her distraught neighbor and all she could think of was what it might feel like to graze her smooth-shaven legs against the coarse hairs on his.

Wrong, wrong, wrong.

"Um—" She swallowed hard. "Where was I?"

"How should I know?"

"Right. That's it." Before plopping down beside him, she'd been about to explain how he could find out his sister was safe without driving hundreds of miles. "There's a very simple way you can not only reassure yourself that Patti's okay, but skip a lo-o-ong road trip with three babies. All you need to do is—"

"I know—call. But the cabin doesn't have a phone, and I already tried her cell. Big surprise, it's not working. Which leaves me calling my friend Ditch, who's the local sheriff."

"Ditch?" She raised her eyebrows.

"It's a long story. Anyway, I tried calling Ditch both at home and at work, and got nothing but answering machines. I left messages for him to call me back ASAP. The town has a hardware store, gas station and a grocery, so I called those, too. Nobody's seen her, but that doesn't mean she's not there. I have to talk to her and see for myself that she's okay."

"I'll tell you who's *not* gonna be okay after being cooped up with three screaming babies all the way to Colorado."

Jed shook his head. "Babies supposedly like cars, don't they? I mean, I took 'em to the zoo yesterday— or was that the day before?" He rubbed his forehead. "See how messed up Patti's got me? I don't even know what day it is."

"All the more reason for you to go upstairs and take a nap. You're in no condition to make that drive. You've been up for days. Now, if you could fly or take a train or if someone else could help you, then—"

"That's it!" he said, turning around on the steps to face her.

Annie crinkled her nose. "What?"

"Someone to help. And I know just the person."

Though Jed looked straight at her, Annie glanced over his shoulder at the pasta-colored wall. A nice sage-green would be a vast improvement.

She gasped when he put his fingers beneath her chin, dragging her gaze right back to him. "You know who I'm talking about, don't you?"

"Um…" She licked her lips. Maybe that wall could be painted celadon. Or pumpkin. Any color that took her mind off Jed's arresting eyes. "If that special some-one is me," she said, "I have a *very* full schedule. I start my new job a week from Monday. So, this week, I have tons of painting to do, ceiling scraping and—"

"I'll pay you," he interrupted. "Name your price. As long as I have that amount in savings, it's yours."

She stared down at her lap where she clutched her knees with a white-knuckled grip. "This isn't about money, Jed."

It was about this crazy yearning she had at the thought of sitting beside him in the intimate confines of a car for the next few days. It was about falling for him—from his laugh to his smile to the fact that he honestly believed four diapers and a few cans of formula were going to get him and three babies all the way to Colorado.

He hadn't even packed a can opener!

He needed her, and what scared her even more was that she might very well need him. But she *couldn't* need him, because just as soon as this crazy road trip was over, his need for a babysitter would vanish, and her need for companionship would be that much stronger.

Her head and heart that much more messed up.

"Annie?" he said softly. "Please?"

She used the wall for leverage to push herself up from the stairs. She had to get away from Jed, from his citrusy smell and his strength and, worse yet, his vulnerability.

Friends told her she worried way too much about other folks' problems and not enough about her own.

Well, this was one time she needed to listen to their advice. Her friends were right. Jed and his adorable crew were trouble with a capital *T*.

She stood in front of the door staring at the doorknob. "I have to go." *I can't allow myself to fall for you.*

She was still too raw from Conner. And she hadn't even begun to sort out the mess Troy had made of her soul. She was weary from missing Grams and from being all alone in this town—and practically the whole world.

Jed stood too, and then he was behind Annie, resting his strong hands on her shoulders.

"Ever since our folks died," he said quietly, "Patti's been my responsibility. She was a good kid—the best. She was also the *worst* teen. I've been through hell with her. The night she gave up her virginity to the first greasy-haired punk who asked, it was me she came home to. I was the one who held her while she cried. Just like when I found her underneath a highway overpass in a seedy part of downtown Tulsa. She'd run away because she'd gotten mad at me for making her wash the dishes. She was shivering, and I wrapped her in a quilt our mother had made for her fifth birthday. It matched the yellow-and-white daisies on Patti's bedroom walls. When our house burned down, Mom had wrapped the quilt around Patti as we fled."

His hands still on her shoulders, Jed turned Annie to face him, which only upped the stakes of the battle raging inside her. Standing behind her, he was dangerous enough. When he stood in front of her, staring at her, she found that just looking at him was emotional suicide.

She'd already been through so much.

She couldn't open herself up to more pain.

Her move to Pecan was about healing. Making a fresh start. It was about—

Jed took her hands and gave them a gentle squeeze, flooding her with the kind of simple, wondrous, unconditional companionship she hadn't felt in years. Except that it wasn't unconditional; it came with strings.

Strings that would vanish the instant they reunited Patti with her babies.

"I—I have to go," Annie said, turning for the door, putting her hand on the cold brass knob.

"Howie's her husband," Jed said. "He should be with her right now. But I can't find him, Annie. Until I do, I'm all she has. I have to help her. She's all I've got."

Annie swallowed hard.

How had he known?

Of all the words in the English language, those were the ones that spoke the loudest to her heart. It was exactly the way she felt about her grandmother.

"Annie, I'll be the first to admit I've got a milelong streak of pride running through me. I hate asking for help. Even worse, I hate needing help. But in this case—"

"I'll do it."

"You will?"

Lips pressed tight, fighting silly tears of trepidation, maybe even excitement, Annie nodded.

Jed pulled her into a hug, and the sensation was warm and comforting, like slipping into a hot bath. This sure wouldn't make it any easier to fight her feelings for this man.

Releasing her, he clapped his hands, then rubbed them together. "Great! Let me tackle a few quick errands. I'll beg, borrow or steal time off from work and we'll get this show on the road. I'm assuming you'll need to call your folks? Or your grandmother? Or—" he crossed his fingers for a negative on this one "—your boyfriend?"

Annie shook her head. "The only family I have is

my grandmother, and there's no need to worry her with a short trip like this."

"You sure?"

She nodded. Why even broach the subject with Grams? The older, wiser woman would think she was nuts—which she probably was.

"All right then. If you wouldn't mind hanging out here just a little while longer, we'll be good to go. Oh—before I forget…" He took a cell phone from the coffee table and plugged it into a nearby charger. "Is your cell battery fully charged?"

"I don't have a cell phone."

"How come?"

"I'd rather spend the fifty dollars a month on decorating supplies."

He smiled. "I knew I liked you. Finally, a woman who actually prefers an activity to talking."

"I didn't say I don't like to talk." She winked. "I just don't want my conversations to cost more per year than a custom-upholstered sofa and love seat."

Chapter 4

It was nine the next morning before they finally pulled onto Highway 75 leading out of Pecan and into Tulsa where they'd catch Highway 412. Annie had talked Jed into taking a nap that'd thankfully turned into a decent night's rest. Meanwhile, she'd run to the store for a more realistic stock of formula, diapers and diaper wipes, and also managed to grab a little shut-eye for herself while the babies were sleeping.

During her brief time away from Jed's formidable appeal—not to mention that of his niece and nephews—she'd given herself a nice, long pep talk.

Jed was *just* her neighbor.

And yeah, he was gorgeous, but that didn't necessarily mean she was falling for him. She was a big girl. So why was she so confused? Why did she feel that by agreeing to what should be nothing more than a brief road trip, she was essentially giving away her heart?

Could it be because that heart of yours hums whenever the guy's within three feet?

Annie cracked open the map. "Want me to find some shortcuts?"

Both hands on his sister's minivan wheel, Jed shook his head. "I'm an interstate kind of guy. I see no reason to tempt fate."

"Oh." She slipped off her sandals and propped her bare feet on the dash. Admiring her fresh pedicure, she said, "Don't you just love this shade of pink? The silver sparkles look like there's a party on my toes." She glanced his way and caught him rolling his eyes.

Eyebrows raised, he asked, "Do you have to do that?"

"Do what?"

"Get your dirty feet all over the clean dash. I just dusted it this morning."

"My feet aren't dirty—or dusty." She twisted in the seat to display her soles for inspection. "See?"

Barely ten minutes into the trip and the woman nearly had him crashing the car! Jed cleared his throat, thankful for that *keep your eyes on the road* rule, otherwise, he'd be sorely tempted to take the bottoms of those squeaky-clean feet and—

Nope.

Not going there.

This was a family trip.

G-rated all the way.

For an instant, he squeezed his eyes shut and took a deep breath. Did she have any idea that when she'd raised her feet for inspection, she'd also raised the frayed bottoms of her jean shorts? The sweet curve of her behind had him thinking anything but sweet thoughts!

He tightened his grip on the wheel.

"Tell me about Ditch," the constant temptation sitting beside him said.

He was grateful for the change of topic. "What do you want to know?" he asked.

"For starters—" she hiked her feet back onto the dash "—please tell me that isn't his real name."

"Nah. We used to take walks down our dirt road, and every time we heard the tiniest little noise, he'd hit the ditch, sure it was a bear."

She crinkled her nose.

Was it wrong of him that such a simple thing gave him such a peculiar thrill?

"If it *had* been a bear," she said, "why did he think getting in the ditch was going to keep it away?"

Jed laughed. "Good question, which is why the other kids and I gave him such a hard time."

"Poor guy. Did he ever—"

Waaaaahuh!

"What's the matter?" Annie asked one of the boys. "Already needing a snack?" She took a pre-warmed bottle from an insulated bag, tested the formula's temperature on her wrist, then offered it to Jed's nephew, who promptly batted it away. "I'll take that to mean he's not hungry," she said.

Waaaaaaahuh!
Waaaaaaa!

Great. Now Pia had joined in.

"Good Lord," Jed said. "We haven't even made it to Tulsa and already they're crying? I thought babies liked car rides?"

"Most do," she said above the racket, "but I guess these guys are the exception. Well, except for Richard. He's sound asleep."

"How do you know that's Rich?"

"Technically, I don't. But he has slightly thicker eyebrows than his brother, so that helps me tell them apart."

Sure. Why hadn't he thought of that? Jed sighed.

"What? You think I'm making that up?"

"When we make our first stop in Kansas, I'll take a look."

"*Kansas?* I hate to burst your bubble there, but judging by the howling, we're going to have to stop way before we even reach the Kansas Turnpike."

"The hell we will." And to prove it, Jed stepped on the gas.

Five miles down the road at a run-down picnic stop where hot, dry wind rustled scattered litter on the ground, Jed scowled.

All three babies wailed.

"This place doesn't look very clean," he said.

"It's not like we're going to roll your niece and nephews across the pavement."

"Yeah, well, all the same," he said over Pia's especially heartfelt cry. "Maybe we should just—"

Annie unfastened her seat belt and hopped out of the van.

Jed looked at the sun-bleached concrete parking area and the shabby picnic tables and shook his head.

An empty two-liter pop bottle rolled like tumbleweed until it stopped against the carved wooden sign urging folks to *Put Litter In Its Place.*

Annie slid open the van's side door. "Listen to you all," she crooned to the bawling trio. "My goodness. The way you're carrying on you'd think some TV exec canceled *Sesame Street.*"

She unbuckled Pia and scooped her from her seat. After patting the rump of her pink shorts, Annie said, "What's up, sweetie? Your diaper's dry." While talking to Pia, she rubbed Ronnie's belly. "Seeing how they tossed their bottles, I'm guessing they're not hungry, which leaves general crankiness as the cause of all this angst. Come on," she said, awkwardly taking Richard from his seat, too. "You grab Ronnie and we'll take them for a quick walk."

"A walk?" Jed had stepped out of the van and was standing behind Annie. "We were supposed to be half-way to Colorado by now. This is going to completely blow the schedule."

"What schedule?" Two babies and a fat diaper bag in her arms, she backed out of the van. "Think you could help me down from here? I don't want to trip."

Suddenly, Jed didn't just have lost time to worry about, but Annie's soft curves landing against his chest. He caught her around her waist, guiding her safely to the ground, getting himself in trouble with the trace of her floral perfume.

"No, no." He shook off his momentary rush of awareness to remember his argument. "Why are you leaving the van? It'll just take that much longer to load back up."

Already halfway across the lot, aiming for the nearest picnic table, she called over her shoulder, "Could you please grab Ronnie? Now that we're stopped, I'd like to do an official diaper check."

Muttering under his breath, Jed did Annie's bidding, cringing when he reached the table only to find her spreading the babies' good changing pad across the graffiti-and-filth-covered concrete slab.

"What's the matter?" she asked mid-change on Richard, her right hand efficiently holding the gurgling baby's feet while she wiped him with her left.

Pia sprawled on a blanket Annie had spread beneath a frazzled red bud. The little faker was grinning up a storm while gumming the baby-friendly rubber salamander he'd bought for her at the zoo.

"What's the matter?" he echoed, hands on his hips. "These kids are bamboozling us."

Annie shot him an entirely too chipper smile. "Jed, they're just over three months old. There's no way they could systematically set out to mess with your schedule."

"Yeah, well, what else explains *this?*" He held out Ronnie, who was also alternately giggling and cooing.

Annie looked up only to hastily look back down.

She returned her attention to sealing the tapes on Richard's diaper, then resnapping the legs of his short-sleeved cotton jumper.

Why did she have the feeling that a whole lot more than the beating sun and dry Oklahoma wind were making her cheeks hot?

Like the sight of entirely-too-handsome-for-his-own-good Jed wearing Ray-Ban sunglasses, camo-green cargo shorts and a white T-shirt, while holding tiny little Ronnie so tenderly in his arms.

Once he learned to loosen up, Jed would make a great father.

Obviously not to any children of hers—just some lucky woman he had yet to meet.

"Okay," she said with forced cheer, hoisting Richard into her arms. "Pia's bone-dry, so let me check Ronnie's diaper and we should be good to go."

"So she faked all her tears, too?" He sighed.

Annie gave him a dirty look, suddenly annoyed

when she ended up a little too close to Jed in order to give Ronnie's diaper the pat test. "He's dry, too," she said, turning quickly, planning to grab Pia and her blanket, along with the diaper bag.

"Wait," Jed said, his fingertips brushing her forearm.

Even with the breeze, the August air was stiflingly hot, yet somehow each individual imprint of his fingers on her skin felt hotter. She looked at Jed. "Yeah?"

"Thanks."

The breeze blew strands of hair into her eyes, and since her arms were full with Richard, Jed used his free hand to sweep away the stray curls. "What for?"

"What do you think?" He stared at his baby, then hers. "Much as I hate to admit it, you were right. There's no way I could've made this trip on my own. So in case I get too wrapped up later on—thanks."

His grumpy attitude about their first pit stop?

Forgiven.

"You're welcome," she said, afraid to look at him for fear she'd be that much more attracted. "Wanna put Ronnie in his seat while I grab the princess?"

"I'll get her and the gear," he said. "You be the brains and beauty behind this operation. I'll be the brawn."

Beauty, huh?

Settling Richard in his carrier, then climbing back into her own seat to feign interest in the map, Annie realized that trying not to fall for Jed would be about as easy as keeping three babies content for the next eight hundred miles.

"Y'all keep a good eye on those cuties!" The burly tow-truck driver waved, then veered into the heavy stream of back-to-school traffic clogging Wal-Mart's lot.

One arm around Richard, the other around Pia, Jed said, "When I get my hands on that no go brother-in-law of mine, I'll—"

"Calm down," Annie said. "It's only a flat." She took Pia from Jed and placed her in front of her brothers in the three-seat stroller.

Jed snorted. "A flat that could've been fixed on the side of the road in under ten minutes. But *no-o-o-o*. Howie's the only man in the world who lets his wife and children drive around without a spare."

Hand to her forehead, Annie shielded her eyes from the baking sun. "You never know. Maybe they used the spare and haven't had a chance to replace it."

"Don't," Jed said, steering Annie toward the automotive section of the store.

"Don't what?"

"Try making this easy for my sister. Even if that no good brother-in-law was too lazy to replace the tire, Patti knows better. How many times have I told her always to be prepared?"

Annie laughed. "Like you were prepared to call a tow truck by forgetting to grab your cell from the charger? We were lucky that Triple A guy stopped for us on his way to work."

"I told you not to remind me about my cell phone."

"Sorry. Just thought poor Howie needed defending. Besides which, I think you're too hard on yourself. Things happen. You can't always be in control."

Wanna bet?

Yeah, forgetting his phone was a major screwup—right up there with not checking for a spare himself. But no more. From here on out, this trip would be run with military precision.

They'd reached the podium-on-wheels the tire guy

used to write up their ticket. Jed held his jaw tight through the entire ordering process, during which the tire guy explained how the popularity of the back-to-school tire special meant his department was running about two hours behind. But there was a waiting area for their convenience.

"Sir?" the tire guy said. "Your keys?"

Jed fished in his pockets for the gaudy pink rabbit's foot key chain his sister had given him. It wasn't there.

Realizing what he'd done, he groaned.

"Sir? Your keys?"

Annie giggled. "You left them in the van, didn't you, Mr. Always Prepared?"

"Aren't they sweet?" Annie said, eyeing the three sleeping angels while slurping the last bit of cherry heaven from the bottom of her Icee cup.

Jed, who'd just finished checking his messages—or lack thereof—from a payphone, growled.

"Oh, come on," she said. "Would you get over it? Everyone makes mistakes. I lock myself out of my car all the time, which is why I now keep a spare key in a little magnetic box under the front wheel well."

"I've got one, too," he said, "only it's under the truck bed. Fat lot of good it's doing me there when I'm driving my sister's stupid van."

Fingertips aching to reach out and touch him, Annie toyed with a potato chip instead. "Are you more upset with your sister or yourself?"

"What do you mean?"

"I mean, why are you so angry? Are you still fired up about the missing spare tire? Or is your miserable mood more about the keys?"

Ever the pillar of responsibility, even when it came

to his choice in drinks, he took a swig of bottled water. "Just drop it, okay?"

"Now what are you ticked off about?"

Jed pretended to be captivated by a pink, blue and yellow cotton candy display. "Do you think yellow is banana flavor?"

"Yes. And I also think you're avoiding my question."

"How do you know it's banana?"

She sighed. "Because it's my favorite and I buy it all the time. Back to the important stuff. Are you avoiding my question?"

"Absolutely. Now would you mind dropping it?"

"*Excu-u-u-use* me," she said, pushing herself up from the table to put her cup and remaining chips in the trash. Was it just him, or had her hands been shaking when she'd dumped the stuff? "I'll be in the clothing section until the car gets done, okay? While you were off grabbing all that auto emergency stuff, I changed everyone's diaper and filled fresh bottles, so you shouldn't have any trouble watching the babies by yourself."

Right before she left, she snatched a tiny pink Velcro bow from Pia's PJ sleeve and put it in her purse. "It's evidently a choking hazard," she said. "Kind of like looking at you."

"Dude, you got schooled," said a baggy-clothed punk passing Jed's booth.

Huh? Ignoring him, Jed just sat there, watching Annie walk away. Dammit. Why the hell hadn't he said something? He should've tried to explain.

His sister's selfish disappearing act already had him wound tight, but this latest fiasco?

He was now a man on the edge.

Elbows on the sticky table, cradling his face in his hands, he closed his eyes and took a few deep breaths.

Calm down, man.

Keep the past in the past.

Just like his little brother Ronnie's death had been out of his control, so was everything happening right now. That was the bad news. The good news was that all he had to do was hang tight until they got to the cabin, then everything would be fine.

Yeah, right.

Who was he kidding?

Here he'd been snatching peeks at Annie's long legs all afternoon, dreaming of the moment they turned the munchkins over to his sister so he could ask his hot neighbor out on a proper date. But if he kept up this gloom-and-doom routine, she'd refuse to even climb back into the van.

Jed looked down at his niece and nephews—all three of them still snoozing.

After another deep breath, he let the calm of knowing that at least the three of them were safe and content spread through him.

Patti was safe, too.

In the cabin. Probably trashing it with gossip magazines and pop cans and Oreo crumbs.

By the time he got there, the place would no doubt be mouse-infested, but that was all right.

As for his future nightlife...

He snatched a bag of banana-flavored cotton candy from the display.

Time for some major sucking up.

"I'm sorry, ma'am, but I'm afraid you'll have to—"

"No!" Patti cried, fighting to get past the nurse keeping her from Howie's room. "He's my husband. It's my right to know what's going on." A few minutes earlier, she'd been holding Howie's hand, telling him how much the babies had grown in just the week he'd been gone. The room had been peaceful. Silent except for the soft whir of air-conditioning and the sound of her voice. And then that awful beeping had started, and—the rest was too horrible to think about. "I *have* to see him," Patti begged, hot tears stinging her eyes. *"Please."*

"Mrs. Norwood, let the doctors do their work. They'll tell you everything just as soon as your husband is stable."

Patti wanted to fight—really, she did, but at the moment, she was just too tired.

The kind nurse put her arm about Patti's shoulders and guided her into the dimly-lit waiting area that had become Patti's new home.

What she wouldn't give to be back at her old home. Holding all three babies on her lap while Howie changed the TV channel fifty billion times with the remote.

"Are you going to be all right?" the nurse asked, settling Patti into a recliner.

Numb with fear, she nodded.

"Can I get you anything? Coffee? A blanket and pillow?"

My husband.
Please tell me he's going to be okay.

Chapter 5

Twenty minutes later, pride swallowed, Jed found Annie in the women's clothing department, holding up two metallic jogging suits against herself that, in this heat, would bake her like a foil-wrapped potato.

"In case you haven't noticed, it's a hundred and fifteen degrees outside."

"A hundred and *one,* and I don't remember asking for your opinion," Annie said. "Besides, if I wait to buy these until the time of year I'll really need them, the stores will be carrying bathing suits."

"True." Jed laughed. "And it can get chilly in the mountains—not that we'll be there that long, but—"

"Who said I'm going anywhere with you?"

"I got you this," he said, retrieving the cotton candy peace offering from the stroller's back pocket.

Refusing to meet his eyes, Annie shook her head,

then turned back to the jackets. "You hurt me. I barely even know you, yet you really hurt me."

"I'm sorry," he said, slipping in between her and the clothes. "I'll be the first to admit I have issues. Ask any of my ex-girlfriends and they'll tell you the same."

"Well, since none of them are around, how about *you* tell me."

Unfastening the twist tie on the cotton candy, he groaned. "What is it with women and talking? Can't you try to understand that sometimes I get a little worked up and leave it at—"

"Excuse me, but could I please get in there?" A middle-aged woman wearing thick glasses and a Tweety bird T-shirt nudged Jed away from the jogging suits. She looked at Annie. "I see you're buying two," the woman said. "Crazy how we have to snatch 'em all up so early. I've already got most of my Christmas shopping done."

"I know, me too," Annie said, putting the jackets back on the rack.

"You don't want those?" the lady asked.

I don't know what I want.

Five minutes earlier, Annie thought she would've been content with a new sweatsuit and an apology, but now she wanted more. For some reason, the argument back in the snack bar made her think of Troy. It reminded her of the way he'd seemed to deliberately pick fights, then gradually get louder and louder. Yelling and punching the walls and cabinet doors, then eventually punching or slapping her.

What happened at the snack bar was nothing compared to one of Troy's scenes, but—if only for an instant—it had returned her to memories better left forgotten.

"You go ahead," Annie said to the woman eyeing the jackets. "It's too miserable outside to even think about climbing into those."

Obviously, the woman didn't care, as she dove enthusiastically into the rack of clothes.

Keeping a tight grip on the stroller handle, Annie wove through the apparel maze to the purses.

"Does this mean you're going with me?" Jed asked, hot on her heels.

"This means I don't know what it means. Just that the last thing I want to do is stand around and chat about shopping. Jed, I want to—"

"Oh, my Lord! Walter, would you look at this! Triplets!" A white-haired woman with her stout husband in tow crouched over the babies, coochie-cooing and poking them to the point that Annie thought she might have to call for security.

Thankfully, Jed stepped in. "If I were you," he said in a stage whisper, "you might want to steer clear for your own protection. The babies bite."

"Oh, my." Eyes huge, the woman lurched back, clutching her chest. "I've never heard of such a thing. You should take them to a doctor right away."

As the couple wandered off whispering and glancing over their shoulders, Annie wanted to be mad at Jed for telling such an outrageous story, but she couldn't help cracking a smile. Not only had the man apologized, but he had brought her banana cotton candy, then made her laugh. Comparing him to Troy wasn't just unfair to Jed, it was ludicrous.

"You're awful," she said in a semi-serious tone.

"Thanks." He beamed with what she suspected was pride.

* * *

They were just past Wichita, playing a truly wretched kids' CD they'd found in the glove box when Annie dared to ask, "Ready to talk?"

"I thought we *were* talking."

"Sure. About whether or not those clouds on the horizon are producing rain. And whether to choose a McDonald's or Arby's or Taco Bell for our next pit stop. But near as I can tell, we still haven't touched on any important stuff."

Squirming in his seat, Jed said, "I thought you didn't like talking."

"Only on expensive cell phones."

He sighed.

"You told me to ask your exes about your…issues, but conveniently for you, none of them were lurking around the purse department just dying to spill your dirty secrets."

"What do you want to know?"

"Since you asked—" she said, propping her bare feet on the dash, ignoring his glare, "—how about telling me why you and your last girlfriend split up?"

Looking over at her, he said, "And you need to know all of this because…?"

"I put every dime I had on my condo. If we're going to be neighbors, I should know what types of floozies might be skulking around next door."

"*Floozies?* I'll have you know I only date the finest women the town of Pecan, Oklahoma, has to offer. I'm talking primo top-notch. Two former Miss Pecans, three rodeo queens and I nearly married my class's homecoming queen."

"That's an awful lot of royalty." Annie aimed a sweet

grin his way. "No wonder you're proving to be a royal pain in the—"

"Watch it," he said. "There are tender ears present."

The kids' CD launched into a high-pitched, squealing rendition of "Row, Row, Row Your Boat."

"Wow." Annie winced.

In the back seat, all three babies gurgled and cooed.

"I take that back," Jed said. "Carry on. If they actually like this crap, those little ears of theirs can't be all that tender."

"All right, then, you're a royal—"

"Hey, whoa. I change my mind. *I'll* talk. Just don't ruin my Mary Sunshine image of you."

Fluffing her hair, Annie teased, "You think I'm perfect, huh?"

"Oh, I'm sure you have flaws in there somewhere."

"True, but back to yours…"

He tightened his grip on the wheel. "Well, the general consensus is that I'm too controlling."

"You?" Annie widened her eyes. "I never would've guessed."

"Hey, I'm trying to be serious here."

"Sorry," she said, her expression appropriately somber. "By all means, carry on."

"For instance, there was Beth. We were rocking along just fine at around the six-month mark when she announces out of nowhere that she's starting a night course at the community college. She wanted to learn cake-decorating. Well, I'm all for furthering one's education, so I was fine with that. My one request was, since her class didn't start until eight on Tuesday and Thursday nights, that I pick her up and drop her off. There'd been a mugging on campus just a few weeks earlier and I wanted to be sure she was safe."

"Oh, boy," Annie said.

"What? Even a year after the fact, I fail to see what's so bad about that."

"Nothing—if you were her husband. But Jed, if you two were just dating, she probably felt you were trying to control every aspect of her life. She probably thought you wanted to see if there were any hot guys in her class. Or that you'd think she was at some campus kegger, when she'd really been studying frosting techniques."

"Oh, please." Jed rolled his eyes. "First of all, it's a community college, so there aren't any keggers. And second of all, I didn't even *want* to be there. Hell, all I did was sit in the car and listen to all-sports talk radio. It was a total bore, but as her boyfriend, I felt it was my responsibility to keep her safe."

"And you feel it's your responsibility to keep Patti safe."

"Exactly. See? You get it. Why couldn't Beth?"

"Did you ever try to explain your feelings to her instead of just asserting your need to control every situation?"

"Nah. Besides the subject of cake-decorating, she wasn't really big on talk."

"Talk about adorable. Sissy, come on up here and look at these three—make that *four*—cuties." The teen cashier at the small town's pizza joint cracked her gum and winked at Jed.

Jed pretended to be busy with his wallet. He'd already checked his messages, but maybe he should go and check them again until Annie got out of the bathroom.

A girl wearing a name tag that said "Sissy" approached the counter. "Ooh…they *are* cute." She didn't take her eyes off Jed. Great. How old were these two? *Maybe* sixteen?

"Want me to sit with you while you eat?" Sissy asked. "I can, you know, help you take care of your babies."

"Uh, thanks for the offer, but my *wife* should be out any—there you are, *honey*." His back to the counter, Jed winked at Annie. "Is one thin-crust Canadian bacon, black olive and pineapple all we need?"

"Except for my tea, *honey*. Did you order that?"

"Two iced teas," Jed said, relieved that Annie was playing along.

"Okay," the original cashier girl said. At her first sighting of Annie, Sissy went back to the kitchen. "Coming up."

Jed paid and headed for the booth where Annie had set up camp. Thankfully, it was far from the cashiers.

"Thanks," he said, setting their iced teas on the table before easing into the red vinyl seat across from Annie. "That was a mess."

"What was a mess, *honey?*"

"Those two girls. They were coming on to me. Both of them need to go home and play with their dolls."

"And stay away from real men like you?" She blew him a kiss.

"Anyone ever tell you that you've got a mile-long mean streak?"

Smiling, Annie shook her head. "Okay, Mr. Control. What would you have done if I hadn't been here?"

Jed grabbed five sugar packets, gave them a shake,

then tore the tops off and dumped the contents into his tea.

"I'm waiting," Annie said. "Again."

"Truth? I probably would've made up some dumb excuse like I forgot my wallet and left. Stuff like that makes me uncomfortable. I never know what to say."

She put two sugars in her tea and stirred. "All you really need to do, Jed, is speak up. With Beth, you just needed to explain your feelings about wanting to keep her safe. And with those teenage girls, all you had to do was tell them politely but firmly that you weren't interested."

"Yeah, but what you don't seem to get that I don't *like* talking. Makes me itch." He scratched the back of his neck.

"You're so making that up."

Pia started to cry.

"Ah…" he said, removing her from her stroller seat. "Thank you, sweetie." He nuzzled the top of her fuzzy head, breathing in that good clean baby smell.

Which reminded him…

He searched the stroller pocket for the disinfectant wipes he'd picked up at Wal-Mart for just such an occasion. Taking one out, he began to wipe down the table.

"What are you doing?" Annie asked.

"Isn't it pretty clear? The last thing we need is for these babies to pick up a bug."

"But Jed, they're not even sitting at the table. And we're not going to eat here. We're only waiting until our order's ready to go."

"I'd rather be safe than sorry."

"Pia—" Annie said, reaching across the table for her

chubby fists, "—it's my solemn vow to loosen up your uncle by the time this trip is over. Okay?"

The baby gurgled.

"There you go," Annie said. "At least someone in this crowd agrees with me."

"Yeah, well, the two guys think I'm pretty cool, so it's a three-two vote. I don't have to change a bit."

"No, no, no…" Jed said. After checking his answering machine—still no messages—he now stood at the entrance of the World Famous Corn Museum, taking off the corn-husk hat not five seconds after Annie had put it on him. "I told you I'm only here to get the babies calmed down from their latest crying jag. Once they've had a few minutes to chill and forget how much they hate being in that van, we're gone," Jed warned.

"Fine, but what's the harm in having a little fun along the way?" She stood on her tiptoes to plop the hat back on his head. "Smile."

Before he could take it off again, she snapped his picture with the disposable camera she'd bought in the Corncob Hall of Gifts.

"What'd you have to do that for?" The hat was finally off and resting on the table she'd borrowed it from.

"You're the one who bought me this stupid shirt and insisted I put it on," Annie said. "Why shouldn't you look just as ridiculous?" She peered down at the nubby corncob on the white shirt. A caption across the top read I Hope To Be *Earring* From You Soon.

At first she hadn't gotten the joke.

Jed had been the one to explain. Ear of corn. *Earring* from you. *Hearing* from you. He bought her the shirt to remind her that *he* was the funny one. He'd even had the nerve to bring up her lame joke about his fried phone being served with ketchup or tartar sauce.

"And do you know why I wanted you to wear that shirt?" he asked. "Because I have a sense of humor and you don't."

"That is not true," she complained, waving her camera with one hand and jiggling a crying Ronnie with the other. "And I'll prove it by getting these pictures developed and showing them to everyone you know."

"That's not funny. That's blackmail." He tried to look gruff but couldn't hide the lingering smile in his eyes.

Slowly pushing the stroller by a floor-to-ceiling display of facts about corn, Jed whistled in amazement. "Did you know the biggest box of popcorn in the U.S. was over fifty-two feet long? Ten feet wide and ten feet deep? Wonder if it had butter?"

Ronnie wailed louder.

Jed gave his nephew a weary glare. "Have you given any thought to the schedule?" he asked Annie.

"A few more minutes of walking—and he'll calm right down."

Jed returned her reassuring smile with a skeptical scowl.

They walked past another exhibit—this one on the history of corn.

"Check it out," Jed said, pointing to a model village. "The earliest recorded windmills were in seventh century Persia, and they were used for grinding corn."

"Be careful," Annie said, elbowing his ribs. "Someone might think you're actually having fun."

He made a face at Annie, then continued to read each plaque on the remaining exhibits.

Ronnie kept crying.

At the end of the room stood an elderly woman volunteer, dressed in a long-skirted pioneer outfit. "Would you all care for a sample of early settler-style popcorn?"

Annie bit her lower lip.

Here it comes.

No doubt Jed would give the poor woman a lecture on how unsanitary her cooking method was.

"Yes, please," Jed said, accepting a paper sack from the woman, then turning to Annie. "Want one?" he asked an openmouthed Annie.

Even Ronnie must've been shocked by his uncle's surprisingly cordial behavior, as he'd quieted to a whimper.

"Sure," Annie said.

Behold…the power of corn.

He handed her his bag, then got another for himself.

After listening to a short lecture on how the treat was prepared, they moved on to a diorama of corn-husk dolls and different corn ceremonies performed by Native Americans.

Pausing in front of the door that led to the World's Largest Ear of Corn, he said, "After this build-up, I feel there should be a drumroll to mark such a momentous occasion. Here." He took the camera from her. "Park the stroller in front of the sign and I'll take your picture."

Eyebrows raised, Annie did as he'd asked and said, "So tell me, former Corn Scrooge, how is it that in the past fifteen minutes you've gone from corn-hater to corn-believer?"

"I never said I hated corn. I just don't like stopping. We're supposed to be keeping this show on the road. I have to admit, though, this has been educational."

"It wasn't supposed to be educational. Aside from

calming Ronnie, this was just for fun. I wanted to loosen you up, and—"

Jed took a deep breath. "Can we please skip this latest attempt to analyze me and just see the corn?"

"As you wish."

He held open the door, but the stroller forced her in at an odd angle, sending her right under Jed's outstretched arm—right against his chest, into the danger zone of his all-male scent. Luckily, the sight before her was so awe inspiring, Annie just wanted to get a closer look.

Gripping Jed's hand in excitement, she said, "Have you ever seen anything like this?"

He shook his head. "Can't say I have. Annie, I've gotta tell you, I'm not sure why someone would build something like this, but I'm impressed."

Towering in the middle of a glass dome—surrounded by a thirty-foot circle of the greenest, most velvety-soft grass Annie had ever seen—stood what undoubtedly was the world's largest ear of corn in all its yellow glory. The thing was so tall, that in order to see the very top, Annie had to bend her head back so far it hurt.

Up in the cavernous room's rafters, barn swallows chirped.

"Damn," Jed said, hands braced on his hips. "How do you suppose they made this thing?"

It just so happened that the husband of the popcorn lady—he'd proudly informed Jed and Annie of this fact—was more than happy to fill them in on every riveting detail of the three-story plaster corncob's creation.

At the end of his tale, the man said, "Local legend has it that any couple passing through here must kiss each other under the Corncob Arbor for good luck in the rest of their travels."

Jed cleared his throat. "We're not, um, really a couple. We're just friends."

"Doesn't matter," the gray-haired man said. "If you don't kiss the lady, odds are you'll have a flat within twenty miles of the museum."

Annie's palms were sweaty against the vinyl stroller handle and her pulse all of the sudden wasn't so steady.

Would Jed really kiss her just because of some silly superstition?

Much to her secret shame, she hoped so!

While Annie scolded herself for even thinking such a thing, the old man eyed a gold pocket watch he'd taken out of the pocket of his faded overalls. "Four forty-five. You two better get on with it. The museum closes in fifteen minutes."

He wandered off, and Annie released her breath. "That was close."

"What?"

Playing it cool, she tucked her hair behind her ears. A nervous giggle spilled from her lips. "You know…"

"No, I really don't." He took a step closer.

"That thing about the kiss," she said, letting the inquisitive baby squeeze her index finger instead. "Could you believe how that guy was pressuring us? Jeez, the way he was going on, you'd think—"

And then all thinking stopped when Jed kissed her.

Soft, exquisitely warm, his lips met Annie's in a maddening maelstrom of emotion she couldn't begin to define—didn't *want* to define. She just wanted to appreciate it for the pleasant surprise it was.

When Jed stepped back, a grin playing about the corners of his mouth, she brought trembling fingers to her lips.

"You heard the man," he said. "It's a tradition. What else could I do? You don't want to spend another three hours at Wal-Mart waiting for our next tire change, do you?"

"Um…no. Of course not."

"Ready to get back on the road?" Jed asked, looking at his now sleeping nephew.

"Sure. I guess. But…shouldn't we talk?"

"Nah." He dropped his arm across her shoulders in such a way that she wasn't sure if he meant the gesture as a show of casual affection, intimacy or just plain friendship. Whatever it meant, Annie could scarcely breathe, so aware was she of his presence and the lingering taste of popcorn on her lips. "After all this excitement," he said, "I'm kind of sleepy," he said. "Would you mind driving while I catch a few z's?"

Chapter 6

Patti squeezed her eyes shut, praying for strength.

Howie had suffered an allergic reaction to one of his many medications, but his doctor promised he was improving.

Unfortunately, her husband's health was only the start of her problems. She'd tried calling Jed at least twenty times but kept getting his stupid machine or the voice mail on his cell.

Where was he?

What had he done with her babies?

"Oh, Howie," she whispered, clasping her sleeping husband's hand. "I wish you'd never taken that job. I wish I'd said let's sell our big house and the minivan and all my shoes and clothes. I'd be happy living in a tent right now if it meant the five of us could be together."

Hot tears sprang to her eyes.

She didn't bother to wipe them away.

What was the point?

Lately, her cheeks never seemed fully dry.

She leaned forward, resting her head against the soft white cotton blankets on Howie's bed. She held his hand to her cheek.

"Get better, sweetheart. I need you to help me find our babies."

Annie had plenty of experience driving vans.

The day-care van.

The preschool van.

So it wasn't the actual handling of the large vehicle that had her in such a tizzy.

Glancing at the passenger seat, the cause of her nervous stomach softly snored. How dare he kiss her like that and just fall asleep! Were they ever going to talk?

All three babies were snoozing, too.

Looking back at Jed, Annie realized that in spite of her frustration with him, he'd never looked better. At least in the short time she'd known him.

Even with his long legs folded beneath the dash. Even with his arms crossed and his head cocked at what couldn't be a comfortable angle, he still had a latent power she found devastatingly attractive. But with sleep had come peace and vulnerability—a trait she got the feeling he'd rather die than show during his waking hours.

And he'd trusted her enough to let her take the lead on their mission.

Any number of things could go wrong.

Another flat.

Engine trouble.

Taking the wrong road.

And yet he'd ignored all these possible disasters when he handed her the keys. Was she making progress in her quest to loosen him up? If so, that was great. But why did she care? It wasn't as if she'd reap any benefits from the new-and-improved Jed Hale once the trip was over.

Her lips tingled.

She turned up the air-conditioning and aimed the nearest vent toward her.

So what if she was thinking about the kiss?

And the crazy, wonderful, unexpected glimpse into what it would be like to come home from work every day and step into his open arms...

Why had he kissed her? Did he do it because their museum guide had goaded him into it?

If so, why did Annie feel sad that Jed hadn't kissed her for another reason?

An infinitely better reason.

Like the plain and simple fact that he'd found her impossible *not* to kiss!

"I don't suppose you know where we are?" Jed asked Annie, shading his eyes against the bright early-evening sun.

She finished strapping Pia into the stroller. "We're at the only two-story cow in the continental U.S. made entirely out of beer cans."

He groaned. "Please, God, tell me this isn't happening. Please tell me there isn't another beer-can cow somewhere outside the continental U.S."

"I wasn't going to stop," she said, "but then Pia laid one heck of a smelly egg. Since the place is open twenty-four/seven, according to the billboards I saw, and since it's got clean restrooms and changing tables, I figured we should stop. Why not stretch our legs and do a diaper change?"

"Sure," Jed said. It made complete sense. If you were out of your mind!

"Well?" she asked. "You coming?"

He rubbed his eyes with his thumb and forefinger, then climbed out of the van.

On the way to the giant fenced pen that held the cow, Jed noticed signs boasting live rattlesnakes and scorpions just inside, right along with peanut brittle and taffy.

"That's quite a combo, huh?" he said to his smiling companion. "I always enjoy having a good wad of taffy in my mouth when I'm checking out rattlesnakes."

Annie tugged at Jed's hair. "Quit being such a grouch. Can you imagine how long the creator of this cow must've worked?"

"Yeah, and can you imagine how he did it—drunk as a skunk on all that beer?"

"For that—" she gave his arm a pinch "—you're going to buy me taffy *and* peanut brittle. And we're going to keep to the schedule, so you're going to look at every single snake, scorpion and beer can in this building in under ten minutes."

"Wow," Annie said as they walked through the cow's belly. The freshly diapered babies happily gummed teething rings in their stroller. "This is even more impressive than I'd hoped. I never thought we'd be able to walk around inside. The giant corncob people need to step up their exhibit. This is much more fun than looking at it from the outside—even if it does smell like sour yeast."

"Yeah." Jed ran his fingers along the dusty row of cans that served—according to a hand-printed sign—as the cow's large intestine. "I was just thinking the same thing."

"You were not."

"Sure, I was." He almost succeeded in keeping a straight face. "Especially about improving the corncob. If the corncob people really want to draw in the masses, they should perform weddings in the cob, just like they do here."

"They do?" She wrinkled her nose.

"Why Annie Harnesberry, you haven't been reading all the signs?"

She stuck out her tongue.

"Look." He pointed to another handwritten sign. "It says so right here. For the low, low price of fifty bucks, we can get married by a real live justice of the peace and have a beer toast over white cupcakes and white-chocolate-covered pretzels."

"You're so making that up," Annie said, nudging him out of the way to get a better look.

"Puh-leeze. I'm not creative enough to make this stuff up."

Annie giggled. She read the sign, and sure enough, he was telling the truth.

"Does someone owe me an apology?"

"For what?"

"For accusing me of lying—right here in the sanctity of the beer-can cow's belly."

"No way."

"Yes, way," he said, easing her up against the cow's ka-thumping heart—which was actually beating, courtesy of a looped sound effect.

Annie fought for her next breath. Did he have any idea how much trouble this playful side of him caused? She couldn't think straight. Had she been too hasty in her decision to steer clear of *all* men?

"You know," he said, "there *is* one way we could remedy this situation."

"I, um—" Annie licked her lips "—didn't know we had a situation."

"Oh, yes, we do. It says so right here on this other sign."

"Which one?"

"The one that says it's bad luck if we don't kiss in here."

"Really?"

"Hey, I told the truth about the marriage ceremonies, didn't I?"

"Y-yes." Jed's breath was warm and sweet-smelling from all that taffy and peanut brittle they'd eaten while gawking at the snakes.

Annie knew kissing him would be a bad idea, but she couldn't help craving one more taste of his lips. Just one more kiss, and then she promised to stay away.

No more hair tugging.

No more pinches.

No more looking at him—well, maybe that was a little extreme, but—

Jed took the decision out of her hands by pressing his lips to hers in a decadent display of kissing perfection.

A contented moan caught in Annie's throat as she pressed herself against him, craving his touch, his strength. He urged her mouth open and she let him in, deepening their kiss with a thrilling sweep of tongues.

Pausing for air, Jed touched his forehead to hers.

"We've got to get back on the road. What are you trying to do to me?"

"Me?" She laughed. "I was just thinking the same about you."

"So what're we going to do?"

"That's a no-brainer. First, we'll only make rest stops at places that don't encourage kissing. And second, if crying babies do force us to stop at places like that, we're forbidden to read the signs or listen to the buttinski guides."

"Sounds like a plan to me."

"Good." Annie smiled. "We agree."

"Definitely. I'm just going to need one more kiss."

"Nope," Jed said an hour later at a standard-looking burger joint near Flamingo, Kansas. In a town named Flamingo, it was a wonder no enterprising local businessman in Pecan hadn't tried to make his fortune from a giant bird made of pink bubblegum wrappers. "We'll have to go someplace else."

"What do you mean someplace else?" Annie said above the roar of all three babies crying. "I realize you've been sleeping, but this is the only restaurant I've seen in a while. It might not be the cleanest, but…"

"Then you must not have been looking."

Annie turned away.

Could she have been more wrong about Jed's rehabilitation?

"Look how dirty this place is," he whispered in her ear, giving her chills when his warm breath settled around her. He gestured at an ant-covered scrap of hamburger bun that had fallen onto the muddy footprints at the base of the order counter.

Dust and a city of cobwebs lived on the silk ivy that decorated the cash register.

Ew. "Okay, but—"

"Can I take your order?" a twenty-something pregnant brunette asked above the babies' unanimous howl. She winced. "Dang. I'm glad I'm just having one. Bet you all never get any sleep."

Annie smiled politely. "Sometimes it's rough."

"You all know what you want?"

"Nothing, thank you," Jed said, taking hold of the stroller. "We've gotta get back on the road."

"Wait a minute," Annie said, fishing Pia out of the stroller. "I'll have a bag of corn chips and a bottled water."

"That's it?" the girl asked.

Annie nodded.

Jed scowled before storming outside.

Meeting him at the van a few minutes later, Annie said, "You didn't have to be rude. You could've ordered something that came prepackaged."

"Why?" he asked, taking both boys out of the stroller.

"Well...because it's polite."

"Right. And it's polite for whoever owns this joint to run such a messy ship? And what about when I was being polite back at the last fast-food place by pretending we were married so I wouldn't hurt those two girls' feelings? Remember how you were all for me standing my ground?"

"That's different," she said, kissing Pia's forehead.

"How?"

"Well..." *Because maybe when other females are attracted to you, I want you to be more vocal in your brush-offs!* Okay, so she was wrong. Her actions didn't make sense, but then, not much did these days. Especially her attraction to him. She cleared her throat. "You're missing my point."

"And what would that be?" he said over the collective crying of the babies.

She shot him a look. "Give me those two."

"I can calm them myself."

"Then might I suggest you do it?"

Annie opened the van's side door and slipped Pia into her seat. Her diaper was dry, so a bottle made her content.

She took Ronnie. He had a dirty diaper, which she changed on the passenger seat, then she gave him a bottle, too.

Richard had a dry diaper and didn't seem to be hungry, so she held him against her chest, humming one of the songs off of that awful kid's CD while nuzzling the top of his fuzzy head.

Jed slammed a pay phone back on its cradle and stalked off to pout beside the only tree within a hundred miles.

"Now what's the matter?" she asked, sandals crunching in the gravel parking lot.

"Nothing." He crossed his arms.

"Let me guess," she said. "Still no messages, and you can't stand it that I didn't blindly follow you out of the restaurant?"

A muscle twitched in his solidly clamped jaw.

"Bingo."

He sighed.

"Yahtzee."

"Stop," he said. "It's no secret that I'm usually the one running the show. But contrary to what your shade-tree psychiatrist brain evidently thinks, it's not because

I like it, but because—" he looked sharply away, then said in a voice barely loud enough for her to hear "— that's the way it's always been."

"But it doesn't *have* to be," she said just as softly, stepping up behind him, curving her fingers around his arm. On the outside, he was steel, but on the inside, Annie suspected he was cream-filling soft. Hurt. What'd made him like that? Was it the death of his parents? Was it a result of Patti's rebellious teen years? Why did Annie have the uneasy feeling that there was something more? "Look, Jed, I know we're basically strangers, but in this case, maybe that's a good thing."

Jed laughed. "How so?"

"Well…"

She licked her lips, and it no longer mattered that she'd annoyed the hell out of him only minutes earlier.

The sun was setting in a fiery blaze across the western sky, and Jed was sick of fighting. What he really wanted was another kiss. His brief taste back at the beer-can cow hadn't been enough—not nearly enough.

"Maybe," she said cautiously, "you could try letting your guard down around me. I mean, since we're getting to know each other, you could practice trusting me the way I trust you."

"You trust me?"

"Duh. If I didn't, do you think I'd have left my home to come all this way with you?"

The sun streaked the sky with orange, yellow and violet. Pretty as that sunset was, it didn't hold a candle to the warm glow in Annie's eyes. The faint aroma of her floral perfume rose above the weary scent of baked earth.

Cupping Richard's head, Jed said, "You mean that, don't you?" He didn't meet Annie's probing gaze.

"I wouldn't have said it if I didn't."

"Okay, but *why* do you trust me? I'm a train wreck. Start to finish, I've bungled this entire mission. How can you feel anything for me but disgust?"

"This mission is nowhere near finished. And second, if you think you've bungled caring for the babies— remember that I've had years of training and experience. You've had a few days of sporadic babysitting. Give yourself a break, Jed. You can't expect to be an expert at everything."

Her words made sense.

His feelings didn't.

After his parents died—and even before that, when his little brother died—Jed had to be everything to everyone in some ludicrous attempt to make up for Ronnie's death.

He always had to be in control, because if he wasn't, he might lose something else. Someone else.

He had to save every helpless person from every fire.

He had to save his niece and nephews from their mother's refusal to grow up.

He *had* to do all of this, but suddenly, he no longer knew how. He was afraid, confused and overwhelmed. He'd been on his own for so long, and honestly, he was tired. Tired of always being in control. Of being the parent. Of never allowing himself to have fun.

The sun had set, and all that remained of the show was a faint orange glow.

Straightening his shoulders, he said to Annie, "We'd better get back on the road. Hand me the keys."

He'd be tired later.

Right now, he had to find his sister.

Chapter 7

"Mmm...where are we?" Annie asked, rubbing her eyes, then stretching. Except for a yellow glow spilling in from a lone parking-lot light, the van was dark, chilly and brimming with the achingly sweet scents of babies and Jed.

"The Fill'er Up and Go station at mile marker four-seventeen. We need gas. This place opens at six."

The glowing green numbers on the dashboard clock read 2:37 a.m. "Oh."

"I'd keep driving, but the empty light came on a few miles back. There's an awful lot of nothing out here. I don't want to spend the next week walking if we run out of gas."

"Makes sense," she said through a yawn.

"Why don't you go back to sleep?" he said. "I've got this covered."

"Why don't we both sleep?"

"You go ahead. I don't want to risk snoozing through this place opening."

Annie snorted.

Even though she could've slept until Christmas, she said through another yawn, "I'm not all that tired, either."

"Isn't it a sin for preschool teachers to lie?"

She shrugged.

How could it be a sin to lie when that wicked-handsome smirk of his left her wide-awake and humming with awareness of how cramped the van was. And how all she'd have to do to once again be in his arms was lean a little to the left.

"You hungry?" Jed asked.

Loaded question. "Uh-huh. How about a ham-and-cheese omelet with hash browns and a side of pancakes?" Annie said.

"Mmm. I like your taste in breakfast."

"How far are we from Denver?"

"Three or four hours, give or take a few depending on how long the critters in back decide to sleep."

"It's pretty miraculous that they let us go this far without stopping."

"You don't think they're sick, do you?"

Annie sighed. "What I think is that they've finally worn themselves out from all the screaming they've done today."

"Don't you mean yesterday?"

Annie stuck out her tongue.

"Go back to sleep," he said. "I'll handle this."

"Why don't you let me?"

"Let you what?"

"Stay up. I'll make sure we're awake when the gas station opens."

"Haven't we already been over this?"

"Yes, but since I don't have a clue where your cabin is, you need to be alert to drive in the mountains. Therefore, it makes the most sense for you to sleep now, and me later."

"Yeah, but—"

"If you agree that I've made an excellent point, does that mean you actually relinquish a bit of your almighty control?"

He rubbed his whisker-stubbled jaw. "I didn't say that."

"True, but I dare you to deny that's what you felt."

"Why did I ever open the door that first day you showed up at my condo?"

"Hmm…" Annie beamed. "Could it be because you needed me?"

"You promise to wake me the second this place opens?"

Annie gave him the same look she would've given one of her preschool students hell-bent on licking the fingerpaints.

He closed his eyes. "See you in a few hours."

"Jed?"

Annie shook him gently.

"Jed, you need to wake up. The station owner just turned on the pumps."

He slowly came round to find himself staring at a vision way better than that omelet he'd been craving earlier. How'd the woman manage to look so good wearing nothing on her face but a sweet smile?

"What time is it?" he asked.

"Six-thirty. The owner got a late start. He said he was up all night with his dachshund, Cocoa. She had three puppies."

"Oh." He straightened behind the wheel, then looked over his shoulders. The babies were gone. "Where—"

"Outside, they started fussing a little after five, so I got them out and walked them around."

"Why didn't you wake me? That could've been dangerous."

"What?"

"Walking around in the dark."

"What was going to get us? Other than that pack of yipping coyotes that finally knocked it off, there's not a whole lot to worry about out here."

"Yeah, well…" He opened his door and stuck his foot out. "You just should've woken me, that's all."

Annie jogged around to Jed's side of the van.

The babies were in their stroller, parked ten feet away on the store's covered porch. All three were drinking from their bottles.

"Face it," she said. "You can't stand the fact that we all survived the night without your help."

"That's crazy talk." Jed slipped his hand under his T-shirt and scratched his stomach. "I knew all along you'd be fine." Right. Which was why he'd faked sleep until accidentally falling into the real thing.

He had to get to his family cabin immediately. He couldn't let Annie get some softhearted notion that he needed a few more hours of sleep. He couldn't believe he'd gone and messed things up yet again by actually falling asleep. But Annie had done just as he'd asked and woken him when the gas pumps were turned on.

Only hours earlier, he'd wished for someone to lean on and here he'd found that person in the petite and perfect form of Miss Annie Harnesberry.

What else could he lean on her for?

Did he have the courage to try?

"Well?" she said, hands on her hips. "I'm waiting."

"For what?"

She coughed. "Your apology?"

Man, she looked good. The soft morning sun backlit her curls. Her eyes and skin glowed not from makeup, but from good health.

Just following his gut instinct without weighing the outcome of his actions, Jed pulled Annie in for a good-morning kiss. Looking at her and at his contented niece and nephews, it was suddenly a *good* morning.

They were safe, and in a matter of hours, he'd know his sister was safe.

At that point, he'd work on saving himself.

How?

By opening himself up to let Annie Harnesberry in.

"Hey, Annie?" This time Jed was shaking her awake.

She opened her eyes slowly and stretched. Her breasts strained against the thin cotton of her white corncob T-shirt. "Hi," she said with a lazy smile that tugged on his stomach and regions below.

"Hi." He smiled back. "We're in Denver. Still hungry for that omelet?"

She nodded. "Babies okay?"

"Freshly diapered and probably ready for their next meal. I got the formula can open, but I can never get the plastic liners to fit or fill them without making a mess. Would you mind doing that part?"

"Not at all." In fact, Annie was flattered he'd asked.

She made the bottles and the five of them walked toward the IHOP just off Interstate 70 that would take them into the mountains.

Pushing the stroller, Annie hung back while Jed opened the door, then ushered her inside with his hand warmly, solidly, on the small of her back.

The restaurant smelled heavenly—of sweet syrup, bacon and spicy sausage. Her stomach growled.

"How many?" the hostess asked.

"Five," Jed said.

"Will you be needing high chairs?"

He looked to Annie.

"No, thank you," Annie said.

The hostess grabbed two menus and showed them to a large corner booth well away from the other diners.

Once she'd taken their drink orders and left, Jed said, "Think she's afraid of us dive-bombing her potential tips?"

Grinning, Annie said, "Maybe. But I like it better over here anyway." She doled out the bottles to the babies and tried to ignore the little voice that told her just how perfect this whole morning felt.

Jed's handsome face had been her first official sight of the day, and it was a good way to start. Something about the vibe between them now, about the way they seemed to be operating not as Jed and Annie, but as a team—a couple—felt right.

Not once had she felt like this with Troy or Conner. After what they'd put her through, she'd been afraid she'd never truly feel at ease with another man.

But here she was. Allowing Jed's smile to launch a whole new batch of cautious hopes. It wasn't fair of her to constantly urge him to share his woes when she hadn't opened up to him, either. But somehow she couldn't do it.

Not yet.

But soon.

Jed unfolded his napkin, used it to wipe the dribble from Ronnie's chin. "They must've been hungry."

"Has your sister introduced them to solid foods?"

Reddening, Jed feigned deep interest in a packet of sugar.

"Okay, mister. Spill it. What have you fed these guys that you weren't supposed to?"

"Nothing too exciting. Just a little ice cream at the zoo."

"And..."

"Maybe a few French fries."

"French fries? Jed! They could've choked!"

"I was right there. I mashed them with my fingers. I'm not letting anyone choke on my watch."

"That's it?"

"I, um, gave them a bit of a milkshake on the way home from the zoo. I just put a little in their bottles. And they had some licks of a dill pickle. I love 'em. I was curious if they would, too."

"No wonder they were fussy when I first showed up. Their stomachs probably hurt."

"From a few bites of people food?"

"You have to introduce solids into an infant's diet very slowly. You can't just start feeding them junk food."

"Yeah, well, I say that's how it should be done."

The waitress returned with two iced teas, then took

their order for omelets and link sausage. They decided to share an order of pancakes.

The second after the food arrived, Pia and Richard got fussy.

Annie started to tend to them, but Jed said, "You go ahead and eat. I'm used to eating my food cold down at the station."

"You sure you don't mind?"

"Do I look like I mind?" he asked, a baby on each knee. He made goofy faces at both.

Pia giggled.

When Annie had been with Conner, he'd never once offered to let her eat while he took care of Sarah. She'd been the one to calm the baby, cut Clara's meat or make sure Ben used his napkin.

Looking back, Conner and Annie hadn't operated as a team at all. But considering how things had ended between them, was that really a surprise?

"Why so quiet?" Jed asked, bouncing the smiling duo on his knees.

"Just thinking."

"Oh, no. As much as you've made me spill my guts lately, don't think I'm letting you off that easy."

Annie fiddled with the syrup dispenser. "I was just comparing you to a guy I used to date—not that I think we're dating or anything."

"Sure."

"It's just that…" Suddenly, she couldn't seem to focus on anything but Jed's lips. On how tenderly he kissed. "He turned out not to be a very nice guy. And you…"

"Happen to be very nice?" His wide, welcoming smile warmed her inside and out.

"Yes," she said. "You're *very* nice, and probably very

hungry. Here—" she held out her arms "—why don't you let me take those two."

"But you're not done."

Thinking of Conner had stolen her appetite. "Really," she said. "I'm full. You eat now. Then we'll get back on the road."

"Okay." He awkwardly stood to hand the babies off to Annie. In the exchange, his strong, warm fingers inadvertently brushed the sides of her breasts. The warmth of his breathy laugh, combined with the heat and goodness of the babies, confused her further.

She loved nothing more than infants.

What she couldn't do was mistake that love for her growing attraction to Jed. She wasn't interested in anything but her work and redecorating her condo. She didn't have room in her life—let alone, her aching heart—for another man.

It just wasn't time.

She hadn't had enough space to heal.

Jed kissed Pia on the top of her head, then Ronnie on top of his. He looked into Annie's eyes. Deeply. Thoroughly. Hungrily. No matter how hard she tried not to respond to his message, it was in plain view for all the world to see.

I like you, Annie Harnesberry.

Do you like me, too?

Without a word, he leaned forward and gently pressed his lips to hers.

"You taste sweet," he said. "Like blueberry syrup."

Terrified of what she might find next in his golden-brown eyes, she looked down.

"Now what's the matter?" he asked. "Didn't you want me to do that?"

She shook her head, then nodded. "I—I don't know."

Maybe the problem was that she'd very much wanted him to do that. Despite knowing she had no business letting him this close.

And not just physically close.

A few kisses she could handle.

Maybe.

But emotionally?

Inside, she felt like melted cheese. Ooey and gooey and incapable of doing anything but molding herself to him. Was she attracted to *him* or to her idyllic picture of him? Was it the total package? The image of him as a loving father to three children? A loving partner to her?

The reality was that they were strangers.

She knew nothing about him.

He knew nothing about her.

So how come all she wanted to do was learn *everything*? She wanted to know him fully, spiritually, intimately. The way only a wife could.

"Annie?" He began to kiss her again, but she backed away. "Did I offend you?" he asked. "If I did, I'm sorry. I never meant to—"

"Please," she said, wanting to put her hand on his arm but struggling to restrain herself. "This kiss—all of them—have been nice. Better than nice. It's just that maybe we ought to present a platonic front for the babies."

Jed raised his eyebrows. "They're old enough to know about kissing?"

"No, but—" Both babies tucked close, she sat down. "Go ahead and eat. You don't want your omelet getting any colder."

He took a bite. "I ticked you off, didn't I? I knew it."

"Knew what?"

"I came on too strong. You're probably right about us keeping it cool in front of the kids. But to give you fair warning—as soon as we pick up that no-good sister of mine, be prepared for some serious wooing."

As the minivan gobbled the miles to Jed's cabin, Annie tried to sleep, but how could she with a loaded word like *wooing* between them?

Although she should've told Jed right then and there that she wasn't interested in dating anyone right now, she hadn't been able to get the words out of her mouth.

No, she wasn't interested in casual dating, but *wooing*?

That was an entirely different issue.

The old-fashioned word implied holding hands on long walks through Pecan's many parks. Rowboat rides at the city lake and bouquets of pink cabbage roses. Late-night phone conversations. Sharing popcorn at the movies...

"Just a couple more hours," Jed said, startling Annie from her daydream of what would happen *after* the movies.

She blushed. "Un-until what?"

He flashed her a funny look. "Are you okay?"

"Um, sure. Perfect." Especially since men hadn't figured out how to read female minds!

"Good. Anyway, I was just saying we should be at the cabin in about two hours."

"Great." They'd get Patti and at least have a chaperone for the trip home. But wait a minute. Annie's stomach lurched. Patti would've driven Jed's truck to the cabin. If Patti took her van and the babies home, that would leave Annie alone in the truck with Jed.

A misery-filled whimper came from Richard in the back.

Annie reached behind her and jiggled his seat. "Hang in there just a little longer."

Waaaah huh waaaaaaaaahh!

Jed sighed. "So close, and yet so far…"

Now Pia joined in.

Then Ronnie.

"Sorry," Annie said, giving Jed's shoulder a sympathetic pat that wasn't supposed to result in her palm tingling. "But it looks like our trip's been extended again."

"This is beautiful!" A few minutes later, Annie was rubbing baby heads while trying to catch a glimpse of the postcard-perfect view of snowcapped mountains cradling a shimmering lake.

There hadn't been anywhere to pull over on the steep interstate, but now they were approaching Dillon, a small town just north of Breckenridge.

Annie opened her window. It'd been mid-nineties in Denver, but it was in the seventies up here. The air smelled too good to be real. A blend of pine trees and water, earth and sun.

"Ooh!" Annie squealed. "Not only is this place gorgeous, but there's an outlet mall." Forget the mountains—check out the size of that Liz Claiborne store! "I wish we weren't in such a hurry. I could do some serious damage to my finances there."

"Watch it, buddy." Jed cursed under his breath when an SUV with camping gear piled on top cut him off, then did a U-turn. "Nice. Why don't you just skip the road and try driving on the median?"

"Goodbye, mall," Annie said. "Maybe we'll get to know each other next time I'm in town." If there ever was a next time.

Jed pulled into a gas station. "Shall we divide and conquer?"

"Sure. Want me to do babies or the gas?"

He sent a truly pained look over his shoulder into the angry pink-and-blue mob in the back seat. "Guess."

"All right, gang…" Annie unfastened her seat belt to climb into the back. "Looks like I drew the short straw, so work with me here."

She felt diapers. One—*ew*. Majorly loaded. The other two seemed okay. "Pia, dahling, let's get your latest surprise cleaned up."

She took the infant and changing pad to the second bench seat. Jed stood right outside the window pumping gas.

He waved.

Grinning, Annie stuck out her tongue.

He returned the favor.

She held up Pia and wiggled the baby.

Jed pressed his nose to the glass and made a silly face.

Eyelashes still wet from her recent tears, the baby girl giggled.

So did the big girl. "Your uncle's a charmer, isn't he?" she said softly, commencing with the business of unsnapping the baby's britches.

Pia cooed.

"Ah, so you agree?"

Luckily, Pia's brothers must've sensed their sister's change in mood, since they quieted, too.

"Agree with what?" Jed was back in the front seat.

"None of your beeswax. This is private girl stuff."

"You two making fun of me?"

"Maybe." Annie wiped the baby's bottom. Whew. For such a tiny bottom, it sure packed a potent punch.

"Girl," Jed said, "you stink."

Pia smiled.

"I'm gonna check for messages." He pointed to a nearby pay phone.

She waved him along.

Annie had to pause for a moment to counteract the affect of Jed's leaning over the seat in all his glory. Had there ever been a more gorgeous man?

Annie finished her task as quickly as possible—not so much to avoid the smell, but because being so close to Jed was just too darned hard. It made her think crazy things. Like how much fun it would be to cuddle up with him on rainy spring nights or snowy winter mornings.

When Jed returned and Pia was strapped back into her carrier, Annie asked, "Do you want me to drive?"

He shook his head. "I need something to do with my hands. I'm starting to feel antsy about what we might find."

"You don't think Patti's hurt, do you?"

"Nah. But I'm sure she's badly shaken. I know my sister. She needs me now—more than ever."

Chapter 8

Patti eased her fingers around her husband's neck, hugging him as close as possible without causing him pain. "I've been so scared," she said.

"'Bout what?" His voice still scratchy from the tube they'd only recently removed from his throat, Howie laughed. "I'm a Mack truck. Nothing's gonna keep me away from you and our babies."

"I love you," she said, giving him another light squeeze.

"So," he asked, once she stepped back, "when are they springing me from this joint?"

"The doctor said she's going to move you out of ICU in a couple hours, then you'll probably be here at least another week on the regular floor."

"A week?" He tried to lift his arm to scratch his head, but it obviously hurt too much.

Patti did his scratching for him. "Once they get you into a regular room, I'll see if someone can wrangle me hair-washing supplies."

"Don't go to any trouble."

"Trouble?" She teared up but managed to give him a wavering smile. "Do you have any idea how awful the past few days have been?"

"Sorry."

"Just wait till you get healthy enough for me to pummel you, mister. *Then* you'll be sorry."

She hugged him again.

"I shouldn't have been driving that late. I'm just glad I only banged myself up and not someone else."

"Why were you driving, anyway?"

"To get to my next sales call ahead of schedule, which would get me back home to you and the babies ahead of schedule. Speaking of which, how are my angels?"

"Good question." Patti put her hands on her hips. "As soon as I finish giving you a piece of my mind for being so careless with yourself, that brother of mine is going to hear a word or two about the fine art of returning phone calls."

A muscle in Jed's jaw kept twitching, and it was bugging the hell out of him. Almost as much as the winter-ravaged dirt road that led to the cabin.

But the babies seemed to enjoy the constant bumping. They hadn't been so happy since he'd fed them all that ice cream at the zoo.

He gripped the wheel harder.

Man, he was nervous.

He didn't want to alarm Annie, but what if Patti was

up here thinking about something drastic like committing suicide? Where had he failed in raising her? He'd done the best he could, but evidently that hadn't been anywhere near good enough.

The van hit a particularly nasty mudhole, jostling him all the way to his bones.

The babies gurgled happily.

"She's going to be fine," Annie said.

"What?"

"Your sister. She'll be okay. We'll probably find her lounging in the sun with a good book."

Jed's heart and mind reeled. He'd only known Annie a few days, and yet they were so in tune.

But were they really?

Was it the urgency of their situation that made him see things that weren't there?

"What's the first thing you'll say to her?" she asked.

He glanced at Annie and saw how she'd rested her arm on the open window. How the sun glinted golden off the fine hairs. How the cool, pine-scented mountain air ruffled her curls.

He was freaking out, but look at her.

So comfortable with her bare feet propped on the dash; he'd long since given up trying to cure her of the habit. She was so calm. So not at all like the chaotic images that flashed in his mind.

Patti with slit wrists.

Patti lifeless and overdosed.

Patti crumpled at the base of a cliff.

He pressed a hand to his forehead.

This had to stop. The whole control thing. He had to trust that Patti wasn't crazy, just hurting. He had to trust the woman beside him to help. Whatever they found, he wouldn't have to weather it alone.

As if reading his mind, Annie put her hand on his shoulder. Such a simple touch, but it meant the world.

"Thank you," he said, afraid to look at her.

"You're welcome."

Most women he'd known would have acted coy.

Thank you for what? they'd ask, wanting, *expecting* him to give more. Turning his thanks into a complimentfishing expedition for themselves. And it wasn't that he didn't want to show how grateful he was, but at the moment, he lacked the emotional energy. Annie was different. She intrinsically understood his mental exhaustion. As soon as this ordeal was over, Jed planned to demonstrate in a hundred different ways how much her blind faith and trust in his mission had meant to him.

"Are we almost there?" she asked, removing her hand from his arm.

"Yeah," he said with a tight nod, pulse raging. "A few more turns and we'll come upon the lake, then the cabin."

"What's it like? The cabin?"

Bless her, she was trying to take his mind off the prospect of what they might find, hoping to ease his tension with small talk. Jed took her up on her offer. "It's pretty sparse. Log construction. One bedroom. And since it's inaccessible in the winter—the whole cabin, not just the bedroom—" he winked "—we just have a fireplace for heat."

"How about the important things? Electric? A flush toilet?"

Seeing the worried furrow on her forehead made

him smile. "Yes, and yes. Although the power up here has a mind of its own."

She laughed. "Sounds like a beach house my parents used to rent."

They rounded the last curve, to be treated to the sight that never failed to stir his soul. On this cloudless day, the lake wasn't filled with water, but with midnight-blue diamonds. Most of the snow had melted from the mountains that embraced it, except for a few dirty white patches above the tree line.

Palms sweating, heart hammering, Jed turned another curve, the one leading to the cabin, to Patti. "Here we are."

"Where's your truck?" Annie asked as he pulled into the crude dirt trail that served as the driveway. "Think she parked around back?"

He turned off the van, frowning. "I have no idea. But then I can't imagine why she's even up here, so what do I know? Maybe she went to town for supplies?"

Annie unfastened her seat belt and lowered her feet from the dash. "I'll bet that's it."

Checking quickly in the back seat, Jed saw that all three babies were wide-eyed and ready for action. Damn. Why couldn't they choose *now* to sleep?

"Go ahead," Jed's savior said. "I'll get this crowd into their stroller."

"No, let me help."

"Really. I'll be fine. You go on." There was her small hand on his shoulder again, her touch infusing him with strength.

He took a deep breath, then opened his door.

Half out of the van, he looked at Annie.

The corners of her lips were raised in a hopeful

smile. "These guys'll be fine on their own for a few minutes. Want me to go with you?"

Swallowing hard, he nodded.

She checked the safety straps on the babies' carriers, gave them each a teething ring to gum and walked around front to meet him.

The place was eerily quiet.

A pair of mountain bluebirds tweeted and a light breeze shushed through the pines, but other than that, there was silence. It unnerved Jed, and he took Annie's hand. "My sister's loud. She always has the TV or radio on. Says it's background noise."

Annie squeezed his hand.

Together, they crunched up the path that led to the cabin's wide front porch. A couple of rockers usually sat out here. They stored them inside when they were gone.

The rockers weren't out. And that bothered him.

"It's beautiful here," Annie said. "How do you stand going home?"

"Once that first snow hits in September, it's easy enough to head down the mountain to places where it's still ninety."

They mounted the five steps.

Dust.

Yellow pine pollen.

Cobwebs.

Everywhere.

It was obvious that no one had been in or out of the cabin's front door in a while. All the shades were drawn, too.

Jed dug the cabin's key from the front pocket of his shorts. Reluctantly releasing Annie's hand, he took hold of the padlock on the door, then fit in the key.

It popped open with a click.

He took the lock from its faceplate and opened the creaking door.

"Patti?" he called into the darkness. "Sis? You in here?"

Nothing.

"Maybe, she's in town like you said." Annie crept up behind him.

"Yeah." But he knew from the faint smell of a long winter's dust that Patti hadn't been here at all.

He suddenly felt dizzy. Weak in his knees.

He set the lock on the dust-coated kitchen table, pulled out one of the chairs and sat before he fell down, pushing the heel of his hands against hot, stinging eyes.

He'd been so sure she'd be here. And if she wasn't at the cabin, where was she? Where else could she have gone?

Annie eased her arms around his neck, her breasts pressing against his back. She rested her cheek on top of his head. "We'll find her. I'll help."

"Where could she be, Annie? Where could she be?"

"I don't know," she said, voice scratchy, "but I promise you, Jed, we'll find her. There has to be some logical explanation. No woman in her right mind would up and leave three gorgeous babies who need her."

"That's just it," he said. "What if she *isn't* in her right mind? What if—"

"No. You're not going to think that way. It won't solve anything. Until we hear different, we're going to assume she's fine. Maybe she's lost or something."

"Yeah—it's the *or something* that gets me."

"Jed…"

"Okay, I get it. Positive thoughts. Now, let's lock this place up and get back on the road."

One of the babies started to cry.

"Are you kidding me?" Annie looked toward the van. "Jed, neither of us has slept more than a few hours for the past three days. The babies need to be out of their seats or the stroller for more than fifteen minutes at a time. I promise, we'll leave first thing in the morning, but please, let's just stay here for the night."

An hour later, sweating from the effort of cleaning thick dust from every surface in the cabin, Jed asked, "Are you sure you want to go through all this trouble for only one night?"

Annie glanced around the cabin with its lovably shabby brown sofa and chairs and the mismatched assortment of knickknacks that added up to a wonderfully eclectic home. Suddenly, she'd never been more sure of anything. She belonged here, with Jed, helping him find his sister.

"Yes," she said, putting her open palm on the cool, knotty-pine kitchen counter. "I feel kind of sorry for the place. It reminds me of some giant toy that used to be everyone's favorite, but then got abandoned for something better."

"Nah," Jed said, scrubbing the last of the pine-plank floor. "That wasn't the way it happened at all. This place will always be special. Back when Mom and Dad were alive, we used to spend entire summers up here. Me and my little brother—"

"I didn't know you had a little brother."

"I don't."

"But you just said…"

Instantly, Annie saw Jed's entire demeanor change. He went from gently scrubbing the floor to wiping it so hard that if he wasn't careful, he'd rub right through. "Forget what I said. Sometimes I have a really big mouth." He finished, then stood to fling the bucket of soapy water off the back porch.

Both doors to the cabin were open, as were all the windows, letting in a crisp-smelling breeze that should've aired out not only the cabin's musty-dusties, but their heads. It should have. So why did Annie get the feeling that Jed was hurting—and hiding more than ever?

"So after all we've shared, that's it? You're essentially telling me to mind my own business?"

He stood just inside the door, filling it with the breadth of his shoulders and chest. Backlit by the fading late-afternoon sun, Jed's face was a study in grim shadows. Annie wanted so badly to reach out to him, but how? He looked at her and stepped onto the small back porch.

Jed slipped his hands into his shorts pockets.

They should've gone to a motel. As much as he loved this place, it's obviously no good for him. Too many memories. And now that Patti wasn't here, there was too much pain.

And then there was Little Miss Walking Therapy Session. Without her saying a word, he could tell what she was thinking.

Really, Jed, you'll feel better if you open up.

Please, Jed, talk to me. Let me help.

Ha. What she refused to understand was that he was beyond help.

Life had dealt him some pretty crappy hands and that

was just the way it was. But in life, you didn't have the luxury of folding or trying a new batch of cards.

In life, you get what you get and don't pitch a fit.

"Jed?"

"Dammit, Annie, why don't you understand that I don't *want* to talk about my dead brother?"

Eyes welling with tears, she brought her hands to her mouth. "All I was going to tell you was to look down. You have an admirer."

Embarrassed, ashamed, he did look down, only to get a much-deserved kick in the pants. Pia had escaped her makeshift playpen and now lay on her tummy, pretty-as-you-please, there beside his dusty Nikes.

She looked up at him, her innocence stealing his breath. How could he grouse about his lot in life with such a miracle right here in front of him?

Yes, his brother had died.

Yes, after that, his parents had drunk themselves into oblivion, dying in a senseless car wreck that had more to do with his father's inability to say no to vodka than anything else.

He scooped up Pia, hugging her fiercely.

He began to walk. Off the porch. Across the over-grown yard. Down to the lake's edge.

On the rocky shore, he allowed long-overdue tears to fall.

Tears for his mom and the red bandanna she'd worn over her hair up here at the cabin, because she didn't want any neighbors dropping in on her when she didn't look her best. Dad had always given her hell for that, considering their nearest neighbor was a good five miles down the road.

A twig crunched, and he hugged Pia harder, praying Annie wasn't standing behind him, witnessing his emotion.

He was a man, dammit.

A man totally in control of his life and surroundings.

From a few feet beside him, Annie said softly, "When I was little, I always dreamed of coming to a place like this. My parents were never all that keen on camping, though. They were more the Holiday Inn type. Remember how popular those used to be? For my eleventh birthday, my folks made sure they were back in town. They rented two rooms in the motel closest to where we lived. I got to invite three girls for a sleepover, and we spent practically the whole night splashing around in the indoor pool. My birthday's December fourteenth, so that was quite a treat. Birthday cake and poolside pizza with a grumpy sky threatening to snow. Boy, let me tell you, that party elevated my social status by a good mile. Anyway, this is a really nice place you've got here, mister. Not quite on par with a Holiday Inn, but I'm loving it just the same."

She put her hand on his shoulder, and that was his undoing.

He wanted to stay strong.

God, he wanted to stay strong, but he was too tired. He needed help. He needed Annie.

Turning to her, Pia still in his arms, he crushed Annie in a hug, the squirming baby between them.

Annie hugged him back as best she could, and they stood there for the longest time, hugging, not saying a word, while tears streamed down his cheeks.

This woman, this enigma, was so damned good for him.

Just when he thought he knew what she was going

to say, Annie went and said the opposite. Just when he thought she'd scold him for not opening up, she pulled him in deeper into his heart, forcing him to open up whether he wanted to or not—at least to himself.

And how great was that? She didn't seem to care how he worked out his problems. She only cared that he did, and that he came back to her when he was done.

How could he have known her for a mere few days when it felt like a lifetime?

From where would he find the courage to tell her he had to stop seeing her when the time came to take her home?

For she'd become an addiction he would have to stop. He was no good for her. Always trying to be in control but failing.

She'd be much better off without him.

Trouble was, he got the feeling that without her, *he* might never be better again.

Chapter 9

"Ugh." Annie lugged in the last awkward packs of diapers and wipes. On their way out of town, Jed had accused her of packing *waaaay* too many baby supplies, but since they were spending the night in a place that might as well be a thousand miles from the nearest Baby Depot, she was happy to have erred on the side of caution.

"Is that everything?" Jed asked on the porch, rubbing his lower back after setting down his heavy load of formula.

The creatures who drank all that formula were inside, indulging in their latest nap.

"I think so," Annie said. "Oh—what about our stuff? Want me to get it?"

"Nah. I'll handle it."

While he walked to the van, Annie stood on the porch, hands on the rail, enjoying the light conifer-scented breeze that brushed curls against her cheeks.

Wow, what a beautiful place.

Even though it was only six, the mountain's shadow crept into their sheltered valley, creating the illusion that it was later in the day. Time for a crackling fire in the stone hearth. For marshmallows and sharing stories.

The cabin and the land around it were magical.

Straight from a more innocent era, like those old Doris Day and Rock Hudson movies, where trouble was having one's hat blow off in a sudden wind.

She sighed. If only things weren't so complicated now. Jed was still worried about Patti. But what was Patti worried about? Was her marriage not as great as it seemed? Was she mired in an epic case of postpartum depression?

If *she* were Patti, Annie could've done a lot of thinking up here.

Annie swallowed painfully.

She had never felt so helpless as she had back there beside the lake, when Jed had poured out his soul with just one heartbreaking look into his eyes.

The man was eaten up inside, and she had no idea what to do.

Maybe that was why she got along so well with babies.

When they cried, all it took to fix them was the basics.

They wanted to be cleaned.

Fed.

Held.

Men, on the other hand, were a total mystery. Sure, she and Jed had shared a few wonderful kisses, but that moment down by the lake, that had been much more intimate.

For just an instant, when he'd turned to her, reached out to her and only her for comfort, he'd been emotionally naked. She'd wanted to help him so badly, but how? Where did she begin to—

"That's the last of it," Jed said, clomping onto the porch, carrying their overnight bags.

"Looks like the cab light's still on. Want me to check it?"

He glanced over his shoulder toward the van. "Nah, I think it's just the angle of the sun."

Are you feeling better? she wanted to ask, but didn't have the nerve.

"What's for dinner?" Jed asked.

She blinked back hot tears.

So that was how it was going to be. He'd pretend what'd happened earlier hadn't happened at all, but because she couldn't bear to see him in that much pain again so soon, she'd let him go on pretending.

For now.

But not forever.

As his friend, she owed it to Jed to see him through his troubles with Patti, then help him handle a few of his own.

Isn't that considerate of you?

Like she didn't have problems of her own?

"Dinner, huh?" Thinking two could play the avoidance game—at least for one more night—Annie pasted on her brightest smile. "Dinner, huh? How about Canned Good Surprise followed by Stale Road Food?"

"Sounds good." He set the bags next to his feet and pulled her into his arms.

She rested her cheek against his chest and listened to his heartbeat, his breath.

What was happening between them?

What was her fascination with this man?

She hardly knew him, yet she felt as if she'd always known him.

Jed ran his fingers through her hair, and her throat ached with the tenderness of his touch. With her wish that life could be different. That love could be different. That neither had to hurt.

The pleasure and pain of it was devastating, and Annie squeezed him for all she was worth.

"I couldn't have done this without you," he said. "How can I thank you?"

Gazing up at him, tears pooling in her eyes, a smile playing on her lips, she said, "You just did."

"Out with it," Jed said several hours later in front of a crackling fire. "Where'd you learn how to whip up a meal like that out of nothing?"

Annie rolled her eyes while putting fresh socks on each baby. "It was just baked beans and canned ham. My grandmother taught me that crushed potato chip trick."

"Yeah, well..." He took the next baby on the assembly line and slipped Pia's chubby arms and legs into soft, pink pj's. "Next time you see her, tell her I like it."

"I will." She cradled Richard close and kissed him just above his ear. "You are so adorable. Do you have any idea what a heartbreaker you're going to be?"

"I can see it now," Jed said. "Us getting a call from his first-grade teacher telling us how he spends every recess chasing all the girls."

"Don't you mean Patti and Howie?" Annie asked.

"That's what I said." *Wasn't it?*

She looked so beautiful right now with her hair glowing in the firelight. She made him want his own family.

His own wife, who'd never run out on him the way his flaky sister had. Annie would be a great mother. What else would she be good at?

"Do you have any idea how kissable you look?" he asked.

Laughing with eyes that were luminous and inviting, she shook her head.

"What do you think we should do about it?" he said, fingering one of her curls.

"Quit goofing around. We still have to get these guys and gal tucked in for the night."

"So? What's so tough about that?"

"You think they're going to fall asleep like magic?"

"A guy can dream, can't he?" Just as he'd dreamed of how his life might play out with her living in his home instead of next door....

"I've always liked dreams," Annie said softly.

Together, quietly, efficiently, in the coordinated motions of an old married couple, Jed helped Annie put the babies into the playpen he'd unearthed from the back of the van.

"They're perfect, aren't they?" she said, shyly reaching for his hand.

They'd set up the temporary crib in a corner of the bedroom where it was dark except for a milky swath of moonlight over three, blanket-wrapped angels.

Annie shivered. "Do you think they'll be warm enough in here?"

"Has anyone ever told you you worry too much?"

"Yes, but—"

Jed stopped her with a kiss.

Nothing fancy. He just wanted to show her how much he looked forward to the rest of their night.

She groaned, and the vibration of it against his chest pushed him over the edge. To hell with the restraint he'd been hanging on to.

He wanted her, needed her—*now*.

And he was so damned glad she felt the same.

Still holding hands, Annie led him into the living room, straight to the fire, then past the fire, then—what the...? "What are you doing with that Scrabble game?" Jed asked as she took it from a shelf. "I thought we were going to make out."

"How'd you get that idea?"

"Well, the way you kissed me back there, I assumed—"

She pressed her finger to his lips. "That's your biggest problem, Jed. I may worry too much, but you assume too much."

"No way is *muzjiks* a word."

"Sure it is," Annie said. "It's a plural variation of the spelling of *m-u-z-h-i-k*."

"Which is?"

She grinned. "A Russian peasant."

"Right. Should've known."

"One-hundred and twenty-eight points."

"I quit."

"But you haven't even played your first word."

"And I'm already so far behind, there's no way I could ever catch up. Can you think of a better reason to quit?"

"Now where's your competitive spirit? My grandmother and I play Scrabble all the time. She's so good, though, I have to study the *Scrabble Dictionary* on my lunch breaks."

"Well?" he asked, grabbing a handful of the Jiffy

Pop popcorn they'd found above the fridge. "Do you win now?"

"I wish." She laughed. "I've *never* beaten her."

He sighed before placing d-o-r-k. "Has your grandma ever entered any tournaments?"

"Before her hip went bad, she was the Oklahoma state champ. But I don't think she's played much since her surgery."

"And what does that make you? Some kind of Scrabble hustler? Luring unsuspecting innocents such as me into—"

"Oh—" she said, nearly snorting her cocoa up her nose from laughing. "Let me get this straight. You—Mr. Kiss a Poor, Helpless Preschool Teacher in the stinky old belly of a beer-can cow—you are calling yourself an innocent?"

The size of his smile took her breath away. Had there ever been a handsomer man? A man she wanted to kiss as much as she wanted to kiss him? He was a mischievous boy and at the same time all man. A hard, muscled man. Although she knew better, she craved the taste of his delicious lips.

They each played five more words, and with every new draw of letter tiles, Annie grew more confused. What was she doing? Joking with him? Flirting? Was there something in the crisp, clear mountain air that made her forget her vows to stay clear of all men—and in particular, one as seemingly perfect as Jed?

They planned to head straight home in the morning. Once they got there, her good judgment would surely return, but until then, she was tired of being good. She was tired of playing Scrabble. She was tired of pretending she didn't find Jed incredibly attractive.

Still, tired as she was, she had to remember she was wary of nursing another broken heart. Already, no matter how hard she'd tried to fight it, her feelings for Jed went miles beyond what she'd ever felt for Conner or Troy.

Which was why, right now, before the fire glowed any softer, before they shared one more mug of cocoa, she needed to call it a night.

Feigning a yawn, she said, "I'm beat. Ready for bed?"

"Sure, but there's a problem."

"What?"

"Have you forgotten there's only one bed?"

"You can have it," she said. "I don't mind crashing on the sofa."

"Yeah, well, I mind. How about we share the bed?"

She folded the Scrabble board in half and let the tiles slide into the plastic bag they'd been stored in. "You think that's a good idea?"

"What's the matter?" he asked. "You don't trust me to keep my hands to myself?"

Oh, she trusted *him,* but she feared she couldn't trust herself. What if she rolled up against him in the middle of the night, basking in his warmth, his strength?

"Come on," he said, putting the screen in front of the dying fire. Finished, he held out his hand. "Let's get some sleep."

Not for the first time that day—or even that week—Annie followed her heart instead of her brain. Linking her fingers with Jed's, she let him lead her to bed.

"Rise and shine, sleepyhead."

"Already?" Annie yawned.

Jed laughed and kissed her forehead. "Shoot, the

babies have already been up for hours. We're all fed and diapered and packed. All the van's missing is you."

"Why didn't you wake me?" she asked.

He trailed his finger so gently down her cheek she wasn't sure he'd touched her at all.

Hugging her down pillow, Annie recalled the long wonderful night she'd spent cuddled next to him. Had they met at a different time under different circumstances, maybe he'd still be in bed beside her.

"You looked so peaceful," he said. "I thought I'd just let you sleep."

Her stomach growled. She put her hands over it and blushed. "I don't suppose you brought breakfast?"

From the nightstand, he took a plate of the remaining peanut brittle they'd bought at the beer-can cow. "Sorry. This is all we had left—unless you have a craving for baked beans. In which case, I can open a fresh can."

She shook her head. "I love sweet stuff for breakfast. I'll pretend this is crunchy pastry."

"That's the spirit." He started to fold the playpen but didn't have much luck.

"Let me help." Annie said, slipping out from under the light down comforter that'd kept the chilly mountain night at bay.

In under a minute, she'd folded the playpen and slid it back into its carrying case.

Jed crossed his arms. "Woman, you delight in making me look bad, don't you?"

Grabbing her overnight bag on her way to the bathroom, she winked. "I'll never tell."

Five minutes later, she'd tucked her hair into a ponytail, slapped on a hat, brushed her teeth, washed her face, and changed into khaki shorts and a University of Oklahoma sweatshirt.

Back in the living room, she put her sneakers on. "Where are the babies?" she asked Jed as he stood in the front door. "I haven't even had a chance to hug them this morning."

"They're in their car seats. I have to admit, I'm a little antsy to get home."

"I'll bet by the time we get there, Patti's going to be the one worrying about you."

He took a deep breath. "I hope you're right—not that I want her to be worried, but—"

"I know."

The living room was gloomy with all the shades drawn and the dust covers back over the sofa and chairs. Had it really been just last night that the place had felt so inviting?

"Looks like you've thought of everything," Annie said. "Want me to strip the sheets off the bed? You probably shouldn't leave them on dirty."

"I grabbed them while you were in the bathroom."

"Okay…" She took one last look at the idyllic cabin she'd never see again. "I get the hint. Let's go."

Hand on the small of her back, Jed guided her from the house. She struggled to keep her composure.

Even though she hardly knew this guy, and had no emotional ties whatsoever to this run-down cabin, Annie knew she wouldn't forget the short time they'd shared.

Cooking that strange mix of canned foods for a dinner that'd actually tasted pretty good. Bathing the babies one by one in the chipped white porcelain sink. Laughing over Scrabble. Sharing that big old wrought-iron bed, and just as she'd feared, rolling into Jed's arms in the night. Only instead of hating it, she'd loved it. And she irrationally wished she could do all of it again.

Jed opened the van's passenger-side door for her.

Once in her seat, Annie promptly swung around to say good-morning to the three cuties chomping on teething rings. "I missed you," she said, touching the nearest hand.

"Believe me," Jed said, climbing into the seat beside her. "They missed you. I didn't think I'd ever get their diapers changed. Every time I thought I was finished, some wise guy—Richard—had to go again."

"Is he sick?" she asked, slipping off her sneakers to park her sock-covered feet in their usual position on the dash.

"If you're asking if he had the runs, his poop looked normal enough to me."

"That's good."

"I'll say. The last thing we need is a sick baby." He put the key in the ignition. "Ready?"

She nodded. "Let's go find your sister."

Apparently, the van had other ideas. Instead of turning over, the engine made a funny clicking sound, then nothing.

"Dammit," Jed said, thumping the heel of his hand against the wheel.

"What's wrong?"

Leaning his head back, he groaned. "Remember yesterday afternoon when you asked if the cab light was on?"

"Uh-huh."

"I'm guessing it was."

Chapter 10

"Sheriff Franklin here," a man said over the phone. Static on the line made him sound far away.

"Ditch. Thank goodness I got you!"

"Patti Schmatti?"

She cleared her throat. "I go by Patricia now, thank you very much."

He chuckled. "Still touchy as ever, I see."

"Yes, and if you could actually see me, my scowl would tell you I'm calling for a serious reason. Jed's missing. And he's got my babies."

Ditch laughed. "Patti, Jed's not missing. He's looking for you. He asked me to check if you were at the cabin. I called to tell him you weren't, but I guess he decided to take matters into his own hands—as usual."

Fingering the pearls around her neck, Patti quickly told him what'd happened with Howie, and how he'd improved so much over the past twenty-four hours that his doctors were releasing him within the next few days. "I swear, sometimes I could throttle Jed," Patti said. "Anyway, would you please, *please* run up to the cabin and see if he's there? And if he is…" She imagined herself throttling her brother. "Tell him to get my babies home ASAP."

"Are you sure you've got enough to drink?"

Jed brushed off Annie's latest offer of a second water bottle with a quick kiss to her cheek.

"It's only a twenty-something-mile hike back to the main road," he told her for the third time. "From there, it'll be easy to find a ride the rest of the way into town."

"Be careful," she said, cradling a blanket-wrapped Pia to her chest while Richard and Ronnie watched from their playpen, which had been set up temporarily on the sun-flooded front porch.

When he'd discovered the dead battery, Jed had felt like pitching the mother of all fits. But how could he when he had no one to blame for this latest disaster but himself?

"You be careful, too," he said. "The last thing we need is—"

"I know, I know," Annie mocked his deeper tone. "The last thing we need is a sick baby, or one getting hurt."

Despite himself, he grinned. "You'd better watch that sass."

She grinned right back. "Are you going to make me?"

"Don't tempt me," he said, "or I'll just stay here forever and we'll forget all our troubles and live off the land."

"Hmm…" She put her index finger to her lips. "It's tempting except for the fact that we're down to a one or maybe two-day supply of diapers and formula, and since there's no cow handy and I'm not exactly…" She looked down and blushed. "Good grief." She landed a light swat to his arm. "Would you just get going?"

With one final wave, he set off down the road, tennis shoes crunching against frost-hardened dirt.

Even though he could see his breath, he was plenty warm once he got a half mile or so into his walk.

He'd made this hike for fun when he was a kid. Now, though, it was a major pain.

When Annie asked about that cab light, why hadn't he at least checked it? It would've taken only a second. Wasn't he the one who was supposed to be in control?

Right.

Not since the night his brother had died in that fire and he'd been helpless to save him had Jed felt more out of control.

And what kind of person was he wishing he could stay on this mountain with three adorable babies and one beautiful woman when Patti could be in serious trouble?

Not willing to answer his own questions, Jed marched on, losing himself in the scent of pines and the task at hand.

For now, he didn't have to worry about anything more than putting one foot in front of the other. He had to get through this hike, then he'd worry about Patti. And after that he'd worry about how he wasn't nearly good enough for Annie. But at the same time, he wasn't nearly strong enough to let her go.

Not that he even had her.

But he wanted her.

And he wasn't just talking about sex.

Since meeting her, for the first time in years, he'd thought about what he wanted to do with the rest of his life.

He wasn't content to remain a bachelor forever, but with other women, he hadn't known how to tame the controlling beast inside him.

It was obviously no big problem for Annie that he wasn't always the most easygoing guy around, which made him think that despite his not deserving her, Annie saw something redeemable in him.

Knowing there might be light at the end of this latest tunnel quickened Jed's step.

The sooner he got to town, the sooner he'd get back to Annie.

Famous last words.

Whether it was the altitude or that he wasn't fit as he used to be, Jed felt like hurling, passing out or just plain collapsing—not necessarily in that order. Perhaps all that running hadn't been such a good idea.

Making matters worse, he'd stumbled a ways back and dropped his water bottle. Just his rotten luck that it fell on a jagged rock that had punctured the plastic. He'd never admit it to her, but Annie had been right. He should've taken a second bottle.

He was hunched over, hands braced on his knees, when he heard the best sound ever—an engine headed his way.

Glory, freakin' be.

He glanced up to see his good friend Ditch's squad

car. "Jed?" Ditch called from his window. "What the hell are you doing?"

"What's it look like I'm doing?"

Ditch laughed. "Having a coronary on the side of my road. Get in."

"Thanks." Jed climbed in on the passenger side.

Reaching into a small cooler between the seats, Ditch pulled out a grape pop. "Want one?" he asked, holding out the dripping can.

"You still drinking this crap?"

"Are you turning me down?" Ditch asked, snatching it back.

"Not on your life." Jed took the pop and opened it. "At this point, I'd be happy to drink motor oil as long as it's cold." He finished half the can in one gulp. "Damn lucky coincidence running into you. What're you doing up here?"

"It's no coincidence," Ditch said, putting the car in gear and starting back up the mountain. "I heard from Patti this morning."

Jed choked on his pop. "As in my sister, Patti?"

"One and the same."

"Did she happen to tell you where the hell she ran off to, so I can hightail it over there to—"

"Whoa, bud. Cool down. It isn't what you think."

"Oh, that she ran off on her kids like—"

"Cool it, man. Like I told you, it's not what you think."

"Well, then, what is it? Did she go off with another man? She—"

"She's been in the hospital."

Jed's stomach fisted. "What happened? Is she all right?"

"It's not her, it's Howie. He was trying to make it to his next town ahead of schedule when he fell asleep and slammed into an oak. Patti said she tried to call, but couldn't get you. Then something happened with the hospital phone lines. Anyway, she's safe. Howie's on the mend. And she's been beside herself trying to find out if her babies are all right." Eyeing Jed for a moment, Ditch said, "Look, knowing Patti's reputation, I took the liberty of contacting your pal Ferris in Pecan and her story checks out. He's been trying to call you because he found your truck at the Tulsa airport. Jed, she was telling the truth. This time she wasn't just running away."

Jed brought his hand to his aching forehead.

No.

No way this was happening.

No way could he have screwed up this badly.

Jed thumped his head against his window.

"So let me get this straight…" Ditch laughed so hard he started to snort. "You *had* to find her yourself, right? Didn't trust anyone else to do the job?"

While his supposed friend continued to howl, Jed turned away.

"Well, one good thing came out of it. At least I got to see you. It's been a while. Marthe'll be thrilled. 'Course you'll have to let her cook for you tonight. You know what a kick she gets out of feeding the world."

"It's not just me I dragged up here," Jed said, head and heart pounding with regret.

"Well, sure, the babies are invited, too. Marthe would rather see them than either one of us, anyway."

"There's someone else," Jed said.

"Oh, yeah?" Jed's old friend shot him a sideways

glance. "Well? Who? Did you hire some grandma to help out with the triplets?"

I *wish.* "Her name's Annie. She's a neighbor."

"Oh? Grandma-type neighbor or hot neighbor?"

Hot. Very hot.

Jed shrugged. "*Just* a neighbor."

Ditch started in again with his snorting. "*That* kind of neighbor, huh? Damn, looks like for once we're going to have some decent entertainment round here."

Annie's new friend Marthe put her feet up on the porch rail and sighed. "It's sure good to have Jed back. Ditch never volunteers to do the dishes."

"Oh?" Annie said, taking a swig of the peach wine cooler Marthe had brought. Marthe had indigestion and was drinking Sprite.

"If you ask me," Marthe said. "He's out to impress you."

"No, Jed's just being polite."

Laughing, Marthe patted Annie's knee. "I took you for smarter than that. Nope, I've known Jed all my life, and he's never been that keen on housework. Billy!" Marthe shouted to her seven-year-old son. "Get off that stump right now!"

He didn't.

"Excuse me," Marthe said. "Time to get mean before he falls and we spend the rest of the night in the nearest emergency room."

While Marthe stomped off the porch and through the small forest that was the front yard, Annie took another sip of her wine.

No, Jed wasn't out to impress her with his offer to clean up after dinner. He was trying to compensate for dragging her all the way up here for nothing. Little did he know, this was the best time she'd had in years. The day had turned out to be truly enjoyable once she'd heard that Patti and her husband were okay.

Soon enough, they'd have time to head home.

Soon, she'd start her new job and spend her evenings redecorating instead of listening to Jed's booming laugh—the one now drifting through the cabin's open door.

What a wonderful sound.

The whole night had been filled with laughter, and this new playful side of Jed's personality was potent. Was it the norm for him? Or was he on an artificial high after hearing that his sister was safe?

Marthe, Billy in tow, walked back up onto the porch. "You get inside and stay there until I say you can come out."

"But, Mom, I—"

"Now," Marthe said, hands on her hips. "I already have a stomachache. The last thing I need is to stand here arguing with you."

Chin to his chest, the little boy did as he was told.

A wink, followed by a quick grin at Annie, showed the drill-sergeant mom was all bark and no bite. "Ditch is so lax in discipline. Seems like I'm always the bad guy."

"Overall, though, both of your kids seem very well behaved. Especially Kayla. I can't believe the way she's looked after the babies all night."

"Yeah, she loves little ones. Ditch and I have thought about having more, but financially, it's all we can do to keep clothes on two. I'm not sure how we'll manage when they start college. You and Jed ever talk about having your own brood?"

Annie was glad she'd already swallowed before hearing Marthe's question, or the shock of it would've left her choking on peach-wine cooler. "W-we hardly know each other. We're just neighbors."

"That may be," Marthe said, "but I've got a sixth sense about these things. You two are in it for the long haul."

Not wanting to argue with Marthe, Annie decided to let her think whatever she liked. Marthe might have a sixth sense, but Annie had a keen sense of realism.

"I need a back rub after all that hard work," Ditch said, strolling onto the porch, Jed behind him.

"Is that my cue?" Marthe asked, casting her husband an indulgent smile.

She stood, and took Ditch by the hand to guide him to her chair. Once he was seated, she began to rub his shoulders and neck.

Ditch closed his eyes and moaned.

Annie turned away. Somehow, the scene felt too intimate for her to watch. They were so obviously in love that it almost hurt to look at them.

She wanted what they had.

Jed stepped up beside Annie and she was suddenly very aware of his sheer size. He smelled of lemony dishwashing liquid and faintly of Marthe's barbecue ribs. "Do you need a back rub?" he knelt to ask, his breath tickling Annie's ear.

She shivered.

"Cold?"

No. More like disturbingly aware. No other man

had ever made her feel such pleasure just by asking a question.

If only she didn't doubt his intentions. If only she had the courage to ask him if what he'd said back at the giant corncob, about wanting to date her after they got home, was true. What if he said yes? And what if he didn't want to wait until they got home? What if tonight, right here in this cabin, he kissed her long and leisurely until her toes curled with pleasure?

Had she really praised herself for being a realist a few minutes ago?

"Mom!" Billy cried. "Can I come out yet?"

Marthe laughed. "Oops."

"You'd make a lousy cop," her husband teased. "Imagine if you treated prisoners as badly as our poor, kids."

"Oh, right," she said, smacking him on his red-haired head. "Like the kids and I haven't spent all afternoon decorating cookies for the Founder's Day parade. And yesterday, I drove that cherub-cheeked little demon into Denver so he could have the right baseball cleats."

"Watch out, Jed." Ditch laughed. "Protect your bachelorhood at all costs. Or else you'll end up like me— broke and completely whipped."

"I'll keep that in mind," Jed said, laughing too as he and Marthe went inside.

"Mom?" Kayla met her mother by the door. "Can we *pleeeeeease* keep the babies? They'll be good, and I promise to do everything for them. Hailey could come over and we could babysit together. It'd be good practice for when we're allowed to babysit by ourselves."

"Fine with me," Marthe said, "but you'll have to ask Jed. He's their temporary daddy."

Kayla turned her sweet smile and big brown eyes on Jed, and he was a goner. "Are you sure that's what you want to do?" He asked. "They're a real handful."

She nodded solemnly.

Marthe winked, and said, "Besides, now that you don't have to get back right away, this'll give you two a much-needed breather before the trek home. Why don't we take the van. We'll stop by the store on the way home and get you stocked up on baby supplies. Tomorrow, all you have to do is drop by the house, grab the triplets, and then you'll be ready to go."

Jed scratched his head. "Sounds like a great plan, but I still say it's an awful lot of work. What do you think, Annie?"

Annie gulped.

What do I think? That a night alone with you in this romantic setting could be trouble. "Um, maybe the triplets ought to stay here? They've got so much stuff."

"Then I guess it's a good thing Kayla and I brought our men," Marthe said. "Billy, Ditch, help us load the van."

Chapter 11

"That was nice," Annie said after waving goodbye to their company. She carried the cup Billy had used for his soda to the sink.

"Yeah. Ditch and Marthe are good people." He shook his head. "I can't believe how those kids have grown."

"That Kayla sure is a cutie." She turned on the warm water, holding the cup under the flow while running a soapy dishrag around the rim. In a pitiful few seconds, the cup was rinsed and dried and tucked beside its friends in the cabinet, leaving Annie not quite sure what to do with her hands.

Jed knelt to grab a napkin from the floor. He put it in the paper sack they'd set up for trash. "Kind of strange around here without the babies, isn't it?"

Yeah, Annie thought with a pang of sadness.

Look at us.

Without the triplets between them, they didn't have

anything in common. Nothing to talk about. Did that mean they weren't supposed to be more than friends?

Jed chuckled. "Let me rephrase that. Strange in a *good* way. We never get the chance to finish a conversation with my niece and nephews around. When you were telling me this afternoon about your plans to decorate your new classroom like a giant underwater scene. I was going to say how cool that sounded but Ronnie interrupted, demanding his diaper be changed that second."

"Really?" Annie said, busying her fingers with a stray curl. "I thought you just didn't know a polite way to tell me my idea stinks."

"Heck, no." He braced his palms on the opposite side of the island. "In fact, if you don't mind, I'd like to help out. I'm pretty good with tools. Maybe I could build one of those reading lofts you sometimes see in kindergarten classrooms. We could paint it to look like a coral cavern underneath."

"Th-that would be great," Annie said, charmed anew. How come every time she thought she had their relationship—or lack thereof—figured out, the man had to go and confuse her?

Jed flashed Annie a smile so handsome that she had trouble finding her next breath. "So?" he asked. "You gonna give me another shot at reclaiming my Scrabble honor?"

"Sure you're up for it?" she teased.

"Damn straight. Last night, I didn't even try. Tonight, you're toast."

An hour later, seated in front of a crackling fire, Jed groaned. "Please tell me I didn't just get whomped again."

Grinning as she slid the letter tiles into their bag, Annie said, "If that's what you want to hear, that's what I'll tell you. But there's no way you'll ever beat me. I've got too much of my grandmother's Scrabble blood pumping through my veins."

He rolled his eyes, then surprised her by taking her hand. "Thanks," he said, his voice a throatier version of its normal timbre.

"For what?" She gave his hand a squeeze, releasing it to tuck the game board into the box.

"For making me forget—at least for the past hour— what an unbelievable fool I've been."

She made a face. "I wouldn't go that far. Over-the-top concerned, sure, but not foolish, Jed. You love your sister. Because of that love, you put your own life on hold to search for her. What's wrong with that?"

"Anyone ever tell you you're too good to be true?"

"Nope. But I do get told to mind my own business. To get my own life. My girlfriends at the school where I used to work got tired of me always giving my two cents' worth about their relationships with their husbands or how to discipline their kids when I didn't have either."

The fact that she knew almost everything about Jed, but had told him precious little about her own rocky past, gnawed at her conscience. He deserved to know. *Everything.* But she couldn't open up. Not quite yet.

Jed brought her hand to his mouth, palm up, and kissed the sensitive center.

She shivered inside.

"Do you ever want any kids, or a husband?" he asked, his warm breath on her hand causing even more internal distress.

She nodded. "It'd be awfully lonely living the rest of my life alone."

"What kind of guys do you date?"

"What is this?" she asked with an easy smile. "The Dating Inquisition?"

"Sorry. Guess that's just my knuckleheaded way of asking if I'm your type."

"Stop!"

"What?"

"Putting yourself down. For the record, yes. At times on this trip—namely in unsanitary fast-food restaurants—you got a little domineering. But aside from that, you've been thoughtful and caring and—" She stopped just short of adding wickedly handsome to the list.

She traced the worried furrow of his brows. "Let it go, Jed. Whatever's bothering you about Patti, forget it. I can see it's still eating you up inside."

"That's just it," he said, leaning against the sofa and staring into the fire. "Sometimes I'm afraid that this compulsion to control everything is all I have... Remember how I mentioned that our house burned down when I was a kid?"

"Yes," she said quietly.

"I was sound asleep when Mom screamed at me to get up. Not many people had smoke detectors in those days, but my parents woke up because Mom had bad asthma and the smoke made her cough.

"Their room was at the top of the stairs. Next came Patti's, then mine, and my little brother Ronnie's room was all the way at the end of the hall. By the time Mom grabbed Patti, she was coughing so hard she could hardly breathe. Dad yelled at her to get outside. Dad got me and held my hand till we were outside. There was snow on the ground and I can still feel the icy-wet ground soaking my socks."

"Oh, Jed..." Annie placed her hand over her mouth. "I'm so sorry."

"Oh." He laughed sharply. "That's nothing. It gets better. After leaving me with Mom and Patti, Dad ran back in to get Ronnie, but it was too late. The stairs were gone. The firemen weren't there yet. I remember hearing their sirens, but they were still far away. Dad ran around the side of the house to get a ladder and prop it up against Ronnie's window, but the ladder was buried under the snow. He dug and dug screaming for me to help. I did the best I could, but it wasn't enough."

Jed started to cry.

Tears hadn't helped him that night any more than they did now.

"I kept waiting to hear my little brother crying. He was only four. He cried a lot. But the only sound was the wail of those sirens. By the time firemen got there and busted through Ronnie's bedroom window, he was dead. Smoke got him—not fire. I just stood there, staring. Dad said, 'Why didn't you help me dig, Jed? Why didn't you help?'"

Annie sat on the floor beside him, slipping her arm around him. "What a horrible thing to say. But Jed, you know your father didn't mean it. He must've been out of his mind with grief."

"Yeah, that's what he said later when Mom yelled at him, but it didn't matter. It was already too late. Things were never the same after that. The house I'd lived in my whole life was gone—along with all the memories of good times. Dad started drinking. Mom's asthma got worse. I began to help around the house more and more until I felt like I was the parent and my folks were the kids. Hell, maybe a part of me was a little relieved the night they died. How sick is that? At least after they were gone, I stopped having to make excuses for them to Patti. I used to tell her Dad was too sick to come to her softball games when, in reality, he was soused. I didn't even tell him about her games for fear he'd embarrass her in front of her friends. And Mom…she could've tried to get better, but she wouldn't take her medicine. I wanted so badly to fix it. Them. Me. To make everything better. Nice. Happy. The way it was before Ronnie died.

"I thought that if I worked hard enough, I could bend life to my will. For a while, with Patti, it worked. But everything went bad when she hit her teens. I wasn't her parent. Tupac was. Hellhammer and Black Flag. I was just the guy who kept her from doing what she wanted. The more I tried to control her, the more out of control she got. That's why I came up here now. I had to drag her back. I had to at least try." He covered his face with his hands. "That's the only way I stay sane."

Annie sighed before pulling him into her arms. "I'm so sorry," she said, stroking his hair. "So, so sorry."

"I didn't tell you so you'd feel sorry for me," he said. "I can handle it. All of it. I just need a breather, you know? Time to catch my breath."

"I know, Jed, I know." Cradling his face in her hands, she kissed his forehead and cheeks and nose. "What you have to realize is that Patti's a grown woman now, not a wild teen. No matter how hard you try, you can't control her any more than you can the weather or a flat tire or a dead battery." Smoothing his hair back from his forehead, she said, "Once you understand that no one—not even a man as strong as you—can control every aspect of his life, you might be able to conquer your fear of losing control."

"If only it was that easy," Jed said with a pained laugh. "Do you think I haven't tried?"

"Listen," she said, watching his tearstained face. "As an experiment, try controlling me like you have every other aspect of your life."

He shook his head. "I don't know what you mean. I wouldn't do that to you. I couldn't. I respect you too much."

"That's good news," she said with a wavery smile, tears pooling in her eyes at the fear that she might lose her nerve and not follow through on the outrageous act she had in mind. "Because if you try to stop me, we won't have nearly as much fun."

She unfastened the top button of her blouse, then the next and the next.

He groaned. "Annie, please. You don't know what you're doing. I didn't tell you all this to make you think I'm some charity case."

"Did I say you had?"

"No, but—"

She pressed her lips to his—hard. She forced his mouth open, nipped at his tongue. She was unbuttoning the rest of her shirt when he put his hands on hers.

She thought he was helping at first, but then she saw he actually intended to stop her.

"Good boy," she said softly.

"Excuse me?"

"You just proved my point. The experiment failed. I want to make love to you, Jed. No matter how hard you try, you can't control that."

"Are you *sure* this is what you want to do?"

"You don't want me to have my way with you?"

For the first time in a while, he grinned. "I didn't say that. I'm just, you know, not accustomed to a woman taking the lead."

"Yeah, well, get used to it. I can't believe I'm admitting this, but Jed Hale, from the first moment I saw you, all I could think of was how good it would feel to be held in your arms. I've got a past, too. And deep down, something's telling me that only a man as honorable as you can heal me. Make me whole."

Cupping her face, he asked, "What happened?"

She was suddenly laughing—and crying. Kissing him. Burying her fingers in his hair. "Heal me, Jed. Please."

Aside from the time it took to tug off his T-shirt and help Annie lose her top, Jed never broke her stare. At least not before muttering, "Oh, crap."

"What?"

"Protection. I mean, I know I'm clean, but I'm not the kind of guy who carries condoms in my wallet."

"It's okay," she said. "I'm on the pill—and I'm also *clean*." Feet tucked beneath her, she reached around to her back to unfasten her bra. When her breasts were free, she watched in wonder as Jed sucked in his breath.

"If I'd had any idea you were hiding all that under those T-shirts of yours," he said, "I would've seen about getting them off you a long time ago."

She giggled. "We've only known each other a few days."

"Right. A few *agonizing* days." He nuzzled her neck, starting a delicious new batch of shivers. "You think I haven't been wanting you? If we hadn't been saddled with my sister's kids, I would've put the moves on you in that smelly old beer-can cow."

"You did."

"Did what?"

"Put moves on me in there."

"Are you talking about that measly kiss? Honey, that was nothing. You're not going to believe what else I have in store."

"Mmm... I can't wait."

And she didn't have to.

Jed stood, then scooped her into his arms, carrying her to the bedroom where he eased her onto the bed and settled beside her. "Wanna know why I was up so early this morning?"

She nodded.

"Because lying next to you got me so damned hot I thought I was gonna explode. It was easier to just get up than lie there rock-hard."

"Wanna know why I didn't want to wake up this morning?" she asked, straddling his waist, then raining kisses on his chest.

"Oh, hell, yeah."

"Because I wanted to snuggle up next to you, but knew I shouldn't."

"Why not?"

"I wasn't sure if you liked me for *me,* or if you were afraid you couldn't handle the babies without me."

"Are you crazy?" Jed asked, flipping Annie over so that he was on top. The room had been dark, but he switched on a bedside lamp. "I want you to look into my eyes when I say this. Annie Harnesberry, you are the *total* package. Sweet, gorgeous, funny. The fact that you also happen to be great with kids is just a bonus."

"Really?" she said, scarcely able to trust her ears. "Do you mean that?"

"Hey," he said, toying with one of her curls. "What's this sudden insecurity? Does this have to do with the creeps you used to date?"

She nodded.

"Well, you're with me now. And I promise, you'll never have to worry about another single thing ever again."

His promise was another attempt to control matters that were completely out of his control, but for the moment, she chose to ignore his backsliding. Besides, it was kind of hard to scold him when his touch made it impossible to even think.

Jed woke to a stream of sunlight warming his legs and a wild, wonderful woman warming his chest. Damn, how such a small person managed to hog such a large bed and all the covers he'd never know—not that he was complaining. As far as he was concerned, after the night they'd just shared, she could have anything she wanted. Including his heart.

He rubbed a night's worth of stubble on his chin. Was he actually thinking the "L" word after only a few days?

He frowned.

Probably not. But in the meantime, he wouldn't fight it.

For much longer than he cared to remember, he'd presented a happy face to everyone, while Patti's antics shredded him up inside. Now, after hearing Annie's take on the matter, he realized he'd given his sister all he had to give. And that was enough. She hadn't run off and abandoned her children like he'd originally feared. She'd gone off to nurse her sick husband.

How could he fault her for that?

The beauty beside him stirred.

"Good morning," he said, running his open palm along the rise and fall of her back.

"Yes, it is." She grinned.

Good Lord, what the woman did to him with just that smile. Part of him wanted to stay up here forever, never giving the outside world a chance to intrude. Another part of him wanted to slide a ring on her left hand and show her off to all his friends.

"Am I holding us up again?" she asked, her voice sexy-husky with sleep.

"Nope. I figure with Patti not due home for a few more days, there's no hurry. We can eat Marthe's leftovers for breakfast, then leisurely pack up and get the babies."

She pouted.

"What's wrong?" he asked, tracing her down-turned lips.

"I was hoping for a repeat performance."

"Already?"

"Not up to the challenge?"

He laughed. "Them's fightin' words. Prepare to be dazzled."

Dazzled? Lounging in bed, waiting for Jed to deliver her breakfast, Annie decided that what they'd just experienced was more in the realm of miracles.

She stretched and yawned, utterly content and as pleased with her cozy knotty-pine surroundings as she was with her companion.

They'd been without the babies for a whole night and morning, and look how well they were getting along. All her doubts about him not liking her for *her* were just silly insecurities. Leftover baggage from Conner that she needed to get rid of. As for her failed marriage to Troy, never had she been more determined to banish that disaster from her mind.

This was a morning for fresh starts.

"Hungry?" Jed asked. He carried a meagerly filled plate of leftover ribs and potato salad.

The sweet scent of Marthe's barbecue sauce made her stomach growl.

"Guess so," he said with a lazy smile while Annie put her hands over her noisy belly.

"Excuse me," she said. "I'm hungrier than I thought."

"What time do you usually eat breakfast?" he asked, setting the plate at the foot of the bed, then helping her sit up, bunching pillows behind her back.

"Six. I hardly ever sleep this late."

"Yeah. Me, neither."

"What do you eat?"

"You mean like am I a cereal or oatmeal kind of guy?"

"Right," she said as he set the plate on her lap, helping himself to a plump rib.

"I like bagels and cream cheese," she said. "Scrambled eggs, too. But believe me—" she said, grabbing a rib "—these work just fine."

"Good. Well, I'll leave you in peace to finish up."

Stay.

She wanted to say the word, but how could she when he was evidently eager to make his escape? Still, she had to say *something.* "Don't you want more to eat? I mean, there's not much, but we can share."

He shook his head. "I'm fine. Really, you take your time, and I'll start packing."

So this was it?

Fate's little kick in the pants to remind her not to get too comfortable?

Suddenly no longer hungry, Annie looked at her plate and wanted to cry.

After last night…

This morning…

Jed had been such a perfect lover. He satisfied her every need and deeper desires she hadn't even known she'd felt. How could she have misread him so badly? How could she have ignored all the warning signs that'd raged through her mind?

Her conscience laughed. *How could you have been so stupid? Do the names* Conner and Troy *ring any bells?*

Jed was nothing like them, but that didn't mean they'd make a perfect couple. Or that being with him was a magic ticket to happiness.

If anything, it could be just the opposite.

Chapter 12

Jed slammed the cupboard door above the sink.

Dammit.

What was wrong with him?

Why wasn't he in that bedroom right now, sharing ribs and more kisses with the woman of his dreams?

Because he wasn't good enough for her.

God, look at the way he'd rambled on in there about stupid stuff like what she ate for breakfast.

What could he offer a woman like Annie?

A lifetime of dealing with his neuroses?

Ah, now those he had plenty of. Searching for his sister had turned into a total disaster. If he'd just stayed calm the way he did at work, instead of getting all freaked-out, they wouldn't have made this trip.

And then what?

He would never have gotten to know Annie beyond neighborly waves across the breezeway.

Frowning, Jed worked double-time packing the rest of their stuff.

Maybe never knowing Annie would've been best....

"Sure you've got everything?" Jed asked, glancing at Annie. He climbed behind the wheel of Marthe's red Jeep, then pulled his door shut.

No, Annie wasn't at all sure she had everything.

In fact, she was pretty certain her heart was being left behind.

"Do you think there's something still inside?" Jed asked when she'd settled onto the seat beside him but hadn't closed her door.

She swallowed the knot in her throat.

Yes. She'd left the feel of his kisses and his handholding and touching her breasts. The feel of him being so deep inside her she'd forgotten where she ended and he began.

"Nope," she said, closing her door, then wiping tears from her cheeks so she could face him with a bright smile. "I'm all set to hit the road."

To get back to her safe, quiet condo where no paint would charm its way into her life only to leave her embarrassed, confused and alone.

"Great." He clapped his hands and rubbed them together. Did he have any idea how his eagerness to leave shattered the beauty of everything they'd shared? "Let's go."

Sure, let's go... So they could be that much closer to home, where she'd once again nurse her bleeding emotional wounds. Alone...

"So?" Marthe asked with a big wink. She held a steaming coffee mug in her left hand and nudged Annie with her right elbow. "Did all that by-yourselves time ignite any sparks?"

"What sparks?" Annie asked, hoping her new friend would drop the subject. She scooped Pia from a high chair. The baby smelled like her pink lotion and the sugar-sweetened rice cereal Marthe and Kayla had fed the triplets for breakfast.

"Oh, come on. You two couldn't wait to get us out of there. Well? Did Jed kiss you? Did more happen? Come on, girl, spill it."

"Sorry." Annie kissed the crown of Pia's downy head. "We just spent a quiet night playing Scrabble."

"Don't you believe her," Jed said, entering the dining room from the kitchen to casually rest his hands on her shoulders. "There was nothing quiet about the way she beat me."

Why was he doing this?

Pretending everything was great between them when nothing could be further from the truth?

Marthe said, "She ought to play King Murray over in Leadville. As far as I know, no one's ever beat him. Why don't you two take a day trip over there? Kayla and I will watch the babies. King's been off his feet for a few months now. He loves getting company."

"Who's King?" Annie asked, thrilled to have the topic off Jed and herself.

"Cantankerous old miner," Ditch said, doughnut to his mouth. He strolled in from the kitchen through the same door Jed had. "Old guy'll outlive us all. There's no real hurry to get back," he said. "How about it? You can take Marthe's Jeep. Head over Mosquito Pass. On a weekday, there should be hardly any traffic."

"What do you think?" Jed asked Annie.

Spending more time alone with him in this idyllic mountain setting—even one more day—was out of the question. Her spirit couldn't take it, knowing that their ultimate breakup was coming as soon as they got home.

Wishing she could shout her true feelings, she simply shrugged. "Sounds like a good time, but we probably ought to just head home. I've got to get my classroom ready and I still haven't completely unpacked at my condo."

"You're right," Jed agreed, crushing Annie when he didn't try to change her mind. "I need to get back to work, too."

"Aw, you guys are no fun." Marthe held out her arms. "At least give me a few more minutes with this cutie."

Annie handed Pia over.

Ditch said, "Come on, then, let's check your oil and tires. When Zane installed your new battery, he said you'd been burning oil."

Jed shook his head. "Patti and Howie bought the van used, but it's only three years old. I can't believe—" He'd been about to rag on his sister and brother-in-law for not taking better care of their vehicle, but stopped himself. No more. As Annie had said the night before, it was time to let his sister go. She was a grown woman. If she didn't care that her van burned oil, neither should he.

See? He was slowly but surely getting a handle on this control thing.

"Ready?" Jed asked Annie, wishing she'd taken Marthe and Ditch up on their offer to watch the triplets just one more day. Her decision was the right one, but that didn't make her apparent rejection of him any easier to bear.

While Annie and Marthe checked the house for stray

baby items, Jed shook Ditch's hand and thanked him for all his help.

"Forget it," Ditch said. "I didn't do anything you wouldn't have done for me." He leaned in closer to Jed. "Marthe's gonna kill me if I don't get the inside scoop. Did you and Annie, uh, hook up last night?"

Jed made a face. "Jeez, Ditch, has anyone ever told you that your social skills are sadly lacking?"

His old friend rolled his eyes. "I'll take that as your wounded male pride telling me not only didn't you get any, but your odds for the future aren't looking too good, either. Too bad…" He made a clucking sound. "The two of you are cute together. Annie and Marthe seemed to hit it off, too. I was hoping maybe we'd get to see more of you."

"Oh, you'll probably be seeing plenty of me, just not Annie."

"Ouch." Ditch winced. "Didn't even make it to first base?"

Jed slapped his friend on his back. "Buddy, I didn't even make it on the field."

Nearly a hundred miles from the cabin where she'd allowed herself to fall for an amazing guy who only wanted her for her babysitting skills, Annie slipped off her sandals and propped her feet on the dash.

The heat radiating from the van's windows grew uncomfortable.

Just like the silence between her and Jed.

"The babies seem to be riding better," he said in the tunnel through Loveland Pass.

"It's probably the cereal Marthe fed them for breakfast. Solid foods sometimes help infants sleep."

"Oh." Outside the tunnel, he turned off the van's lights. "How come Patti hasn't been trying that?"

"She might have, which would explain why they were so put out with us. They wanted a more substantial meal than formula."

"Oh."

That's all you can say? Oh?

Annie gritted her teeth.

How could he stand the tension? That morning, they'd been in each other's arms, and now, they talked less than when they were strangers.

Had their night together been nothing to him but a quick roll in the hay?

Jed veered the van onto the side of the highway, and parked on the wide shoulder. "Out with it."

"Out with what?" she asked, traffic whizzing by. A monstrous tractor trailer made the small van shudder. "Is this safe?"

"I'll tell you what isn't—this brick wall you've been making me bust through all morning. If I ticked you off about something, tell me. Don't just sit here glowering the whole ride home."

She crossed her arms. "I'm not glowering."

"The hell you aren't. Look, I'm a big boy. Now that you've had a few hours to think about it, if last night and this morning were a mistake to you, I can take it. Just tell me. We'll agree to keep things casual once we get home."

"Oh, you're a big boy, all right. Big enough to give me what was obviously nothing more than a *thank-you* lay for my babysitting services?"

He flinched. "Please tell me you didn't just say what I think you did, because—"

From the back seat came a whimper. Judging by the

low-pitched sound, it was Ronnie. Annie glanced over her shoulder and, sure enough, it was him. She jiggled his carrier, then got a teething ring from the diaper bag.

"Annie? I'm still waiting for an answer."

"Just stop it, Jed. As you've so graciously pointed out, we're both adults here. I don't know what I expected from you—if anything, maybe that you'd at least sit and have leftovers with me. But *nooooo,* you were in such an all-fired hurry to get away, you couldn't even stand to share a meal, let alone a conversation more meaningful than what we eat for breakfast."

He dropped his head back. "You've got to be kidding. That's what you're upset about? The fact that I didn't eat breakfast with you?"

"You wouldn't have found it a little upsetting if the tables had been turned?"

"Okay…" He reached for Annie's hand and gave it a squeeze. She wanted to snatch it back to the safety of her lap, but physically, emotionally, she couldn't. Just this simple touch meant so much. "First off," he said, "you can't imagine how badly I wanted to stay in that bed and share leftovers with you. But the problem was, if I had eaten that food, there wouldn't have been any for you."

"You mean that's all there was?"

"That's what I just said, isn't it?"

"But there were plenty of ribs left over last night."

"Three a.m. snacks?"

"Oh." Now *Annie* was the one with no comment. How had he done it? The creep. Now she felt bad for scraping her meal into the trash.

"I was trying to be a good guy by leaving you to your feast. And that's why I now have raging heartburn from the dozen doughnuts I put away at Marthe and Ditch's."

"And that's my fault?"

"Heck, yeah."

Despite herself, she grinned, although she was far from convinced that altruism was the full reason he'd left her alone in the bed.

"Look at me," she said.

"Why?" He looked out his side window at a passing red car, instead.

"Because, after all we've shared, I think you owe me that much."

Since he didn't turn away from the window, he obviously didn't agree.

"All right, then," she said with a deep sigh. "You can do it without looking me in the eyes."

"Do what?"

"Tell me your supposed fear of my impending starvation was the only reason you left me alone in that room."

"God, woman." He slammed his palm against the steering wheel. "What do you want from me?"

"The truth." Every bone in her body urged her to jump out of the van and run when Jed had hit the steering wheel, but she stood her ground.

She was no longer a scared newlywed.

He wasn't Troy.

When Jed finally looked at Annie, her gaze was solidly on him. The instant their eyes met, she knew she was on the right track. The man was definitely lying. And if they had to sit here on the side of the road until Christmas, she intended to find out what he was lying about.

"Oh, hell," he eventually said. "You're not going to let this go, are you?"

She shook her head.

"Okay, then, the truth is that you looked so damned beautiful…lying there with your hair all messed up and nothing on but my ratty old sheets. I felt I should've given you more. That I should *be* more."

"You're kidding, right?"

"Do I look like it?"

Judging by his down-turned brows and lips—no. Jed still held her hand, and she tightly gripped his.

Annie asked, "Don't you have a clue how much I've come to care for you?" She shook her head again, glancing out the window while swallowing new tears. "I mean, when I first met you with all those crying babies in your arms, I was captivated. But then the more I saw you in action…going off to work, where you save the world one house, one family, at a time. And then how you tried to save your sister… You're a special breed of man."

Releasing her to cover his face with both hands, Jed said, "I should've just kidnapped you today. Taken you over to Mosquito Pass to give you the pleasure of letting my friend, King, soundly whomp your sweet little butt."

"I would've liked that," she said.

"Then why didn't you say so?"

"Because I thought you didn't want to."

He groaned.

"What's wrong now?" Annie asked.

"It's a good two hours back to the cabin. By the time we get to Marthe and Ditch's to drop off the babies, it's too late to get out there today."

"True. But as Ditch pointed out, now that we know Patti's okay, and she's not due home with Howie for another couple of days, there's really no rush."

Except that every second she was with him, she fell a little more in love.

Annie suddenly had a tough time finding her next breath. *Love?* Was that what made her stomach hurt and feel wonderful at the same time? They'd weathered their first fight and Jed had been the one to start the healing. What kind of man did that?

A very special man, just as she'd told him.

A keeper.

He put the van back in gear and did a U-turn at the next exit.

Annie's pulse hammered a little more quickly.

Granted, Jed's words had been ultrasweet, but that didn't mean he was ready for marriage. Neither was she. She'd just recovered from a crushing blow with Conner, and before that, a disastrous marriage to Troy.

Those things pretty much guaranteed it wasn't love she was feeling, but a giddy, strange mixture of emotions ranging from relief—because this trip had taken her mind off her more pertinent troubles—to a physical yearning for more of Jed's kisses.

Yes, she should've told Jed that the idea of going to meet this King person was nice but that she really ought to head home.

She had things to do.

A bathroom that needed painting.

So why did absolutely nothing in the world sound more appealing than driving over a mountain to play Scrabble with a man who might very well beat her as badly as her grandmother did?

Why? Because all of that would happen with Jed by her side.

Chapter 13

"*Aaarrgghhh!*" Annie cried. "Slow down. We're going to crash!"

Jed laughed. "You need to relax. I've done this a hundred times. Trust me, we'll be fine." She stopped screeching, but still had a white-knuckled grip on the support handle built into the dash.

On this stretch of road before the summit, the ruts in the dirt road were particularly deep—in some places, three or four feet. Jed would never tell Annie, but the drive was proving to be more challenging than he'd expected. But that was okay, because once the day's diversion was over, he'd have another night alone with Annie back at the cabin.

"Do you see how far down it is over there?"

He glanced in the direction Annie pointed. "That's nothing. I've been on old mining trails up the sides of sheer cliffs."

"Yeah, well, maybe I'd be better off back at the out-let mall."

"You didn't have enough of that yesterday?" They'd stopped off on the way back to the cabin. Jed had told Annie that he wanted to get the babies out of the car for a while, but he'd really stopped for her. Jeez, their first time through, she'd looked at the place like a dog catching sight of a bone—only it wasn't bones she was after, but bargain-priced clothes and purses.

He'd lost count of the hours he'd spent sitting out-side dressing rooms jiggling the babies in their stroller. But looking at the hot little denim miniskirt and tight pale-blue T-shirt she had on today, Jed had to admit that every one of those hours had been worth it.

"A woman can never get enough shopping. Remem-ber that, and any woman will adore you forever."

What if I don't want any woman, just you?

He shook his head lightly. The altitude must be affect-ing his reason. They'd gotten along better than ever since their talk, but they still had some incredibly large barri-ers between them—his pigheaded need to be in control.

Who knew where the next few days would lead? And when they returned home, she'd probably be asked on a ton of dates by rich single dads who could afford the steep tuition at the private preschool where she worked.

They'd be professional men who never came home reeking of smoke, even after a shower.

Guys who didn't work twenty-four-hour shifts and didn't have soot under their nails.

"You're awfully quiet over there," Annie said. "Is that a sign that this road is in worse shape than you've been letting on?"

"Nope." But *he* was in worse shape. Why couldn't

he just live in the moment and let the future sort itself out? Lots of women liked firemen. Why should Annie be any different?

Because she was.

Different from most women—*better*—in every conceivable way.

"Are we almost to the top?"

"Yep. And from up there, the view is going to make this bumpy ride worth it."

"Promise?"

"Absolutely."

"All right, then, I'll try to relax. But between worrying that we're about to slide off the mountain and wondering just how badly I'm going to be beaten at Scrabble, I have to say that this hasn't been the most peaceful of days."

"It's not supposed to be peaceful, remember? This is my revenge for the way you crushed me again last night." He'd started the game in the lead, but then he'd caught a whiff of the end-of-the-day scent that was all Annie. A little sweat, a little baby lotion, a whole lot of temptation to resist.

"Hey—it's not my fault you kept drawing bad letters."

Right. No more than it'd been his fault that he'd kept getting distracting peeks down her shirt. Had it really been less than twenty-four hours since he'd tasted what now he could only dream of?

"Yeah, well, you just wait," he said. "King's going to beat you so bad you'll cry—not that I'm looking forward to that part."

"You're mean," she said, sticking out her tongue.

"Check out that view, then tell me I'm mean."

He floored it to get the Jeep over the last big rise, then they'd arrived.

For as far as the eye could see, green forests accentuated the snowcapped peaks. Jed had climbed many of the mountains in the area. Others he'd four-wheeled. But none of those adventures meant as much as being here with Annie.

He parked the Jeep next to the wooden sign serving as a memorial to Father Dyer, a man who'd brought not only religion to the mining town of Leadville in the late 1800s, but mail.

Openmouthed, Annie climbed out and slipped on a light denim jacket. Hand to her forehead, she shaded her eyes from the sun. "Oh, Jed, it's amazing. I feel like we're alone on top of the world."

At this time of day, on a weekend, the spot would be covered with sightseers, but on a Wednesday, Annie and Jed had it all to themselves.

He wanted to lace his fingers with hers and draw her into a kiss, but things were almost comfortable between them again. Why risk doing anything that might harm their fragile new bond?

As good as their relationship currently felt, he couldn't help wondering if they'd somehow gotten it backward by sleeping together so soon. Their making love had been great, but at the same time, it was probably a mistake.

Did Annie feel the same way? Was that part of the underlying tension between them?

Jed had never been the type to casually sleep around. Making love implied a certain level of commitment. He and Annie were practically strangers, yet on a soul-deep level, he'd never felt closer to a woman.

"Thank you for bringing me here," she said.

"Thanks for coming."

"Are you okay?" she asked, nudging his arm.

"Sure. Why? Do I look sick?"

"No. You're just awfully quiet. In fact, you've been quiet ever since I thought we patched things up."

A gust of wind took her OU ball cap.

She shrieked and laughed as she tried to catch it, but the wind sent it skittering across the rocks.

Jed chased it down, then perched it back on her curls. "I forgot to tell you back at the cabin, but you look cute in that."

"Thanks."

"You're welcome."

"Well?" she asked, not looking at the view but at him. "Are you going to tell me what's bothering you?"

"For starters—" he tugged on the bill of her cap "—I bring you all the way up here and all you want to do is analyze me."

"I'm not analyzing you, Jed. I'm showing an interest in your thoughts and feelings. There's a difference, you know." Her kissable lips frowned.

Jed frowned right back. All the signs were there— he was in deep trouble.

"Are you ticked that I ate the last doughnut for breakfast?"

He rolled his eyes.

"Did I snore or hog the covers?"

"What's the matter with you? Why do you have to keep harping at me when we're in this beautiful setting?" *Why can't you just step into my arms and let me hold you while we take in the view?*

"I'm not harping."

"Then what do you call it?"

Annie looked away from him to hide her irrational tears.

What she called it was frustration!

Honestly, how many hints did she have to give the guy before he'd hold her hand or kiss her? Ever since they'd made love, it was as if he'd adopted a hands-off policy, and it was driving her completely nuts.

"Why won't you kiss me?" she finally blurted.

"W-what?"

"You heard me."

"Okay, I haven't kissed you because I thought we weren't going to do that anymore."

"Says who?" She stubbornly raised her chin.

"Me." Jed turned his back on her, mounting a steep dirt trail.

"Oh, so Mr. Control has the final say on everything—including matters of the heart?" Annie chased after him, one hand on her hat, the other holding the flapping halves of her open jacket.

"I didn't hear mention of any hearts." He kept right on walking.

She kept right on chasing. "Yeah, well, if you'd been listening, you'd know I didn't imply any specific hearts, just the general premise."

He stopped and turned to face her. "And if *you'd* been listening, you'd see that I want to kiss you—a lot. But I'm no fool, Annie. Your body language says it loud and clear—hands off."

She laughed. "Really?"

"Yes, really."

"Sorry to bust your ego there, fella, but you might want a refresher course in Body Language One-Oh-

One, because ever since you were so honest with me yesterday—not to mention your patience at all of those outlet malls—I've thought of nothing but doing this…"

On tiptoe, Annie seized initial control of their kiss, but then Jed swept his strong fingers under the fall of her hair, cupping her head, tilting it to get their lips at a better angle. He urged her mouth open, caressing her tongue with his. Waves of hunger and need shimmered through her.

She crept her hands up under his T-shirt, gliding her fingertips along the warm, smooth skin of his back.

"Woman," he said on the heels of a groan. "You make me crazy."

"Ditto," she said before he started to kiss her all over again.

Next intermission, he asked, "Why are we always fighting when this is so much more fun?"

"New pact," she said.

"Let's hear it."

"Kiss first. Bicker later."

"Why do we have to bicker at all?"

"Good question. Let's kiss some more. Maybe that'll help us figure it out."

"You're late," King Murray said the instant he jerked open his door. He sat in an antique wicker wheelchair with a red flannel blanket across his lap. His white hair, beard and bushy eyebrows would have made him look like a cross between Santa and Colonel Sanders—but King didn't sport the requisite smile. "And from the whisker burn around that poor girl's lips, you should've shaved before mugging her in broad daylight."

"Nice to see you, too." Jed gave his old eccentric friend

a hug and made formal introductions before asking, "How do you know I kissed Annie today and not last night?" He slipped his hand reassuringly around her waist.

"What kind of fool do you take me for?" King slammed the door to his sweltering tin shack. He clicked five dead bolts into place. Great. Nothing like spending an afternoon locked in a sauna that reeked of wet newspapers and pipe tobacco. The guy could afford better, but he'd get all cantankerous when pressed to make improvements to his abode. He said he liked it just the way it was. Jed figured who was he to tell the old coot any different?

Jed smiled. "Expecting silver bandits?"

"You can never be too safe," the old man said, jerking his head toward the curtained-off entrance to his mine. "Doc says I'll be out of this chair soon. Come October, I aim to have a whole new shaft open. Once news hits town of the vein I'm gonna find, folks'll be linin' up to be my new best friend."

"Yeah, well, until then, how about a game of Scrabble?"

King snorted. "I've already beat you five ways to Sunday. What's the matter, need a little more stomping on your pride?"

Jed rubbed his palms together. "You're playing Annie, not me."

The old man roared with raspy laughter. "Me play that stick with curls? Not worth my time. Go on, both of you get lost. I've got plannin' to do on where to sink my next shaft."

"Not so fast there, Mr. Murray." Still ticked by his whisker-burn comment, Annie reached into her purse, grabbed her wallet, then slapped a twenty onto the nearest table. "Care to take me up on a friendly wager?"

While the old man gawked at the money, Annie winked at Jed, who seemed equally surprised to find a preschool teacher placing bets.

King cleared his throat. "Take a seat at the kitchen table. I'll get the board. Oh—do you like polka?"

Four hours and four Scrabble games later, Annie was up by eighty bucks—despite the accordions blaring from hidden stereo speakers. While King took a bathroom break, she whispered to Jed, "I feel awful taking his money. Is he on a fixed income?"

Jed chuckled. "The old coot's a millionaire ten times over. He was a Wall Street bigwig before he took up mining."

"For real?"

"Have you had a good look at the mantel?"

Annie looked in that direction and saw what she'd assumed was a Van Gogh print. "No way," she said, marching over for a better look. Up close, the painting's colors glowed.

"He's got a Monet over the john," Jed said. "I don't know if you noticed while answering my phone, but that Gauguin over my bed is the real deal. Marthe and King had this big art discussion one day, and she mentioned I liked that painting. My next birthday, it came to my place via FedEx. Marthe said he bought it from some museum. Off part of the mine is a wine cellar where he stores vintage champagne. Come New Year's, he's a real popular guy. Throws one great party."

"Sounds like fun," Annie said. "I'd love to go if— well, you know what I mean." She tucked her hands in her pockets for the short walk back to the table.

"If we're still together?" Jed asked.

She shrugged.

"Do you want to be?"

"How should I know?" she said, playing it cool despite her racing pulse and the knot in her stomach that felt as if she'd driven her car down a steep hill at sixty miles per hour. "We're practically strangers."

He took a step toward Annie, blasting her with his charming grin. "We didn't feel like strangers the other night."

With him so close, so handsome, so charming, so flirty and fun, she wasn't sure how to reply. Luckily, she didn't have to.

King rolled back into the room. "One more game, Curl Girl. Double or nothing. What do you say?"

From what she'd learned about the guy, Annie suspected he might be setting her up. One-hundred-and-sixty bucks bought a lot of paint. "I don't know," she said. "That's a great deal of money."

"Chicken?"

"No, but come on—I'm a preschool teacher. My job's rewarding, but not exactly lucrative."

He grunted, then wheeled over to a cheap metal filing cabinet and pulled open the creaky bottom drawer. He fished something out, shut the drawer, then wheeled back. "How about this to sweeten the pot?" From out of a velvet pouch he withdrew a bejeweled egg.

Faberge?

She gulped. "Is that what I think it is?"

"Bah." He waved his hand in dismissal. "Got three more stashed around here somewhere. Wife liked 'em real well."

"Did she die?"

Jed coughed. "I've heard the Broncos are going to have a great season."

King glared at Annie. "The no-good wench said I

spent too much time underground and not enough with her. She left me. Married some fool nightclub singer down in Phoenix." To Jed, he muttered, "If you ever tell anyone I said this, I'll flat out deny it, but son, once you two hitch up, make sure you don't spend too much time on the job. Work enough to pay the bills, but remember—you've got to tend your flowers."

"My *flowers,* huh?" Jed shot a wink Annie's way. "Does that mean I get more than one?"

Back at the cabin, over a dinner of deli sandwiches, chips and giant dill pickles, Annie eyed her Faberge egg. "I still can't believe he just gave this to me. The thing's got to be worth a fortune."

Jed shrugged. "It's only money. King was crazy for his wife, he just didn't always show it. She was a blonde. I suspect you remind him of her, otherwise he'd have whomped you five out of five games instead of letting you win."

"Oh—you think he *let* me win?"

"That's what I said, isn't it?" He dabbed the corners of his smile with a yellow paper napkin. "Because what Marthe and I failed to tell you, is that while you're good, he's *nationally ranked* good."

"So the whole day was a setup?"

"It was supposed to be," he said, before taking a bite of ham sandwich. "Who could've guessed King would actually take a liking to you? He hates everyone."

Reaching across the table, Jed laced his fingers with Annie's. "You wanna be in my garden? I'm going to take old King's advice and tend my flowers well." He waggled his eyebrows.

"Beast."

"Your beast if you'll have me."

"Yeah, but for how long?" she whispered, shocked

that she'd asked the question, dizzy from the pace of her heart.

"How long do you want?"

"You're talking in circles."

"So are you." He raised her hand to his lips.

Closing her eyes, Annie willed her pulse to slow. How many sides did the man have? Here was yet another. A soft, romantically teasing side that she adored every bit as much as his many others.

"Do you think you could stand being mine for a month?"

Unable to speak, she nodded.

"How about two?"

She nodded again.

"Want to be my date for King's New Year's party? We could head out right after Christmas. Ski Copper Mountain and Breckenridge, then—" He stopped himself. "Listen to me. Taking over your holidays when I know you've got family obligations."

"Yes. My grandmother."

"So you probably don't want to do anything for New Year's?"

She wrinkled her nose. "I'm thinking we might want to work on our communication skills."

"That's a given, but you still haven't told me if you're penciling me in for the holidays."

Slipping her arms around his neck, she pressed her lips to his, telling him in the plainest way she knew…

Yes—to skiing and New Year's and most anything else he might want to offer.

Chapter 14

There, beside the small oak table where their meals sat, half-eaten, Jed drew Annie to her feet, sliding his hands to the small of her back, deepening their kiss with bold strokes of his tongue.

"I'm not even sure how it happened," he said, "but I love you, Annie Harnesberry. We've both had some tough times, but somehow this—*us*—feels right."

Her cheek against his chest, she nodded, surrendering herself to the feel of his heartbeat, so steady and sure.

Yes, a tiny voice inside still warned her to be careful—not to jump into something she wasn't ready for. But then the voice of reason kicked in, reminding her that Jed was nothing like either of the men who'd hurt her so badly before.

Like Troy, Jed wanted to be in control, but he proved every day that he didn't *have* to be. He never hit when he didn't get his way. He didn't even yell.

And when she'd asked Jed if he only wanted her around as a sitter for his niece and nephews, his answer was all she could ever hope for and more.

So as she watched him unfasten the buttons of her denim jacket, did she feel ready to make an unofficial commitment to Jed even though she barely knew him?

Yes, because she *did* know him.

In her soul.

Where it truly counted.

He eased her jacket off her shoulders and arms, draping it over the back of her chair.

She shivered, and he ran his large, warm hands up and down her shoulders. "Cold?"

"Uh-huh."

"Nervous?"

"How did you know?"

"Your lower lip quivers."

"It does?"

He nodded, outlining her mouth with the tip of his index finger. "And your pupils widen."

"Sorry," she wasn't sure what else to say.

"I don't want you to be sorry," he said. "I love that about you. That I know what you're thinking."

I love that about you, too.

"Do you want to know what *I'm* thinking?" he asked.

She nodded, and he skimmed his finger lower, down her chin and throat. Making a sharp right at her collarbone, he etched a new path under her thin cotton T-shirt to the strap of her bra. Slipping his finger underneath, he said, "With your consent, I'd like to take you to bed, then just hold you all night long. Does that sound okay?"

"More than okay… Perfect."

* * *

Never had Annie awakened happier or more content, as if all was right with her world.

Jed lay on his back beside her, broad chest bare. His hair was always spiked and messy, but this morning especially so. Was he one of those who moved around a lot in their sleep? She'd slept so soundly beside him, she didn't have a clue.

She curved her hand over his shoulder, grinning when it didn't reach even halfway around.

At the time she'd left him, Troy's size had frightened her. Jed's size had always made her feel more secure.

She closed her eyes and sighed, reflecting on how much her life had changed in less than a week's time.

In a roundabout way, Jed had proposed, and she'd accepted.

"What's got you so deep in thought?" he asked, startling her.

Hand to her chest, she said, "Jeez. You scared me to death."

"Sorry." He drew her into his arms. After kissing her forehead, he moved on to her lips.

"Mmm…you're forgiven."

"Thanks." After a few minutes of holding her, he asked, "Hungry?"

"Not really. You?"

He shook his head. "I'm actually not feeling so hot."

"You don't think you're coming down with something, do you?"

"Nah. Just nerves."

She scooted up in the bed to see his face better. "About what?" *Not us, I hope.*

"There goes that quivering lip of yours," he said with

the slow, sexy grin she'd come to love. "Trust me, this has nothing to do with you, okay? I'm wondering what I'm going to say when I see Patti."

"What do you mean? Won't you simply be happy to see her?"

Bunching a pillow under his head, he shrugged. "Of course, I'll be glad she's home safe, but it's more complicated than that."

"How so?"

"It just is. But it shouldn't be, so I'll shut up."

"You don't have to on my account. Go ahead, explain how you feel."

"That's the thing," he said, drawing her against him, playing with one of her curls. "I don't even know myself—except when it comes to how I feel about you."

"Which is?" she teased.

"Good." He kissed the crown of her head. "Very, very good."

"I'm going to miss you," Marthe said, practically suffocating Jed with the strength of her hug. Ditch helped Annie gather and load the last of the baby gear.

"You've hardly seen me," he said, hugging Marthe back.

"I know, but somehow just having you here feels like old times. Like back when we were kids, hanging out all summer. No responsibilities, just fun." She swiped at a few fat tears.

"Hey," he said, "I already told you Annie and I will be back for New Year's. She wants to fix her grandmother up with King."

Laughing through her tears, Marthe said, "Annie told me. I think it's a super idea."

"So why are you still crying?"

"Oh, God, Jed. I'm pregnant. I've suspected it for a while, but I just took one of those home tests this morning. Ditch doesn't know yet."

"Why the tears?" Jed asked. "He's going to be thrilled."

"No," she said. "We can barely afford the two we have." With Sponge Bob blaring on TV, she cried all the harder, leaving Jed not sure what to do. Of course, he held on to her for dear life, but what could he say? The financial aspect of having kids was a sobering fact.

While he couldn't be more pleased about how things were going with Annie, he'd made love to her twice without protection. She could be pregnant. Sure, he had savings—more than enough to feel comfortable asking Annie to marry him, *if* and *when* it came to that point. But he didn't have nearly enough to raise and support a baby—or babies—of their own.

But if Annie told him on the drive back to Pecan that she was expecting his son or daughter, he'd be thrilled despite any financial hardships they'd encounter. And so would his good friend Ditch when he heard the news about the latest addition to his own family.

After telling Marthe just that, Jed said, "Do you want me to break it to him for you?"

She sniffled and shook her head. "I think I'll farm Kayla and Billy out to Ditch's mom this weekend, then let him know over a steak and baked potato—plenty of butter. He's always in a good mood after eating butter."

"Aren't we all?" Jed said with a laugh.

"I think we're ready." Annie stepped up behind Jed, slipping her arms around his waist. "Mmm… I missed you."

Marthe cast Jed her first real smile since they'd arrived. "I can't wait to make Ditch pay up on that thirty-minute massage he owes me for losing our bet."

Easing beside Jed, Annie said, "I still can't believe you two bet on whether or not Jed and I would—Marthe? What's wrong? You look like you've been crying."

"Wh-where's Ditch?" she managed to ask.

"Outside with the kids," Annie said. "Billy got gum on one of the front stroller wheels, so Ditch is making him scrape it off."

"He's such a g-good father," Marthe said, starting to cry all over again.

Annie was instantly by her side, putting her arm around her friend's slumped shoulders. "Please tell me what's wrong."

Marthe did.

And when she'd finished, Annie snatched a paper towel from the counter and wiped her cheeks. "I think this is fabulous. You two are great with kids. Why shouldn't you have more?"

"B-because they cost a fortune. There are medical bills and clothes and lessons and college and—"

Annie said, "Wait here. I've got just the thing to ease your mind."

Annie left the room and returned with a black velvet pouch in hand. "Once we're gone, I want you to open this. It's yours."

Marthe's eyes widened as she accepted the gift. "It's heavy. What is it?"

"Your first baby gift from me to you. Now, stop worrying and start celebrating. Babies are supposed to bring joy." Annie kissed her friend's forehead, then told her how much she'd miss her with a heartfelt hug.

* * *

They'd said their goodbyes, loaded up the babies and were on their way home, but even fifty miles down the road, Jed couldn't believe what Annie had done for Marthe and Ditch.

He finally asked, "Do you have any idea how much that egg must be worth?"

"I'm hoping it's enough to buy a truckload of diapers and several years college tuition."

"I'd say it's worth a damn sight more than that. What made you give it away?"

Annie lifted those adorable feet of hers onto the dash and wriggled her toes. "A pretty selfish reason actually."

"Okay, let's hear it."

With a smile, she asked, "Why should I tell you?"

"Because after all we've been through, we're a team. And that's pretty much a rule in all team sports—no secrets kept from other team members."

"Oh, well, in that case…" The cocky look she gave him made him want to pinch one of her pink-tipped toes.

"I'm waiting," he said, slowing to take the next curve on the winding road lined with ponderosa pines and stands of aspen.

"With us so happy, I couldn't stand seeing Marthe so sad. I figured, what the heck? It wasn't as if I'd even had time to become attached to the egg. And anyway, I figure King would approve of my decision."

"I figure you're right. So? What did you think about Marthe being so upset about her pregnancy?"

"I can't say I blame her. Finances are something to consider."

"Yeah, I thought so, too."

"Plus, there's the whole age issue. Kayla and Billy are already half-raised. It's got to be scary thinking you have your child-rearing days almost behind you, and then starting over again."

"You do want kids, though, right?" The second the question was out, Jed wished he hadn't asked. He'd broached the subject the other day when they'd been fooling around, but this time he was serious. What if Annie said no?

"Absolutely."

His shoulders slumped with relief. Good. He wanted kids, too. Maybe not today, but soon.

"You?"

When he nodded, her expression brightened.

And together, babies for once contentedly napping, Annie and Jed rode out the miles that brought them closer to their futures.

"You're not pregnant, are you?" Jed asked just past the exit for the Denver International Airport.

"What?" Annie looked at him sharply, brushing away tears.

"You're crying. And it hasn't been that long since we heard Marthe's news."

Annie rolled her eyes. "No. I'm not pregnant—at least, I don't think so."

"So what's the matter?"

"Look in your mirror. The mountains are so beautiful. How can you stand to leave them?"

Jed laughed—not because he thought she was being silly, but because he understood how she felt. "Patti and my mom always cried when we left. Dad never knew if they were crying because our vacation was over, or because of their feelings about the mountains."

"Maybe a little of both," Annie said, blowing her nose on a fast-food napkin she'd found between the seats. "I didn't expect to have so much fun. This might sound a little odd, but since we're members of the same team…"

"Yeah, yeah," he said, eyes smiling.

"I know this trip was good for you in that it jolted you into realizing that Patti's capable of looking after herself. It was also good for me. The past few years haven't been all that great, and I was beginning to think I'd never trust again."

Jed reached across the space between them, and locked his fingers with hers. "Thanks. After what Patti put me through, you can't know how much that means to me. For a while there, I felt like I was going out of my mind."

"Patti might not know it, but she's very lucky to have you."

"Right about now, *I* feel like the lucky one."

From the back, one baby started to cry, then another and another.

Jed groaned. "I had to go and jinx us, didn't I?"

"Hey," Annie said, pointing to a run-down billboard in the shape of a giant sunflower. "Look on the bright side. We're only fifteen miles from the world's only working car made entirely from sunflower seeds—excluding the engine, of course."

"Oh, of course." Jed smiled.

"Annie, honey, wake up." Jed lightly shook her awake.

Hands prayered beneath her cheek, her legs drawn

up in what appeared to be an uncomfortable position beneath her, she said, "Where are we? What time is it?"

"We're home. And it's about three in the afternoon." After getting a late start the previous morning, they'd taken their time, and even spent the night in a motel outside Salina.

Annie inched into an upright position so slowly, it made Jed cringe.

"What hurts?"

"Everything," she said. "Remind me not to fall asleep sideways again."

"Gotcha. But you were so out of it after that last diaper stop, I think you would've fallen asleep standing on your head." He grinned, smoothing his hand across her rumpled curls.

"So we're really home? As in Pecan?"

"Yep. I already put the babies inside. I just left the van running with the air on so you wouldn't bake. Compared to that perfect mountain weather, being in this heat again pretty much sucks."

"We could always go back."

"Believe me, if it weren't for the twenty or so messages from my captain, the second we get hold of Patti, that's exactly what I'd suggest we do."

"You're not in trouble, are you?"

"Nah. The boss just gets cranky in all this heat."

"But isn't he used to it? He's a fireman."

"Good point," he said. "The next time I feel like going on a suicide mission, I'll be sure to bring that up."

"How are you doing?" Annie asked at about eight, rocking Pia in her arms.

Patti and Howie's plane had landed in Tulsa at six-forty, and they were due at Jed's apartment any minute.

Jed shrugged. "I'm all right. I'll be better once I've got you all to myself, though."

She laughed, relieved to see him able to joke about their situation. Truthfully, she'd been worried about how his meeting with Patti would go. The way he'd first talked about letting his sister have it had spooked her.

Before hitting her, Troy had yelled—loudly enough that the last time, the time he'd sent her to the hospital—the neighbors had called the police. If they hadn't, who knows where she'd be now? Or if she'd even be alive.

Truck lights shone through the slats of the mashed-potato-beige vertical blinds on Jed's windows. She made a face. "We've got to get you some color in here."

"What's wrong with my place?"

"Everything," she said. "Where should I start?"

A car door slammed shut

A few seconds later, another.

Annie watched helplessly as a muscle popped in Jed's jaw. What was he thinking? "Is there anything I can do to help?" she asked.

Hand possessively on her bare thigh, he said, "Don't leave me."

She nodded just as a knock sounded on the door. "Jed?" a woman's voice called out. "It's us."

Chapter 15

Jed looked at Howie's crutches, bruised cheeks, black left eye and right foot in a cast. He knew that as awful as Howie looked nearly a week after the accident, he must've really been bad off when his sister left town to be with him. But an hour of watching Patti coo over her babies, acting as if nothing had ever happened, filled him with slow-burning frustration.

While Jed was in the kitchen getting everyone Cokes, playing along with Patti's *everything's normal* routine, he couldn't stop from replaying the desperation he'd felt. The sheer knife-edged panic that'd seized him the moment he'd realized something serious had happened to his sister.

He'd had the same feeling when his little brother was in the house dying. The same feeling when his parents had died and when Patti became a wild teen, running with the wrong crowd, determined to destroy her life before it'd even begun.

He looked up and Patti was in the kitchen. Grinning up at him with her glass held under the ice dispenser on the fridge, she said, "Some excitement, huh? Aside from the fact that Howie was hurt and my ankle's sprained, I haven't had such an adventure since—"

"An *adventure?* You think this week was an adventure?"

She waved off his concern. "Good grief, Jed, stop being such an old grouch. You know what I mean. The adventure of it. All this flying and driving and trying to get in touch with each other. In retrospect, it's been quite exciting. Maybe we ought to do it all again, only—"

"Dammit, Patti!" Jed smacked his palm against a cabinet door. "This is so typical of you. Every grandma and her poodle has a cell phone these days, but—"

"Speaking of which, where was *your* cell while all of this was going on?"

Count on Patti to bring up his mistake when he was in the middle of bawling her out. Glaring at his feet, he said, "My phone was back here, but we're talking about you. About how you didn't reach me before I left for the cabin. You just left me here with three infants. *Me.* A bachelor who doesn't know the first thing about babies. And you just took off, without even trying to get word to me, what—"

"I did try! At least fifty times. Do you want me to list them all? One, at the airport, only you weren't home. Two, at—"

"Knock it off!" Jed raged, unable to keep his anger with her at bay.

In the living room, Annie jumped. The last time she'd heard yelling like that was with Troy.

Howie moaned. "Oh, no, here they go. Jed means well, but where Patti's concerned, he's never learned to let go."

"She's all he has."

"I know," Howie said. "It's the same for her with him. I mean, I know she has me now, too, but it's different with Jed. They have a strange bond that I'm still trying to figure out."

Jed railed on. "This has to be your last stunt, Patti. The last time you're going to act like a child. Running off without telling anyone where you were going was just that—childish. No matter what the circumstance. What if the babies had been older? Old enough to know that Mommy was gone, and worry that she might not be coming back? What could I have told them?"

"I'm sorry," Patti said, her voice broken. "I didn't *not* call you on purpose, Jed, any more than you purposely forgot your cell. You act like I deliberately set out to push your buttons. God, you always think the worst of me."

"I think I'll go referee," Howie said, reaching for his crutches.

Annie clasped her fingers tightly on her lap, glad the babies were upstairs sleeping.

"That's just it!" Jed roared. "You've done a crap-load of button-pushing in the past, Patti. Remember the time you called me wasted from Jasper Henning's party? You asked me to come and get you, then you took off with Greg Davis. You didn't come home for three days. And how about the time you—"

"Shut up!" Patti fired back. "I'm not a messed-up kid any more."

"No," he said. "You're mother who thought nothing of hopping on a plane without—"

Annie squeezed her eyes shut.

What was she doing?

Jed's raised voice sounded remarkably like Troy's.

Her ex-husband yelled first, and hit later.

Was that how it would be with Jed? After all, if he yelled at his sister, what was to stop him from yelling at his girlfriend—or his wife?

Annie knew better than to have fallen for him. How many warning signs had she chosen to ignore? His controlling nature. His seeming perfection. And now the yelling.

It was all the same.

How blind was she? How dumb?

Had she learned nothing in the past five years? All along she'd been worried that Jed only liked her for her skills with the babies. Ha. That was nothing compared to the dark truth she was now finding out.

Troy had begun their relationship making Annie believe he was the answer to her every prayer. He'd bought her flowers and candy and sung her sappy love songs on karaoke night down at their favorite local bar.

Annie grabbed her purse, then crept out the front door.

"You dumb, bitch. I told you to get light beer. You know I'm in training for that bodybuilding show at the gym."

"I'm sorry, Troy. They were out of light. I figured this would do."

"Yeah, well you figured wrong." He slammed his fist
against the wall, creating one more dent among many.

*Cringing inside, always inside herself, Annie fussed
with the dish towel that hung from the rack beside the
sink.*

So pretty.

She'd just focus on the pretty pink cabbage roses.

*The towels had been a gift from her grandmother,
who'd warned her about Troy. Grams told Annie she
was marrying him too fast. That she was trying to escape the pain she felt over losing her grandfather, then
her parents to another overseas assignment. Looking
for shortcuts to achieve her dream of starting her own
family.*

Bam.

*Instead of the wall, Troy turned to Annie, smacking
her hard across the face. "The next time I tell you to
get light, if State Line's out, go to another store. You
know I had a bad day down at the plant. Why do you
want to go and ruin my night, too?"*

"I—I don't," she said, slipping further inside herself.

*He hit her again. "Get the hell out of here. Don't
come back until you've got the right beer."*

Annie hadn't bothered coming back at all.

In the Emergency Room, she'd filed a police report.
The next day, divorce papers. With no children, and
practically no shared property, the matter was settled
soon enough—especially since Troy already had his
next female punching bag in line.

Annie tried to warn the girl, but it hadn't done any
good. Charmed senseless by Troy's good looks and
honed body, Heather could have cared less about any-

thing other than snagging the man she thought he was, rather than the nightmare Annie knew him to be.

Minutes later in her condo, door closed and locked behind her, Annie quickly repacked her duffel bag, snatched her car keys and left Jed much the same way she'd left her husband five years earlier.

Quietly.

Without a fuss.

Forever.

Jed stood in the kitchen, legs shaky from delayed relief. His anger with Patti came from loving her so damned much, and she knew that. He pulled her into a hug.

"Aw," Howie said, hobbling into the room. "I figured it'd only be a few minutes before you two made up. And for the record," he said to his wife, "I agree with your brother. If you'd pulled that stunt on me, I'd have called every cop from here to the Grand Canyon."

Patti rolled her eyes. "Both of you lay off. I get it. Believe me, if anything like this ever happens again— which I pray it never does—I'll hire singing telegrams if that's what it takes to get word to you."

"Thank you," Jed said, giving her an affectionate pat on the back. "That's all I ask." Glancing at the glass in his hand, he said, "Jeez, I came in here to get Annie a soda, but I was so mad at you, I forgot all about her. I'll be right there with your drink!" he hollered.

"She's great," Patti whispered. "Perfect for you. And here you are complaining about me running off, when you should be thanking me. The two of you never would've gotten together without me."

Jed gave Patti one of his famous big-brother frowns.

Teetering on one crutch, Howie slipped his free arm around his wife, and said "Honey, I wouldn't press your luck."

"Listen to your husband," Jed said, Annie's cola in hand as he headed back to the living room—only to find that she wasn't there.

Since the door to the downstairs bathroom was open and the light was off, he assumed she'd gone upstairs to check on the babies.

Patti and Howie were making out in the kitchen so Jed left them, taking the stairs two at a time to see about getting some action of his own.

"Annie?" She wasn't in his room.

Or the bathroom.

Or the guest room where his niece and nephews were still asleep.

Halfway down the stairs, he shouted, "Patti, is Annie with you?"

Silence.

Back in the kitchen, Jed walked in on a hot and heavy scene. "Dang, guys, get a room."

"Good idea," Patti said with a giggle. "Howie, I'll pack up the babies, you start hobbling to the van. By the time I'm done, maybe you'll be there."

"Ha-ha. Is she always this mean to sick people?" Howie asked Jed.

"Unfortunately, yes." Jed flipped on the laundry-room light. "Where the hell could Annie be?"

"Maybe she went to get something from her unit?" Patti headed upstairs. "Give me a hand. I'm sure she'll be right back."

By the time Jed got his sister, brother-in-law and their triplets out the door, it was pushing ten o'clock.

Not only was Annie not in her condo, but her car wasn't in the lot. He searched his place for a note, thinking she might've gone to the store.

No such luck.

What would make her take off like that without saying a word? That was Patti's style, but definitely not Annie's. She was as responsible as they came.

She probably hadn't wanted to interrupt his reunion with his sister, and had just run to the store for milk and bread.

He sighed. Hadn't they played enough *Find the Missing Loved One* this week?

No matter how impossible it seemed, that was what Annie had become. His loved one. His lucky charm. His everything. What would he do without her?

Fighting an all-too-familiar mounting dread, Jed hoped he'd never have to find out.

In the meantime, he picked up the TV remote, found an Atlanta Braves game, and sat down on the sofa to wait.

"Don't worry, Grandma! It's just me." Annie stood in her grandmother's front hall and punched the code to stop the chirping alarm. She breathed in the cinnamon potpourri that had always given her a sense of calm and well-being. Yes, this was her true home, and Annie never wanted to leave it again.

"Land's sake, girl," Grams called out. "What are you doing here at this time of night?"

"I missed you," Annie said, forcing a smile and an upbeat tone to her voice. "So I thought I'd come up for a visit."

Her grandmother turned on the hall light, ruining

Annie's cover of darkness. "You've been crying. Come on, let's get you some cocoa, then tell me all about it."

"There's nothing to tell."

Lips pursed, the white-haired woman said, "You've never successfully lied to me. Don't think you're going to start now. March."

Thankful to have someone else take charge of her disastrous life, even briefly, Annie did as she was told.

At midnight, Jed called his friend Ferris down at the police station.

After dispatch put him through, Ferris had the nerve to laugh at Jed. "You mean to tell me you've already lost another woman?"

"Dammit, Ferris, this isn't funny. Annie wouldn't just take off. I know her like I know myself."

"Yeah, but do you know her as well as you know your own sister? You kind of screwed the pooch on that one, pal. If you'd been patient like I asked, we would've found Patti probably before you and your new lady-friend had hit the state line. I left you at least a half-dozen messages. If you hadn't forgotten your cell, we could've—"

"I know, I know. Saved me an eight-hundred-mile useless trip." Jed rubbed his forehead. He missed all those messages because, as it turned out, he'd used the wrong remote code. He'd take that one to the grave! "Believe me, I know better than anyone that I screwed up big-time."

"You said it." His friend's sarcastic tone undoubtedly matched his equally condescending expression, which Jed could picture all too easily.

Jed was well aware that his friends thought he was an idiot, but he had to defend himself.

"Annie's different," he argued, fully aware that he sounded insane. "I can't explain it. It's a gut feeling. She's the only woman for me, man. But she's gone. It's been a few hours already, and—"

"Right." Ferris chuckled again. "We'll keep an eye out for her car, but after what happened with Patti, your reputation's mud around here, pal. If you find any signs that she might've been abducted or is in some other kind of trouble, call me back and I'll be glad to help. Otherwise—"

Jed hung up the phone, and convinced himself that he didn't really have to throw up. The sudden waves of nausea he felt were all in his head. Just like the gnawing worry that he'd been wrong about Annie. That she wasn't the woman he'd first thought her to be.

If that turned out to be true—what then?

How would he cope with her living right across from him?

Every opening and closing of her door would remind him how foolish he'd been to so blindly trust her?

The control freak in him knew better. The romantic in him needed to butt out.

How can you even think that? What if she's hurt? What if she needs you? Where's your sense of loyalty? Compassion?

Hoping to permanently squelch that damned romantic side of his, Jed searched his wallet for the slip of paper with a number he'd used once, then dialed it.

Someone picked up on the third ring. A familiar voice said, "Jed?" His heart sank when he recognized Annie's grandmother instead of the woman he loved.

He'd spoken with Annie's grandma once before—
right before their trip. Call him old-fashioned, but he'd
wanted to introduce himself. Ask permission.

"Yes, Mrs. Harnesberry, it's me. Sorry to call so
late, I just—"

"Annie's here, and she's crying. Did you hurt her?"

He toyed with the buttons on the alarm clock next
to the phone. God, Ferris and the other guys at the station were right to think he was an idiot. What was the
matter with him?

"If I did hurt her," he said. "I honestly don't know
how. One minute I was chewing out my sister, then Patti
and I were hugging. I apologized to her for getting all
bent out of shape. She forgave me. So then I went to
find Annie, to apologize to her for letting my frustration get the better of me, but she was gone."

Annie's grandmother sighed. "Do you promise that's
all that happened? You didn't hit her?"

"*Hit her?* What kind of monster do you think I am?
I might have some kinks to work out, but my idea of
therapy isn't hitting girls."

"That's all I needed to know."

"Yeah, but—"

"Do you love my granddaughter?"

Was this a trick question?

"Well?" she asked.

"I'm not sure how it happened so fast, but yes," Jed
said, "I do love Annie."

"Did she tell you anything about her first marriage?"

"She was married?"

The older woman cleared her throat. "Do you like
chicken and dumplings?"

"Yes, ma'am."

"Good. Me, too. Be here at six o' clock tomorrow night, and I'll make you and my granddaughter a big batch." Click.

She'd hung up, leaving Jed more confused than ever.

"Who called?" Annie asked, towel-drying her hair.

"What do you mean?" Grandma Rose didn't look up from her nightly crossword puzzle.

"I thought I heard the phone ring."

"Who would call at this hour?"

Jed.

To explain what there was no explanation for.

But he didn't even know where she was, let alone her grandmother's phone number.

"You're right," Annie said, lowering herself onto the sofa, then raising her feet so she could rub her cold toes. What was her problem? Ever since leaving Jed's, she couldn't get warm.

"Ready to tell me all about it?" her grandmother asked.

Not until she'd figured it out for herself.

Chapter 16

The next morning, Annie sat in a wash of sunshine in her grandmother's breakfast nook. Outside, it was probably already ninety, so why did the house feel as cold as the morning after Christmas?

She felt let down.

The presents were all unwrapped.

She'd gotten socks and underwear instead of a Barbie Dream House and new art set.

There'd been so much promise with Jed. All the glitter and potential for lifelong happiness. But Troy had looked pretty good in the beginning, too. She hadn't married him knowing he'd turn out to be wife-beating scum.

Annie slid her fingers into her hair, pulling hard.

How could she have been so wrong about Jed?

First, she'd believed he was like Conner, using her to

watch Pia and Richard and Ronnie, only to find out that he was much worse. And the whole time they'd been together, he'd hidden his dark side from her. All along he'd pretended to be someone he wasn't.

He said he loved her, but even that was a lie.

Everything. Every kiss, touch, glance.

Every conversation that seemed to unite them had only led her that much closer to seeing—

"That coffee sure smells good," her grandmother said, ambling through the kitchen door. "Did you make enough for two?"

"Try about two dozen."

"Rough night?" Grandma Rose asked.

"Rough life," Annie said.

"Ready to talk?"

Even though she wasn't, Annie knew her grandmother would eventually get to the bottom of her morose mood. She might as well get started on the torture of explaining.

She took a sip of coffee and fiddled with the sugar dispenser.

"Well?" her grandmother probed.

Sighing, Annie said, "I know you were probably expecting some big, hairy story, but the condensed version is that I met this guy, thought he was the one, and he turned out to be no different from Troy."

Lips pursed, her grandmother shook her head. "Is this Jed we're talking about?"

"Yeah. How many other guys do you think I could fall for in under a week? Wait a minute… I never told you about him. How could you—"

"I have my ways," her grandmother said, moving across the kitchen for one of the yellow mugs hanging from beneath the upper cabinets. "This is the same guy who yakked my ear off on the phone. He was getting my permission to take you traipsing off to Colorado."

"He *what?*" It was a good thing that Annie's mug sat firmly on the table, or she would've dropped it.

"I didn't tell you?"

"Uh, no."

Grandma Rose waved her hand as if the bomb she'd just dropped hadn't just rocked her to the core.

"Do you know what this means? He knows where I am. He's done one of those lunatic Internet searches on me, and now he'll probably turn into some stalker, and—"

"Stop." Her grandmother rested her gnarled hand atop Annie's smooth one.

When had her best friend gotten so old? What was she going to do when her grandmother was gone?

"Annie, doll, your instincts were right about this one. At least I thought they were, since I got the same impression of him. He didn't find my number on the Internet. He simply called information. When he phoned me, he explained who he was and how he'd asked you to go with him to find his sister. I was worried at first, so I asked if he'd meet me for a quick coffee, since I only live an hour away from Pecan. He even brought the babies with him. One look at the love and fear for his sister in that young man's eyes, and I knew you were in good hands. I saw—"

"Don't you think it's weird that he didn't tell me about meeting you?"

Shrugging, her grandmother said, "I thought it was weird that that you didn't even take the time to tell me you were leaving the state with a stranger. Jed said he didn't want you to know he'd been up here, because he was afraid you'd think he was being silly. And judging by your expression, he was right. But think about it, *Anniebug*. What kind of man in this day and age actually cares enough about a woman to ask her grandmother's permission before he takes her on a road trip?"

"Mind games." Annie tapped her temple. "Don't you see? He wanted you to believe he was all nice and polite and considerate. But that's only on the surface. Inside, he's a self-confessed control freak—just like Troy. Last night he was yelling. I know what comes next."

After pouring herself a cup of coffee, Annie's grandmother joined her at table. Eyes shiny with unshed tears. "They should have locked Troy up and thrown away the key for what he did to you."

"Finally, something we agree on."

"Not really," her grandmother said. "At least, not for the reasons you think."

"What? He's a monster. That's a given."

Grandma Rose took a napkin from the holder in the center of the table and pressed it to her eyes. "Yes," she said after blowing her nose. "He's sick because of what he did to you physically, but what he's done to your heart, Annie—that's the true crime. You've given him such power. Your every thought and action is so tainted by what he did that you can't even trust your own innate sense of right and wrong. Yes, your Jed likes to be in control, but unlike Troy, who needed to be in control to raise his own pitiful self-worth, Jed's needs center around ensuring the well-being of the people he loves. Like his sister. And you, Annie. *You*."

Slowly shaking her head, swallowing the lump at the

back of her throat, Annie said, "But you weren't there last night. You didn't hear him yelling at Patti."

"And you didn't, either. Because if you had, you'd have known that he apologized to Patti, then gave her a big hug."

Eyeing her grandmother, Annie asked, "And you know this how?"

"Remember how you thought you heard the phone last night? You did. He called, and—"

"Jeez, Grandma, whose side are you on? Have you listened to a word I've said? *He yelled.*"

"Just like I'm yelling, Annie! People argue. Get over it. Now who's the control freak? You can't cocoon yourself into a little sterilized box where there won't ever be any pain, baby. Yes, it'd be nice, but it's unrealistic. That's mostly why I'm angry at Troy—for destroying your view of the world and making you believe all men are bad. Sweetheart, please, open your heart. Trust yourself to believe in goodness again. At least where Jed's concerned, consider giving him a second chance. I'm not saying you should run out and marry him tomorrow, but just talk to him. Explain about Troy and what you went through."

"What if I can't?"

"Can't what?" Grams asked. "Talk to him?"

Annie nodded.

"That's your choice. I'm not going to force you to talk. Neither will he. But so you know, I invited him for dinner. Tonight at six. Chicken and dumplings. Your favorite."

"I'm not hungry."

"Good." Dabbing at the corners of her eyes, her

grandmother pushed back her chair and stood. "That just means more for the rest of us."

Behind the wheel of his truck, hot wind ruffling his hair, Jed should have felt better.

All he really felt was tense.

How could Annie have kept her marriage a secret? And even worse, the fact that she'd been hitched to a wife beating jerk?

Where was the guy now?

Jed had never considered himself the violent type, but right about now he wouldn't mind introducing that bastard to his fist.

He steeled his jaw.

Tightened his grip on the wheel.

If Annie wanted to talk about it, what would he say? Was he strong enough to help her through that kind of pain?

A sad smile raised the corners of Jed's lips, as he thought, yes. For her, he'd take on the world—even if that world happened to be inside her head.

"Don't you look pretty," Grandma Rose said when Annie walked into the kitchen, which smelled divine with supper simmering on the stove.

"Thank you." She'd changed from shorts and the corn T-shirt Jed had bought her into a pale pink sundress.

*I Hope To Be E*arring *From You Soon.*

While changing, she'd closed her eyes and ran her fingers over the cob's nubby surface. She remembered that day. That first kiss.

She'd been so happy with Jed before finding out the

dark truth. So then why, if he was as awful as she'd started to believe, had Annie still been wearing the shirt? She should give it to charity. That was what she'd done with everything Troy had ever touched.

Her grandmother's words came back to haunt her.

Was the reason she hadn't thrown the shirt away more complex than she'd imagined? Deep down, did she already know her hasty assumptions about Jed's character were false? Could she have been wrong? Was he the opposite of Troy? Was Jed's yelling an isolated incident?

Kids bickered at school all the time.

Her parents had petty arguments and then made up. Even her grandparents. Okay, she acknowledged that Jed had the right to be upset with his sister—but to yell at her?

Annie rubbed her bare arms.

She should have worn something more substantial than this flimsy sundress. She was cold. Would she ever feel warm again?

The doorbell rang.

Her heart lurched.

"He's early." Her grandmother put the lid on her biggest pot, then whipped off her apron and set it on the counter. "Give this a stir every few minutes, and be sure not to burn the rolls."

"But—where are you going?"

"Scrabble club." She kissed Annie's cheek. "Bye, sweetie. Have fun."

"But—"

Someone knocked on the back door.

"Good," her grandmother said. "There's my ride."

Whoever it was knocked again.

"I'm coming, Lu! Keep your shorts on!"

"Grandma Rose, you can't just—"

"I might be late, so don't wait up."

How could her grandmother do this to her?

As if the woman had read her mind, she poked her head back around the kitchen door and said, "Oh, and in case you're wondering, this is something Dr. Phil calls tough love. You've got to tell Jed about Troy, sweetie. Don't let your fears of the past ruin your future." She blew her a kiss, and then she was really gone.

Fear pressed heavily against Annie's chest. She wasn't sure what she was more afraid of—Jed or how he'd react to the knowledge of her first marriage.

After having some time to think about it, Annie had to wonder if her grandmother was right. Maybe Jed was the great guy she'd first thought.

So if Jed wasn't the reason she'd run away, then what was she running from? Her own fears and insecurities.

What if Jed thought less of her once he found out about the creep she'd married?

Pulse thudding in her ears, Annie's eyes darted around the room.

She had to get out of here.

She could drive back to her condo.

Yes.

That was a great plan.

Run.

Hide.

Her purse was on the hall table, but what had she done with her keys? They had to be here somewhere. She yanked the leather bag open wide.

In the zipper compartment? No.

The only thing in there was Pia's pink bow. How many times had she put it on the little angel, only to have it slip off? And that was how it'd ended up in here that day at Wal-Mart when Annie had decided it was a choking hazard.

The doorbell rang.

She looked up, and saw Jed peering through the window beside the door.

Her mouth went dry.

"Hey," he said, his voice muffled but still dearly familiar.

Oh, God, why had she left him?

He wasn't a monster like Troy.

He was her dear, sweet Jed. She didn't deserve him. She didn't deserve anyone, she—

The door creaked open. "You scared the hell out of me," he said, walking inside, then easing the door shut behind him. "Why didn't you tell me about your ex?"

She bowed her head. "My grandmother has a big mouth."

"I don't know about that. I like her big mouth. I think you're right—we really do need to fix her up with King."

"Oh, Jed…" Annie crossed the short distance to him, flinging her arms around him in a sobbing hug. "Please, just hold me."

He did. Tightly and sweetly.

"Wh-when I heard you yelling at Patti," she said, "I—something inside me snapped. I'm not sure what happened. My marriage to Troy has been over for years. It barely lasted three months." She paused for breath, then went on, unable to stop the flow of emotions and words. "Grams was sick. She'd been diagnosed with breast cancer and I thought I was losing her. I thought I'd be totally alone in the world. But then I met Troy at this party and he seemed like the answer to my prayers. I was so vulnerable and he took care of me. But there were signs. When Grandma lost her hair, he made fun of her with his friends when he thought I wasn't listening. At first, they were little things, but I should've paid attention. I knew he was bad, Jed, but I was so insecure, so afraid of being alone. But with him, I learned there are some things scarier than being alone."

She began crying again. Hard, racking, ugly sobs. Jed simply held her. Eventually he scooped her into his arms and carried her to the sofa where she'd sat just last night fearing her life was over. Only now she knew it'd only begun.

"We're going to slow things down," he said, smoothing her hair back from her forehead, kissing her eyebrows and cheeks. "If it's okay with you, I'd like to take you on at least a hundred dates. Then, when you're convinced I would never—*could* never—hurt you, I want you to think about—just *think* about—being my wife. Could you do that?"

Still crying, but now tears of joy, she nodded against his chest. He smelled so good. Like hot summer air and mountains and forests...

Snug on his lap with her arms around his neck, Annie released years of tension. He was so gentle and so strong. Strong enough to protect her and their children and her grandmother and Patti and her husband and children and the whole of their wonderful new combined family.

And Annie had become stronger. She'd finally forgiven herself for getting involved with losers like Conner and Troy.

And suddenly, there, in Jed's arms, she was no longer alone, but united with many.

She no longer wanted to spend her Saturday nights reading decorating magazines and painting her bathroom. She wanted to sit at laughter-filled tables, playing Scrabble or cards or talking until they ran out of stories to tell.

But because they'd all have each other, there'd be more stories.

More laughter.

More love.

"What's going through that head of yours?" Jed asked.

"How happy I am. But also how sorry I am for ever doubting you. I heard you raise your voice and…just lost it."

Wiping her cheeks with his thumbs, Jed said, "If you'd bothered to tell me about your ex, I would've known not to raise my voice around you. None of this would've happened."

She shook her head. "You can't walk on eggshells for me. That's not fair."

"Well, you can't go on being afraid."

"I know. That's why I want to talk to a professional about this stuff. What we have is too special to risk losing because of ghosts in my head."

"Does your ex live around here?"

"Last I heard, he moved out to L.A. trying to be a personal trainer to the stars. His body was all he ever cared about. He wanted me to stand around looking pretty. He didn't appreciate it when I wanted more."

"Is that why you never went on to further your degree?"

"Yes. Dumb, huh?"

A sad laugh escaped him. "Considering what you'd been put through, it sounds more like self-preservation."

"Just hold me," she said. "Hold me, and if I ever flip out on you again, remind me who you are and what we share."

"Will do," he said, cradling her even closer.

He held her and held her until her pulse slowed and her eyes dried. Until she felt confident and ready to face the world.

"I hate to ruin this moment," he said, "especially when you feel so damned good up against me, but is something burning?"

Annie jumped from his lap. "Grandma's chicken and dumplings—and the rolls!" She ran into the kitchen with Jed right behind her. "I hope we're not too late to save it. She worked so hard."

Jed slipped an oven mitt on his hand and lifted the pot's lid. "Looks all right to me," he said.

Annie nudged him aside. "It can't be." She took a wooden spoon from the counter and gave the foul-smelling brew a stir. "Ugh. Grandma's going to be so upset."

"What's the matter with it?"

"Look." She stepped aside to let Jed see the inch of brownish gunky black lining the bottom of the pot.

She turned off the oven. A peek inside showed her the rolls hadn't fared much better.

Jed hefted the pot off the stove and placed it in the sink, filling it with hot water. "I'm pretty hungry, now that I think of it. A home-cooked meal would've really hit the spot."

"I'm not as good a cook as grandma, but she keeps

her pantry and freezer stocked. I could scrounge up something."

"Are you sure? We could go out." He put his hand on her bare shoulder and she leaned into his touch. Warmth. Blessed warmth.

Suddenly it was Christmas Day all over again, but this time, she got everything she'd ever wanted. Her deluxe art set. The Barbie Dream House and matching Ken.

Only his name was Jed.

And he was hotter.

Way hotter.

Annie opened the freezer door and said, "Let's see—steaks, chops, spaghetti, waffles."

"Let's do breakfast for dinner. You do the waffles. Got any eggs? I make a mean omelet."

While she unearthed waffles, Jed started a game of fridge Twister, reaching under and around her in the fridge to find the eggs. And in such a simple act, such a simple blessing, Annie knew she had finally found her new family, her home.

Epilogue

Four years later

Despite the rowdy sports-bar atmosphere in the theater room where hundreds of spectators had assembled to watch that year's crowning of the National Scrabble Champion, Annie clamped her sweaty hands together, and nibbled the inside of her lower lip.

Three-year-old Olivia squirmed in her seat. "Mommy! This dress itches."

"I know, sweetie," Annie said. "It'll just be a little bit longer until Grandma Rose and Grandpa King's game is over."

"Who do you think's going to win?" Jed asked, scooping Liv out of her seat and onto his lap.

Annie winked. "My money's always on Grandma, but after she beat King so soundly last year, I feel sorry for him."

Liv tucked her head full of blond curls under her daddy's chin and closed her gold-flecked brown eyes.

The sight of her daughter snuggled up against Jed never failed to warm her. How had she gotten so lucky? How had they all gotten so lucky?

King and her grandmother were vying for the title of National Scrabble Champ, but once the gloves came off, they'd be that much more in love. King had finally struck his silver vein, and Annie's grandmother had been right there beside him. After hitting it off at King's New Year's party, the two became inseparable. After a six-month whirlwind romance, they'd married and had a gorgeous ceremony at the top of Mosquito Pass.

When the two of them weren't doing the Scrabble circuit, they were star speakers of the amateur prospecting conference circuit.

Annie was in med school, earning her child psychiatry degree. The commute and school hours were long, but Jed was always willing to help—at least when he wasn't working. He was on his way to becoming Pecan's fire chief.

Patti held her hand in front of Ronnie's mouth. He spat a purple wad of gum onto her palm.

"Ew." Annie grimaced.

"Hey, a mom's gotta do what a mom's gotta do." And what a great mom Patti had turned out to be. She was a whirlwind of cookie-baking and volunteering while Howie had taken a managerial position at Pecan's bread factory.

"Oh my gosh." With her clean hand, Patti grabbed Annie's forearm and squeezed. "After that last word, they're tied. Have they ever had a tie score this late in the game?"

"I don't know," Annie said. "Grandma's the pro, not me."

While the ESPN host and expert Scrabble co-host talked about strategy and odds, Annie closed her eyes and willed the match to be over. Winning this year's title would mean a lot to King, but it would also mean the world to her grandmother.

Liv asleep in his arms, Jed leaned close to his wife. "After the big victory party, how about you and me give the rug rat to my sis, then play our own championship game of strip Scrabble?"

Swatting him, Annie said, "How can you say that at a time like this?"

Grinning, eyes bright with laughter and love, he said, "I had to do something to get your mind off the outcome of this game. You do realize it won't be the end of the world for either of them if they lose?"

"I know, but—"

He stopped her latest round of worries with a spell-binding kiss.

Wild cheers went up around them along with enthusiastic applause signaling the end of the game.

Jed paused their kiss long enough to ask, "Who won?"

Now it was Annie's turn to smile. When it came to having the perfect husband, child, friends and family, the answer to that question was a no-brainer. Who won? "Me."

* * * * *

SPECIAL EXCERPT FROM

⟨H⟩HARLEQUIN
SPECIAL EDITION

*Skylar Davis is grateful to have her late husband's dog.
But the struggling widow can barely keep her three
daughters fed, much less a hungry canine. Kyle Mitchell
was her husband's best friend and he can't stop himself
from rescuing them. But will his exposed secrets ruin
any chance they have at building a family?*

Read on for a sneak peek at
Their Rancher Protector,
*the latest book in the Texas Cowboys & K-9s miniseries
by* USA TODAY *bestselling author Sasha Summers!*

"Even the strongest people need a break now and then. It's
not a sign of being weak—it's part of being human," he
murmured against her temple. "As far as I'm concerned,
you're a badass."

She shook her head but didn't say anything.

"Look at your girls," he insisted. "You put those smiles
on their faces. You found a way to keep them entertained
and positive and with enough imagination to turn that
leaning wooden shack into a playhouse—"

"Hey," she interrupted, peering up at him with red-
rimmed eyes.

"I was teasing." He smiled. "You're missing the point
here."

"Oh?" She didn't seem fazed by the fact that she was still holding on to him—or that there was barely any space between them.

But he was. And it had him reeling. The moment her gaze met his, the tightness and pressure in his chest gave way. And having Skylar in his arms, soft and warm and all woman, was something he hadn't prepared himself for.

Focus. Not on the unnerving reaction Skylar was causing, but on being here for Skylar and the girls. *Focus on honoring Chad's last request.* Chad—who'd expected him to take care of the family he'd left behind, not get blindsided and want more than he should. How could he not? Skylar was a strong, beautiful woman who had his heart thumping in a way he didn't recognize.

"Thank you, again." Her gaze swept over his face before she rose on tiptoe and kissed his cheek. "You're a good man, Kyle Mitchell."

Don't miss
Their Rancher Protector *by Sasha Summers,*
available August 2021 wherever
Harlequin Special Edition books and ebooks are sold.

Harlequin.com

Love Harlequin romance?

DISCOVER.

Be the first to find out about promotions,
news and exclusive content!

Facebook.com/HarlequinBooks

Twitter.com/HarlequinBooks

Instagram.com/HarlequinBooks

Pinterest.com/HarlequinBooks

You Tube YouTube.com/HarlequinBooks

ReaderService.com

EXPLORE.

Sign up for the Harlequin e-newsletter and
download a free book from any series at
TryHarlequin.com

CONNECT.

Join our Harlequin community to
share your thoughts and connect
with other romance readers!
Facebook.com/groups/HarlequinConnection

HARLEQUIN

Heartfelt or thrilling, passionate or uplifting—Harlequin is more than just happily-ever-after.

With twelve different series to choose from and new books available every month, you are sure to find stories that will move you, uplift you, inspire and delight you.